THE CROW MAIDEN

THE CROW MAIDEN

Sarah Singleton

Cosmos Books, an imprint of **Wildside Press**
New Jersey . New York . California . Ohio

THE CROW MAIDEN

Published by:

Cosmos Books, an imprint of Wildside Press
P.O. Box 45, Gillette, NJ 07933-0045
www.wildsidepress.com

For more information, contact Wildside Press.

ISBN: 1-58715-324-6

For Joe and Pauline

CHAPTER ONE

At the Swallowhead Spring, five old willows tower above the River Kennet, trailing thin, supple strands in the clear water. The spring rises at the bottom of a grass bank, and trickles through a tiny vale of succulent grass into the river. The earth is soft and boggy. Fleshy green stalks of reeds and nettles rise from the rich mud. The trees are tall and twisted, leaning across the waters with thick boughs covered with coarse, greenish brown bark. Their limbs interlace. The bent lower branches are festooned with ribbons and colourful scraps of cloth, a couple strung with bells that clink in the breeze. High up, some accomplished climber has adorned a tree with a set of silver chimes, glinting in the sunlight. On the first morning of May, the maidens peel off their jeans and jackets to paddle through the mud and bathe in the chilly waters. They tie new ribbons to the trees. Wishes. Bright, satin wishes rippling in the cold spring breeze.

    Katherine was sitting on her bed, alone. Beyond the window, the square view was broken by the parallel lines of the telephone wires, running along the block of terrace houses. The bright, brilliant blue sky unrolled an endless, changing vista of faraway clouds, low on the horizon. Every few minutes, the stillness was cut by the tight, black rush of swifts flying in front of the house. It was nine o'clock in the evening, the beginning of June. The hours of light were stretching deeper and deeper into the night. The child was asleep, at last, and Katherine's energy ebbed and dissipated in the new calm of the house. Now, however, a small insistent voice seemed to call from the wide world beyond the window—come out, feel the rush of the sap rising, the slow sink into twilight, this quick June, this summer...I can't go out, she thought. Of course not. Leave Niamh with Paul? He'd manage, of course, but would it be fair, after his trials at work today, for me to leave him babysitting while I go out and enjoy myself? She felt a faint, satisfactory sense of relief for so neatly concluding the little voice could be disregarded. The hold of lethargy was strong. It was always easy to do nothing, to succumb to the confinement of the house. She was tired. A heavy weariness had become a condition of being. Niamh was a fitful sleeper, often waking every couple of hours through the night. Sleep came to Katherine like a brief, black pool, dreamless, from which she was snatched to instant alertness by Niamh's first tentative grizzles in the dark. For months her sleep had been shattered. She inhabited a grey half-world, aching always for sleep, to slip away into an ocean of peace undisturbed. She gazed at the framed patch of sky, where the distant clouds turned and glistened and the first, faint edge of moon showed white in the distance.

The itch remained. Katherine rose to her feet and walked to the window. The vista opened before her, houses and gardens, the trees green and fresh with young leaves, the last lilac blossom purple and white, drifting with a faint perfume. Apart from the occasional passing car, the street was quiet. The pavements were deserted. Was everyone sitting inside, moribund? She opened the bedroom door.

"Paul?" she called.

"Here," she heard from the tiny back bedroom, his office. Was he still working? So it proved. He was busy at his computer.

"What are you doing?"

"A letter," he said, still typing. "I'm replying to Waltham MP again, the bastard. About the bypass."

"Of course," she nodded. The walls were covered with maps, postcards, pinned up letters, quotations written out, and architectural plans. The largest map, pinned above the computer, marked the proposed route of the new bypass with a wide red line through the land. The sun shone brightly through the window. Paul had partly closed the cane blind but still fingers of golden light stole through and touched the desk, the piles of paper and magazines. Katherine buried her hands in her waistcoat pockets.

"I thought I might go out for a walk."

The staccato rhythm of the keyboard did not flicker.

"What, now? Yeah, okay. See you later."

"Keep an ear open for Niamh, won't you."

"Of course."

Still Katherine hesitated.

"You don't mind?"

"Mind? Why should I?" Paul had stopped typing. He looked irritated. She was interrupting his thoughts.

"Okay then. See you later."

Paul had already resumed his typing. She headed downstairs and out the front door. She climbed in the car. As she moved from the shadow of the terrace, the evening sun struck her in the face with a soft warmth. So where to go? She headed south-east, to the wide Roman highway, towards the long barrows, to Avebury and Silbury Hill. She parked the car in a layby and headed across a field to the Swallowhead Spring. Lumps of flint, knobbly like white fists, littered the moist chalky soil beneath her feet. The field rose in a gentle slope to the west, and the rays of the sinking sun edged the bright green blades of young wheat with a translucent glow.

Katherine edged down the steep bank towards the spring. Since her last visit, at dawn on May Day, the nettles had burgeoned and she had to pick a careful path through the bristling emerald heads. On a flat stone at the spring's head, someone had left a small chunk of amethyst and a crudely modelled Mother figure, white clay thighs and enormous breasts. It had no head though, no thoughts. Its consciousness was cradled in its belly, in the womb, the space for gestation and birth. The wind rose and the bells clinked. Katherine gently replaced the Mother and trod carefully through the mud to the river. Looking up from the sucking earth, she saw three wicker shapes hanging from a river branch above the river. She edged closer, and the icy spring water leaked into her boots. The first was a perfect globe. The second was a human figure, and the third, twisting slowly above the water, was a large hoop twisted with fading flowers.

Then behind her she heard the hoarse "wah wah" of a crow, and turning, she saw the glossy black bird perched at the top of the bank, disregarding her and hopping across the flints in the wheat field. Maybe she should bathe in the waters. That May morning three women had submerged themselves amongst the rippling reeds, but the morning had been bitterly cold, and pulling back, laughing uncertainly, Katherine had shaken her head and refused. But tonight? The evening was still mild. The fading light was stretching into the long, eerie midsummer gloaming, not day or night but a muted, shadowy space in between. She looked quickly about her, then pulled off her boots and socks, tottering clumsily. She undressed and draped her jeans, shirt, and waistcoat over a branch. Then she edged her way through the deep mud at the river's edge. It squeezed up through her toes. She sank to her ankles. She stepped into the river, onto the sharp, stony river-bed. The water was fiercely cold. Even as she continued, up to her knees, it took her breath away, and her body began to tremble violently. She forced herself onwards, keeping one hand on the willow branch. In the middle of the river, the water just about reached her waist. She took a deep breath and plunged herself down into the river, face first into the bitter, icy water where the stones shone on the bottom and the water weed rippled in the currents. Then—up again, gasping for breath and shaking with cold, but triumphant.

"I did it!" she cried aloud. "I did it! I did it!" Swiftly she began to wade out of the water, but a movement at the top of the bank above the spring had her frozen still, in fear and the most acute embarrassment. Who was there? Had they seen her? Heard her cry out like that? Despite the cold she remained motionless. She peered up through the branches to see if there was someone there. A figure stepped out. A young woman. Still, Katherine was mortified, to be caught so foolishly, so vulnerably naked. She staggered through the mud and grabbed for her clothes, but too late. She knew the girl had seen her, seen her thin, bony body, her golden skin turned yellowish and sallow after the winter and the cold, enduring spring, seen her gaunt breasts and the stretched wrinkled skin on her belly where not so long ago Niamh had nestled and grown.

Katherine's elation disspiated in a moment and she hastily pulled on her clothes again. Her jeans were smeared with mud, and her shirt clung to her wet body. The river water dripped from her hair over her face. She smiled a false polite smile at the intruder, who smiled back quite unapologetic, and stood waiting for Katherine to emerge. As she walked out through the nettles, the girl faced her, with a serious smile.

"Hello, " the girl said. "I've been waiting for you." Her manner was intimate.

"Yes?" Katherine said, wiping her face.

"Will you come to the fire? Share a drink?"

Katherine hesitated. She didn't know what to say.

"Um, okay," she muttered, uneasily. She wanted to be home, and safe, but foolishly she had committed herself. The girl turned to lead the way. She took her along the hedge and over an old stone stile into a small copse, only half a dozen trees, and in its centre a dark brown shelter, and old tarp pulled over a dome of springy saplings.

"I'll get the fire going," the girl said. "You must be cold."

"Not too bad." But Katherine squatted by the fireplace and peered into the depths of the bender. The girl returned with more wood and started up a little fire. She rested a blackened kettle across two of the chunks of stone forming a ring around it.

"I'll make us some tea," she said. Inside the copse it was dark, and Katherine began to fret about her return home. Paul might be worrying.

"Okay, thanks. But I can't stay long. My partner and daughter are at home. They'll be wondering where I am."

The girl smiled at her. As the kettle heated up, Katherine's eyes grew accustomed to the darkness in the trees and she could see her host more clearly. Younger than Katherine, maybe only seventeen or so, she was short and slight, her hair very long and matted, utterly black. Her eyes were dark too, and her skin brown, coarsened by outdoor living, prematurely aged. She wore grubby clothes, layer on layer, leggings, long embroidered skirt, waistcoat glinting with tiny mirrors, a huge jumper hanging off her shoulders. Around her neck she had half a dozen necklaces, strips of cord and leather hanging with small stones and shells, the quick silver glint of a half moon. Amongst the matted ropes of her hair were long, slender plaits decorated with feathers and beads.

"How long have you been staying here?" Katherine asked. The girl shrugged.

"A long time."

"To be by the spring? Like a guardian?"

"Something like that."

"Well, I'm Katherine. What's your name?"

"Crow."

"Crow? Crow. That's a good name. Was it you who put up those lovely wicker things by the river?"

Crow shook her head. She handed Katherine a chipped tin mug. The knuckles of her hand were dark with grease and dirt. As she leaned over towards her, Katherine caught the scent of earth and grease and woodsmoke. They sat quietly for a minute or two, sipping the strong tea. It left a strange aftertaste in Katherine's mouth, like soil. She began to feel warm again, and invigorated, though her damp hair still smelled of riverwater and she could feel crusts of mud between her toes in her boots.

"I'd better be going," she said. "They'll be wondering where I am."

"No they won't. Stay for a while. Enjoy yourself." Crow put another piece of wood on the fire, and as it fell into the flames it knocked a cloud of red sparks into the air. Katherine watched one drift to the ground, where it lay on a stone and glowed, pulsing slightly. When she looked up again she realised that beyond the circle of the fire it had grown very dark, and above their heads the moon was shining brightly. She began to sense the movements of the trees around her, the gentle ripple of the branches in the breeze and the whispering of the leaves one against the other. They seemed to form a protective cove, arching above the little camp like pillars, but alive, sensitive—long, swaying bodies curved around the two warm people on the ground. Katherine gazed deep into the fire, at the golden, gleaming flames, the flickering tongues breathing heat around the charred logs. She looked up at Crow's still, beautiful face, where the shadows danced from the fire. She tried to speak, but found her words were sucked back by yawning spaces in her mind. She gathered her wits.

"What was in the tea?" she asked, clutched by a sudden fear. What was happening? How would she get home? Was she about to be assaulted and robbed? Her pulse began to race. But Crow remained calm, looking intently into her face.

"Get past them, your fears," she said. "Crow's special brew. What you wanted, isn't it? Look up."

Katherine lifted her face from the warm, enclosed radius of the fire and the trees to the great, vaulting sky, to a drift of stars.

"How far do your senses reach?" Crow asked.

"Right into space. I can see stars. From millions of miles away, I am touched by stars." Then suddenly she was aware of movement closer at hand. She looked down from the heights and saw dark forms moving round the edge of the trees, and she retreated behind a barrage of fears again.

"No-one will hurt you, Katherine. And in our circle here, they can't even touch us. But they want you. They want you to walk with them."

"Who are they?" she said, in a whisper that still seemed to echo off the trunks of the trees.

"The little people, the dark folk, the old tribes. All of these."

Katherine heard a low chorus of whispers from the figures circling the trees. She could make out no words. She felt faces pressed against the borders of their little camp. In a quick flicker of the fire she thought she saw a hideous head, a twisted goblin mask with fleshy lips and slit goat-eyes. The shadows moved and instead a glimpse of a slim, alluring youth, utterly captivating, with locks of dark green hair. It disappeared. There was laughter.

"The faeries," she said. Crow nodded.

"But I'm afraid." Part of her was already lost to the people beyond the trees, but a heavy weight held her down.

"What about Niamh? I can't leave her. I can't abandon her to chase my dreams."

"No-one will know you have gone. They walk outside time."

"So that's it? I can go and everything will be the same?"

"I didn't say that. A sacrifice will be required on your part. Something precious. You can not take without giving in return. A balance is required."

"Niamh."

"Niamh is not yours, to hold or surrender. She belongs to herself. No harm will come to Niamh."

"What then?"

"I can't say. You must take the chance. You must decide."

Katherine struggled to master her thoughts. Around the trees, the movements of the people grew more urgent, the whispers were louder. She felt a growing compulsion to go to them. Equally, a solid core of resistance held her where she was.

"Crow, I am afraid."

"And the man at the gate of the year said?" Crow replied. Her voice carried scorn rather than sympathy. "Do you need a light to show you the way, or a known path? Or will you step out into the darkness? What are you afraid of releasing? What stops you committing yourself?"

Still Katherine hesitated, but she felt strangely flayed by Crow's words, as though Crow could see into her mind, into her weakness.

"What has been your impulse?" Crow asked. "Since the day began, what has driven you?"

"Facing action or inaction, I have acted," she said. "Yes, I see the pattern. At each step I have broken out. Consciously I have decided to move."

Crow nodded and drew back. She fiddled with one of her necklace strings and untied it. Then she leaned forwards and tied it around Katherine's neck. As Crow's arms enveloped her, the black ropes of hair fell across Katherine's face. Her clothes stank of old leaves. Then Katherine sat back, her eyes shining. She stood up and turned away from the fire. She walked out towards the dark, towards the open space. The people closed in around her.

CHAPTER TWO

Paul Matravers stopped typing and looked up. Niamh was crying. He realised she had been crying for several minutes, and he had been so absorbed in his writing he had not even noticed the loud, insistent baby complaint. She wailed again, and a prickle of irritation ran down his spine. Where was Katherine? Why didn't she see to Niamh? Beyond the pale electric glow from the screen the room was dark. Outside, a faint prickle of starlight glinted in the sky. Paul remembered that Katherine had gone out for a walk. Had she still not returned? Niamh, silent for a moment, screamed suddenly. He sighed, angry with Katherine for her absence. Then, spurred by Niamh's shout of fear he strode to her bedroom.

As soon as he switched on the light, an unexpected flurry of black feathers began to crash around the room. He withdrew in alarm as a bird hurled itself with a great thump at the window, which stood ajar. The bird—a crow—half fell to the floor and flapped again in a frenzy. In fierce panic it clawed at the glass. Would it shatter the pane? As Paul edged forwards, the crow dived clumsily. It flew around the room, bashing into the walls and emptying the contents of its bowels onto the carpet. Paul pushed the window wide open and stepped back. With a clatter of wings, the huge beast flew out into the darkness.

Paul took a deep breath. Suddenly the room seemed very still. On the walls were colourful postcards and pictures, reassuring fluffy animals were piled in a heap on a chair. Above the cot a mobile spun gently, four brightly painted wooden parrots. In the cot itself, a small girl stood holding the bars, staring across at him with wide saucer eyes.

"Niamh, are you okay? Did the bird scare you? Did it hurt you?" He lifted her out of the cot and held her close to him. He pressed his face into her shoulder and breathed the scent of her soft, warm hair. To his intense horror, she stank. He recoiled in shock.

"Niamh? What's that awful smell?"

Niamh, held at arm's length, gazed at him calmly. Gingerly Paul drew her closer, wanting her sweet, clean child perfume. He was assailed again by a dreadful odour of rot, like decomposing garbage. Nothing like the usual baby smells of dirty nappies, regurgitated milk, spilt food. The reek drifted from her apparently unsullied, rosy skin, and even at arm's length, he could barely keep a straight face. He dropped her back into her cot.

"Good grief, Niamh. What's happened? Did the bird crap on you too?" He looked at the carpet where a trail of foul white and yellow ooze shone stickily in the electric light.

"Bloody hell, Katherine, where are you?" he muttered. Vaguely alarmed, Niamh began to cry a little in her cot. Paul ran for some tissue to wipe up the mess. By the time he returned, Niamh was calm again, sitting motionless. Once he had cleaned up the carpet he went downstairs to the bathroom and filled the bath. He poured in large quantities of bubble bath till the foam rose in white hills to the taps. Then he carried Niamh downstairs, guiltily averting his face from her. He undid her sleepsuit, removed her still-clean nappy, and plonked her in the bath. A look of alarm flitted across her face but then she played happily, splashing in the bubbles.

Paul squatted on the tiled floor, leaning on the side of the bath and watching her. Niamh was small and slight for her eighteen months. Looking into her face Paul could see his own baby self. Her bright blue eyes were his own. Her strong, square face his too. Only her hair was different. It was a deep brown, almost black, and curled like a doll's.

Niamh stood up in the bath and put her small wet hands on his cheeks. Paul smiled. But still he could smell her. He reached for the soap from the sink and carefully washed her from head to foot. The he shampooed her hair, rinsed and rinsed it with clean water from the tap. At last, he pulled out the plug and lifted her onto his lap, where he dried her. To his dismay he could still detect the dreadful rotting smell. Fainter, yes, but still distinct. He could bear to hold her close to him again, but her delightful baby smell had vanished. The stench lingered around her body.

He carried her up to the cot, made sure her sheets and blankets were clean, then settled her for the night. When he went back downstairs it was eleven thirty. A mixture of annoyance and anxiety clouded his mind. Where was Katherine? He suspected she had called in on friends, probably at the squat in the old cottages, and involved herself in a conversation. But on the other hand, it was not like her to be so late, to leave him with Niamh so long without a word. Paul headed up to bed but he was uneasy. He found it hard to sleep alone.

He woke in pitch blackness. Someone was hammering on the front door. Without a thought he leapt out of bed and ran down the stairs. He opened the door. Katherine was standing on the doorstep. Her face was black and shadowed. Her hair hung in a dark curtain. He could not see her eyes. She held out her hand to him, and smiled. Her teeth glinted oddly. He took her cold, white hand, and she walked past him into the house. She led him up the stairs, to their bedroom, and opened the curtains so that moonlight poured into the room, pale and faintly yellow on the walls. The bald, ivory moon reflected in the mirror on the wall. Katherine drew Paul towards her and slipped her arms around him. Apart from a tee shirt he was naked, and her cold hands pressed into his buttocks and thighs. He was immediately aroused. He stood motionless as she took off her clothes. Then he felt the pressure of her breasts and belly as she pushed against him. She nuzzled his neck, reached up to kiss his face with a strange, hot mouth that tasted of fruit and earth. A prickle of sweat broke upon his body. He ached to move but his mind was held, spellbound, as she licked him with a rough tongue, like an animal. Paul closed his eyes and let the pressure of his own desire flicker out along his limbs like flames. How good it felt. How could he have forgotten so soon the intensity of these feelings? The months of broken nights and weariness, Katherine's turning away from his desires to those of the infant. She had stopped wanting him. He never doubted that she loved him, but hell, he had too much dignity to pester her. He hadn't realised how much he had suppressed himself, how much he had dulled his senses.

Katherine pulled him down to the bed and sat across him, drawing him deep inside her. He froze momentarily. She felt different. The heat of her flesh was intense but he felt as though he had thrust into moist earth. Katherine took him deeper. He reached his hands up to her breasts. He looked into her face, the high, wide cheekbones, the faintly oriental symmetry, seeking to meet her gaze, to find communion, but her eyes were closed. Her twisty gold-brown hair fell onto his face as she moved on him. He could barely contain himself, and his mind swam into a dark fog where quick vivid pictures flashed before him. He saw a red steam ship move upon the clear waters of a mountain lake. He saw a thorn bush upon the stony beach of a winter sea. Then the fragments were snatched away, and the blackness in his mind exploded in the red heat of consummation. He heard himself shout, once, and then he lay still, sweating, Katherine's limp body heavy upon him. The bed seemed to heave. He put out a hand to steady himself, and Katherine reared up from him. As she moved away, ribbons of unsavoury odour tumbled down from her mouth, her hair, her armpits. The very pores of her skin began to drip the dreadful rotten smell that had infected Niamh. Paul pushed her off and jumped from the bed, but the stench was relentless and Katherine began to laugh as he recoiled.

"What is it? What is that smell? What have you done?" he cried, flinging off the bedclothes and opening the window. As he turned, the moon at last illuminated Katherine's face. She stopped laughing and lifted her gaze to his. Her eyes were as green as emerald, and the pupils were slit, reptilian. She licked her lips, not sensual, but coarse, like a dog just fed. Then, neatly, impossibly, she jumped though the open window.

"Katherine!"

He was sitting up in bed. The light was faint and grey. It was six o'clock and he was alone. Katherine had not been back. He remembered—the dream?—with a faint sense of shock. The window was still open. He rehearsed the scene over and over in his mind till it ceased to sting. He felt intensely tired. He allowed himself to feel angry with Katherine for absconding. Then he worried. Was she dead in a ditch somewhere? Should he call the police? How he was to get to work, and what about Niamh? From the next room he could hear her stirring. Just as she began to cry the telephone rang. He grabbed Niamh from her cot and ran downstairs. When he picked up the phone he could hear two voices in the background, and the acoustics of a call box.

"Hello? Paul?"

"Paul here."

"It's Jan Blessing. Look, Paul, it's Katherine. She's at the cottages. I think you should come over."

"Is she okay? Has she had an accident?"

"No, she's okay." He heard a muffled conversation at the other end of the line.

"How can I come over?" he said. "She's got the car."

"Look, something weird's happened. Walk over. It's only a mile across the fields. I can't really explain now, the money's run out. See you soon." The line went dead.

CHAPTER THREE

It had been a Saturday, a clear, golden day in spring. The light in the early morning was the colour of wine, and the fragrance of the blossom was almost sufficient to cover the smell of exhaust fumes. Joseph Hoblyn woke at seven, disturbed by the sound of his uncle Dave coughing in the bathroom. Dave worked most Saturdays. He coughed for several minutes, as he did every morning. Dave was only in his late twenties, but he smoked incessantly, and every morning Jo was woken by the rough, painful noise of his uncle seeming to cough his lungs from his body. Jo imagined gouts of foul, black catarrh heaving from his mouth, though it didn't stop him smoking himself.

When Dave had finished in the bathroom Jo sank back into sleep. He woke again an hour later when Jackie got up and the two kids began to tear round the house. Still he waited. He knew Jackie would take them off to her mother's for the morning, so he lay awake in bed for another hour, though he stirred himself sufficiently to light a cigarette and put a record on. At last he heard the back door shut. When he knew he had the house to himself, he dressed and walked downstairs to make a mug of tea. The cigarette had taken the edge off his hunger so he decided to skip breakfast. His friend Steve had promised to call round in the afternoon, but till then, he had no plans. He sat back in his room and played the same record again, recalling the fun of the night before, drinking at the wine bar.

He had made his room a haven. Cut-outs from pop magazines and record sleeves adorned the walls. Pots of gooey nail varnish, hair spray cans and cases of make-up covered the dressing table. Upon the window sill, beside the china mug in the shape of a breast, he had a wooden jewellery box filled with ear-rings and silver necklaces. Next to the stereo stood his uncle's old video recorder, a hulking, often unreliable machine. False cobwebs from the joke shop dangled from the ceiling.

He mooched downstairs to check out the videos Dave had hired the night before. Two were porn movies, with fleshy pouting girls on the cover. The third was a horror video, dripping blood and tacky gothic lettering for the title, 'The Torture Garden.' Mildly curious he put it on, and began to watch the hammy special effects, hearts torn from bodies, power tools biting into soft, screaming victims. He thought he knew all of the horror titles at the video library, but this was a new one. The warm, tawny sunlight filtered through the net curtains, but Jo was locked into 'The Torture Garden'. As the film proceeded he became more engrossed. A gang of tearaway American teenagers were camping out at their local haunted house, as a dare. One by one, they succumbed to the awakening evil, the spirit of a dead murderer who had once owned the house. Not an original plot, Jo considered, but the adventures of the punky teenagers thrilled him, and the swinging chains, and the blood on the power tools, and the hands reaching out of the flames, and the close up shot of a goth girl's head exploding in a cloud of blood and brains. When the tape ended, he rewound it and put it back in its box. He would take it out of the video shop himself and watch it again soon.

Jo essentially lived in his bedroom. He made brief forays outwards—occasional trips to the seven-day store at the end of the road, to buy cheap make-up, hairspray, and cigarettes, to hire out a handful of horror videos, which he watched in the night when his landlord-uncle and family had gone to bed. And every Friday night he made his way to a nearby pub, or a club in the city if he was feeling flush, to eek out his benefit on a couple of halves of lager, which were sufficient to provoke a drunkenness of sorts. He never ate much, and the drink went straight to his head. He was immensely tall, well over six feet, and emaciated. He had an absolute horror of obesity and often his dreams were filled with images of fat, nightmares of waking with floods of excess flesh hanging around his body. So he forced himself to the opposite extreme, and lying on his bed, he could count the bones of his body. He was skeletal.

Apart from a few brief trips to the store, and a couple of hours in the pub on Friday night, his only other exodus from the four walls of his bedroom was the fortnightly trip to the dole office to sign on. So he dreamed away the hours and days and months on his own. He could lose himself in huge, convoluted voyages in his brain, fantasies about rock stars, about becoming a model and earning fame and admiration. His dreams made up his life. He was twenty two.

He spent inordinate painstaking hours in front of a long, cracked mirror, recreating himself in the image of his heroes, bright Sputnik quiffs and fishnet, effeminate chart popsters, theatrical black gothic. And then he would wash all the makeup off, and lie on his bed again, filling his head with increasingly bizarre dreams. He began to wear elaborate underwear, stockings and suspenders. He bought a black basque, all frivolous lace, from a charity shop. He filched posters of new teeny popsters from magazines at the newsagents, pictures of bright, crispy lollipop girls with golden curls, and he dreamed how he might become them, how he might live in their bright, golden, lollipop world.

When his mother had moved to Birmingham with a new boyfriend, Jo had stayed behind. Bristol was the only home he knew, and anyway, his experience of stepfathers was not altogether positive. His mother was an attractive woman, and Jo had always thought her glamorous and exciting. He could remember being sent to the door to lie to the men trying to collect their debts, and at the time it had seemed like an adventure to cover for his mother's love affairs. Looking back on it now, he was puzzled and a little hurt. He could also remember taking his little sister to his bedroom and turning the music up loud so she would not have to hear their mother and stepfather arguing. He left school when he was fifteen and the stepfather told him not to bother about exams, as he could get him a job in a factory. Jo did as he was told. Besides, he had never enjoyed school very much.

So then his mother moved away, and he found a tiny bedsit. When the factory closed down, he lay alone on his bed and decided he would die. He swallowed two bottles of aspirin and closed his eyes. He woke up three days later with a searing headache. Utterly isolated, he cried bitterly for hours. Then he packed his two boxes of possessions, and moved in with Dave and Jackie. Dave was his mother's brother, but he didn't know them very well. They were amenable landlords and happily soaked up his housing benefit. They didn't bother him much, and he didn't bother them. His world shrank to the four walls of his bedroom. In the real world he was nothing—but in this space—he could be anything.

But slowly his outside life had improved. Bit by bit the group of black-clad, leather-jacketed young people at the pub in town coalesced into a union of friends. A new wine bar, the Chapel, opened in the city centre where local bands played in the basement. They gathered to drink and dance and share their records, books, horror videos. They visited each other's houses. Jo was no longer alone.

Steve did not arrive till after six. Jackie and the kids returned in the afternoon. Jo was lying on his bed when Jackie called up to him. He heard her talking.

"Go on up," she said, "he's in his bedroom."

Steve thundered up the stairs.

"Sorry I'm so late," he said. "I had to help my dad in the shop." He was shorter and stockier than Jo, but looked just as painfully young. His hair was coloured with the same cheap hair dye, a strange bluey black, and it was sticky with hairspray. Grinning, he drew out four cans of beer from inside his leather jacket. Within half an hour they had turned up the music and were trying to dance in the few feet of space not filled by the double bed and the dressing table. When Jackie moaned at the noise, Steve suggested that they head for the Chapel.

"No money," Jo said. Steve had a tenner in his jeans pocket.

"Got it from my Dad for helping him today. I'll buy you a drink," he said. Jo smiled.

"Let me get ready first. I need to put some make-up on."

"Hey, put some on me too," Steve asked him. "Give me some eyeliner."

It was another half an hour before they left, plastered with mascara, purple eye shadow and red lipstick, tipsy and giggling. They staggered down to the bus stop, singing songs and shouting out at the evening sky. There were several other people waiting at the bus stop, all dour and silent. One, a huge, thickset man, saw the suspenders through the rips in Jo's jeans and shot "queer" out to him in a voice full of malice. Steve and Jo heard and laughed together, like school boys, and the man turned away from them to his companions.

Once in the city, they headed straight for the wine bar and down the steep stairs to the basement. Already, three of four familiar faces were present and although the band had not begun, music was booming from the jukebox. Steve bought more drinks, then disappeared to talk to a girl he was keen on. Jo sat on his own for a time, and the effects of the beer began to wear off. Although Steve had bought him a pint, Jo nursed it carefully. Steve was unlikely to buy him another, and as he had no money of his own, he had to make it last all night.

Faintly bored, Jo reached into his jacket pocket for a set of tarot cards bound in a piece of black silk. He wiped the slopped beer from the table with his sleeve, and began to play Patience. He played with only half his mind on the game. As people came and went, he realised he was waiting for something. For someone? He lit another cigarette. He had only two left to last till the next day. He felt restless. He scooped up the cards again, finished his drink, and headed over to Steve.

"I'm off," he said. "I can't hack it tonight."

"Okay," Steve nodded. Jo waited for a moment, as though expecting Steve to join him, but Steve looked quite happy where he was with his young lady, so Jo turned away and headed out into the night air. The Chapel was situated on the fringes of the city centre, not sufficiently commercial to attract the custom of the glossy money-happy revellers, who were now heading for the city's major nightclubs. Jo struck a course through the thick of it, looking at the drunken girls staggering down the street arm in arm, and the wary groups of young men, cropped hair and hands stuck in pockets, affecting a swagger but instead projecting unease and a barely suppressed violence. As he walked, he noticed a dark mark beneath his feet on the pavement. He looked more closely, and realised it was a bloody footprint. There were more, leading up one of the side streets. It made him wince, thinking about the bare, injured foot that had left such a signature on the cold paving stones. How much blood had there been? Without thinking, he followed the footprints—only the right foot had made marks—and walked along a narrow street away from the desperate, pleasure-seeking crowds.

It was very dark. None of the street lights seemed to be working. He didn't recognise the street, though the form of the city was ingrained in his heart. He had never been anywhere else. The footprints petered out. Just ahead, light from a plate glass window spilled yellow upon the pavement. It was a small cafe, though the red plastic chairs were all vacant. A thin, grey-haired man was cleaning the counter at the back. As Jo peered through the window, a woman's voice made him jump.

"Looking for someone?" An old woman. He hadn't heard any footsteps. She was very short and bent, her head bound with a scarf, and over a jumble of other clothes, she wore a voluminous coat that trailed on the ground.

"Uh, no," he said.

"Are you going inside?" She stared up at him. She was carrying three enormous carrier bags stuffed with bits and pieces. A bag lady. Was she hoping he would buy her a hot drink?

"No. No money."

"Let me buy you a cup of tea then," the woman said. Jo hesitated. Was she religious? It wouldn't be the first time. He thought he must look like someone in need of salvation. Every now and then someone would try and shelter him, wave a bible or a hare krishna pamphlet at him, try and feed him up.

"Okay," he said at last. "Best offer I've had all night."

He held the door open and she manouevred her bundles inside. She selected a table, and fussed over her possessions, bidding Jo watch over them while she ordered the tea. Then she shuffled off to the counter. He watched her spreading out a handful of copper coins to pay for the drinks, so he drew out his tarot cards again, and began another game of Patience. If she was intent on the salvation of his soul, that should wind the old dear up quite nicely.

She returned with two mugs and a small packet of biscuits. She saw the cards spread out across the table and pushed them aside to make space for the tea.

"Hey!" Jo said, as a handful tumbled to the floor. He picked them up.

"You don't need them," she said. She took off her enormous coat and sat down on the other side of the table.

"Here's your tea."

Jo took the proffered mug and added three heaped spoons of sugar. As he stirred, he looked at the old lady. He had thought she was old. Now it was hard to tell. She had thick, very black hair. Her face was brown and deeply wrinkled. He guessed she was well over seventy, though he wouldn't care to hazard a guess at her exact years. When she smiled at him, he saw she was missing two front teeth. He tidied the cards into a pile.

"You don't need them," the woman repeated, shaking her head. Jo put them into his pocket. The old lady began rummaging in one of her carrier bags, and eventually drew out a small embroidered handbag.

"Have you got a cigarette, love?" she asked. With a sigh, Jo drew out his packet, with the two remaining cigarettes. She took one, and he had the last. The old lady opened the handbag and tipped the contents on the table.

"This is what we need," she said. There were metal bottle tops, bits of bone, stones, fragments of broken jewellery, some old keys, a couple of plastic dolls no bigger than a thumbnail.

"Take them," she said. "Cast them on the table."

"What? Are you going to tell my fortune from this lot?"

The old lady laughed and shrugged, looking strangely girlish for a moment.

"Okay then. I'll give it a try." He gathered together the fragments of glittering rubbish and rattled them together in his large, thin hands. He let them trickle in a heap upon the table. One of the tiny dolls fell last, and lodged upon the top of the pile. The old lady peered at the arrangement, smiled with delight and clapped her hands together.

"Just as I thought, oh yes," she said. "A friend will need your help. A friend in the green wood."

"What friend?"

"I don't know her name. You'll know when the time comes."

"It's a her then. I suppose that narrows it down slightly."

The old lady ignored him and continued with her reading.

"She may need my help too," she said. "She will also want this." She reached again into a fat plastic bag and lifted out a figure, carved from a piece of dark wood. She thrust it at Jo. On the top of its head a wisp of greasy black hair was stuck with an odorous blob of some sticky substance.

"Yuck," he said. "Are you sure about this? You want me to take it?"

"Give it to her."

"Ah yes, to the mysterious lady. Okay. Did you really need all these bits and pieces to tell my fortune? You knew it anyway."

The old lady smiled.

"If you can see far enough, you can read events in the pattern of weeds at the roadside, in the shape of a tree, in the folds of a child's clothes. I can see a world in a grain of sand. Or a swirl of tea-leaves. A little showmanship is not out of place though. A ritual has its worth."

Jo realised she did not sound so much like a bag lady any more. She was standing up, gathering her possessions.

"How do I find you again?" he said.

"I'll be around."

"So what so I have to do? To help this friend-in-a-wood?"

"What you usually do. Nothing. Absolutely nothing. Wait and see." She walked away from the table and out of the door. When Jo picked up his tea, he found it was stone cold. He left the cafe. Outside the sky was growing pale with the dawn. The streets were deserted. He shivered, suddenly very hungry. He began the long walk home.

CHAPTER FOUR

Owain walked along the bottom of the valley, where grey boulders littered the thick grass, each one marked with coins of lichen—lemon and white and copper brown. From the end of the valley the humped backs of the rocks resembled sheep, lying heavy in the meadow, amongst the red clover and cowslips.

To the west, the little valley levelled out, and a copse stood at its end, a stand of beech trees, hazels and a dense hedge of blackthorn overgrown for years. In the copse was a small mound, marked on the map as a barrow, though it was hard to see unless you were standing on top of it. Up in the branches of the trees, very visible, were half a dozen makeshift human dwellings, made of rope and tarpaulin, and pieces of mismatched wood.

As Owain passed the copse, the sun disappeared below the gentle hills, and a gleam of light from a paraffin lamp stole through the chinks of the door flap of one such construction thirty feet up, clinging to the boughs of a sleek beech. The flap opened briefly, and a slight figure appeared in silhouette. The paraffin lamp was extinguished and the girl began to descend. She moved from branch to branch slowly, but with an accuracy and grace that spoke of long familiarity. The last branch was eight feet or so from the ground, and the girl used a rope to make the final drop to the ground. She brushed off her hands and turned from the copse, nearly walking into Owain, whose quiet, even tread had not informed her of his presence. She started in alarm. In the fading light it took her a moment to work out who he was.

"Owain," she said. "You gave me a shock. I didn't hear you."

"Sorry."

"Are you going to the house?"

"For a bit," he said. "I'm not staying though, Violet. I'm picking up my sleeping bag."

They set off together down a rough track. The old lane led to the main road, and set back from the road, with narrow overgrown gardens at the front, was a terrace of three stone cottages. They were old farm cottages, though more recently two had been converted into one more spacious dwelling. Now a large, makeshift sign in the front garden, painted with flowers and a rainbow, declared, "Welcome. No Road Extension." Violet opened the front gate and walked up the garden path. She tried the front door, but found it was locked. She knocked impatiently. Inside music was playing, some kind of ambient rhythm sounding shallow on a battery-powered tape recorder. Eventually a young woman opened the door.

"Why is it locked, Elaine? They're not going to come for ages yet," Violet said.

"Anytime," Elaine answered, shaking her head. "They could be here anytime. We can't make it too easy. We can't be too careful." Elaine was tall and thin, with sleek, black hair.

She retreated inside, admitting Violet and Owain into a long room illuminated by a dozen candles, which flickered in the draught from the door. The candles stood on the window sills and on the mantel above the fire place. Upturned crates served as tables and chairs. The floorboards were bare. The only real piece of furniture, against which the squatters' rolled up sleeping bags were piled, was a tattered armchair scavenged from a skip. It was occupied by Jan Blessing, Violet's mother. The room did not look cold or inhospitable. Painted on the wall was a huge female figure reaching up with outstretched hands, seeming thus to be scattering stars and flowers, painted upon the ceiling, the walls and the floor. Alongside the candles there were pots and tins full of flowers, piles of stones, bunches of feathers and leaves.

Jan looked up briefly from the joint she was rolling.

"Too quiet up there tonight?" she asked Violet.

The other half dozen tree dwellers had hitched into Marlborough, seven miles away, for the pub. Violet was supposedly on sentry duty, as they never liked to leave the tree houses unattended.

"I feel a bit restless. I should have gone with them. There's a strange atmosphere tonight, you know?"

Jan nodded.

"I know what you mean."

Violet sat on the arm of the chair beside her mother. Nineteen years old, Violet had dropped out of art school after a term. Jan owned a struggling wholefood shop in Marlborough. She lived in a flat above the shop. Mother and daughter had hair the colour of burnished copper, flecked with gold in the shifting candlelight. Jan's was cut at shoulder length, but Violet's hung to her waist and was interlaced with dozens of colourful hairwraps, beads and ribbons. She had a large silver ring through her right eyebrow, and another through her lip. This she sucked disconsolately as her mother lit the joint and began to smoke.

"D'you want some of this?" Jan said. Violet shook her head, and Jan passed it instead to Owain.

"Are you staying here tonight?" he asked.

"Yes," Jan said. "But I'll be heading back early tomorrow. I've got to open the shop." She looked closely at her daughter.

"Are you okay? You look tense."

Violet shrugged, frowning.

"Weird mood, mother. I don't feel comfortable in the tree, but I definitely don't feel comfortable here either. I think I'll go out again. I shouldn't have left the trees unattended. And I need to be moving."

Owain looked up.

"Me too. I'll come with you," he said. "I'm going to sleep down at the other end of the valley."

He picked up a small, dingy rucksack, a sleeping bag and some food. He headed out with Violet.

The sky arched hugely black above them, but the moon was vaguely yellow, casting long shadows beyond the trees and hedges. They walked without speaking along the Old Lane, boots kicking noisily against the stones. Owain rarely slept inside once winter was over. With a rolled sleeping bag and a fly sheet for cover when it rained, he spent his days walking, right across the south of England and into Wales. He had often joined the road protesters, at Twyford Down, Batheaston, Newbury. But he was happiest alone, walking and watching the land. He spent the winter months at Locksbury, working with horses and then in the early spring helping with the lambing. But once the weather had warmed, the long trails beckoned and he was off again. He was in his mid thirties, not tall but fit and physically resilient, with dark blonde hair tied back, and a beard that grew pale, like a Viking.

"Where are you sleeping?" Violet asked.

"Down at the far end. By the big hawthorn hedge—I want to watch the badgers."

"I don't think I'd want to sleep outside tonight."

"I can see things. Tonight—more than badgers, maybe. I don't like being closed in at the moment, not even by the fly sheet if I can help it."

They walked on till they reached the copse. In the darkness the tree houses looked like giant nests amongst the leaves. Owain waited as Violet pulled down the rope and hoisted herself to the lower branch. then quickly she moved up to the bender, and climbed in. She looked out, Owain a dim shape, way down below her.

"I'm okay, Owain. I'll see you tomorrow. Have a good night."

Owain waved and turned from the copse to the stone valley.

Inside her mid-air cave, Violet lit two candles and fastened down the door, attempting to shut out a night that seemed to steal through the chinks in wood and tarpaulin, through the fabric itself. She wrapped herself in blankets, though it wasn't cold, and strained her eyes to read in the poor light.

Outside, Owain walked amongst the rocks. In the moonlight they shone oddly phosphorescent but the shadows behind were dark, impenetrable pools. He saw the dew beginning to gather on the grass, and crushed by his boots it released a fragrant, herby tang. He sensed the same urge to close in, to hide himself, but he fought the desire and consciously looked outwards. He willed the very cells of his body to open to the unexpected sting of the night. At the end of the valley grew the long hawthorn hedge, laced with dogrose and travellers joy. On the ground beneath the tangled branches were the holes and disturbed earth of the badgers' set. Owain had seen them often, emerging after dark and moving amongst the stones. He sat in his familiar spot nearby, partly hidden by a slight rise in the side of the valley, beyond the hedge.

He waited for a long time, while the moon rose high and began to sink again, but the set remained perfectly still, as though abandoned. He lapsed into reverie and a half sleep, wrapped in the sleeping bag against the cold. His mind drifted. He sank into a shallow slumber.

Then in an instant he was wide awake. He looked around, but he could not make out what had woken him. His senses were unnaturally keen. He could not see anything, except the stones and the stars. All around, the valley lay motionless. The air was still. He realised hours must have passed because the moon was now very low on the horizon, near setting. A movement caught his eye, but it must have been a trick of the vanishing moonlight because it seemed to him the stones themselves were turning in the grass. He shut his eyes for a moment, then opened them again to dispel the visual distortion, but it persisted. The phosphorescent shine increased. The air tensed in the valley and an odd exotic smell, vaguely autumnal, sent a prickle across the surface of his skin.

He heard a low, distant murmuring, like the sound of a multitude of voices far away. As he strained to hear, the noise grew slightly louder. The voices became more distinct and faintly he thought he heard laughter, shouts, crying—but the tones were confusing and inhuman. The noise trickled over him, like a tendril of smoke. Gradually the volume increased. Then the noise was all around him. He was surrounded by an incomprehensible animal discourse filled with fragments of song, some he half recognised—here and there words, or pieces of jumbled sentences, musical phrases, shrieking. The sounds seemed to zoom towards him then shoot away again, to be close to his ear, then in an instant, heard from a great distance. The strange smell intensified, a brew of decaying leaves and ripe fruit and the cloying sweetness of jasmine flowers. He thought it something like patchouli, and fenugreek, and the acrid scent of something dead, decaying feather and bone.

Crouched to the ground, Owain's heart beat fiercely in his chest. A rush of fear—a tension in his belly. He willed his body to relax. Was he in danger? His mind thought not, but under the barrage of alien sensations his flesh had a different instinct. He breathed deeply. Once again he allowed his mind to open and uncoil. He looked deep into the darkness.

Movement began. At the end of the valley lights flickered over the stones. An emerald mist drifted towards him, where faint figures seemed to be walking in procession. Then one was in front of him, close enough to touch. A slender green body sharpened into focus—the curve of a cheek, the trails of verdant tresses and smooth limbs—then faded away. In an instant, he saw the faces complete—faces that noticed him pressed like a shadow to the earth. Some smiled, brimming joy. Others bristled with hostility. Passions seemed to wash across their faces in waves. Most walked past, insubstantial, and ignoring him utterly. How beautiful they were, greenish all of them, but underneath rippling as though they contained the light of rainbows within their bodies. But their eyes were cold and blank even as they laughed and embraced.

He found it hard to judge how long the procession lasted. Seconds or hours? Gradually the crowd began to thin. The shimmering procession headed up the valley, past the copse and along the Old Lane. Once they had crested the hill, Owain could not see them any more. The last figures disappeared. For a moment he felt a strange temporal pause, an absolute stillness. Then around him, the earth seemed to sigh and unfold. The breeze picked up and carried away the last faint wisps of the fragrance. From across the fields came the short bark of a fox. It would soon be dawn.

Standing up, glad to be able to stretch his legs, Owain stared up the valley, seeking for the source of his visitation. In the distance—though how distant he found it hard to make out—a last shimmering figure was heading his way. The figure was blurred, striding slowly, with long hair drifting in a wind he could not feel.

Katherine had been walking for a very long time. She began to feel the weight of her body again. She walked as though through a lake of water, her legs half suspended, half incapacitated by the density of the fluid substance around her. Her mind struggled against the barriers which seemed to rise around her thoughts. Was she dreaming? At each step, it seemed that a veil was torn away and the medium around her began to thin. As her vision cleared, so too did her mind. On and on and on. As she moved forwards she was growing closer to wakefulness. At the same time this wakefulness seemed like a shutting down, a narrowing. What was she walking from? As her consciousness began to clear and grow defined, some part of her mind was wailing in protest. Don't forget! it cried. Don't forget, don't let it go. But already she knew that whatever it was, it was slipping away. She was sinking down. The weight was increasing. Almost she could sense the earth beneath her feet. Almost she could feel the cold against her skin—still far away as yet, but reaching for her, dragging her down. She wanted to turn around, to head back to wherever she had some from, but her legs moved of their own volition. Her body had its own direction. Gradually she became aware of her surroundings. The sun was rising, orange and gold above the hills. Its faint warmth on her face pulled her back into her flesh. The damp grass made her feet throb with faint, and then increasing pain. She looked at the stones and the hedges and the fields. In an instant everything fell into place. The last veil tore away and evaporated. She knew where she was. Ahead, motionless, she saw a man standing amongst the stones and watching her approach. Like the man at the gate of the year, like a guardian, an earth spirit, welcoming her return.

"Owain," she said. Her voice sounded alien. The word seemed to hang on the air. "It's me. Katherine."

She stepped towards him and clutched his arm to stop herself from falling. Her feet stung. Her hands were icy cold.

"Sit down," he said. "Here. Put this sleeping bag round you. Did you see them? Is that where you've come from? Were you with them?"

Katherine looked at him blankly. The dawn light was pale and greyish.

"You look different, " he said. "You've got a tan. Your face is golden."

Katherine ran her fingers through hair tangled and matted. She sensed Owain was struggling for words. He was bursting with questions, aching for her to say she had seen them too. Them. Whatever they were. Katherine was not well acquainted with Owain, though she thought they shared an unspoken kinship, a mutual liking She had always wanted to talk to him more. Now they rested in silence for a while, unable to explain their experience but each gaining comfort from the presence of the other. The wind blew coldly. Mauve and white cloud patched the sky. Owain looked tired and heavy.

In the daylight the reality of the adventure was already fading. It was swiftly becoming a dream, half remembered. Katherine clutched Owain's arm again, compulsively.

"It did happen, didn't it?" she said. Owain nodded.

"Yes. But it's hard to hold onto. I'm losing it already."

"Me too." Whatever it was. Had they shared the same vision?

"How long have I been gone? It seemed a very long time. Like months. But it can't have been. What day is it?"

"Friday. June 10th I think."

"Just hours then. Like she said. I was only gone hours."

"She said? Who? What happened, Katherine?"

But Katherine had lapsed again, vague and unfocused.

"I don't know," she said. "I've got to sort my mind out, my memories." She was shivering.

"Let's go to the cottage. Jan's there. It'll be warmer."

Katherine nodded, her face blank. Owain helped her to her feet. He noticed her boots.

"What happened to them?" he asked. Katherine looked down, and at once the pain in her feet flared fiercely. The leather was falling apart. Gaping holes had appeared in the soles, and her feet were covered with mud and scabs and blood. Her clothes were torn and stained. She sniffed.

"I stink, don't I?"

Owain smiled gently. "Don't worry. I stink most of the time."

Suddenly Katherine felt very small and afraid. Not only was she conscious of her bodily presence again, she was intensely and unpleasantly aware that her skin was covered with filth and sweat. Her head itched furiously and her feet were so sore she could barely stand. She felt an overweening desire to peel off her contaminated body and fly off...where? Away, upwards. Then came a crushing thought. Niamh. The remembrance of the child earthed her like a great rock. How could she have forgotten her? Niamh. The inescapable, the unavoidable, the burden and foundation of her life, this love for her daughter. How could she go and leave her?

"I've got to see Niamh," she said, urgent at last. "I've got to see Niamh." Then, regardless of the condition of her feet she strode off through the wet grass that stung and bit into her tattered skin.

CHAPTER FIVE

The light in the bathroom was green and pale, filtered through the web of leaves from half a dozen plants on a shelf above the window, dangling long tendrils. A swirling mosaic dominated the tiny room—the shimmering, twisting body of a mermaid amid waves of ultramarine and cobalt blue on the wall behind the bath. On the wooden shelf beneath the mirror crowded small glass bottles, breathing the perfumes of lavender and orange blossom. Paul splashed his face with cold water and peered at his weary reflection. Grey marks had appeared beneath his eyes. He ran his fingers through his hair, white blonde and greasy, falling in uneven clumps to his shoulders. He was good looking in the bland, square jawed fashion of the men in shirt ads. Like, he knew to his discomfort, the perfect Aryan, the model for a Nazi propaganda poster. But in defiance of his genetic heritage he softened the angles of his face with perpetual stubble. At work his talent and efficiency meant his unkempt appearance was just about tolerated.

Niamh toddled into the bathroom, a yellow plastic dog in her hand. She dropped it into the bath with a loud clatter, then cried out for help when she couldn't reach it again. Paul turned and scooped it out for her. She began to grumble.

"Just a minute," Paul said. "I'll get you something to eat."

She looked at him, then turned, absent-minded, and wandered out. The unfastened end of her white bodysuit hung over her bare bottom like a tail. Paul dressed himself in his habitual jeans, shirt and old army boots. Rummaging through the neat piles of baby clothes, he found a pair of dungarees for Niamh. When he came to dress her, she was in the process of peeing copiously on the rag rug in the middle of the bare floorboards. She looked at the puddle in faint surprise. Paul cursed and grumbled, mopping up the damp patch with tissue. He had to hold Niamh still, as she twisted and protested when he pinned on her terry nappy. As soon as she scrambled to her feet it began to sag dangerously, but he quickly whipped on the plastic pants, holding everything together. When she was dressed he sat her in the high chair with thick slices of bread and honey.

The sun shone through the front window, filling the long living room that stretched the length of the cottage. The floor was dusty and rough. In the rays of sunlight tiny motes turned and glittered. Books on the shelves were illuminated, and the jumble of pots, pieces of bark, pictures and candlesticks on the mantel above the empty fireplace. Perched in the grate was a jester puppet, a crude papier mache head and a mismatched patchwork body. It was one of Katherine's early efforts. The more recent creations lay drying and dismembered on a shelf in the kitchen. A faint perfume of damp and incense was overlaid with the sharp tang of urine from the rug.

Paul made toast for himself but when he took a bite his appetite deserted him. His head ached dimly, and every now and then recollections of his night time encounter flashed into his mind till he felt himself vaguely tainted and soiled. He wanted to wash, as he had washed Niamh the night before. He felt a slight guilt for his intention to skip work. Niamh dropped her plastic beaker to the floor with a clatter. When he stooped to pick it up he sniffed her cautiously. The smell was fainter now, but still he recoiled. He wondered if he carried the odour on his own skin, a contaminating slick upon his body.

When Niamh had finished her breakfast Paul wiped her hands and face with a flannel, then slipped her into the baby backpack. On his way out he telephoned the architect's office in Swindon. It was too early for anyone to be in, so he left his guilty excuses on the answering machine.

The sky was a perfect eggshell blue, still pale in the early morning sun though soon it would be blazing. Now the air was cold and clean and Paul shivered as he locked the front door and felt the breeze upon his bare, white arms. They lived in a small terraced cottage on the west of the village. The plans laid the bypass to the east, cutting a huge swathe nearly half a mile from Locksbury, a two mile stretch of unswerving dual carriageway. At this hour, the village was relatively quiet, though every now and then, a lorry trundled by, and a few early commuters. Niamh waved at the postman and a young boy delivering newspapers. At the back of the bakers shop they caught the smell of hot bread and heard the clanking of metal doors as huge trolleys were pulled from ovens. Niamh jumped in the backpack and pointed, as they walked up the lane to the High Street. Locksbury was large enough to have a bank, a post office and a dozen shops, as well as a handful of pubs and a library that opened two mornings a week. On the corner a small Indian restaurant had recently opened. Just away from the High Street in a small alleyway, was the Gallery, selling a mixture of watercolours, Indian bedcovers and jewellery, postcards, decorated bowls, and even one of Katherine's puppets, a sharp-faced scarecrow leering through the window. As he walked beside the shop fronts, Paul could tick off in his mind how the proprietor of each felt about the impending bypass—who would smile (if the shop had been open) and who would turn away. Grocer, chemist, butcher, florist. To be sure, most were opposed to the new road. They depended on the traffic flowing through the village for much of their trade. The vociferous florist had vowed to lay her generous form before the first digger that appeared, as she envisaged the erosion of her livelihood. Paul recalled how the tree dwellers had cheered as she stood up, all shiny nail varnish and hairspray, to make her resolution at the village meeting. A smile flicked across his face. But the Residents Association—now that was an entirely different kettle of fish. Set up by newcomers to the village, people who worked in Swindon and Bristol and wanted a tranquil rural home, the association had fought vehemently for the bypass. So the village was divided. Passions ran high.

It took him fifteen minutes to walk to the far side of the village. Jan's optimistic mile was going to take him about half an hour. By the time he reached the footpath across the fields the backpack was making his shoulders ache. He wriggled his load and adjusted the straps but still failed to find a comfortable position. From the edge of the village he set off up a field sown with wheat. It was a steep incline, for the village lay in a valley, and Paul toiled without an eye for the attractions of the flourishing hedgerows and the hosts of young rabbits surprised by the walker. When he reached the top of the field Paul could see the valley of the stones, but it was still a fair walk, skirting the edge of more crops, scrambling over an overgrown stile and along a farm track. Climbing a fence into the stone valley field, he headed towards the cottages. As they came into view his initial chill had become a considerable sweat. Niamh bounced in her canvas seat and squealed with pleasure.

Violet opened the door before he knocked.

"Where's Katherine?" he said.

"In the back garden."

She followed him round. He saw Katherine sitting cross legged in the long, dewy grass, gazing across the fields. She was in a bad state, torn and dirty and her hair all matted.

"Katherine? Are you okay? Where've you been? What happened?" He lifted off the backpack and pulled Niamh free. As soon as he set her down, she trotted off to her mother. Katherine lifted Niamh into her lap and held her tightly. There was an uneasy silence.

"Shall I make tea then?" Without waiting for an answer, Violet left them alone. Paul sat down beside Katherine. Somehow she had acquired a tan. Her skin looked vaguely dirty, but beneath it he observed an unexpected, almost unnatural radiance. Her clothes were crumpled. As usual she had silver hoops in her ears, and a tiny garnet stud in her nose. Around her neck she wore the aquamarine he had given her when Niamh was born, but he saw something else.

"What's this?" he said, lifting a necklace lying on her shirt. On a rough thong hung what looked like a little bone, smaller than his finger, highly polished and engraved with spirals and coils. Katherine looked, puzzled, then recollected—what?

She began to cry. Surprised, Paul put his arms around her. Katherine pressed her face into his shoulder, breathing his familiar scent, his heat. Paul felt her tears soaking through his shirt. Niamh, caught between them, yelped and pulled herself free. She tottered through the overgrown garden pulling the heads off dandelions.

Katherine withdrew, sniffing and wiping her face.

"I'm sorry," she said. "I suppose you should be at work. I've really messed things up for you, haven't I. And the car—it must still be at Silbury Hill. Is Niamh okay?"

"She's fine. Tell me what happened."

"It's just coming back to me," she said. She told him how she had bathed in the river—how she had met Crow. She recalled the strange, fierce faces peering through the trees. She told him how she had walked out, to the faeries.

"And now to see your dear familiar faces," she said. "You and Niamh. My flesh and blood family. Such a sense of relief. A homecoming."

"But what happened next? When you say you left Crow?"

"Then—I can't remember. It's like a blackness, a space in my memory. I can't remember where they took me, what happened. It'll come back though, I'm sure, the veil will go. I just have to wait." She turned to Paul. He was struggling on the borders of credulity, trying to be open-minded, but finding the effort a great one.

"You say this Crow girl gave you something in your tea. Maybe it was mushrooms or poppy. More than likely you were wandering round in some kind of altered state till you met Owain."

"Maybe. But I don't think it's true. Anyway, Owain saw them too."

Paul swallowed and drew away from Katherine.

"You don't believe me, do you?" she said.

"Would you?"

"It's true, I promise, I know what it sounds like."

Paul looked again at the bone necklace.

"It's what Crow gave me. Doesn't that prove it?"

"Not really." He turned it over. As he examined the minute decorations a faint but unmistakable odour drifted from the bone. He shuddered.

"What is it?" Katherine said.

"That smell. I know it. From last night. Something weird happened at home. A crow flew into Niamh's room, and afterwards Niamh stank. Then in the night I had a dream that you came home and we made love, but then you had the same smell. Absolutely vile, like rotting garbage."

Katherine looked at Paul, amazed.

"Then how can you not believe me? If this happened at home? Is Niamh okay?"

Paul shrugged.

"I think so. She still smells, a bit."

Niamh was waving dandelions in the air. Her unconfined hair tumbled over her face and the little ringlets gleamed in the sunlight. Paul's heart ached as he watched her. Katherine called her over, sniffed her gingerly.

"Yes. I can smell it. They've been close to her. Funny, I quite like the smell."

"Why would they want Niamh? I thought she was out of this deal?"

"So did I. Does this mean you believe me?"

Paul sighed.

"Maybe. I don't know. I'm still trying to work out a reasonable explanation."

"Why did they want you? A succubus, isn't that what it was?"

"Perhaps I'm your price. Am I precious to you?"

"Of course. Have I surrendered your fidelity? You've been unfaithful."

"A dream, Katherine. You can't be unfaithful with a dream."

But now Katherine looked guilty. What had she been doing?

"I'm not so sure it was a dream," she said.

"Well, what about you? You can't even remember what you did."

They heard footsteps on the path, and realised their voices were raised. They fell into silence as Violet brought tea. She quickly retired to the cottage again.

"This is a stupid discussion."

"Yes," Katherine assented, "we should be worrying about Niamh. What do they want with her?"

"You say Crow promised no-one would know you'd gone. That hasn't been true. How can you believe anything she said?"

"You think they want to take Niamh? Perhaps you were just in time, and interrupted them. Then they went to you instead."

Paul sighed deeply and looked away to the smooth, gentle hills to the east.

"You don't really want to believe all this, do you," Katherine said gently. Paul looked down, pulling restlessly at the damp grass.

"My head—no way. My guts feel different. Afraid. Worried about Niamh. Having a crow in your bedroom, that's pretty strange."

"Yes."

They left Niamh with Violet, and took a lift in Jan's car to Silbury Hill. The water supply to the cottage had been disconnected a long time ago, so Jan brought drinking water to the squatters and the tree dwellers. The boot and the back seat of her car were piled high with plastic containers. Silbury Hill was only five minutes drive away. She dropped them off in the layby where their car was parked. Katherine took her keys from her pocket, but Paul stopped her opening the door.

"Don't you want to see if your Crow is still there?"

"I'm not sure if I do. I don't know what it'll prove either way. The answers are in my head."

"Well, I'm going to look. Do you want to wait in the car?"

Katherine shrugged but when Paul set off briskly across the field she trailed after him. He reached the Swallowhead Spring and climbed down the bank to the river. His big boots smashed down the nettles, but still he was stung, on the thin skin on the back of his hand. He swore loudly and sucked at the skin. Six white lumps appeared, and the patch itched and throbbed, so he plunged his hand in the bitter cold river water.

"Are you okay?" Katherine was standing at the top of the bank.

"Yes," he said sharply. "No. I stung myself, that's all."

"Did you see the wicker things?"

He looked up. Almost above his head, the three shapes twisted from the branches.

"Yes, I see them," he said. "But the third one's not a man, it's some sort of dog or wolf or something."

Up on the bank, Katherine was looking away. Annoyed at having to shout, Paul clambered back to her.

"I thought it was a human figure," she said. They headed for the copse. It was smaller than Katherine remembered. They saw no bender, no sign of human presence at all. The ground was bare earth strewn with a thin layer of last year's leaves and bits of twig. Katherine scuffed through with her boots and found a patch that may or may not have been blackened by fire, and a couple of stones she thought bore traces of ash. Paul was unconvinced.

"But don't you see? I know for sure I met Crow. She gave me this necklace. If there is no trace of her, maybe it does prove that something strange is happening."

"Perhaps."

"You still don't want to believe this? Then what about the smell? You're the one who recognised it."

Paul shook his head. Katherine seemed to sense his irritation and she lapsed into silence. They walked back to the car and drove to the squat. Violet was sitting outside with Niamh on her lap. Niamh was tugging at her necklaces but when she saw her mother she wandered towards her with her arms in the air, wanting to be picked up.

Paul drove them home. Niamh was tired, and after she had eaten some yoghurt she was happy to sleep in her cot. Katherine let Paul run her a bath, and she peeled off her dirty clothes. She lay in the warm water, while Paul fed her biscuits and tea. He was shocked by the state of her feet, though once they were clean they did not look quite so bad. He anointed her feet with calendula cream, and rubbed her face with moisturising cream, smelling of cucumber and aloe vera. It pleased him to take care of her. It didn't happen very often. It was more common for Katherine to be the caretaker, running around after everyone else. He even brushed her hair, though eventually they had to resort to scissors to cut out the worst of the matted locks.

"There's a meeting this evening. At the valley," Paul said cautiously. "I don't mind going on my own if you don't feel up to it."

Katherine ran her fingers through her hair.

"Of course we couldn't miss a meeting," she said. "No, I'll be okay. I want to come. I want to talk to Owain."

Katherine went to bed, as Niamh appeared to be settled for a while. The sheets were cool and clean. She felt cleansed, and gazing at the sky through her window, she was tranquil at last. Paul lay down beside her, and they held each other gently.

"I love you Paul," she said. "I love you." He stroked her hair. They made love very gently. Katherine began to cry again. She felt very vulnerable and exposed. Before...in the other place...what? What had happened?

She had vague recollections, holding Paul like this. The sense of floating like a cloud, a faint longing for pure being, the intoxication of perfect union. So sex was nothing to a closeness she was chasing in her memory—perfect intimacy, complete revelation. Nothing, a clumsy and inadequate pastime, an absurd struggle to overcome isolation. But now, this time, truly their physical communion was something, however inadequate. She had shrunk back into her separate and unassailable self, but here at least, they could make some delicate and tender sign of their intercourse.

In the evening, thin ribbons of cloud drew across the sky and the wind quickened. But it was still warm and at eight oclock the various inhabitants of the tree dwellings, the squat, and friends and supporters from the locality wandered in twos and threes to the stone field for the meeting.

At the cottage the front door blew open again, slamming back against the wall. Paul and Niamh went ahead to the valley. Katherine and Jan waited to meet with a man from the local history society who had offered to give a talk. The speaker arrived a few minutes late, a thin stooped man in his early sixties, largely bald except for a few thin wisps of straw-coloured hair. He smiled and shook their hands, then fiddled awkwardly with a large bundle of paper and leaflets. One of the part-time squatters had agreed to be sentinel at the cottage, as they never left it unoccupied. Jan told him they were leaving, and they escorted the speaker up the old lane to the valley. He was nervous and voluble, but his voice was gentle and Jan tried to put him at his ease. The gathering amounted to about thirty people, with a handful of children running round the stones. They assembled into a circle of sorts, leaving a space for the speaker. Amongst the motley garb of the road protestors, he was conspicuous in his tweed jacket and neat brown shoes, but the people around him smiled and shook his proffered hand.

"Is everyone here?" Jan said. She sat upon a low flat stone, which had come to signify the speaker. She looked quickly around. Further up the valley, a solitary white-clad figure was walking slowly down the slope.

"I don't think we'll wait," she said. "This is Bill Whates, from the Wiltshire History Society. He is going to talk to us about the history of this area, and specifically, what features are likely to be destroyed by the road extension."

She moved from the speaker's stone and gestured Bill Whates to take her place. He smiled, sorted cautiously through some notecards and began to speak. Beyond him, Katherine could see Elaine, in her pale, fluttering clothes, drifting towards the gathering. Her face was downcast, looking slightly sideways to the west, where the sun was sinking.

"I think Elaine's being mysterious again," Paul whispered to Katherine. Katherine shook her head impatiently, but she could see others, every now and then, turning their heads away from Bill Whates and towards Elaine's wandering progress. She felt a quick pang of envy. She didn't think Elaine particularly good looking. Her features were heavy, even coarse, but her long, thin body possessed a languorous grace and her black hair blew against her face as soft as down. As Elaine drew near the assembly, Katherine carefully observed her clothes. She hadn't seen this outfit before. She wore a laced camisole, a small embroidered waistcoat, a thin, gauzy shirt unbuttoned and a long cheesecloth skirt—all white and cream in layers. She wore a fragile Celtic cross on a necklace, the metal glinting on her pale throat. Like a milkmaid priestess—a hippie Tess of the D'Urbervilles. Feeling clumsy and unremarkable in comparison, Katherine resolved to develop a more prepossessing image for herself. She began an uninspired mental trawl through the old clothes harboured in her wardrobe, but a ripple of laughter amongst her companions drew her attention to the present again. She must have missed some amusing remark. Chiding herself for inattention, she turned her gaze from Elaine to Mr Whates. He was recounting the geological history of the area.

"The grey stones are sarsens, or sandstone. They are called grey wethers, meaning sheep, because they look like sheep lying in the grass," he said. "They are the broken down remains of a cap of sandstone which used to cover the chalk. Thousands of years ago palm trees grew in this region, and in some stones you can see the holes created by the roots of those trees."

She had heard it before—they all had. Still, they listened, as though Mr Whates was recounting anew a sacred history, summoning an English dreamtime.

"The valley in which we are standing is not such a splendid example as Piggledene, near Fyfield. Still, it is a charming and unique and worthy of protection. It has been designated an Area of Outstanding Natural Beauty, but this has apparently makes no difference to its fate. You can be assured that the Wiltshire History Society fully supports your protest against the bypass."

When Mr Whates had delivered his speech, Jan asked for questions.

"What about the barrow in the copse? You haven't told us about that." Violet spoke, sitting in the long grass beside Owain.

"Yes, the barrow. It is considered to be an ancient site, but we know little about its purpose. It was always assumed it was a burial chamber, as we find at West Kennet Long Barrow, though a smaller, less significant version. An excavation was attempted some thirty years ago, but very little was uncovered. I'm afraid it wasn't rated important enough, in an area littered with ancient sites, for the road builders to avoid."

"The barrow makes a few appearances in local folklore though." Violet again. Mr Whates agreed.

"According to one story, a hooded figure emerges from the barrow on midsummer morning, accompanied by a white horse. In another, people say if you sit on the barrow at certain times you can hear a woman weeping. There are many similar legends associated with these sites. At West Kennet, the ghost of a priest is supposed to enter the barrow on the sunrise of the longest day, and a big white dog with red ears. There is a myth that Silbury Hill is the burial mound of King Sil, buried erect on horseback, and sometimes he can be seen on a moonlit night, riding upon the hill in golden armour. Completely untrue of course. Sections into the barrow have revealed there is nothing buried in it at all. The mound is more likely to be some kind of monument, rather than a barrow. Still, there are many stories about its possible purpose, and many strange events are supposed to be connected with it. Unfortunately for me, I haven't witnessed any of these events for myself—and that's not because I haven't looked."

"You've been to West Kennet at midsummer?" someone asked. Bill Whates smiled shyly.

"Not for a good few years," he said. "But I did once. On my own."

"I think we may have had a sighting," Jan said. "I think Owain should tell everyone about his encounter."

Owain's face flushed red. He shot Jan a look of hostility. He shook his head.

"Come on. We all want to hear."

Violet nudged Owain. His body tensed with resistance. But he rose to his feet and made his way towards Jan. She ushered him to the speaker's stone. He looked quickly around the gathering, the circle of expectant faces turned towards him. Just beyond the circle, Elaine was sitting too, at once part of the gathering but also ouside it. He took half a roll-up from his pocket and lit it. He was procrastinating. Katherine felt a pang of sympathy. In the light of day, just how hard would he find it to explain his experience of the night before?

"I was sleeping out, in the valley." He spoke slowly, as though his tongue had thickened in his mouth. "I saw some kind of procession. Hundreds of figures moving together through the valley and up along the old lane. They looked like ghosts, not solid, but very brightly coloured. I could hear them too, music and strange songs and voices." He stopped talking. His audience waited in silence. Then, when no further words were forthcoming they turned to one another, unsure how they were ment to receive this account. A young man spoke up.

"Is this for real, Owain? Are we talking about a dream here, a vision? A hallucination?"

Owain shook his head.

"I'd taken nothing, drank nothing, I wasn't asleep. Anyway, Katherine was there too. She saw them as well as me."

The expectant faces turned to Katherine and she was summoned to the stone. Owain slipped gratefully to his place beside Violet, and Katherine described what had happened to her. As she finished, some discussion broke out.

Many of the gathering, adorned with amulets and crystals, disciples of the earth spirit, followers of magic, were aching to believe it. Katherine looked into their faces, and saw how hungry they were for her tale to be real. Still fragile from her experience, she felt afraid. She looked across at Paul and imagined he was silently pleading for her to keep his own encounters to herself. She complied. She sat beside him again and Jan took the stone.

"What do you all think?" she said. The talking died down. After a moment of silence, a girl near Violet stood up.

"I think it's obvious we must do everything we can to protect this place. Isn't this a sign of the valley's importance? Hasn't Owain witnessed some communication that we can't continue to destroy the land?"

Another voice, unidentified, spoke up:

"Are you suggesting we tell the planners they can't use this route because the faeries want it?" A ripple of laughter amongst some—but the girl shook her head with an expression of annoyance. A nearby companion leaned forward and patted her shoulder. Owain looked a little humiliated. The atmosphere of the meeting was not hostile to his story—they were all prepared to accept it, even if they didn't throughly believe it. No-one was laughing at him. Still, no-one would take it entirely on board, either. He glanced over his shoulder at Katherine. She smiled in reassurance.

Katherine sensed discord, and also uneasiness. To the likes of Bill Whates, they might appear as a unified body, but the clutch of protestors at the meeting were a very mixed alliance. Several belonged to local environmental organisations, and formed a practical, rational wing to the group living in the trees—the letter-writing, lobbying, marching people. Paul was the unspoken leader of this faction. They would not be keen to pay much attention to this episode. And seeing as Paul was also secretary of the Locksbury Anti-Bypass Alliance, he was a useful bridge between the main body of local opposition and this more radical group, that had formed around the tree dwellers. However, she, his partner, was the one who had purportedly been away with the faeries. At the other end, a handful of the gathering claimed to repudiate the ways of modern man entirely (though not enough to spurn their benefit cheques for the most part) and were waiting for the not-too-distant time when western civilisation would collapse under the weight of its own greed. To these, believers of spirits and conspiracies, Owain's faery visions would be signs of a collision with the Otherworld. Katherine put herself about half way along the line. Something very strange had happened to her. She knew Owain well enough to believe that he had been affected too. But did she really believe in faeries?

Mr Whates looked curiously animated.

"What do you think, honorable historian?" Jan asked him. He surveyed the assembly with a sly smile and shook his head.

"I'd have to see them with my own eyes I'm afraid," he said. Most of his audience nodded and smiled in agreement and the atmosphere of the gathering was partially smoothed over. Katherine looked again at Owain. He was sitting hunched up, his face downcast. One or two announcements were made regarding the progress of an eviction order served by the county sheriff, to oust the squatters. Jan thanked Mr Whates and invited him to their next gathering. A few people began to walk away from the stone valley, but most stayed to talk and to watch the sunset, the bright coppery flames brushing upon the ribbons of cloud.

As the light began to fade, the atmosphere in the valley grew more intimate. As the last fiery fragment of the sun disappeared beyond the hills, it was honoured by a ripple of appreciative applause. Not far from the copse, in a charred circle ringed by stones, a fire was burning and food would soon be ready—potatoes and carrots, sprinkled with rosemary conveniently growing wild in the cottage garden, baking in foil in the embers. A large saucepan full of onions, lentils, mushrooms and beans, was ready to set on the flames. For dessert, they would eat bananas, split and filled with chocolate melted in the heat.

Niamh was playing with the older children. As the evening wore on, she became tired and crept back to her mother, curling on her lap. Away from the fire the air grew chilly, and Katherine wrapped her in a blanket Violet had fetched from her bender. The sky darkened, and a gibbous moon lifted from the horizon, faintly gold. Katherine looked down at her daughter, the soft, baby cheek pressed against her lap. Her skin was very pale, and seemed to shine faintly in the darkness, like a flower—like the cool petals of magnolia. From nearby she heard the sound of drum beats as two lads, students from the local college, began an improvised rhythm on instruments they had brought along. Despite the hubbub of good natured conversation, Katherine felt isolated. Paul was talking to one of the Friends of the Earth people. Owain had disappeared altogether. Behind her the breeze swayed the trees in the copse, and the clash of the young leaves sounded very loud. The darkness intensified, but it seemed to lie dense on the ground, thickened by smoke, while up in the sky the air was clear and bright, glittering with moonlight and a blaze of stars. Down here, the shadowed forms of her companions seemed huddled and bent, like animals clinging tight and afraid to the face of the earth.

She felt a gentle hand on her shoulder. Elaine sat down beside her. She had wrapped herself in a dark shawl, but in the firelight, the silver around her throat glinted orange and red.

"I loved what you said about the faery people," she said carefully. "I tried to talk to Owain but I can't find him. I think he's wandered off."

Katherine nodded.

"Will you tell me again what happened?" Elaine asked. Katherine felt tired and heavy. Her mind lapsed into vacancy. She forced a smile and wriggled Niamh into a more comfortable position on her lap. Elaine persisted.

"Why don't we go for a wander?"

"I've got Niamh. She's asleep."

"Paul will keep an eye on her." Elaine went over to Paul. Katherine saw her gesture to Niamh, and Paul nodded.

"He says that's fine." Elaine stood waiting. Katherine gently scooped up the child, and placed her on Paul's lap. Elaine began to walk down the valley, and Katherine followed after her, trotting to catch up. She felt slightly intimidated, not knowing Elaine that well. She could not remember ever having a one to one conversation with her before. Elaine kept often to herself, a little withdrawn from the close, intimate community of the other tree dwellers. Indeed, although she had a little nest in the trees, she was often entirely absent for days at a time.

They walked to the end of the valley, then climbed the short, steep slope through the hawthorn bushes. At the top, beyond three strands of barbed wire, stretched a huge field, gently undulating, the young wheat rippling silken in pale moonlit glimmers. The women did not cross the fence. They stood on a small level at the top of the slope, with the dark hawthorn below them. The grass was short and dense, marked here and there with old sheep droppings. The wind tugged at a strand of wool caught on the barbed wire. In one direction they could see right along the valley, to the sharp orange flicker of the fire near the copse.

Elaine turned her back to the valley and gazed out across the wheat field, to the moon swooping up into space. Katherine stood beside her. How clear and pure it was, how open and free. Elaine stretched up, as though she wanted to fling herself from the face of the earth, up and up, to fly into the wide spaces where the light was fierce and clean. She dropped her shawl and breathed the cold air deep into her body as the night chill washed around her flesh. She turned to Katherine.

"Isn't it wonderful up here?" she said, exulted. But Katherine felt small and dark, like an animal shrinking from torchlight. Elaine regarded her with some chagrin. She tried to force a change.

"Isn't it wonderful?" she repeated. "Isn't it better to be alone? Once you can break free of the little social connections. They tie you. You talk to x,y,z and your consciousness, your entire, grand consciousness, is focussed on bits of trivia and gossip. I'm tired of it, you know? I thought it would all be different, coming here, to live in a community like this, but it's turned out all the same. How many planned spontaneous drumming sessions can we cope with?"

Despite herself, Katherine laughed. As she laughed, her reserve crumbled and her mind seemed to break from some restraint. But she felt a little guilty and compelled to respond.

"Oh, I don't know. I love it here. I think the people are brilliant. I like planned spontaneous drumming sessions. It beats the telly."

"Do you know what I mean though? In offices people gossip about who's sleeping with who, about so-and-so's lack of dress sense, about someone else's poor work performance. And it's just the same here, only coated with hippiespeak. This person's a bit earthy, someone else doesn't communicate well, his moon is in a water sign, that person's hard to deal with when he's taken too much speed, but it's understandable when you know about his family circumstances and anyway his pottery is inspired."

Katherine stifled a giggle. Inside, she felt a curious, frightening pit loom open, a physical sensation. Some kind of fear. She did not want Elaine to destroy her happiness with these people, her hope that at last she had found some kind of kindred. But Elaine was relentless.

"I want more, you know? For all the appearance, they are still treading the same old tracks. Even here there's complacency. We don't go far enough. Their minds revolve in the same narrow sphere. The thinking space is limited, the boundaries are closing in. We're all tricking ourselves into thinking this is some alternative way of living, but what have we really got? Half of us on a girl guide's camping holiday in the trees. The rest aren't even committed, they trot home to their prison houses at the end of a meeting and carry on with their careers and modern lives. This is just some little outing, an interlude of new ageness so they can appease their consciences."

Katherine bridled. Was this a thinly veiled personal attack? She took it personally. She nursed it in her heart, and felt diminished. Elaine continued in a similar vein, reiterating her accusations. Her voice was relentless. When at last she paused, Katherine piped up.

"And how are you different? What exactly do you want?" she asked, half choked. Elaine sighed deeply. She stared up, out towards the oceanic wash of stars.

"It's not enough to join a road protest," she said. "You can sit in front of the diggers, you can smoke dope and hang around campfires for the rest of your life and it won't make any difference to the way you think, the way you feel. To be keenly alive, like an animal; to move among the shades and spirits, like a shaman. I am floating on the breath of the universe. My life is an illumination in the void. So how can I bury my subtle senses in mundane routines? Even here, look at them balming their insecurities with their false loving acceptance of each other, making things comfortable. So much mental and emotional wadding." Her speech, a bitter staccato, lapsed into silence. Katherine failed to respond.

After a moment, Elaine breathed in and asked, "Do you think you could find Crow again?"

In an instant it occurred to Katherine that the root of Elaine's outburst of anger and attack was a jealousy that she, Katherine, had apparently been taken by the faeries, while Elaine, the mystic and free spirit, had been overlooked.

"I don't know," she said slowly. "Paul and I went back to the place where Crow pitched her tent and we could find no trace of her. I have no idea how we could reach her."

"Are you utterly convinced this really happened?" Elaine spoke through gritted teeth. For her to disbelieve Katherine's tale of the otherworld was unthinkable, but could she place herself in the position of postulant? Katherine nodded. She also shivered. As the darkness deepened the cold seeped into her body. She sat on the short grass hugging her knees to her chest.

"Look, I'd better get back," she said. "Niamh will be wanting me."

Elaine shook her head impatiently. "She'll be okay. She's with her father, isn't she?"

Katherine felt an ache of concern that Niamh might be fretting without her, but she succumbed to Elaine's will and remained sitting.

"Perhaps we could call them up somehow. A summoning. Maybe you have a link with them."

"I don't know. I can't yet remember what happened to me. I wouldn't know where to start."

"What about the bone necklace? Isn't that a link? Maybe we should meditate upon it. May I have it?"

Unwilling to relinquish it, but afraid she might otherwise seem churlish, Katherine took the necklace off and handed it over. In the darkness Elaine could make out little of the engraving, but she sniffed it dubiously, then pressed it in her palm.

"You're right, it does have a weird smell. Very faint though. It gives off strange emanations too."

"Does it?" Katherine said politely. Elaine closed her eyes and pressed the bone to her forehead. She remained thus for several minutes. Katherine sighed noisily. Wasn't it all a pose? She got to her feet and stomped up and down to warm herself.

"Picking up anything?" she asked. Elaine frowned.

"Maybe. We need a ceremony, an evocation. I have some things with me." She fished around in a small bag hanging from her waist. A stub of candle, a charcoal block and some other bits and pieces Katherine could not make out in the darkness. But she was at once intrigued. Elaine took out matches and lit the candle. The fragile golden flame guttered in the breeze. Elaine positioned her body to shield it from the wind. In its quivering illumination, Katherine watched her place a Mother figurine near the bone necklace, with tiny smooth pebbles to mark the four quarters. She lit the charcoal block with the candle, and placed it, glowing orange, in the centre. She dropped a few grains of incense on the block, where they hissed faintly, and Katherine caught the sharp resinous scent on the cold night air.

"Was it you who put that Mother figure by the Swallowhead Spring?" Katherine asked. Elaine nodded.

"I saw it there the night I met Crow. Last night."

Elaine looked up and smiled with some satisfaction.

"We must meditate," she said. "Remember them, Katherine. See if you can call them again." Elaine shut her eyes. Katherine shivered, and gazed upwards. The mental effort of meditation seemed way, way beyond her. But when she looked again at Elaine, the other woman was regarding her very coolly.

"Don't you want to do this?" Elaine asked. Katherine shrugged, and Elaine became irritated.

"You've been given an amazing gift. You have an opportunity. Take it," she said sharply. So Katherine capitulated. She gazed down at the bone, shadowed in the flickering yellow light. Threads of sweet smoke from the incense, and beneath it a wisp of the stranger perfume from the bone. She focussed inwards, to the black space in her memory, to the lost long hours of the night-time. Here and now she was cold and tired, niggled by concern for her daughter. She made a concerted effort to clear her mind, to push out the stray thoughts that flitted into her mind like bats. She recalled the walk to the boundary of trees, where the creeping, mutable forms of the faeries were waiting. And then...what happened then? She tried to remember. Still she came against the void in her head, like a barrier to a strange realm in the mind. But first confront the mental block. Like a hallowed gateway in a folk tale, the secret doorway with a magic key. How to find it? How to discover the 'open sesame!' that hid from her the contents of her own memories? What was it like? Katherine imagined an tall archway built of honey-coloured stone, the sky blue and open above it, and two wooden gates barred and locked. No. Too grand, too obvious. The image twitched and unravelled. A new image materialised in her mind. Buried in streamers of ivy and travellers joy, the mellow red of an old brick wall. Then, obscured by plumes of dog rose, a tiny doorway. To one side she saw an ornate, rusty keyhole, and on the other—two long, shapely hinges. The doorway stretched up to a pointed arch. Yes, this was it. Beyond the door lay the hidden fields, the pathway into faery lands. She stood before the door tasting the faint breeze blowing from the hidden place. If I put my hand into my pocket, she thought, I will find the key that fits the lock. Then I will remember. Slowly she reached into the pocket, waiting for the cold contact with a long, iron key. Her fingers closed on emptiness. Nothing. She looked all around the door. She peeled back ivy from the wall. Still nothing. She began to hurry. She was failing to control her own fantasy. A distant music, like the faintest strains of a violin, drifted on the wind from beyond the wall. Was this part of her meditation or did it originate in the real world? The sound was so far away she could not quite distinguish. It started up again, a frail stream of music drifting into her mind. She stared at the wall, and it began to shift and mutate before her. In vain she willed it to be still. Bricks piled up in front of the locked door, one on top of the other. She could hear the clack of each brick as it slid into place. The vision had become a bad dream. It had slipped from her control and although she knew this was not reality, she could not bring herself back. Have I fallen asleep, she thought, how do I wake myself up? The bricks built up, till the door was half covered. Then she heard a hammering on the other side. Someone was trying to get out. She heard a fierce shriek. Her blood turned to ice in her limbs. Beyond the wall a child was crying in panic. As she heard the cry, she flung herself against the gate.

"Niamh!" she called, "Niamh!" Relentless, the bricks piled higher and higher. Katherine tore at them with her fingers to no effect. At last the door was obliterated, and the child's voice grew dim. A pale, green form drifted from the wall like smoke, and twisted itself about her limbs. It pressed against her face, touching her mouth in a kiss. When her lips parted it flew into her like a fog, and down her throat. She gagged. She could not breathe. She fell back, choking, fighting for breath. The vision was swallowed in darkness. Then she was free.

Katherine opened her eyes, gulping the cold night air. She was lying on her back looking up at the stars. Elaine's frightened face peered down at her.

"Are you all right?" she whispered. "They were here. They were all around us. You were right, it was all true." Her eyes were wide. Her skin glinted whitely in the darkness.

"You just passed out. You shouted out for Niamh. I couldn't get you back, I was afraid," she said. Katherine breathed deeply. She sat up. Her head ached intensely, and at first she was dizzy.

"Niamh," she said. When she rose to her feet she experienced a head-rush so sharp she nearly fell down again. She stood for a moment, tottering, while the stars seemed to wheel above her.

"I've got to check she's okay. " She spoke as though she was half drunk. Still unsteady, she slid clumsily back down the slope. Elaine was soon lost in the darkness.

Alone, Elaine felt the rapid beat of her heart begin to slow. Should she have gone with Katherine, to help her? She wanted to sit alone, to recollect her thoughts. She could hardly believe what she had seen, but amidst her fading feelings of fear she was quietly triumphant. How she had ached for the Otherworld, how long had she been seeking for the path into the beyond. And at last the unknown had shown itself.

She had been only half confident that Katherine's tale was true. She had never taken much notice of her before, apparently unremarkable as she was. She was more impressed by Katherine's partner, Paul Matravers—although he annoyed her, she recognised he was in some way like her.

They had seen her, the spirits. They had looked into her and made an acknowledgement, she was sure. They were sucked from the ground, like a mist. They had clung to Katherine's skin and Katherine had opened her eyes. But the mind looking out was not hers, and Elaine meeting that gaze was at once frightened and comforted. It already knew her, didn't it? She felt she was remembering a deeply buried dream, a quick sense of remembrance. Then a vision—a glimpse of a woman, dressed in white, cleaning blood-stained clothes in a river.

The faeries. She had been waiting for them. She had long been searching without knowing quite what she sought. Her true life was just beginning.

CHAPTER SIX

Above the chalk downs the clouds drifted like ships through the brilliant blue. Tall, glistening clouds trimmed with silver in the heights, and below, a dark, dismal grey, casting huge shadows across the fields. From the top of the scarp face, Katherine looked across the gentle curves of the landscape. Cloud shadows swallowed fields into darkness, floating towards the west, then cast them once again into fierce sunlight, as they passed on their journey. High up, where the breeze was quick, and the grass flickered soft against her legs, Niamh was toddling about in a dream, with stems of white clover in her fist. Elaine was lying on her belly in the shining emerald grass.

Katherine dropped down. She lay on her front, soaked in warmth, her face pillowed on her arms and blades of grass tickling her cheek as she peeked at Niamh. A cloud covered the face of the sun. In an instant the penetrating heat vanished. Then the wind was bitter. Katherine saw the flesh of her arms rise up in goose-pimples. The fine golden hairs stood up. She shivered and shut her eyes, waiting for the shade to pass. She hugged her jacket tight against her body as the chill began to press into her body. Then the cloud was gone, and again they were bathed in the sun's swift, hot caress.

The two women lay silent and sleepy. Alternately they were bathed in glowing warmth, then doused in cold shadow. Nearby, Elaine's little rucksack contained the remains of their picnic, a couple of apples and Niamh's half empty beaker of juice. They had covered seven miles in the morning, and had at least as far to go in the afternoon to complete their circuit back to Locksbury. Time was getting on. Katherine sat up.

"I said I'd be back by five thirty. To meet Paul when he gets back from work. Shall we go now?"

Elaine turned her face away and made some muffled reply, but remained where she was for several minutes longer. Eventually she sat up too.

"Shall we go out to Marlborough tonight?" she said.

"What, out to the pub?"

"Yeah. When was the last time you went out drinking?"

Katherine smiled and sighed at the same time.

"Not since Niamh was born. Well, not for several months before that. I didn't go out much when I was pregnant. All the smoke. And no alcohol for me. Not much fun."

"Well, come out tonight then. Matravers could babysit."

Katherine felt uneasy about asking him, though he had been out several times in the last fortnight. Mostly to meetings, though many of these were at friends' houses and often involved the cracking open of a few beers at the end of the evening. He could have no reasonable objection. In fact, she recalled, he had urged her to go out more, to enjoy herself. So why did the prospect of a night out boozing fill her with slight apprehension? Though also a measure of excitement.

"She'll be fine, Katherine. Stop worrying, paranoid woman," Elaine said. "You keep running off to her. She's always okay."

Elaine had touched correctly on her fears for Niamh.

"How can you say that? You saw them too. You know they're real. How can you say she'll be fine? I'm not even sure she's fine now."

"And what will they do? And isn't Matravers just as strong a protective force as yourself?"

Katherine shrugged. She was sleeping badly, waking up just before dawn, the sky smoky grey above the horizon. And she would rush to Niamh's cot, to find her daughter lying asleep, her face peaceful though her skin was perhaps a little cold. She seemed well enough.

"Something's not right. But what does that mean? She's here with me, so why am I afraid I'm losing her?"

Niamh approached as Katherine spoke and clambered into her mother's lap, her hair scented with grass and clover. Katherine rubbed her cheek against Niamh's perfect, smooth face. Even now she could smell the faery scent, like a faint perfume on the child's body. And Niamh had changed, hadn't she? In tiny barely perceptible ways. Changes that only a mother could detect—though might this just be her own anxiety, as Elaine had suggested? Wasn't she more remote? Had she become more withdrawn?

Elaine was watching the little scene with some detachment. Although she could be perfectly charming with the little girl, Katherine suspected she found Niamh a nuisance, an impediment to their partnership. But it was time to go. Katherine fastened the child into the backpack and hoisted it onto her back. Niamh smiled and cheered, pointing out to the sweeping blue and silver sky. As they set off walking along the top of the scarp face, Katherine noticed two crows circling above land, high above the fields. The sunlight glinted on their backs.

Paul was already home when at they arrived. His greeting to Elaine was offhand. Katherine tugged a tired, uncomfortable Niamh from the backpack and passed her to Paul while she went to the kitchen and began to prepare dinner. Niamh was grumpy and grizzly. As the pasta boiled, Katherine saw how tired and hungry Paul looked, as he patiently jogged his daughter up and down in to soothe her. Katherine felt guilty again. She had been out enjoying herself all day. Elaine was sprawled across a chair by the window, gazing into space.

Half an hour later they were sat together round the table eating pasta in a thick tomato sauce, with a hastily assembled salad and hunks of rather stale bread. Paul wolfed down his portion and returned for more. Niamh picked at hers, then tipped the bowl on the floor scattering mashed up food across the floorboards.

"We were thinking of going into Marlborough tonight," Elaine said. Katherine shot her a quick angry look. She had wanted to ask him herself. Paul continued to eat for a moment, then he stopped and regarded Elaine.

"Are you talking to me?"

"Yes. Katherine and I were thinking of going out. You wouldn't mind babysitting would you?"

Paul turned to Katherine.

"Is that right? You want me to babysit?"

To her annoyance, Katherine found herself smiling a false ingratiating smile.

"If you don't mind. You said I should go out sometime."

Paul shrugged coldly.

Later, when Katherine was settling Niamh into bed, Paul slipped in behind her and put his arms around her waist.

"I hardly seem to see you alone these days," he said. "Elaine's eaten with us for the past five days, and then you're up talking with her past midnight."

"I know. I must get to bed earlier tonight. It's alright for Elaine, she can lie in."

Elaine had spent the past few nights sleeping on the sofa, when their night-time sessions had stretched into the small hours.

"Has she made any contributions to our food bill yet?"

"Why are you being so petty? She doesn't have an income. I thought you were the communal type. How can you get so uptight about extending hospitality?"

Paul's face tensed.

"How do you know she hasn't got an income? Isn't she signing on?" He paused and breathed deeply. "You're right, of course," he said. "But I don't like her."

"I know. You've said."

"I don't understand why you're letting yourself be led round by the nose."

"I'm not. We're going through this together. You too, remember? Or are you in the denial phase again?"

Paul's face stilled again. Katherine could read the conflict in his mind, his attempts to analyse his motives honestly.

"Then it's alright for me to go out? You really don't mind?"

He shook his head.

Later Katherine left him sitting downstairs with a magazine on his lap, but he didn't appear to be reading much. He looked a bit defeated. Niamh was quiet in her cot, presumably asleep. Elaine and Katherine went upstairs to preen themselves for an evening out. They swigged from a bottle of whisky that had materialised from the depths of Elaine's rucksack. Elaine rummaged through Katherine's wardrobe, and they chatted and joked, bursting into fits of girlish laughter. After nearly an hour, they skipped down the stairs and into the living room in a swirl of colours. Katherine spun around in front of Paul, then stood, self-conscious and twitchy, waiting for his verdict. She was dressed in a long green velvet dress, with a tight bodice stitched with sequins and embroidered flowers. Her hair was twined in a long, loose plait down her back, with quick, curly strands loose about her face, thick and brown but glittering with threads of gold and honey. She was wearing make-up for the first time in months, just a smudge around her eyes, a glint of dusty copper on her cheeks, and the bones below her throat.

"Well? Don't you like it?" she asked, disappointed.

"Yeah. You look great. A bit dolled up for a trip to the pub though?" His voice was thick with something that sounded like disapproval.

"Katherine tells me she hasn't dressed herself up for months. So why not? We thought we'd make it an occasion." Elaine draped herself across an armchair, so that festoons of cream coloured lace fell in artless folds all about her.

"That dress. It's Katherine's too?" he asked.

Dreamily Elaine picked at the decorated cuffs. "Yes," she said. "I love it. Kath thinks it suits me. What d'you think?"

"Looks fine," he said, flatly. Elaine swigged from the whisky bottle, and offered it to Paul. He accepted.

"You'd better head off. It's nearly nine. You'll miss the last bus into town," he said. "Have you organised a lift home?"

"Someone will drop us off," she said.

Katherine ran up the stairs to make a final check on Niamh. When she opened the door the bedroom seemed stuffy and warm. She opened the window, and the cool evening air streamed in. Asleep in her cot, Niamh moved her head and her limbs began to stir. Katherine looked out through the curtains, to the backgardens lined up behind the terrace. In their own little patch, an old apple tree grew in the corner, overshadowing the square of lawn with dark branches. Perched at the top were three crows, restless black shadows in the leaves. But crows had always visited the apple tree, Katherine reminded herself, resisting the temptation to shut the window again. She moved quietly to the side of the cot and regarded the sleeping child. Her forehead was slick with a faint sheen of sweat, and her hair was sticking to her face. In her cheeks the colour was heightened. She had kicked her legs free of the quilt, with its faded decoration of roses. She sighed deeply in her sleep, then was still. Katherine bent over the cot, leaning closer and closer to her baby, till their faces were almost touching. She held her breath, and felt the tiny child breaths warm against her cheek, soft as a feather against her skin. Afraid of waking her, yet unable to resist the temptation, she kissed the soft face. Niamh did not stir. Her body had become quite still, though beneath her eyelids, Katherine could see a flicker. What was she dreaming?

Elaine called up the stairs, urging her to hurry. Katherine moved to the doorway. She looked back, hesitating. She opened the bedroom door wide, but she went back to the window and shut it again.

They had to run to catch the bus. They had only one fellow passenger, a morose old man in a brown jacket, who frowned as they sipped from the whiskey bottle, their lips leaving sticky painted kisses on the glass rim. Outside the fields were yet brightly illuminated, verdure shining in the sunlight. Time after time golden light glittered through the leaves, flooding the windows, as the bus changed direction, winding through the narrow lanes.

When the bus pulled up in the Marlborough High Street, Elaine rose to her feet, slowly pulling an incongruous fake fur jacket around her shoulders. Katherine followed her, smiling apologetically to the old man.

They strode down the road, happily drunk and puffed like peacocks. The High Street was enormously wide—following, Owain maintained, the course of a ley line —lined with shops on either side, a jumble of pretty buildings and variously historical shop fronts. At each end stood a church—one now used as a craft centre, but decorated still with a grand square tower topped with turrets like a castle. At the far end, they turned off left, into the sudden darkness of a narrow alley. The ground was paved, tall, red brick walls to either side. Weeds crept from the crevices in the brickwork. Katherine stopped before a narrow wooden door, and took a deep breath. A sweet scent like honey, and a keen citrus, drifting tendrils over the wall.

She opened the door and they stepped into a garden.

It was not a large place—only as wide as Jan's little shop, and maybe twice as long, but the burgeoning mass of botanical growth dimmed the any sense of confinement. On the paving behind the back door crowds of terra cotta pots were overflowing with herbs and flowers. A dense curtain of clematis bowed the decaying beams of an old pergola, the profusion of pale, mauve flowers hanging in skirts each side. A narrow path weaved the length of the garden between verdant beds, crowded with leaves and stems and blossoms. Baskets hung from brackets on the wall, wooden troughs were crammed onto shelves. In every nook, on every spare patch of ground, pots nestled cheek by jowl, erupting with plants. At the far end of the garden, they saw Jan stooping in the shadows, a hosepipe in her hand, spreading a stream of water across the beds.

"Hey! Jan!" Elaine called. Jan looked up, and waved. As she turned the sun glanced across her hair, burnished copper, and the water droplets glittered.

"Sit down," she said. "I'll be with you in a minute. Put the kettle on."

Katherine and Elaine sat at an old wooden table near the backdoor. Around their feet tubs bristled with several varieties of parsley and basil. Positioned more discreetly by the wall, Elaine noticed several magnificent cannabis plants. She nudged Katherine, and pointed them out.

"Shall I put the kettle on? Or are we sticking to the whisky?" she said.

"Whisky I think. But I'll get some glasses." Katherine stepped through the back door and climbed the flight of steps to the flat. The kitchen was small and dark, with an old fashioned butler's sink beneath the one window, which overlooked the garden. Bunches of herbs hung from the ceiling, and more stuffed the jars that lined the shelves all around the room, along with postcards, pictures of flowers, and odd pieces of crockery. The kitchen was immaculate—perfectly tidy. So much crammed into a small space, quite claustrophobic, yet order prevailed. Katherine found three glasses and took them down to the garden.

Jan was sitting with Elaine when she returned. She looked them both up and down, half amused.

"You two are looking very glamorous tonight. What's the occasion? Chasing men?"

"We were in the mood for it. Dressing up that is," Katherine said. She found herself stifling tipsy giggles. Her hand reached for her glass, and almost knocked it over. Her fingers began to tingle. She took another swig, and replaced the glass, conscious of her unreliable fingers.

"I think I'm getting rather drunk," she said with as much poise as she could muster.

"Me too."

Though to Katherine's eyes, Elaine still looked very much in control of the situation. She talked on with Jan, and Katherine lapsed into a reverie, staring at the sway of the leaves not far from her cheek.

Then they were walking away from the garden, down to the White Hart in the High Street. Katherine gripped Elaine's arm, and understood that Elaine was drunk too, because they were laughing very loudly and whispering endearments to each other. The evening became a haze. They met up with friends from the camp. Katherine was suddenly afraid she was talking too much. They danced to music from the jukebox, earning looks from the more sober-minded patrons, and then an hour must have passed, because suddenly she was walking down the High Street again, and it had become dark. The cold air was a shock. Katherine heard a ringing in her ears, and she wished Paul was with her. Elaine was nearby. She could hear her voice though she couldn't see her, with the company milling about on the pavement. A fellow protestor called a taxi, and Katherine found herself wedged between Elaine and another of the camp residents as the car headed away from the town. Inside the car, the atmosphere was very warm. Katherine leaned her cheek against the cold window, dimly aware of the hedges reeling past the car. She thought perhaps the height of her intoxication was past, and she faintly tried to reassemble her thoughts, before closing her eyes, and lapsing into a circling darkness. She must have dozed off for a minute or two. Someone was shaking her.

"Time to wake-up, sleepyhead." Elaine was half pulling her from the taxi. As soon as she was standing, the car door was slammed shut, and the taxi drove off into the darkness. The two women were alone. As her eyes adjusted, Katherine made out the dim forms of trees, the undulating fields.

"Where are we?" she cried. Then the penny dropped. "Why are we here? I'm supposed to be back at Locksbury. Why did you bring us here?"

Elaine looked annoyed.

"We're at the camp, of course. You agreed. In the pub. You said you wanted to come back here for a coffee with the others."

Katherine was silent. She scanned back across her memories of the evening. It was all very hazy. She was fairly sure she had made no such remark, but she could not be certain.

"Come-on. We're getting left behind." Elaine started to walk up the track. The three lads were already far ahead. Katherine caught up with Elaine.

"I should be home. I promised Paul. What if Niamh wakes up? I'll have to walk back across the fields."

"What, in the pitch black? The kid'll be okay. Stop worrying. Have a drink first."

As Katherine stumbled over the ruts in the Old Lane she considered how difficult it would be to walk back at this time. Of course there was no telephone in the squat, though one or two of the people staying at the spinney had mobiles. Maybe she could use one of those.

Light spilled from the cottage windows. They opened the door and stepped into a quiet crowd. Along the mantelpiece and on the window sills a host of candles flickered as they closed the door behind them.

"Make sure you close the door properly. It keeps on slamming," someone said. Katherine fiddled with the latch. They stood uneasily by the door for a few moments, looking around the room. Maybe twelve people were crammed in, sitting on crates, or on the floor, all very quiet with shadows on their faces. As Katherine scanned the assembly she recognised most of the faces, and a sigh of relief escaped her. The tree-dwellers of course, and a few others who drifted in and out of the community, and a couple whom nobody seemed to know but were welcomed all the same. New people arrived frequently, some stayed for a bit then moved on. Sometimes dedicated environmental warriors, sometimes drifters looking for warmth and company. Occasionally strange, unstable people, refugees from the mental institutions. The gathering possessed an aura of tranquility, and of shy welcome. So why had they looked sinister when she first walked in?

At her feet, Violet was nudging her. After a while Katherine realised that she was trying to pass her a grey-looking spliff. She took it, but handed it straight to Elaine. Then she sank gratefully to the floor beside Violet.

"What's everyone doing here?" she asked. "Have you had some kind of meeting?"

"Not really. I was feeling a bit uneasy, like I wanted to be inside. I came down to the cottage, and everyone else must have been feeling the same thing. Eventually we were all gathered here. The spinney was weird." Violet tossed her hair over her shoulder and sucked at her lip ring.

"In what way weird?"

"That's what we were all talking about. We were remembering what you said had happened. I don't mean to suggest that people didn't believe you, but up there tonight..."

"What, did you see anything?"

"No. Just the light was strange, a shiny twilight somebody said. We all felt edgy."

"Perhaps we should go up there." Elaine had spoken. She was listening to the conversation. Katherine felt a chill in her heart. She most certainly did not want to go up there.

"I can't," she said bluntly. "I've got to ring Paul. I've got to let him know where I am. Do you know if anyone here has a mobile?"

Violet gestured to a young woman sitting on the other side of the room. The phone was swiftly produced. Katherine spoke briefly to Paul. She told him she would walk home early in the morning before he left for work.

"He sounds annoyed. What am I going to do?"

"Stop worrying. Let's go up to the copse."

The door slammed open. Someone swore and rose to shut it again, but Owain stepped in just as the door was closing.

"Hey, sorry mate. I didn't realise it was you. I thought it was the wind."

"Don't worry," Owain said. "It was the wind. Only I was behind the wind."

Katherine hadn't seen Owain since the meeting in the stone valley two weeks before. He had disappeared. Not an unusual occurrence, but still she was curious. He looked very tired and worn. The weathered lines around his eyes were deep. His hair was lank and grimy. He had apparently been sleeping very rough. He scanned the room much as Katherine had. His eyes alighted on her.

"Katherine," he said softly. He squatted beside her. "I think you should come outside."

"Where have you been?" she said.

"Come outside. I'll tell you about it." He looked up. Katherine realised that everyone in the room had tuned in to their conversation. He stood uneasily and walked to the door. He nodded expectantly to Katherine. Very reluctant, she rose to her feet and followed him. Elaine was close behind.

When the women had left, Paul threw aside his magazine and reached for a book instead. He put some music on. But he still found it hard to concentrate. His gaze wandered idly around the room. Beside his feet, in a white cup and saucer, the tea grew cold untouched. When Paul came to himself, he registered that the music had stopped some time ago. As he stirred from the chair to choose another CD, he was startled by a vigorous hammering at the door. For an instant he was anxious, remembering the last visitor who had called in the night, when he was all alone. Then he decided the caller was probably the real Katherine. Perhaps she had forgotten to take her keys. He opened the door. He was confronted by a tall, slightly burly figure in a leather jacket.

"Ah. James. Come in," he said. James stepped in, unzipping his jacket.

"You said it was okay to call by today," he said.

"Yes. Yes, I'm sorry, I had forgotten all about it. What time is it?"

"Nine. I'm a bit late. You look out of sorts. Are you feeling okay?"

"Yes. Fine. A bit tired. I thought it was later than that."

"It's still light."

"Yes, of course it is." Paul looked out of the window, and was surprised to see it was indeed still sunny. "Do you want some tea?" he said. He headed out to the kitchen, carrying the last cup with him. Now he had gathered his thoughts, he felt some relief to have company.

"Katherine out?"

"Yes. Gone to Marlborough with Elaine. One of the women tree dwellers. Do you know her?"

James shook his head.

"Don't recognise the name." He was a few years younger than Paul. An inch taller, and several inches wider, with a thatch of light brown hair and a ridiculous long moustache. He worked for the Marlborough Guardian, a struggling weekly paper with a tiny office above a pet shop. It had two young reporters, and the part-time services of a photographer, who shared his time with a paper in the next town. Although the bypass protest had brought the two men into frequent contact, their original meeting was engineered by Paul's boss, the chief architect, who lived in a grand Victorian villa on the edge of Avebury. James was his lodger. Once, several months previously, Paul had been invited round for drinks and he had struck up a friendship with James, who was then entirely new to the area. They met at the various protest meetings, and often had a drink together afterwards. The relationship had its advantages for Paul, particularly as James was sympathetic to the cause. The bypass protest had received particularly generous coverage in the Marlborough Guardian.

It was the first time that James had called on him at home. He picked up the book left on Paul's chair. It was the United Nations 'Progress of Nations' report.

"You reading this?"

"Yeah. Sort of. I wasn't really in the right frame of mind."

"No?" James scanned the titles on the bookcase near the chair. Marx and Lenin, the old guard, were lined up before Callinicos and half a dozen volumes bearing the title "International Socialism." Then books on Green politics, the environment, the Third World.

"You've read all these too?"

Paul nodded impatiently.

"You're some serious politico. Do I read here the progression of your personal ideology?" James persisted. Paul sensed a slight mockery in his friend's voice. He bridled at the jolly public school boy tone. Though sometimes he found it refreshing—so much in contrast to his own endless conscience searching. He shrugged.

"Anyone can read books," he said. "What difference does it make?"

"You tell me. Does it make any difference?"

"Cut the reporter crap, will you? I don't make any difference. The injustice persists. A quarter of humanity survives from day to day in absolute poverty and here am I worrying about the repairs needed for the damp course. I might as well be reading cookery books."

"No," James said, gently. "You don't just read though, do you? You're at the heart of the road protest." Correctly he had touched upon his friend's preoccupation. "Is this what you've been worrying about?"

Paul sat up straight and shrugged his shoulders, uncomfortable that his feelings should be so transparent.

"Yes, it is, as a matter of fact. I have lately been musing upon my impotence."

James raised an eyebrow.

"I trust we are speaking about social, rather than personal impotence," he said. "I can't imagine the other would be a problem."

Conscious that James rather admired Katherine, Paul allowed himself a smile.

"No, not that."

"Well, what's the problem? There seem to be few spare minutes in the day when you're not writing, ringing, hassling, organising or whatever. D'you think you should be up in the trees too?"

"Perhaps. Suddenly it all seems like a lot of tinkering. I'm not free any more. When Katherine became pregnant everything changed. Two years later, I've undertaken a profession, I've got a mortgage, for Christ's sake I've even got a occupational pension lined up. Bound up. Cabinned cribbed and confined. An admirable middle class family, and it's all so reasonable and sensible, but I tell you, when I start thinking about it my guts begin to heave. So all the other stuff I do, the bits and pieces I squeeze into the spare hours around work, it looks like frilling, the decoration around the edge of passivity and conforming. D'you know what I'm doing at work? Designing pretty extensions for people's cottage homes, so they can have a guest bedroom and an extra bathroom, while not a hundred miles away there are people sleeping on the streets. I mean, whose side am I on?"

"You're only one person. Speaking for myself, I think you have an enviable life. What would you prefer to be doing?"

Paul's face clouded.

"There lies the problem. Surely if anyone deserves my time and support it is my own daughter. What could be more natural and human than to care and provide for my family? The more I dwell on it, the greater the feeling grows. Right in the heart of me I start to think I've done everything wrong. I have failed along the line. I am being judged. I have not made the right choices." Paul had been staring at his hands as he spoke, but suddenly he stopped and looked up, carried away by his own train of thought and abruptly conscious that he might have said too much. He was exposed. Still, his companion's face was sympathetic, though silent for a few moments.

"It sounds to me like you should get religion. Maybe you're suffering from original sin," James said.

"Yeah, I know, or sign up for the schizophrenia ward." He felt vaguely weak and tearful. He sought to regain his composure.

"How about trading these teas for beers?" he said. "I've got a couple in the fridge."

"Okay. Just the one."

Paul jumped to his feet and went out to the kitchen. He was beginning to regret his impulsive communication. When he returned with the beers he steered the conversation quickly to material matters, the next meeting at the stone valley, the progress of the eviction order. James drew out a notebook and wrote some details.

Eventually, he picked up his jacket. Paul looked at the clock and saw to his surprise that it was past midnight.

"I'd hoped to say hello to Katherine," James said, as he headed for the front door.

"Well, she promised to be home in good time. I guess they must have called round somewhere after closing time. I'll deliver your greetings."

James had already donned his helmet and as he sat astride the low, black motorcycle, he nodded, and started up the engine. He waved as he headed off down the street. Paul heard the telephone ring just as he closed the door.

So, another night on his own. He checked on Niamh, who looked perfectly tranquil, and then he went to bed. At least Niamh was sleeping better. These last few nights she had slept right through. Katherine had interpreted this as another sign that something was wrong with her, but Paul was grateful his babysitting duties were a little easier. Still, he found it hard to sleep. The night was hot and he was teased by an endless stream of lustful thoughts. His body ached with desire. Why wasn't Katherine here? Not that it would make much difference if she was. Apart from that one sweet time when she had returned, she still stubbornly shrugged him off. Only now he was beginning to get on her nerves. Ever since that night...he felt possessed. Weirdly, his initial feelings of revulsion towards the stinking succubus had reversed, and now his desire for the creature that both was, and wasn't Katherine held him like a sickness, a disease. He only had to think about her for a moment to feel his pulse increase and his body begin to sweat. He was haunted by the memory of her kiss, her taste of sweet, rotting fruit. Even the repugnant smell he recalled so distinctly had become overlaid with a yearning that ate into his will. How could he so much desire a dream?

CHAPTER SEVEN

Jo had enthroned the wooden doll on his dressing table, amongst the dead spray cans. It was propped against the chipped mirror, surrounded by an orange lipstick halo. Unsettled by the doll's blank stare, Jo had drawn the crooked circle to protect himself from its incessant scrutiny. He could, of course, have thrown it in a drawer but somehow he felt it safer to keep the thing where he could see it. He had tried turning its face against the wall, but then he couldn't tell what it was thinking. Now, at least, he knew it was looking at him. He decked it with scraps of broken jewellery, bits of silver chain, odd ear-rings he knew he would never wear. It began to look like a Christmas decoration. He hoped its power would be diminished if he could demean it. Instead, the gaudy bits of rubbish gained an unexpected glory and the doll began to resemble a resplendent Catholic Christ child, like one he had seen in a picture. Then Jo decided he was charging it with his own devoted attention, and that once he could ignore the figurine, the unsettling influence would diminish. This he had worked on with some dedication. But his efforts at avoiding the doll's gaze failed to banish the feeling that it, not he, was the primary resident of his room. How to rid himself of the intruder? The old woman had told him to do nothing, and assiduously he had done nothing. But how was he going to find the doll's true owner? He trawled through the names of his female friends. He came up with no obvious answers. He pondered the meaning of the green wood the woman had mentioned. He could not remember any encounter in a green wood—when was the last time he had visited a wood? Last summer he had spent an evening with a couple of mates up at Ashton Court. They had shared a chillum amongst the trees and he had suffered a bout of the most spectacular hayfever. His eyes had swollen so much his friends had led him home practically blind. No girls there though, and for him, not much fun. That was the nearest he had been to a wood for as long as he could remember. So he waited.

The answer came to him as he slept. He woke one night hearing himself speak a name. He had been dreaming, a convoluted conversation, the meaning of which slipped away from him as soon as he awoke. He remembered her. Of course.

He looked at the clock on the window sill. It was just past midnight, so he had not been asleep long. He reached out to a drawer and scrabbled for a pen and some paper. He tore off a corner from a notebook and wrote the name upon it. He placed the slip upon the doll's head. The doll, he thought, looked satisfied at last. He sank into sleep again, secure in the knowledge that its pitted eyes were no longer boring into his head.

The following morning he spent an inordinate amount of time grooming himself, crimping and back-combing his hair, applying make-up only to wash it all off again, thinking he did not want to look as though he had made too much effort. Finally he was satisfied he had achieved the right balance, donning jeans and leather jacket, with a serpent necklace he was sure would impress her. He needed to be careful though. He remembered she was touchy and unpredictable.

He headed into the city centre on the bus. He tucked the doll into a black shoulder bag and sat it on his lap as they trundled through the traffic into the city centre. He felt a small tension in his stomach as he envisaged arriving unannouced and knocking on her door. He climbed off the bus and headed out to Bedminster. He walked along Coronation Road by the river, which stank in the warmth of mud and silt. Then he turned left, into the maze of Victorian terraces built around the old tobacco factories. Most had been demolished and replaced with superstores and warehouses. One or two were left, grand, mouldering buildings like red brick palaces, awaiting conversion or redevelopment, though he had read they were still heavily contaminated with chemicals. He turned again, and again, sinking into the maze of roads and houses. He remembered the route well. How long since his last visit? Maybe two years by now. It occurred to him for the first time that she might have moved. Maybe he should have done nothing, like the old woman said. Maybe he was messing things up setting off on a search like this. Then it was too late. He was standing outside a huge red brick villa, on three floors, with a bay window topped by a small turret. The paint on the window frames was chipped and peeling. The front door was ajar. Above it, the word 'Ravenscraig' was chiselled into the stone in gothic lettering, though for the greater convenience of the postman, the number 110 had been painted on the wall by the door.

Jo went inside. The house had been divided into half a dozen bedsits. On his left as he walked in was a rack filled with odd items of post. From a room downstairs he could hear music playing, maybe Hawkwind. He headed up to the second floor. The staircase was uncarpeted. Dust on the bare boards had rolled into clumps, puffed aside by the passage of feet. Strands of cobweb on the rails of the bannister stirred as he walked past. The landing window was coated in grime and flecks of mould. A pot of long decayed tulips decorated the sill. Two doors led off from the top landing. Jo took a deep breath and knocked on the one to the left. No-one answered. He tried again. He knew she might not answer even if she was in the room, but his heart sank with disappointment. It sounded far too quiet. He knocked again, rather harder. The door swung open. She had failed to latch it properly.

"Hello? Anyone home?" He peered gingerly round the door. The room was deserted, and appeared to have been turned over, though he knew it had often looked that way. He glanced over his shoulder, and stepped inside. Crumbling plaster coving decorated the tall ceiling, a naked light bulb hanging from the large rose in the centre. Clothes, papers, and books covered the floor and every available surface. Numerous postcards on the table were propped against the wall. It looked, as it had two years ago, as though the occupant was just in the process of moving in —or moving out. He remembered well the air of impermanence. He moved to the window, that looked out onto the quiet street below. When he turned back, he noticed that the back wall, above the double bed, was covered from top to bottom with pictures. They took his breath away. Greens and blues. Swirls of colour radiating from faces. And what faces. Elvish faces, faery faces—long, thin eerie faces, some half beast, some distorted into monsters. Why had she drawn them? They were sketched in ink, he thought, complex, intricate pictures, the faces streaming with odd patterns from the corner of an eye, from the mouth, tumbling from floating locks. None was symmetrical. Each half of each face seemed to possess a spirit of its own. Guiltily Jo picked up one such picture from the table. It was a little faery woman in a cloak looking over her shoulder. She was strangely childish, as well as sinister, peeping behind her with a face only slightly patterned. He folded it up and put it in his pocket. He thought of leaving a note, then decided against it. If his efforts at assertive action were going to prove so fruitless, he would leave the process in the hands of fate. He shut the door behind him and headed back down the stairs.

Just as he was leaving, the sound of Hawkwind grew deafeningly loud, as someone opened a door.

"You looking for someone, mate?"

Jo turned. A long-haired man in torn jeans and a Grateful Dead tee shirt was standing at the end of the hall. Jo shrugged.

"Don't worry about it. She's not in."

"Who're you looking for? The woman in white?"

"Yes. D'you know when she'll be back?" From inside the room someone passed the man a spliff and he inhaled deeply.

"Why don't you come in and share this?" he asked. Jo nodded and followed him into the room. It was considerably more clean and wholesome than any other part of the house he had seen. French windows stood open onto a brick courtyard. Posters decorated the room, which was tidy and welcoming. Reclining on the bed was a girl with long dark hair.

"He's looking for the woman in white," she was told. The girl sat up.

"Elaine," she said. "I haven't seen her for a couple of weeks. She's out on a road protest somewhere or other. She does come back to sign on though. You a friend of hers? Shall I tell her you called round?"

"Yeah, please," he assented. "My name's Jo. I haven't seen her for a while." He stayed with Elaine's housemates for the rest of the morning. He smoked and listened to their music, and they chatted amiably enough. By the time he left, his mind was thick and his thoughts were slow.

Sitting on the bus back out of the city centre, he drifted, remembering Elaine. Elaine and the green wood, yes. They had dropped acid together in her room. It was his first time. The epsiode had faded far away, but the dope he had smoked with her housemates was bringing it back to him again, then and now, lining up seamlessly as though the time between had disappeared. He was back with Elaine. Not in a bus, but in her room, and after a while not even in her room but elsewhere...

For a time, their thoughts had drifted out together like long thin ribbons, twining round each other, so he couldn't tell who was thinking what There was a roaring in his head. He found he couldn't make out the walls of her room. Time passed. With a huge effort of will he could lift himself out, back to normality, but swiftly he was down again, in the labyrinth, in the black, shimmering, multi-coloured spaces that seemed to have opened up all around him, everywhere, nowhere. And as the endless, measureless minutes passed by he found it harder and harder to pull himself out, to look back into the real world...

"You're a caveman," she had said to him, "a bright, beautiful caveman with a pure little face. You're a tree spirit too, like an elf leaping about in the forests."

He thought she had more composure than he could muster, at that moment, being able to hold on to her thoughts long enough to speak. They sat together for another hour, Jo ranting in odd three-way conversations with himself. Here, in the shimmering world, where he led them through twining forests and empty black spaces.

"Go as far as you like," he said, "I can hold you, I can bring you back." And so although Elaine had visited this land before, she realised that Jo knew it far better than her, that he was a habitue, a denizen. Or maybe more than that, an archangel, in the winding green, afloat in the chasms of space, enthroned, streamers of leaves and branches flowering from his face, his eyes, his mouth. They travelled on, headed outwards. How could he explain the eternity of time it took to travel out again, fighting through the twisted forests, days and years and centuries, through huge, limitless moments, each an interminable stretch of never and forever that swallowed them up and breathed them out?

And then Elaine had decided she wasn't going to take drugs anymore. She told him they messed up your aura. She said she felt guilty for giving him acid in the first place, that she should have known how vulnerable he would be to the allure of its false heavens and garbage-pit hells. They had a long argument and Elaine had said many cruel words that cut him to the quick. He had shouted and gesticulated, and carelessly he had caught her on the jaw with his elbow. He would never forget the look on her face. Already he was apologising, but the fury came into her eyes like a demon. She had lashed out at him with nails and fists. She had driven him from the room screeching with rage. He had not seen her again, but even the two years' lapse had not erased the shame and distress he felt as he recollected the scene, a brand upon his heart. He had loved her after a fashion. She was older than him, and seemed to know so much. He had been her disciple, her devotee. He had worshipped her. Then he had blanked her from his mind. Why did these matters keep coming back? All these threads in his life that seemed so unresolved, that he left hanging. Now apparently he would have to engage with her again. Although he remembered the feel of her satiny hair with a shiver, he quailed at the thought.

CHAPTER EIGHT

They headed up the Old Lane towards the stone valley. Owain walked ahead, his face downturned, his step resolute. Elaine half skipped to keep up with him, a whitish ghost in the dark. Katherine trailed behind. She was still half drunk. It took a conscious effort of will to force each step along the lane. She fell further behind. She was disregarded by Elaine, but Owain stopped at last, and waited for her to catch up.

"Are you okay?" he asked.

"Not really. I'm tired. I've drunk too much. I should be at home with Niamh."

Elaine sighed, but put her arm around Katherine's shoulders.

"Come. This is our amazing chance. Can't you feel them calling us? Open up! Look out! Let it all go, Katherine."

Katherine felt a swift inferiority. Elaine was right, of course, as always.

"Lead on," she said. "Show me your marvels."

They walked on. The night was warm and close. Cloud patterned the sky, swallowing and spitting out the moon so that light burst fitfully upon the land. Owain turned to Katherine.

"Can you see yet?"

"See what?"

"Just keep looking."

They were on the very brow of the hill, the valley black and indistinct below them. The stones were invisible. Katherine could barely make out Owain's face as he stared through the night, body tense, into some beyond she failed to penetrate.

"What can you see?" she asked.

"Look. Look," he said. "I thought you would be able to see it." They fell into silence again. Elaine gave a sudden, loud laugh.

"Yes," she said, triumphant. "Yes, I can see it. The light, like rivers. The shining on the land. Yes!"

Katherine strained her eyes to see, but the vision still eluded her. Could they really see something? Were they colluding in some self-fulfilling fantasy?

"Is that what you see too, Owain? Is this why the others are hiding in the cottage?"

He nodded. Katherine felt despondent. Why was she failing? She shut her eyes and stretched out her arms in a gesture of release. The breeze rose for a moment, she felt her skirt brush against her legs. Her hair blew away from her face. The wind was warm and gentle on her skin, like a caress. She stopped trying to see and instead let her mind fall blank. She remembered the black spaces in her mind, locked off like curious rooms, the pathways to faeryland still within her reach but as yet, inaccessible. Still, they were close. She tuned her ears for the faint music, the high, piercing, violin streams. She reached out for the memories of slim green ghosts. When she opened her eyes, she had at last attained clear sight. Elaine was right. Along the floor of the valley she saw a rivulet of light, a faint glowing seemingly rising from the earth. At first sight it appeared to be still, but then, she could make out an irregular flickering, as though it was indeed a river, as Elaine had said. The light was an indeterminate mixture of green and gold and blue, strands interweaving like the slick bodies of ethereal serpents, and shallow, maybe only knee-deep. As she noted this, Katherine looked down and realised that she was in fact standing in the stream. Its course ran the length of the valley, up to where they stood. She looked back, down the Old Lane, where the stream ran on, down the track, over the main road, and up the field the other side, till it disappeared over the top of the hill. How far did it stretch? Katherine crouched down till her body and shoulders were immersed in the shimmering river. She dipped her face. Could she feel it? Not at first, but as the moments passed, she felt a tingle on her skin. She heard dim, confusing whispers in her ears. She tried to make out words. She understood that the stream was aware of her presence, that it knew her. It pressed thin tendrils into her body, exploring her, touching her thoughts. It formed an insistent familiar whisper. A voice she recognised, an emotional tone. What did it want? It was calling her—come, come and find me, I'm here. Who was here? Who was this? Someone she knew very well. Someone she had lost? Was losing?

Suddenly she was hauled up by the shoulders, strong hands bruising her bones. She choked for breath, like a fish, flailing on a beach. Owain was staring down at her.

"Did I hurt you? I'm sorry," he said. Looking round, Katherine perceived the sky was growing pale. Had she been drifting so long? Her throat was dry and her head throbbed. Her muscles were stiff and cold. She looked into his eyes, huge black spaces, and for a moment fancied she could see deep into the convoluted swirls and pathways of his brain. What was it, after all, this strange, vulnerable bag of flesh, his body, when cradled in its apex was the endless looming space of his mind? She imagined she could crawl through his eyes, and lose herself in the limitless chasms of his dreams and thoughts and memories. When he spoke, the sound of his voice was hard and unreal.

"It's dawn," he said. "Where have you been?" His words were so ineffective and conveyed so little of what she perceived he ment, that she laughed insanely for a few minutes, till hot tears poured from her eyes and her stomach began to ache.

"Where's Elaine?" she asked, though as she spoke she saw her sitting on the grass not far away. Her words seemed just as hysterically funny and she laughed again, Owain waiting good-humouredly till she regained control of herself.

"Well?" he asked.

"I didn't realise so much time had passed. I was listening to voices. "

"What did they say?"

Katherine shrugged her shoulders. She thought for a moment.

"I don't know. I can't remember." But as she spoke, she felt a quick panic, once again, for Niamh. Had she been tricked? Had they in some sense taken Niamh after all? Or was it Paul she had placed at risk?

"I'm going home," she said. "I've absconded again. I'll be in trouble."

"D'you want me to come with you?"

Katherine shook her head.

"Stay with Elaine." She headed off quickly, before Elaine could think of joining her. She felt a surge of relief to be alone. As she climbed over the stile, her dress caught on a splinter of wood. In her hurry, she pulled it fiercely, and a long strip of green velvet tore from the bottom of the skirt. For a moment she was caught, but she tugged and broke free. The velvet hung from the top of the stile, flicking lightly in the breeze.

Owain walked over to Elaine and sat on the grass beside her. He waited for her to speak. Elaine's gaze was unfocussed. For a few minutes she ignored Owain's presence. She picked at the grass. Then she turned her attention to Katherine's diminishing form as she strode across the fields towards Locksbury and home.

"You ever seen the film Edward Scissorhands?" she said. Owain nodded.

"Katherine makes me think of it. She's got a strange and magical persona locked in her mind, like Edward up in the castle at the end, but she chooses instead to live a normal life in the suburbs, nice and safe."

Owain didn't reply. He felt uncomfortable being drawn into something that sounded like a criticism of his friend but he was also slightly flattered by the confidential tone of Elaine's voice.

"Not like you," Elaine said. "You really are an unfettered spirit. You just move around, don't you, just walking everywhere, like Merlin."

He half smiled, a little self conscious.

"I work in the winter though. With the horses. And sheep. I'm not free all the time."

"That's different. That's real work, with animals, in the open. And then for the rest of the year you can do exactly as you please."

As Elaine continued to pick at the grass, he took the opportunity to look at her more closely. Despite a night without sleep, in the open, she looked remarkably composed. Her skin was the pale cream of ground almonds, with the faintest freckling across her nose and the top of her cheekbones. Her eyes were bright blue. Her long eyelashes were jet black, like her amazing, heavy hair that fell in such soft, glossy ripples about her shoulders. Elaine was conscious she was being admired. She looked sideways at Owain, and made her own brief assessment.

"Where did you disappear to? These past two weeks? I wanted to talk to you about the things you had seen," she said.

"Around. I needed some time to think. I knew it was just the beginning. I wanted to look around and learn more."

"And did you?" she said. Owain nodded.

"Will you show me?"

He nodded again, not looking at her.

"Good," she said, jumping to her feet. "But first I need to eat. Come with me. Come to my bower and we'll have food, and then you can take me on your pilgrimmage."

They walked together to the copse, where the birds were singing but the tree houses were still very quiet. Elaine stripped off her dress and draped it over a water barrel on the ground. Then, clad only in her big boots, white leggings and little vest, she began the long climb to her eyrie. She was a cautious climber. She had ropes attached to each of the boughs that formed a staging post on her climb. She was never without a handhold. Owain watched and noted exactly where she put her feet, where she gripped the branches. At last she reached platform on which her dwelling was based. She turned round and gestured for Owain to follow. He had climbed to numerous tree houses before, but never to Elaine's. It was a hazardous and testing business, even though he was fit and agile. He took his time, tested each step, for although he had seen Elaine use exactly the same place just seconds before, he knew he was rather heavier than her, and he didn't want to take any chances.

The tree was a tall, smooth beech, so climbing wasn't easy. When at last he joined Elaine on the platform, he was sweating and a little out of breath. Now at least he knew the path, and the next climb would not be so tortuous. The tree houses were all constructed in a similar fashion. At an accommodating bough mismatched planks of salvaged wood had been lashed with ropes to make a base, as, honouring the tree, the protestors declined to hammer nails into the living wood. Then upon the base a huge, dark tarpaulin covered a frame of springy hazel branches. Elaine unfastened a flap to form a doorway and led the way inside. They did not have much space. There was sufficient headroom for comfortable sitting. Her possessions amounted to a few brightly coloured cushions, a sleeping bag, a washing bowl, a handful of books and writing materials, and a small pile of clothes. The tarpaulin was lined on the inside with mismatched pieces of fabric, to prevent condensation, and for insulation.

Owain sat cross-legged upon a cushion. Elaine rummaged in a basket for orange juice, apples, bread and cheese, all a little stale. They ate together in silence. Elaine pulled out extra clothes from the pile, a shirt, waistcoat, a jumper. Then she curled up like a cat on her sleeping bag and shut her eyes. Within a few minutes, her breathing became slow and regular, and Owain realised she had fallen asleep. He was helpless with worry for a few minutes. Should he go? Should he leave her to sleep for a while? She had made no indication that she wanted him to go. He lay down on his side in the little remaining space, careful not to touch her, and for a while he watched her face as she slept. Then weariness overcame him too and he dozed on the hard boards, his head resting on his arm.

He awoke some hours later, hearing voices and laughter. The tarp's door flap had come unfastened, and it blew in the wind, flapping noisily. The leaves shifted all around them, suspended in the air. For a moment he fancied he was on a sailing ship, that the hiss of the leaves was the endless, restless motion of the sea, that the flapping tarpaulin was a huge sail rippling in the sea breeze. Looking through the opening, the light was bottle-green as the sun shone brightly through the foliage. He lay still for a while, seeing Elaine was peacefully asleep, still coiled on the sleeping bag. He guessed it was about mid-day. The voices came from below, from the ground. He thought he heard Violet and a couple of her friends. They were probably checking the ropes and ladders, the fastenings on their benders, ensuring the security of their homes so many feet above the ground. The essential routine had become a ritual, a time for the tree-dwelling protestors to gather and talk. Still, Owain felt no compulsion to move. He was warm and languorous, with the filtered sunlight shining in upon his face and an unexpected feeling of peace settling upon his body. He allowed himself to drift, floating across the oceans aboard his galleon, tucked in this tiny cabin, on the great, shifting body of the sea.

At last Elaine awoke. She stretched and yawned. She pushed her hair back from her eyes, and regarded her guest.

"Shall we go?" she said at once. Owain sat up, ready to depart, though first Elaine washed her face with a little water from a bottle in her basket, and combed her hair. Then they made their descent to the ground. The others were gathered round a small fire near the copse, drinking tea. The two new arrivals were greeted, but Elaine did not stop to talk beyond returning their salutation. Owain walked past too, aware that his new connection with Elaine would be noted and discussed. They headed for the stone valley. Once they were out of sight of their companions, Elaine fell in beside Owain.

"So where do we begin?" she said. They walked briskly. The sun was fierce, and Elaine shed her jumper so her arms were bare. Owain noticed that her pale shoulders were lightly freckled too, and that although she was thin, her bones looked rather large and heavy, almost like a man's. He cleared his throat.

"Tell me what happened to you last night," he said. He remembered very well what he had seen, Elaine skipping and dancing in the stream, possessed, and Katherine crouched like an imp, paralysed beneath the flow of light. He had stood to one side, out of the stream, and watched them. He saw the river of light stretching out across the land, forking and meandering, following a course and gravity of its own. He was well acquainted with it.

They walked beyond the valley. Elaine did not speak for a time, though Owain gathered she was thinking intently, from a tense frown that flickered across her face as she walked beside him. They skirted a field where the wheat was knee-high and the bright green blades were soft and lustrous in the sunlight. Beneath their feet the earth was cracked and rutted. They walked beside a dark hedge that threw out thin, barbed whips of dog-rose. The flowers, suspended on the woody lashes, fluttered like pale butterflies trapped, pink and helpless, amongst the thorns. In the undergrowth campion laced the grass. They were obliged to walk single file, and they proceeded in silence. At the end of the field, Owain found a fence topped with rusty wire and they climbed over into a meadow where the hay had been cut, and now lay drying in long, neat piles. Elaine walked beside him.

"I didn't see faeries," she said. "Not this time. It was connected with them though, wasn't it? When I stepped in I wanted to move. That's what it felt like to me, motion, and I felt that if I could move fast enough I could be obliterated, I could be free."

"Is that what you want? Obliteration? Is that freedom?"

"I am sick of self," she said. "Sick of ego. The illusion of separation. Modern man's made it into a religion. In the man-made system the ego rules as lord. All the grasping and cowardice and hanging on, all the fears. If we could only cease our struggles to prove our worth, if we could be silently sure of it, and realise that the anguish and frustration is bred in this man-made world, and that the larger life, the Earth and skies, is flowing and embraces us all. That is my freedom."

"Did you find it? In the stream?"

Elaine shrugged, disconsolate and sad.

"No. But I could feel it. It was there I'm sure of it. I couldn't move fast enough. And then instead I saw my dream again, my ghost."

"What dream?"

"When I was dancing, trying to catch up, I kept seeing the woman by water, a form rising like mist from the light. The woman in white, like me, scrubbing clothes in a river. But I couldn't see her face. If I could have passed her...but everytime I thought I could lose myself in the stream she kept appearing before me."

"Like a gatekeeper," he said.

"Yes," she said. "I'm not ready. Is that what you think?"

This time Owain shrugged.

"I don't know. What do I know?"

"I think you know a great deal," Elaine said. Owain looked away across the fields, not knowing how to respond.

"You know where I am, where my heart is. You're the same, aren't you?" she asked, her voice a little querulous, but also quivering, as though she might be on the verge of tears.

"Look around," she said. "You see it too. The hidden growth of flowers, the changing weather and the colours in the sky. I can't conceive of anything more precious when I see the endless subtle change of hue and shape to be found in wild plants. It's hard to understand the power of the creative force that urged this world into being, and no matter how many grey mouths tell me to face reality, or mock my vision, I'll hold onto it because I see it so clearly, the natural world so beautifully poised. How could mankind ever have turned away and demanded more and crammed his life with things of little use or value? Why does he trash his mind with trivia and garbage, and miss the endless beauty all around?" She peered at Owain. He made no response, but he wanted her to carry on.

"To be guardians of this planet," she said. "To find our place and live according to it, ever conscious that it was freely given and also to give back in love and creativity of our own...to recognise this magic, this song, which we are part of. Are they going to beat this out of me? Will I, one day, see only dreariness and grey myself because I have become dreary and grey inside? It's so easy to lose your way. One false step and you're swept away in the delusion, taking the sentence of our insane society. I've got to hold on to what I feel inside. If I give up, if I adopt someone else's vision of reality, I am lost."

"You don't have to give up. You make your own way," Owain said. Elaine sighed.

"You seem so much stronger than me," she said. "I winge and verbalise incessantly, and you just get on with it." Owain did not know how to answer. She seemed so far beyond him, like a bird, an aerial spirit aspiring upwards, while he stood solid upon the ground, like a great tree, unmoving and inarticulate.

"They get jobs. They live in prison houses, living vicarious, frightened lives through the television. They willingly give allegiance to the greater organisation, along with their own power and energy. In surrendering they relieve themselves of the responsibility of creating their own lives. They lose the ability to stand on their own, to root their faith in their own strength. They are supported and guided and fed. You know, they can almost believe the opinions they voice are really their own and not those subtly absorbed from those around who let them know what they should be thinking and doing." Elaine stopped for a moment. She held up her hands, gesturing to the land. She was silent for a moment.

"It is very peaceful here," she said. "But elsewhere—too much noise. And too much activity, feeding our senses during the modern day, and then the passive anaesthetic of tv at night. Everyone else is doing the same so the individual gains a sense of ease that comes with acquiescence. But he has given up his most precious gift, the final strength to live consciously as a free thinker, to explore life for himself. Or herself. To discover it freely, to be related to others in a joyful spontaneous way where each individual is appreciated for his or her unique gift. We are so fortunate, to live in this time where we have time to question without the physical pressures of just surviving day to day. Why has it become so easy to forget what we're really here for?"

Owain listened attentively. Her voice possessed an understated anger. He thought he knew these things. Hadn't he, like Elaine, turned away from the lures of security and conformity? It had been no conscious decision. His meandering path had unwound before him, and unthinking he had followed it. He owned very little because his desires were small. He lived from one day to the next, and his life had resolved itself quite naturally into the cyclic seasons of walking and working. Even so, there was something about the quality of her voice and the intensity of her yearning that affected him almost bodily. He felt a rebellious rising in his heart. Was he a free thinker? An adventurer? Or was he no better than the half-awake cattle, like the ones they passed drowsing by the hedges? He felt a quick envy for her restless, destructive intelligence. He experienced an unexpected guilt. Elaine lapsed into pensive silence. Owain felt his mind reeling.

They walked for several miles. They skirted fields sown with wheat and barley and kale, then forced a path through tangled, forgotten lanes, as the heat increased and the wind dropped away to nothing. Owain led them over a high wooden fence, then down the steep, ashy embankment to the abandoned railway line. The embankment, patched with a scree of loose rubble, was covered in cropped grass and rabbit burrows. As the the two people began their descent, half a dozen rabbits skipped instantly into the ground. Elaine slithered downwards, through the hazel trees and hawthorn bushes at the bottom, till at last she stood beside Owain on the old railway line. It was so overgrown they were enclosed in a green tunnel, in cool, dappled shade. Owain set off down the line. They arrived at the round, black mouth of a tunnel. Standing at the entrance, Elaine shivered in the damp stone breath stealing from the darkness inside.

"What's here?" she asked. Owain stepped into the tunnel, gesturing that she follow him. She grabbed hold of his sleeve and crept in behind him. Instantly the sunlight fell away and they were swallowed by the earthy chill emanating from the corroded bricks lining the curved walls of the tunnel. As they entered, a stream of bats flitted around them in the shadows. They halted half way through. Ahead and behind, the circular light of the world outside glittered gold and green. They stood still for a moment or two, and eyes slowly adjusting to the dark. Elaine looked up. The walls had been painted—on the sides of the tunnel, and up above their heads. White lines resolved themselves into symbols and patterns. Some kind of pentacle, embellished with broken spirals, crosses, incomprehensible glyphs. They spread from this central pentacle for many feet all around the walls, a shifting web of disjuncture. Elaine looked to her feet and saw they were standing in a second pentacle, painted roughly on the ground, skewed beneath its elevated partner. And hanging from the tunnel roof, in the centre, just above, something was dangling on a short chain, a still, broken form she struggled to make out. The body of a lamb, very decomposed, almost mummified, a tiny skeletal body. She turned away.

"I feel sick," she said. "My head's reeling. Take me out." She clutched onto Owain's arm, tottering. But she steadied when she gripped his warm hand. She shuddered.

"What a horrible place. Why did you bring me here? Who did this?"

Owain, unpeturbed, led her from the tunnel back out into the sunlight. Once they were outside, the black mouth hid its contents again.

"How did you find it?" Elaine asked.

"I walk everywhere. I sense where these places can be found."

Elaine walked some way from the tunnel before sitting on the embankment, in the shade of the hazel trees. Owain sat beside her.

"Who did it? Black magicians? A coven of New Age pretenders? Is it real?"

"It's been there for years," Owain said. "I believe the place is tended though. From time to time I find candles, new offerings. I think maybe only one or two people look after the place. Is it real? I could never sense any real power there, if that's what you mean. Except that created by the ill-will of those who think they might like to cause harm and hurt. It's a pretty petty kind of harm though. Bad fortune on unfaithful lovers, that kind of thing."

Elaine looked impressed.

"How do you know this stuff? Do you pick it up, are you psychic?"

Owain laughed.

"No," he said. "One night when I was down here I followed a couple of young ladies and listened to what they were saying. They weren't the ones who set it all up. Maybe the ones that did had a greater understanding of what they were doing."

"Which is what?"

Owain declined to answer right away. He stood up.

"Come," he said. "You have more to see." They climbed up off the old railway line and headed on across the fields again.

They covered miles. Owain's pace was unrelenting, and he hardly broke a sweat. Elaine lagged behind. Finally she complained she was hungry and becoming light-headed. Despite her pride, she was obliged to ask for a slower pace. She made it a demand, and Owain felt guilty for having overlooked her needs. They walked into a small wood, edged by a little stream spreading across rocks and pebbles. The moist earth on its shores was pocked with the hoof marks of the cattle. One huge chestnut beast was drinking as they passed. A cloud of flies buzzed around its head. As they headed into the wood, they crossed a low brick bridge, spanning the stream in three small arches. The old footpath headed uphill through the trees. A deep litter of decayed leaves covered the ground. On each side of the path an ancient drystone wall was rotting back into the land, covered with dense moss. Old hawthorn trees thrust roots through the wall in a slow, destructive grip. Tree and stone were locked together, an embrace that tightened over decades. Here and there it had caved in, leaving piles of broken rock to be swallowed by mud and moss. At the crest of the hill, in a coat of rusty ivy, two stone columns stood like portals on the lane.

"D'you like it?" Owain said. Elaine breathed deeply, absorbing the scent of leaves and stone and mud.

"Yes," she said. "It's a great place. But what's the connection with the tunnel?"

Owain leaned against one of the columns, tall enough to reach his shoulders. He stroked his pale beard. Then he looked at Elaine.

"Paths," he said. "Journeys. Like you said in the stream—movement. Do you know how long humankind has travelled the earth? I was reading somewhere about a new archaeological discovery that made our ancestors even older than we've been taught? They've found flakes of rock in Ethiopia that are two and a half million years old but agriculture has only existed for about ten thousand years. You know, I have a vision of the ancient tribes, those hundreds of thousands of years, constantly moving around the earth on an endless pilgrimmage. Their lives were in every sense a journey. I have an image of the tribes gathering at the sacred places, and then dispersing again, their human feet treading the tracks, sensing within their path from the energy in the earth. Charging this energy with their own dreams and their movement. Like the Earth's nervous system, and we are bits of Earth, become conscious."

"And somehow now we've broken away," Elaine cut in. "We've become disconnected. Maybe before, we were in harmony with the Earth and beyond, to the universe unfolding, and the great circular dance of the planets and the stars."

"I don't know what happened," Owain said. "I just know about the paths. I can feel them. I walk and walk and I feel the energy beneath my feet. That is what we saw last night, the streams of light across the land. They are everywhere. They meet and fork at the old monuments and the high hills. I can feel understand it better than any language. The land speaks to me through my bones. The tunnel—that lies on one of the paths, only now it has been broken and corrupted by whoever had sufficient understanding and malice to want to do it. And this path, it lies on one too. There are levels and levels. You can see roads, unavoidable tarmac and noise. Then there are places like the Old Lane and the stone valley, still discernable on a map though not what you'd call dedicated highway. Then places like this, an odd bit of wall or a stone or pillar to show it was once a path. And then if you know how to look, there are hidden signs, paths more deeply buried though I can find them if I look."

Owain stopped speaking, and his manner changed. He was standing straight. His eyes shone. He felt marvellously powerful. He realised he had freed himself from his feeling of inferiority to Elaine. He felt a ripple of energy across his skin, down his arms, and his fingers and feet began to tingle. He smiled at her. He walked a little way from the path, until he reached a point where the tingle became an intolerable itch. He stamped his feet. Then he squatted and began to dig about in the debris beneath the trees. Elaine followed him and watched with considerable curiosity. He dug down into the soil for several inches, till his hands were covered in dirt. Then he discovered something, that looked like a stone. He scraped it clear and lifted it from the ground. He had uncovered half a sheep's skull, the jaw still showing a few teeth.

"How did you know that was there?" she asked.

"My special talent," he said. "Sometimes I know where bones are buried. I'm a bit of a dowser I suppose. Sometimes I can find water, or metals. It comes and goes. Some kind of sensitivity. Not much use though, finding bones." He dropped the skull back to the ground, but Elaine stooped and retrieved it. She was impressed.

"You really are like Merlin," she said. "I think you are the most magical person I have ever met."

Owain laughed and blushed.

"I don't think so. It's all in here," he said, pointing to his chest, and then pointing to his head, "and not much up here."

"Just the opposite to me then," Elaine sighed. "With me it's all mental. Mental and emotional. I know I'm not rooted, not earthed. Maybe we could be Merlin together, a collaboration."

"Maybe we could. Do you want to see more? There are many more places I could show you. I could teach you all the paths round here, we could walk them together." Owain skidded to a halt. Elaine was silent and for a moment he was afraid he had assumed too much. But Elaine turned to him and smiled.

"I would like that," she said. "But right now I'm very tired. I don't think I'm as fit as you and we've got a long way to walk back. And a meeting at the valley."

Owain complied. They walked back to the old path and descended through the trees.

CHAPTER NINE

They were late. Paul was supposed to chair the meeting, and he was greatly annoyed to find everyone sitting and waiting for his arrival. The sky was a level grey, and intermittent showers fell in a fine, light spray, so the protestors had spurned the valley and assembled instead in the cottages. The room smelt of damp clothes and warm, unwashed bodies. James was sitting to one side of the room, notebook at the ready, talking to Jan Blessing, but he waved at Paul and Katherine and stood up to greet them. Katherine sat beside him, and Niamh climbed from her arms onto his lap, tugging the biro from his hand and trying to scribble on his notebook.

Paul scanned the assembly. Maybe twenty people were gathered in the room. He knew most of them. Owain and Elaine were sitting together at the back. Violet, in a cascade of braids and glinting with rings, was next to her mother. Paul was slightly nervous. The Locksbury Anti-Bypass Alliance were a much easier group to handle. As secretary he organised the agendas, wrote the letters and made the calls, and once the meeting began, he handed over the reins to the chairman, a former World War Two submarine commander, much respected by the village. At those meetings, everyone knew when they were supposed to contribute, when they should sit and listen. The tree-dwellers and their supporters were altogether a more itinerant and chaotic assembly.

He began by announcing that the eviction order might be served at any time during the next few weeks, at which point battle would truly commence. This prospect both excited and frightened the meeting, but they all knew that the current situation was a temporary idyll, a pause for peace and boredom before the real confrontation began. Somebody suggested that they draw up a campaign plan but this was shouted down. A number of people eyed James distrustfully.

"Not now. We might find all our plans on the front of the paper tomorrow."

Paul shook his head.

"I think you will find that James is on our side on this one," he said. But he deferred to the will of the meeting and agreed that they would have to discuss the details of their resistance on another occasion. He was well acquainted with the paranoia that stirred within the protestors. People came, people went. There were always several new faces at each meeting, a few unknowns, and suspicions circulated about spies, police infiltrators and agents provocateurs. James put his hand up.

"What can I write then? That you are putting together a plan of resistance? That you will confront the bailiffs?"

"Well that's hardly a secret," Paul nodded. "Has anyone any objections to him quoting us as saying that?" More murmurs. Nobody disagreed. Paul braced himself to broach the next topic.

He stood and waited for quiet to descend, and then he said:

"We need more money. We need to pay Jan for her petrol, for all her running around for us. We also need money to pay for Nigel's solicitor's fees. It would also be useful if we had a fund for this purpose in case any of us needs legal representation in the future."

Nigel, a long-term tree dweller, had been charged with criminal damage after an ill-considered attack on the car belonging to a director of the road building company. He had tipped paint all over the windscreen and scratched 'No New Roads' in the metallic blue paint of the bonnet. Unfortunately he had been observed and videoed by the car's owner, and consequently had a court appearance in a few weeks' time. He had been bailed on the condition that he kept away from the protest site, but still he was much in evidence, and although few of his fellows applauded his action, they were all keen to help him out.

"Has anyone any ideas how we might raise money?" Paul asked.

"What about your Anti-Bypass group in the village? Isn't that their field? They've got stacks of money," somebody suggested. Paul shook his head.

"They've already given us quite a bit. I don't think we can ask again for a while."

From the back of the room he heard Elaine's voice, quiet but crystal clear, as she spoke to Owain.

"I won't do any work. Except fruit picking," she said piously. Paul, in bondage to his mortgage and career, bristled at her words. He addressed her personally.

"Well, how would you suggest we raise money? Do you think we can let Nigel down?"

Elaine looked at him coldly and shrugged her shoulders.

"Maybe we could organise some event. A fair, a play or something," she said.

"A fair. We'd need an entertainments license, I think. From the council," he said.

"Oh, stuff them. They're trying to evict us anyway. What difference would it make if we held a fair? It would be fun. We could hold it on Midsummer's Day."

The suggestion was met with words of approval from the gathering but Paul shook his head and sighed impatiently. He tried to speak again, but Elaine's idea had inspired a considerable response. At last he managed to make himself heard.

"Midsummer is only a week away," he said. "How could we manage anything by then?" Elaine looked at him blankly, but Jan turned to Paul and said:

"It might not be such a bad idea. I don't mean anything formal or too organised. We're not going to have time to set up tombolas or whatever, but all sorts of people will be coming to this area for the solstice. Maybe we could invite them to a gathering in the valley, print out some kind of flyer. I could put up a poster in the shop. Ask people to bring some form of entertainment, or stuff they have to sell. We could cook up lots of food for them to buy, and ask for contributions to the cause."

Paul discerned a faint but perceptible excitement amongst the protestors. A midsummer fair—a gathering of the tribes, a chance for a little revelry and intoxication perhaps. He doubted the possibilities for money-making at such an event but he succumbed to the general mood. He agreed that he and Katherine could create a flyer and a poster. The rest was up to the individuals involved. Everyone would be expected to make some contribution. Jan enlisted Violet and a couple of her friends to organise food. The propect had acquired a momentum of its own, and Paul relinquished his position as leader of the meeting to squat beside James and Katherine. He addressed James.

"Be careful what you write about this," he said."Don't bill it as a fair. Write that we will celebrate the solstice as part of the protest, something like that. But you could send the photographer on the day. It might make some good publicity."

"Will you mention it to your other group? In the village?"

"We haven't got another meeting before then. But I could make some phone calls, ask people to spread the word."

"Are you going to join in?" James had turned to Katherine. She was in a dream, stroking Niamh's hair, and didn't hear his question.

"What? The fair? Yes, I'll do something," she said. Paul glanced over. He was irritated by her state of distraction.

The meeting seemed to be breaking up, and James suggested that he take them for a drink. Katherine demurred, saying she had to put Niamh to bed. Katherine herself looked deathly tired, though she urged Paul to take up his offer. Paul agreed, still not looking at her.

"I have a few things to clear up here first," he said. "Do you mind waiting?"

"Then why don't I take Katherine home, and meet you at the pub?" James suggested.

"On the bike?"

"I've got the paper's car. I'm working, remember."

Paul nodded, and Katherine rose gratefully to her feet. Paul walked over to Jan without another word.

Katherine followed James out of the house, to the car, parked in the lane. She fastened Niamh's car seat in the back with the seatbelt, then sat in the front.

"You look tired," he said, as they drove.

"Exhausted more like. A bit hungover too. My own fault."

"You were out with Elaine? I called round on Paul last night. I missed you."

Katherine smiled and looked away.

"We had a good time," she said. "Unfortunately Paul's pissed off with me because I didn't get in till dawn."

"I see. I thought the atmosphere was a bit chilly. Still, I'll do my best to cheer him up for you."

"Thanks. I would appreciate that."

They completed the drive in silence. Niamh fell asleep in her seat. When they pulled up outside the house, James carried the seat inside, Niamh still slumbering. Carefully Katherine unbuckled her daughter, and took her upstairs to her cot. When she came back down, James was in the kitchen making cups of tea. She was a little irked, but also flattered that he sought her company. They sat in the living room together. James slurped noisily through his moustache. Katherine laughed.

"Why are you still wearing that ridiculous thing?" she asked.

"A bet," he said. "It's got to last a month. Don't you like it?"

"I'm not all that keen on moustaches, but I do like yours in a strange kind of way. You look a bit like a DH Lawrence coalminer. You should get some braces and a cap."

"Maybe ah will lass," he said. She laughed.

"I should forget the comedy Notts accent though." When she rested her head on the arm of her chair, James put his mug down and said he would head for the pub. Katherine followed him to the front door. Just before he left, he kissed her cheek and gave her a warm hug. He was nearly as tall as Paul, but heavily built, and for a moment Katherine was engulfed. Then he was back in the car and Katherine headed upstairs to bed. She had an early appointment for Niamh the next morning with the doctor. What exactly was she going to say? She ran through the list of worrying little changes in her daughter... she caught a faint aroma from the bone necklace around her neck. She took it off and placed it on the floor beside her bed. As she did so she heard Niamh move restlessly in the next room, and she slipped it on again, the fetid-sweet smell at once repulsive and reassuring.

The gestation of the Midsummer Fair was swift. Paul and James chatted together in the White Harte and toyed with ideas for a flyer. At the squat, a group of women devised plans for music and circle dances. In the tree dwellings, Elaine drew out a book about the Mummer's play and worked on amending a script. Violet spent the night at her mother's flat, where they decided on a menu of cheap food they could easily prepare. They were all inspired.

Owain walked alone along the valley, watching the trails of light flickering across the land. Nobody had mentioned the subject at the meeting, nobody talked about it at all, though the stream passed along the Old Lane, and the front door continued to bang. It frightened him. They would walk back up to the trees later on, right through it. He knew some of them could see it—or sense it, at least. The path had always been there of course, but something more was stirring. He couldn't understand their complicity. Were they hypnotised? It seemed that even here, amongst the mystics and free spirits, a peculiar inertia existed. They could pretend nothing was happening. Forgetting did not even require an exercise of will, the events were just slipping from their minds, and instead they latched onto distractions, like the fair, suggested, in all madness, by dear sweet Elaine. And in the shadow cast by their heedlessness what was going to emerge? It struck him as he walked, that perhaps the paths had become rips, spaces through which other energies could emerge. From faeryland? Whatever that might be. Perhaps these ancient paths were even more than he had thought. Maybe they were charged by more than the walking and dreaming of thousands of years. They were faery paths too. He had seen them himself, though the memory was slippery and elusive. Perhaps the paths were the point of contact between the two places. He wished Elaine was with him to share these thoughts. She had a quick mind, and she would believe him. He thought of heading back to the copse, and calling on her, but his legs carried on of their own accord and in the rhythm of walking he found his thoughts were stilled. He headed on west.

CHAPTER TEN

Elaine worked on the mummer's play into the small hours, straining her eyes in the flickering light of a candle in a small lantern. She huddled in her sleeping bag, copying lines from her book, crossing out, re-writing, reading again. When at last her mind broke free of the task she had set herself, the candle faded, and the grey light of the early morning began to steal through the chinks in the floorboards. She slept fitfully for an hour or two, notebook and pen still gripped in her hand. When she woke, she assembled a few belongings and stuffed them into her bag. Then she wrote three names at the top of her script, tucked it in an old envelope and addressed it to Katherine. She climbed down from the tree house, and headed off down the Old Lane.

Two crows perched in the tops of the trees, cawing hoarsely as she passed, swaying with the branches that heaved underneath them in the breeze. It was still very early. The sun was low above the hills, and the wind was brisk, plucking at her clothes and hair, tugging pale, ragged clouds across the sky. She placed her envelope on the step outside the old cottage door, and peered quickly through the window. It seemed she was the only one awake. She had the world to herself for a time. Or so she thought. When she turned from the house back to the Old Lane she saw a horse-drawn vehicle had turned off the main road and was heading towards her. For a moment or two she stayed where she was, obscured by the overgrown hedge near the garden gate. She peeped round cautiously, not eager to become embroiled in any form of human contact when her immediate intention was to fly the nest for a time, to escape. The dull clopping of the pony's unshod hooves grew louder and Elaine realised she would have to emerge or else look ridiculous skulking in the hedge. She stepped out. The pony threw its head up and snorted with surprise, stopping right in front of her. It was a handsome little beast, piebald, with a long black mane covering its neck, and white feathers on its legs. It sniffed her cautiously. She smelt its breath, warm and sweet with grass, and the faint perfume of the worn leather harness, the thick, black straps on the old bridle and blinkers. Then Elaine looked up from the pony to the cart, where three young men were sitting on the front staring at her. She was momentarily at a loss. She didn't recognise them.

"Is this a hold up?" one of them asked, breaking the silence. The other two laughed. Elaine maintained her composure.

"Three of you is a lot for this little pony to be pulling isn't it?" she said coldly. The first man shrugged his shoulders.

"We've not come far this morning. He's only walking," he said. At first glance Elaine had supposed they were the usual traveller type, long hair and mismatched clothes, come to join the protest for a bit, looking for a space to camp. But there was something else. She looked into their faces, and looked again, from one to another, until she realised she was staring like an imbecile and abruptly she turned away. She stood to one side to let them pass.

"We've come for the solstice. For the fair," the first man said.

"News travels fast," she replied. The man nodded. He flicked the reins across the pony's back so that it walked forward a step or two, and the men on the cart were alongside Elaine.

"So how did you hear about it?"

"Word gets around. You know," he said. She looked up into his face. His skin was very pale and fine, and his hair was black, streaked with copper. He had bright green eyes. In fact he did not look like an outdoor dweller at all. Neither did his companions. They all wore faded patchwork clothes, a motley of worn velvet, russet, gold and peach. Two of them were wearing faded top hats, with feathers tucked in a band around the brim. Then Elaine heard a faint, metallic tinkle, and suddenly she laughed.

"You're Morris men," she said. "You've got bells around your knees."

The men glanced at one another.

"Like I said. We've come for the fair."

"And where's the rest of the side? You must have more than three."

"They're on their way," the green-eyed man said. "I suppose we will be seeing you around?" Elaine paused for a moment. The prospect of staying at the site suddenly seemed more tempting. The three men were all smiling at her very genially. But she broke free.

"In a few days," she said. "I've got some things to do. But I'll be back before the solstice, so I'll see you then?"

They grinned and tipped their hats, and the cart headed on up the lane. Elaine watched the pony amble away. Morris men? She refused to think about it too hard. She put her bag over her shoulders and headed onto the main road. She hitched a lift into Marlborough, and then caught the early morning coach into Bristol.

As the coach headed down the motorway she stared out the window. Dreamily she ate an apple she found lying dusty and bruised at the bottom of her bag. When the coach pulled up at the station, she climbed down to the stained pavements, the air heavy with diesel fumes and felt a familiar wash of elation. She walked past the queues of patient travellers, past a couple of tramps sitting blank-faced by the subway, and then she was striding through the city sunlight, across the pavements where early shoppers mingled with smartly dressed office folk hurrying for work. At last! She could breathe again. Oh, yes, she loved the land and the plants and her little home in the tree. But the city had its own attractions and here she was anonymous. She was liberated. Nobody cared what she was doing, and amidst the mass of people she could move and think without the unending pressure of the eyes and ears and analysis of the close and claustrophobic tribe at the protest site. And other strands needed to be broken. Owain, of course, the beginnings of attachment, not to be tolerated. Katherine, heavy with her endless cleaving to the darling infant. No, she could shrug them off, all of them. They were not essential. She could be free.

She walked swiftly to Southville, through the narrow streets to Ravenscraig. As soon as she walked through the front door she drew out an address book from her bag and made a call from the payphone in the hallway.

"Rosie?" she said. "It's Elaine. Out tonight? Come round here, early. I've got some vodka that needs attention." When she had made her arrangements, she skipped upstairs and locked herself into her room. She had to sign on, eat, sleep—mundane activities in readiness for the night-time, when she could shine.

Rosie was expected soon after six. Elaine lay in the bath, in a dream, cleansing a week's accumulated dirt from her skin and hair. The steam was heavy with jasmine oil, sweet and musky, and the sharp scent of thyme, crushed and sprinkled in the bath water. She soaked and relaxed, like a mermaid in a rock pool, with her hair sleek and wet like jet across her shoulders. From the room next to the bathroom she could hear music, the faint, low thrum of a bass line. She felt a faint, rising excitement. Soon Rosie would be here and the party would begin. No more bad dreams, here in this other world, away from the self-enclosed headfuck protest site. No more false faery promises, no more magic pathways that now seemed like foolish fantasies, a paranoid mental closing down. What kind of trip were they all on? Why had she allowed herself to collude in Owain's delusions, in Katherine's post-natal voyages of guilt? She could cast it all aside. The site was one small space, and now she was on the outside of it.

Someone hammered on the bathroom door.

"Have you finished? You've run out of time," came an irritated female voice.

"Okay. Just a minute," she called back. Outside the door was pinned a piece of paper with the bath rota written upon it. Elaine knew she had over-run her slot, but she lay in the bath a few minutes more. When she had dried, she put on her dressing gown and headed upstairs to her room. Rosie arrived a minute later, carrying a large travelling bag, which she dropped on Elaine's bed. They embraced warmly, grinning with anticipated excitement. Rosie drew a large bottle of Vermouth from her bag, and poured a generous helping into two chipped mugs.

Rosie was the latest in a line of drinking companions. Elaine reflected wearily that, as she was now twenty seven, she had been clubbing on and off for ten years. Friends had come and gone, joining her for a year or two, then moving away, or settling down, or tiring of the scene for one reason or another. But here she was, still, the long-enduring free spirit, not stolid or resigned enough to call it a day yet. What else was she to do when her heart itched for intoxication and escape?

Rosie had turned out to be one of her more enduring companions, and their friendship went back several years. She stood a head shorter than Elaine, a delicate girl with wrist bones thin as toothpicks, and a huge mane of bright tangerine hair that tumbled halfway down her back. For the next few hours they drank and talked and laughed. They obliterated the true lineaments of each other's faces with make-up, teased out their hair. Rosie clad herself in black patent vinyl, a little dress laced at the back, her waist tiny, her hair huge and stiff with hairspray. She added several inches to her height with a pair of thigh boots, teetering on pointed heels. Elaine donned an old wedding dress, bought from a charity shop and cruelly butchered so the pale tulle skirts drifted in thin shreds. The bodice was made of shimmering ivory silk, the long sleeves low on her shoulders, embroidered with pearls, buttoned at the cuffs. She wore boots laced to the knee, painted her lips dark red, her eyes wide and black, so she fancied she a looked like a gothic cleopatra. As they drank more, they laughed longer and louder. Elaine played the Doors on her tape recorder at such a volume that the people next door began to bang on the wall. When the vodka and vermouth had finally been consumed, they left Ravenscraig and headed into the city. They were tranfigured—bright with alcohol, created in a new likeness. They laughed, with cruel, belittling amusement, at the teeming masses who went out clubbing in the same (or near enough) jeans and shirts they wore everyday. Why bother going out as yourself, they agreed, when you can go out as someone else? Why go out partying all drab, when you can don, like an actor, a dozen different personae, to test and try and enjoy? Why be everyday and dull when you could be brilliant, like a bird of paradise?

The swift downing of vodka and vermouth had them both on the verge of throwing up, but by the time they had walked to Coronation Road their stomachs were resigned to the alcoholic burden, and the liquor sent strange veins of exhiliration pulsing through their bodies. They caught the bus and checked through the dozen absurd rituals that indicated to them just how significant the evening's events would be. The number of fellow passengers, the type of ticket, the response of the bus driver—all these marked out like clues to be read just how much pleasure they would have. And then they whispered and laughed with each other, perfect intimates, to consummate their friendship with the secret jokes and words and songs that marked the magical borders of their realm. And when the bus stopped in the city centre, they strutted from the bus and out across the square, to mingle with the crowds of rowdy people all out for a night of drink and celebration. In the middle of the square, mounted on tall black horses, a couple of affable policemen monitored the stream of brightly coloured, intoxicated revellers. In the cool of the night, Rosie buttoned up her sumptuous fake leopard skin coat, and tossed her orange hair over her shoulders. As they walked up through the pavements the girls were met with a roar from a coach load of visitors to the city's nightspots, and they laughed, buoyed up by the noise. They were dressed to entice and allure, but felt instead they were armoured like gladiators, ready for battle.

They headed straight for the club. It was situated in a narrow street five minutes walk from the city centre, in an old warehouse, a warren of monochrome rooms and bars and music. On arrival they marched straight for the dance floor, spending a half hour or so gloriously drunk and for a brief, fleeting moment feeling, yes, now I am alive, as though this momentary obliteration of self was the chief aim and end of all their efforts, as though by reaching the elusive intoxicated edge they had accomplished some longed-for and wonderful nirvana, before sinking to normality again, or else tumbling straight over the self same edge into complete, shameful oblivion, like the sad shadows propped around the edges of the club.

The two women left the dance floor to buy more drinks. Rosie filled her plastic cup with ice cubes from a black bucket on the bar, already sticky with puddles of spilt beer.

"Can you leave some of that for me?"

Rosie looked up and saw the speaker was a tall, thin man in a black military jacket and a white shirt. His hair was longish, slicked back off his face. He looked like a pirate from a romance.

"You want some ice?" Rosie asked, flicking her hair, issuing a challenge. She kept her eyes fixed on the man's gaunt face as she picked out a piece of ice from her cup and slipped it in her mouth. She turned her face towards his, and he bent down over her to receive the cold fragment from her lips. He drew back.

"I think I want some more," he said, turning his attention to Elaine. Rosie smiled. She passed her the cup. Elaine took a piece of ice too, and held it lightly between her teeth. It tasted sharp and sweet with rum. The pirate pressed his hot mouth against hers and took the ice. Then again it was Rosie's turn, then Elaine's. She felt the heat of his tongue in her mouth as he kissed her. This time he didn't let go. He put his arms around her waist and kissed her more intently than before. Elaine submitted for a moment, till she realised that Rosie was no longer beside her. Elaine broke away, laughing, leaving the pirate behind, and she scanned the darkened room for her cohort. Then, with a swift sense of disappointment she saw that Rosie had abandoned her to the pirate because her own boyfriend had arrived, with a couple of mates. Rosie was sitting on his lap, locked in an embrace. Suddenly isolated, Elaine wandered about, watching the other dancers for a while. Within a few minutes she realised how swiftly her elation had dwindled and disappeared. Rosie was lost in her man's arms. Was this what all their painting and preening and alcoholic exhiliration had amounted to? Was that oddly revolting snog the culmination and grail of their quest in the city? A hail of lights fell incandescent around the dancers. As the first bars began, half the dancers left the dance floor, to be replaced by a stream of newcomers from the murky platform around the edge. Elaine half stirred herself, but the alcohol in her body had become, tonight, a weight of lead and lethargy instead of the path to euphoria. She noticed a black and purple haired youth not far from her, slumped on the floor. When the track started he showed signs of life, but he also failed to make it to his feet. But why had he caught her attention? He turned his head away from her and threw up on the carpet. Elaine wrinkled her nose in distaste and turned to the dance floor again, where a group of goths were twirling in slow, stately pirouettes, cigarettes poised artfully in ringed fingers, eyes downcast and cultivating an air of inward contemplation, oh bittersweet land of opium dreams. Androgyny, the sensuous allure of basques and belts and elaborate, unnatural hair. But tonight it was all falling flat. They had gathered to conspire in a fantasy, but it was fixed and defined, just as much as a business man in a suit. Though—of course—considerably more poetic. They shared a brief illusion, creating a theatrical set piece. But Elaine was suddenly bored of it, her dream crumbling to dust in her hands. It had nowhere to go. It was a stagnant pool, a frozen moment. Of course it has nowhere to go, she countered herself, that is exactly what it is about: There is nowhere to go, we are sitting in the ruins, dancing at a Masquerade till the inevitable Red Death makes an end to each and every one of us, exposing the skull behind the jewels. So in the abstract, Elaine could still feel the subtle attractions of the pageant. The world was racing to its destruction—or so it seemed from the news, from the mutterings of the older generation—so let's get our kicks before the whole shithouse goes up in flames...But in practice—well, she, for one, was beginning to think she did have somewhere to go. She could feel her soul shifting, amidst the weight of her diamonte, eager to be on the move again. Somewhere there was some kind of path, if only she knew where to find it. Going somewhere—but where? Unconsciously, she realised she was looking at the youth with the black and purple hair again, only this time, he was returning her absent gaze. For a moment the alcoholic haze cleared from his eyes, and briefly Elaine and Jo looked straight at each other.

Elaine could not suppress a shiver.

"Jo?" she said. Though, of course, he could not hear her above the music. She gestured to him. Jo staggered to his feet and slouched on the chair next to hers.

"Elaine," he said, "Elaine, I knew I'd be seeing you soon." He had to put his face next to hers in order that she could hear him. His breath was foul with beer and sick. A few strands of hair were caught in his mouth. Elaine pushed them away from his face.

"Oh, Jo," she said. "You don't change, do you?"

He grinned drunkenly and shook his head.

"You look so pretty, but you smell awful. Shall I get you a drink of water?" she said. Jo nodded.

"I've got something for you," he called as she walked away but Elaine didn't hear him. When she returned with the water he was virtually unconscious. She tried to wake him up, feeding him sips of water, until it was time to leave. Rosie appeared carrying their coats.

"A friend of yours?" she asked, looking at Jo.

"An old friend. He's in a bit of a state. I think we'd better take him back to Ravenscraig." As they left the club, descending the steps to the pavement and the dark street, Elaine heard someone walk up beside her. A thin white hand gripped her arm. She pulled away quickly, and turned to face the man she and Rosie had flirted with earlier in the night, the pirate. He was now wearing a long leather coat. She could see his eyes shining.

"My ice ladies," he said. He focussed on Elaine. "Why don't you come home with me?" He bent forward towards her, and put his hand gently on her shoulder. He was close enough for Elaine to feel his warm breath upon her skin. Rosie and Jo stood waiting, a discreet step away. Elaine realised with irritation that she was faintly tempted to take him up on his offer of hospitality. Then she pushed his hand aside and shook her head angrily. She followed her friends down the steps, not looking back. Rosie called a taxi and they drove back in silence. The taxi driver eyed Jo suspiciously, worried that he might throw up in his car. But Jo remained only partially conscious, and the two girls had to manouevre him up the stairs to Elaine's room. He curled up on the floor, mumbling to himself, but by the time they had made cups of tea he had gathered his wits sufficiently to sit up and take heed of his surroundings.

"So here I am again," he said. "Hello, Elaine. Hello..."

"Rosie."

"Hello, Rosie. I've been waiting to see you, Elaine. I've got something that belongs to you. I was given it, you see, and I think it's for you," Jo said.

"What is it?"

"It's a sort of doll—a magic doll I think, made of wood. It was given to me by an old bag lady, for my friend from the green wood. You remember the green wood?"

Jo was talking too quickly, only just coherent, but Elaine began to feel uneasy. She nodded.

"Yes. Do you have this thing with you?"

"No. But I'll bring it over tomorrow. I'll be glad to be rid of it."

"Why's that?" she said. She shivered.

"Hard to say. It's quite a strange doll. Anyway, did you girls have a good time tonight?"

Rosie nodded. Elaine shrugged her shoulders.

"Not brilliant," she said. "It's wearing a bit thin. I'm getting fed up with the assumption that I'm hoping to get laid."

"You dress up like that and then moan that men aren't attracted to your soul?" he grinned. "So what! Enjoy the attention." But Elaine scowled, and Jo was afraid he had said too much. He shrank visibly.

"Do you have a blanket I could borrow?" he asked quietly. "I think I'd like to go to sleep, if that's all right with you."

They all settled down, Jo on the floor and Rosie on a campbed. Elaine lay awake a long time, staring through the darkness, afraid of an intuition that she had not escaped after all. How can you escape yourself? Her dreams were waiting, and when she sank into sleep at last, she was back by the river, where the woman scrubbed bloody clothes in the water.

CHAPTER ELEVEN

Katherine lay awake in bed, waiting for Niamh to cry. It was seven thirty. She heard the front door slam as Paul departed for work. The curtains were open. She lay, propped on a pillow, sipping the tea he had made, watching the swift passage of the clouds in a sky bright as sapphire. She wondered again why Niamh was sleeping so much. It was worrying. She had composed these worries, each in itself insignificant, into a careful list that alarmed her in its entirety. Paul was less convinced. She was making a fuss over nothing, he had told her. She was mistaken, fussy, even neurotic. He spoke with authority, and Katherine almost believed him. Then he went away, and once she was alone again, her fears overcame his reason. Sometimes Niamh's gaze was fixed so very far away. Sometimes she seemed like a stranger. Was this what every parent felt, meeting the unfathomable stare of their offspring? Shouldn't there be some vital connection, some recognition? Instead she wondered what alien thoughts were flickering through the child's mind, when Niamh seemed to sum up and dismiss her mother in a shiver of her little body, in a contemptuous sniff. Maybe she was unstable, imagining this tiny girl was conspiring against her. Katherine finished her tea and still Niamh was quiet. She flung back the covers, and peeled off her tee-shirt. She lay on her front in a puddle of sunlight on the bed, her skin soaking in the golden heat. She drifted back to sleep for a time.

When she woke again it was eight thirty. She jumped out of bed in a panic and pulled on her clothes. She had to be at the surgery in just half an hour. She opened the door into Niamh's room, and was surprised to see her daughter was awake—sitting up in her cot turning the pages of a book. The little girl squealed at her mother, jumped to her feet and held out her arms to be picked up. Katherine scooped her out of the cot, dressed her, and took her downstairs for a swift breakfast. They arrived at the surgery a couple of minutes late.

The doctor was a strong, good-looking woman with hair the colour of slate. A computer terminal shared desk space with an abundant white geranium. Bookshelves lined one wall. While the doctor typed in details, Katherine scanned the titles and noticed to her surprise 'A History of Witchcraft' and Fraser's 'The Golden Bough'. On the walls were several photos of the doctor's beautiful daughters on their horses.

The doctor swivelled on her chair to face Katherine, and Niamh.

"How can I help you?" she said. "You've come about Niamh?"

"Yes. It's nothing specific. I don't think she's ill. I've noticed changes in her behaviour over the past few weeks and it has been worrying me."

The doctor adopted an expression at once serious and sympathetic.

"Can you describe these changes?" she asked.

"She's started sleeping all night. In fact, she's sleeping a lot more altogether. This morning she didn't wake up till half past eight, and before she used to wake me up every three hours and then refused to sleep after six in the morning."

"What a relief. Why should that worry you? It's not exactly a problem," the doctor said. "I have dozens of parents coming to me for advice on getting their children to sleep more. What else?"

"She's eating less. In fact she hardly seems to eat a thing. I don't know how she manages."

"Not uncommon at this age. They start to get very fussy. She doesn't look underweight, and if she is fairly energetic I shouldn't upset yourself too much about it. Worrying about their eating is just likely to aggravate the situation. You don't want to make a scene."

Katherine took a deep breath and cleared her throat before she spoke again.

"She smells peculiar," she said.

"In what way?" The doctor focussed intently on Katherine.

"She has an unusual odour. Like rotten apples. Smell her yourself."

The doctor leaned forward and lifted Niamh onto her lap. It was the nearest she had come to examining the little girl. She sniffed her hair and neck.

"I can't smell anything. Whereabouts does she smell?"

"All over," Katherine said, but her heart began to sink. The doctor sniffed again, but still she failed to detect anything out of the ordinary. She looked at Katherine more closely.

"My partner can smell it too," Katherine said hurriedly.

"Any more changes you want to tell me about?"

Katherine sighed.

"She just seems different," she said. "I can't exactly put my finger on it. She seems a long way off sometimes. She still cuddles me and wants me, but her mind—I don't know what she's thinking at all."

"I don't think any of us know what our children are thinking," the doctor said wryly, her eyes alighting on the photographs on the wall. "I shouldn't worry. It sounds like Niamh has had some kind of developmental spurt. She's acquired a new sleeping pattern. Picky eating is very common. Just relax a bit, they all do things in their own way, in their own time."

From the cadence of the doctor's speech, Katherine gathered this was a rote pronouncement, often trotted out to over-anxious parents.

"You don't think she might have some kind of autism?"

The doctor shook her head.

"Absolutely not. She's fine. Really."

Katherine gave up. She nodded blanky and rose to her feet. She picked up Niamh and turned to leave the room.

"Thanks for your help," she said. The doctor dug in her drawer for a paper bag of jelly babies, one of which she gave to Niamh just before she left. Niamh smiled and stuffed it in her mouth. The doctor stroked the little girl's head.

"Nothing wrong with you, is there?" she said, giving Katherine a swift glance. Katherine walked from the surgery. She felt the unspoken "your mother's got the problem" prickling her conscience. Maybe it was true.

When she returned to the house she was welcomed by a huge pile of washing, and a floor covered with toys and dirt and spilt food. Paul never complained, but she knew it annoyed him when the inevitable chaos spread around the house. She curled in an armchair in a haze for a few minutes, distantly aware that she ought to make an effort, but unable to muster the energy to do it. Apart from the rattle of Niamh playing with a plastic till, the house was quiet and still. From the back garden she could hear the whistle and rattle of starlings squabbling in the tree. The day spread before her, empty, beside the housework, till Paul returned sometime after six. She felt a pang of loneliness. Elaine had left a space, after their few days together—an intense time, a deluge, a sharing of thoughts and dreams and fits of laughter. Katherine pulled the baby backpack from the cupboard under the stairs and stuffed a bag with a few bits and pieces for Niamh. She put Niamh in the backpack, hoisted it upon her shoulders, and headed out the front door. She walked through Locksbury and set off across the fields. The cleaning would have to wait.

The stone valley was quiet. The grass was long and wet, flecked with buttercups. As Katherine stepped amongst the stones, her jeans were soaked with dew and clung to her legs. Could she still sense the faery path? In the daylight nothing was visible, and the chill in her legs arose from a more mundane cause. Nothing physical then. She walked on, towards the copse at the top of the incline. Amidst the foliage she could make out the dark lumpen forms of the tree houses. Then in the corner of her eye, she thought she saw someone walking beside her. She looked quickly, but no-one was there. She strode on. Niamh jumped suddenly in the backpack, causing Katherine to stagger. Niamh chuckled and bounced again. Katherine stopped and spun round—this time catching sight of her stealthy pursuer. He had ducked behind her, grinning at the child.

"Owain!" she said. "You scared me. I thought you were..."

"One of the faery folk? Maybe I am."

"Don't say that."

"I'm sorry. I was teasing Niamh."

They continued towards the copse side by side. They both stopped below Elaine's dwelling.

"You're looking for her too?" Katherine asked, a dismaying twinge of jealousy in her voice. But who was she jealous of? Owain did not appear to have noticed. He was peering up through the leaves.

"It looks pretty quiet to me," he said. "Do you think I should climb up and see if she's there?" Katherine nodded. On this, his second ascent, Owain climbed quickly and confidently. When he reached the platform, he called out to Elaine. When he received no answer he peered into the bender.

"She's not there," he called down. "Some of her stuff's missing too. I think she might have gone off again." He began the descent. Katherine sighed with disappointment. Owain jumped the last few feet from the tree, and landed with a thump beside her. Despite his agility, his face was damp with sweat and Katherine caught a breath of masculine sweat, slightly earthy, as he turned to her.

"Shall we scrounge a cup of tea from the cottage?" he said. They walked on down the Old Lane. Owain talked to Katherine about his walk with Elaine, about the old paths and his idea that perhaps these paths ran at once in the world they knew, and in a parallel, connected world from which the faeries had emerged.

"Like this, you mean?" Katherine said. "Listen: 'On the bank of the river he saw a tall tree: from roots to crown on half was aflame and the other green with leaves.'"

"Where's that from?"

"The Mabinogion. You know, old Welsh stories? The green leaves represents the mundane world, and flames are the magical faery realm, still vitally connected."

They drew to a halt outside the cottage. Katherine saw a piebald pony tethered in the garden by the side of the house. A shiver seemed to run up Owain's body.

"What's the matter?"

"I don't know. I feel prickly."

"Whose pony is that?"

Owain shuffled uneasily.

"It wasn't here yesterday," he said. Katherine opened the gate and they walked up the path towards the cottage. Katherine headed for the pony. As she approached, she saw three people sitting beside a fire, near a small cart, on what was once a stretch of lawn.

"Hello," she said. "Have you just arrived? My name's Katherine. This is Owain."

Owain walked up beside her. The three men stood up. Katherine was all smiles and warmth, shaking their hands, introducing Niamh, whom she loosed with relief from the backpack. Katherine held Niamh up, helping her to stroke the pony's soft nose. Niamh squealed as it huffed on her face and nuzzled her hair.

"Would he mind if I sat her on his back?" she called. No-one answered. Katherine saw to her amazement that the newcomers were involved in some kind of stand-off with Owain. They were all staring at each other, not speaking. Katherine moved to stand beside her friend.

"Do you know these people?" she asked him.

"No," he said shortly.

"Is there a problem here?" One of the men had spoken. He was not tall—about the same height as Owain, but very slightly built. Katherine thought his face unnaturally white, though as his hair was obviously dyed so black and red, perhaps this emphasised his pallor. He looked at her with eyes as green as apples. She found him extremely attractive. Niamh wriggled in her arms. She realised she was gripping her far too tightly. She put her down.

"You haven't told me your names," she said. She tried to stop herself grinning inanely.

"We're Morris men. We don't tell our names," green-eyes said. The other two nodded.

"You're not like any Morris Man that I've ever seen."

"No? How about these then?" Green-eyes pointed to their feathered top hats, he lifted his leg and shook it so the bells around his knees began to jingle.

"What shall we call you? Morris Man one, two and three?"

"You give us names. Names we can borrow and return. Nice names, though—not numbers."

"You're a slippery lot, aren't you?" Owain said. The menace in his tone surprised Katherine, used to his habitual reserve and gentleness. She, on the other hand, found herself squirming and giggling like a schoolgirl.

"Owain!" she said sharply, dismissing him. She looked carefully at the three men. Green-eyes seemed to be the leader.

"You can be Spring," she said. The other men were remarkably similar to Spring in appearance—both small and slight, long-haired, dressed in shabby motley. The second man, who had blue eyes, and indigo streaks in his hair she dubbed Summer. The third, dark brown and russet, became Autumn. They were satisfied with their names and thanked her.

"But who shall be Winter?" she asked. "Are there more of you?"

Spring inclined his head, and told her that yes, the rest of the side would be along in time for the fair. Throughout this conversation, Katherine was aware that the Morris men kept glancing over at Owain, that he seemed to unnerve them. What was the problem here? She found them utterly charming. But Owain tugged her away.

"Come-on," he said. "We mustn't barge in on these gentlemen. Let's get our tea."

She followed him a little unwillingly to the cottage. Niamh was as little pleased as her mother to be abandoning their new friends so soon. On the doorstep, Katherine found the big brown envelope addressed to herself. She recognised Elaine's writing. They knocked on the door. Violet answered and let them in.

"Have you seen the new people?" she said, as soon as they crossed the threshold.

"Yes! Gorgeous, aren't they? When did they arrive?"

Katherine and Violet disappeared, chattering, into the kitchen at the back of the cottage. Violet already had a fire lit in the hearth in the front room, and emerged in a couple of minutes with a kettle full of water, which she put over the flames. Owain felt his hands itch. The Morris men caused him acute unease. He was aware of their proximity, even through the thick stone walls of the cottage. Who were they? Astonishing feelings of hostility were bubbling up within him. Were they faeries? They were a great deal more substantial than the faeries he had seen before, and those earlier phantoms had not provoked the same instinctive aggression. Certainly the Morris men seemed to be flesh and blood—though also otherwordly, he was sure of it. And the two foolish girls twittering like birds, helpless to their allure.

Katherine came back in and opened the tipped the contents from the envelope.

"A note from Elaine," she said. "She's gone back to Bristol for a couple of days. She's left her phone number for emergencies—that's a new one—and she's worked out a Mummer's Play which she wants me to type up and photocopy. What a nerve!" But she smiled, and sifted through the scrawl on the notebook pages.

"It looks like you're in it, Owain," she said.

"Me?"

"Yes. She's got you earmarked for the Fool. It's the main part."

"The Fool. Of course. But I'm afraid not. I'm no actor. No way."

"It seems she has pre-empted your objections. It says here: 'Tell Owain this is not a play, but a ritual in dramatic form.' She's put me down for the Old Woman. Charming."

"There is absolutely no chance of me being in a play. Anyway, she's disappeared back to Bristol. How she going to rehearse?"

"It's only a short ritual-in-dramatic-form. She says it will only take us a day to practise, and that she'll be back soon. If you've any objections, take it up with her then."

Owain shrugged hopelessly. He could feel himself being roped in, but he blanched at the mere idea of performing. Would he allow Elaine to bully him into such humiliation? Probably yes, he thought humbly. At the moment he felt there was very little he wouldn't do for her, if she asked him.

More immediately, he had to talk to Katherine about the self-styled Morris men. She was poring over Elaine's incomprehensible handwriting. When the kettle boiled, Violet made them rosehip tea. Owain found he was unable to drink it. He was assailed by a distinct feeling of nausea, which he connected with the strangers outside.

"Have they come into the house?" he asked Violet. She shook her head.

"No. They said they wanted to set up camp outside."

Owain remembered something. He opened the front door and peered upwards, to an old horseshoe nailed upon the top of the door frame.

"Iron," he said. "They're not supposed to like iron."

"Morris men?" Violet said.

"No. Faeries. Nor stones with holes in, apparently. I've no idea why."

"You think our Morris men are faeries?" Katherine asked. "They seem pretty corporeal to me. Is that why you didn't like them?"

"Maybe. But I do know that they're not right. I can feel it." His hands were shaking.

"What about the faery smell? I didn't notice it," she said. Violet giggled.

"Can I go out and sniff them? Please?" she asked. "Excuse me, my friend thinks you're fairies, so I want to smell your perfume?"

But Owain scowled, and Violet fell silent.

"Where's Niamh?" Katherine asked, looking round the room. "Owain, you left the door open."

She scooted out of the front door, hunting for her daughter. She headed straight for the pony, remembering Niamh's fascination with the beast, and thinking of its hard hooves and Niamh's soft little body. She heard her laughing. The Morris Man, Spring, had Niamh in his arms. He flung her up in the air and caught her again, in the time-honoured fashion of a doting father. Katherine reacted with traditional maternal anxiety.

"Be careful with her!" she shouted, running up to Spring and pulling Niamh from his arms. Niamh, deprived of her sport, began to grizzle. Spring looked hurt.

"I was being careful. I wouldn't hurt her," he said. "She was enjoying it. Put her down." Meekly Katherine placed Niamh on the ground again. Spring squatted down.

"Come to Daddy," he crooned. "Come to Daddy, little girl."

His voice sent a shiver through Katherine. Was it fear or desire? Katherine was also half mesmerised. But she broke free.

"You're not her Daddy," she said shortly, but her voice was choked.

"Am I not? We're all family here, aren't we? We're all part of each other."

Obediently Niamh climbed into his arms. For a moment they both looked at Katherine, Niamh and Spring, and in a shock Katherine thought she did see a kinship between them. Spring stepped towards her, bestowed Niamh as though she were a gift.

"Care for her well," he said. "She's a beautiful child." As he reached out to her, his green eyes fixed on hers, Katherine caught the faintest wisp of a familiar scent. Sweet corruption. River mud and flowers. Then it was gone. Had she imagined it? Spring's gaze fell to her chest. He picked up the bone necklace, looking puzzled for a moment. He let it drop.

"We're all family," he repeated. "We're all part of each other." He turned away from her, to his companions. They were sitting by the fire, talking quietly. Katherine picked up the backpack, put Elaine's envelope in her bag, and told Owain she was heading back home. He joined her for the first part of the walk, as though he was sensitive to her alarm—and eager to move beyond the aura of the Morris men. She told him what had happened as she marched down the valley.

"I think you might be right," she said. Her voice was shaky. "Right about the new people. I've got to get away from here. I've got Elaine's phone number. I'll ring her. Maybe she'll let me stay with her for a couple of days."

"Maybe. Elaine's pretty cagey about her other life." Owain seemed loathe to let her go. "I could do with some support here, you know," he said. "No-one else knows as much as you about this."

"What do I know?"

"You were there, weren't you?"

"But I can't remember anything! Niamh's got to come first. I must take her away from here."

Owain nodded and sighed.

"Okay. I understand," he said. "But you'll be back soon. We're part of each other, remember?"

Coming from Owain, the same words sounded reassuring rather than sinister. He put his hand briefly upon her shoulder as he spoke. In his touch she felt the calm of winter fields, and the resilience of rock. She breathed deeply. Then she turned away and headed across the fields.

CHAPTER TWELVE

Paul arrived home late, tired and hungry, irritated by the long drive through the Swindon traffic. He endured every working day in a state of tension. His instinct for hard work and meticulous attention to detail struggled hour by hour with a deeper feeling that he was expending his efforts on something unimportant and unworthy. He was extremely good at his job, but he shrugged off praise and commendations. He devoted hours of painstaking energy and skill to a project, but refused to take any pride in the outcome. How could he congratulate himself for top-notch plans, when the fruit of his labour was another set of four bedroom executive homes in the wealthy Wiltshire villages? Even as he sweated over a new scheme, he would be totting up material wastage, energy consumption, the loss of green field sites. On the wall above his desk at the office he had pinned a huge and highly detailed plan for a sustainable village. It had taken him months to complete. It hovered before him like a muse, a constant reminder, while he developed yet another plan for a cottage extension or retail unit. Around the sustainable village were pictures of houses and schools from eco-architecture magazines, follies in wood and beach pebbles, emerging from the ground in organic swoops and curves. The practice was small—three partners and three employees, of which Paul was one. The partners were well aware of Paul's interests, and made an effort to cater to them, but work of any kind was hard to come by. In the meantime, Paul scoured the relevant magazines for design competitions, for openings in a more sympathetic field, but as yet to no avail. He slogged on. His heart ached. His employers sensed his restlessness and, keen to retain his services, allowed him considerable leeway when it came to using the office photcopier, telephone and fax machine for his various good causes.

He walked in the front door, expecting the usual chaos—a tired and grumpy Niamh, a disordered house. Or Katherine might be chatting over cups of tea with some friend or other, forgetting the time, unprepared for his return. Instead he was welcomed by a most delicious smell. On the table in the living room Katherine was placing a huge lasagne, alongside a mountain of salad and garlic bread steaming from the oven. She had even opened a bottle of red wine. Niamh, clean and scrubbed, was dressed in her pyjamas all ready for bed. Even the house looked a little less deep in crumbs and dust than usual.

"What's the occasion?" he asked. Katherine gave him a nervous smile, hovering around their daughter.

"Nothing special. I'll just put Niamh to bed. Do you want to dish up? I won't be a minute." She held out the little girl for Paul to kiss. He dutifully embraced her, instinctively holding his breath as he did so. Niamh was not in the mood for his cuddles and pushed him away, so Katherine took her upstairs and put her to bed.

When she came down Paul was already eating with considerable energy. Katherine had downed a glass of wine before his return, and her thoughts were a little fuddled. But as she ate, her mind cleared, and when their plates were empty she headed straight for the major topic—her plan to stay with Elaine.

"Just for a couple of days," she said, irritated to hear the appeasing tone in her voice. She could see Paul's face tense up. A frown flickered across his face.

"Is that what all the dutiful wife stuff was about?" he asked. "Of course you can go. You didn't need to go to all this trouble. I'll be fine."

"It doesn't seem fair, I suppose—me swanning off to Bristol while you have to go to work."

"And then come home to an empty house, you mean? No, it doesn't, does it? Still, I don't want to keep you chained to the kitchen, do I? I'm a feminist, remember?"

"Yes," she assented, still unhappy. "And anyway, I'm not going for a holiday—I feel the need to go away for Niamh's sake. I think we need a change of environment." She recounted her tale of the visit to the surgery, and later, the arrival of the Morris men and Spring's strange rapport with their child. Paul listened attentively, but his expression was hard to read. He did not make an immediate response. They cleared up the dishes together, and settled in the armchairs to finish off the wine. They drank in silence, Katherine observing that her partner was deep in thought.

"We're creating a great conspiracy here, you know," he said at last.

"What d'you mean?" Instantly Katherine felt defensive. She quelled the slight shrill in her voice.

"Okay—will you just hear me out for a few minutes? With an open mind, as you keep telling me."

Katherine took a large swig from her glass and nodded her head.

"On the one hand, we could be witnessing a troubled explosion of sinister faerie forces from a parallel world. On the other hand—"

"We might be making it all up?"

"Will you listen to me for a few minutes please? Let's consider all the various incidents. You go walking with the Little People after drinking dubious tea. You can't remember anything till you woke up the next morning, admittedly a bit the worse for wear. It is quite probable this traveller girl gave you something in the drink, that you wandered round confused and disorientated for a bit before ending up in the stone valley. A bird invaded Niamh's room. I had an erotic dream. No proof of anything supernatural yet?"

"What about the smell on Niamh? That wasn't a dream. She still has it."

"The doctor couldn't smell it."

"You're suggesting we're experiencing a shared sensory delusion?"

"Maybe. Or maybe she does smell a little weird, and that's just how she smells. The doctor said she was fine, didn't she?"

Katherine was obliged to agree.

"Now," he continued, "Owain thinks he witnessed a faerie procession. How do we know he didn't dream that? He told you he was asleep before he saw it. Elaine claims she saw some kind of apparition around you, but we know she's been something of an acid casualty—doesn't her description of those events sound rather like some kind of flashback? Now some Morris dancers have appeared and you have no reason whatsoever to presume they are anything out of the ordinary except Owain's intuition and your very personal interpretation of a mundane event with Niamh. Have you noticed how every so-called incident is witnessed by one person only? On each occasion there is a perfectly valid explanation. Instead of accepting this, you and Owain and Elaine have fabricated an elaborate fantasy, and every new incident you use to embroider and enhance this creation."

"There is one 'incident' you are forgetting—one I shared with Owain and Elaine."

"Yes, your co-conspirators. You're referring to the streams of light across the land—Owain's song-lines. I can take some of his ideas on board. I'm sure he is right about energy flows, there are many kind of magnetic fields in the earth. And even I've seen the stones in the valley look vaguely phosporescent."

"You think we saw the rocks glimmer in the moonlight?"

"You think your explanation makes more sense?" Paul poured himself the last of the wine. Katherine pondered for a few moments.

"I think it is part of the nature of these faery encounters to be slippery and elusive," she said. "Have you noticed how hard it is to keep the events in your mind? Exactly how well do you remember your 'erotic dream'?"

"I rarely remember my dreams. Okay, hardly at all—except that you keep reminding me about it." Paul realised with a pang this was not entirely true. He was still obsessed by the succubus, though of course it might just be Katherine he desired. They wore the same face after all. Perhaps the succubus was a dream fantasy—his partner and true-love transformed so that she desired and wanted him as he did her. Yes, he was haunted by desire, but he blamed this on his partner's refusal of his attentions. Was it so surprising that he felt so perpetually frustrated? So, on this score too, he could rule out faery intervention.

"When you meet a leprechaun you have to keep your eyes on it, remember?" Katherine said. "They are tricky and cunning, and will do everything in their power to divert your gaze—your attention—and then they disappear and you lose the pot of gold. I think that's just what the faeries are like. The moment you're not focussed on the event, it slides away. You forget it. A faery encounter doesn't stick in your memory. Now you see me, now you don't. Maybe that's why they confine their manifestation to one person at a time—it adds to the confusion. It makes you doubt your own mind."

Paul laughed:

"You've got me there. Damned if I do and damned if I don't. If only one witness was present, if there's a rational explanation, it proves it must have been faeries because faeries like to trick and deceptive. Okay. Let me be credulous. My explanations of these happenings are so logical and probable that, you tell me, they prove quite the opposite. So have you any idea why all of this is happening?"

"Owain and Elaine have been talking about this. Elaine suggested that it was the bypass—the destruction of the old pathway to make a modern road, gouging into the earth, all that stuff. Then Owain pointed out that many of his 'songlines', as you called them, have already become modern highways without any ruptures to faeryland. Then she suggested, on not unrelated lines, that mankind has become so out of touch with the Earth, so dislocated in spirit, that his actions are tearing the balance between the material and the immaterial world."

"And is this what you think too?"

"Perhaps. But I look at it on a more personal level. Every incident so far has been in some way related to a mental or emotional imbalance on the part of the observer? Niamh for me. Elaine's hunger for escape. Owain's obsessive wandering."

"And my overweening libido?"

"Your thwarted passion altogether—in your work, your aspirations. Your frustration."

"In short, you're saying we're all nuts? Doesn't that rule out the need for faeries?" Paul said.

"No. I'm suggesting that the faeries might feed our weaknesses. Or else they feed on them. What if the protest site is the key, situated on an old pathway, full of strange people—dis-ordered people—sensitives, drop-outs. Outsiders—but also passionate and magical. Maybe this concentration has triggered the breach."

Paul listened attentively. He had a quick, curious mind and Katherine's ideas provoked him pleasurably. He smiled.

"It's an interesting explanation. But allow me to remain agnostic for the time being."

They were sitting close together. The intensity of their interchange had kindled intimacy. Katherine put her arms around him.

"You can go to Bristol if you want," he said gently. "Whatever the root of our difficulties, I fancy a change of scene might do you good. I'll hang out with James. I've got plenty of work to do."

"Okay. I appreciate it. I want to go as soon as possible. Elaine wasn't in when I rang this afternoon but I'll try again in the morning. And if she's amenable, I'll take the coach from Marlborough." Katherine kissed him on the cheek.

"Bedtime, isn't it?" he said.

"Ever the optimist. Yes. It is getting late." Katherine stood up and headed for the bathroom.

Katherine was lying on her front when Paul slipped into bed. She turned her face turned away from him. He climbed in on top of her, rubbing his face in her hair, kissing the back of her neck. She could·feel his erection pressing into the back of her thighs. It occurred to her that the smell of her necklace was adding to his arousal. He kissed her shoulders, slid off her and turned her round to face him. Katherine tensed involuntarily. He pressed a knee between her legs, pushing her over on her back and pressing himself against her. Just as Katherine decided that she ought to make an effort at enthusiasm, a wave of fearful images rose up in her mind. Terrible, appalling thoughts. Mutilation and rape. As Paul weighed down on her she saw young girls in Africa and the Middle-east pinned to the earth while elders sliced through their sensitive flesh in obscene rituals of female circumcision. She saw gangs of soldiers, the force of fists and boots on flesh, the callous beatings, the lust for destruction. The endless reports, the interminable catalogue of suffering, the perverted, incomprehensible use of sex, most intimate of acts, as a means to hurt and humiliate. The images poured into her head, as though she had tuned in to a brutal frequency of hatred and pain. She tried to stop the thoughts. She tried to conjure up her love for Paul, desire, but she was flying in the face of a storm. Her mind blanked. Her body began to sweat. With a great shudder of revulsion she threw him off. Immediately the flood of images subsided.

"What? What was that for?" Paul cried. His voice betrayed anger—also hurt, rejection. Katherine turned away from him, curled up.

"I'm sorry," she said. "I'm too tired, okay?" What else could she say? That his amorous attentions made her imagine rape and torture? What sweet things lovers say...He would think she was sick. How could she argue with that? What was wrong with her? Her heart beat fiercely in her chest. Beside her Paul was wriggling and restless. Eventually he jumped up and stomped downstairs, leaving Katherine alone in the bed. She felt the pressure ease off. She waited for calm to descend. What kind of trick was this, filling Paul with unabating desire, while she was afflicted with horror? Was this the payment they demanded, the price of an adventure she couldn't remember? Or another symptom of her mental instability? She remembered the doctor's scrutiny, though perhaps she had imagined that too. Paranoid about Niamh, disconnected from Paul. Her life was full of fractures...

She didn't hear Paul return to bed, though when she woke the next morning he was beside her. She dressed and packed her bag before the alarm woke him for work, praying for Elaine to be in. She called her early. Elaine sounded very distant, complaining of the hour, and a hangover. The little family ate breakfast together, though few words were spoken. Then Paul drove them into Marlborough, dropping Katherine and Niamh in the High Street before he went to work. It was early and the town was quiet. The sun rose above the rooftops, molten copper. The sky was a brilliant blue, with tiny trails of cloud the colour of lavender. Already the heat was fierce. As soon as the baker opened, Katherine bought fruit buns for the journey. She handed one to Niamh, who sat on a wooden bench in the shade, swinging her legs, as they waited for the coach. Katherine was unable to keep still. She was wearing a green velvet jacket, black jeans and a close-fitting black lace shirt, but she quickly shed the jacket, wishing she had chosen cooler clothes, sandals instead of big boots.

When the coach drew up, she manoeuvred bag, backpack and child up the steps and sat near the back. It was a new experience for Niamh, but she remained calm upon her mother's lap for the first half an hour, still dozy after her early morning awakening. They headed down the motorway, Katherine pointing out cows in the fields, barns and houses, and as they drew near the city, a flotilla of hot air balloons, rising crimson, bottle-green and cadmium in the sky. She chatted to her daughter, but her body still ached to be moving. Would the fractures fade, or was she taking the faeries with her? The coach turned onto the M32 and carried them into the city. The traffic was slow, the roads choked with commuters heading in for work. The bus dallied in queues. The temperature increased despite the whirring of the fans, and Niamh's face was beaded with perspiration. Katherine itched and sweated. She peered out of the window at the smartly dressed people on the pavements, crisp white shirts and ties, young women in tight skirts and jackets. They seemed so very complete. Niamh began to fret, climbing on and off the seats, longing to run along the gangway, struggling from her mother's grip, till at last the coach pulled into the station and they disembarked.

Katherine took out her streetmap. She debated whether to take a taxi, but decided to save the money and go on foot. She put Niamh in the backpack, picked up her bag, and headed off across the city to Bedminster. It was a long, hot walk. Along Coronation Road the river stank of sewage, the slick mud-banks revealing here and there the half buried skeletons of supermarket trolleys. The traffic trundled past, noisy, trailing fumes. Niamh sank down, observing her new surroundings without comment. Katherine fixed her eyes on the pavement and strode on, mindless. As they wandered into the smaller streets the din began to abate. Katherine lifted her head and began to look about. Her arms ached and her back was soaked with sweat. Her vision began to tremble. It occurred to her that the spirit of the city was a great dragon, coiling on the land. Every now and then the glint of a red brick in a wall was a scale in the dragon's body. As the sun glanced off a window she fancied she saw the dragon's eye, that it was well aware of her movement through the maze of its body. And here in the labyrinth she would find Elaine, fair damosel in white, though hardly in need of rescue. More likely the damosel was whispering mischief in the dragon's ear...

She found Ravenscraig and banged on the front door. The house towered above them, like a castle, with its single slender turret atop the bay windows. According to the directions, the damosel did live in the topmost tower. The brick walls radiated heat. They sought refuge in the shade of porch, smelling of dust and decayed plaster. The house seemed deserted. She waited several minutes before banging again. Nobody answered. She took off the backpack and lifted Niamh free. Eventually a young man with long hair and a tie-dyed tee shirt opened the door. He looked barely awake. Katherine smiled apologetically.

"I'm looking for Elaine?" she said. The man rubbed his eyes and nodded. He stepped back from the door to let her in.

"Top floor," he said. "Tell her to answer the front door herself if she's expecting guests."

"Okay. Sorry I disturbed you." She shouldered her child and belongings. Below her feet, in the hallway, the floor was patterned with tiles. Grimy chequers of red and emerald, a border the colour of buttercups. At the bottom of the stairs a wooden arch was decorated each side with the face of an angel, painted and overpainted so many times their features were blurred and indistinct. With Niamh wriggling under one arm, Katherine set off up the stairs. The house was deep in dust, the walls covered with yellowing woodchip paper, peeling off around the windows. The air was still and stale. When she arrived at the top floor she could hear music from inside the room, the skewy voice of Nico singing 'Sunday Morning'. She knocked on the door and called out:

"Elaine?" She heard movement inside, and Elaine opened the door. The two women embraced warmly as Niamh trotted into the room.

"Come in! Isn't it hot? You found me okay then?" Elaine stepped back into the room. Katherine picked her way across the debris in the room, dropped clothes, half packed bags, a scattering of books and papers. The room smelled of drink and hairspray, though Elaine had opened the window to freshen the air. Her mutilated wedding dress was flung on the floor.

"Are you going somewhere?" she asked, eying the disorder. Elaine laughed and shook her head.

"It always looks like this," she said. "I'll clear you some space, don't worry." She pushed magazines from an armchair, so that Katherine could sit down.

"Pretty," Katherine said, picking up the dress.

"Keep it. If it fits. I don't think I like it anymore."

"Did you enjoy your night out?"

"It was okay. I went with my friend Rosie? You just missed her."

The sun caught on a crystal, scattering tiny rainbows on the white walls. After the dark ascent through the dust and cobwebs, it was dazzling.

"What a room!" Katherine said. "You're like Morgan le Fay, with a tower in the clouds." She surveyed her surroundings.

"My god, did you draw all those?" Katherine had spotted the gallery of faeries on the back wall. "They're brilliant! I didn't know you could draw." She stood up for a closer look, peering at the legion of fantastical asymmetric faces.

"You couldn't possibly have done all these since you returned." For a moment Katherine was suspicious. "How did you know? You said you'd never seen them before."

"I've been looking a long time. I knew they were waiting for me. I knew."

"Are they waiting for you? Is this all about you then? A touch of egomania perhaps?"

But Elaine's face twisted in quick retaliation.

"No!" she snapped. "That's not what I ment. Just that I have long been aware that something like this was going to happen to me. I could feel it. See for yourself. I've been drawing and painting them for over a year. They've whispered in my dreams. I've been holding on to the conviction that if I kept myself free long enough, a new path would open up. I had to keep myself disconnected and unfettered." She moved towards the window and gazed out across the rooftops, the ranks of houses stretching on towards the horizon.

"Anyway," she said darkly, "there is more. I did have the urge to escape—like you. I thought that leaving the protest site, the sacred circle, I might find the influence falling away. It hasn't worked like that. We are the sacred circle."

"'Which way I fly is Hell; myself am Hell.' Like Satan in Paradise Lost," Katherine said. "I know what you mean. Even here in the city."

"But it's not hell, Katherine!" Elaine urged. "It's my dearest wish! Loosen up, we are blest!" She turned to the window again, and fiddled uneasily with something on the sill. She turned round.

"What do you make of this?" She handed over a piece of shaped wood. Katherine received it gingerly. It was a crudely carved figure, a few threads of dark hair congealed on its head.

"It looks like a voodoo doll," Katherine suggested carefully. "Where on earth did you get it?"

"From an old friend of mine, Jo. He stayed here too—hence the mess. He collected the doll for me this morning. He was given very specific instructions to give it to me, by a mysterious fortune-telling bag lady."

"It's a good story. But what's it for? What are you supposed to do with it?"

"I don't know," Elaine said. "But I'm sure this is connected with what is happening in Wiltshire, and I do know that we're supposed to find this bag lady again." Suddenly she shrieked:

"Niamh! Katherine, get that child away from my stuff!"

In the moments of the adults' inattention Niamh had chanced upon a bag of cosmetics lying on the floor and had tipped the contents in her lap. Katherine grabbed her daughter and retrieved Elaine's property.

"Don't worry," she said. "No harm done. Look, shall I tidy up a bit? You can hardly blame her for playing with the stuff when it's littering the floor."

Elaine muttered something under her breath, but agreed to make cups of tea while her guest cleared some space. She headed downstairs to the communal kitchen, while Katherine began hanging clothes in the wardrobe, picking up pens and books. After a few minutes she heard a knock on the door.

"Come in. It's open," she called. A tall, thin man crept cautiously through the doorway.

"I'm looking for Elaine," he said nervously. "Is she out? I got her some milk. Shall I come back later?"

He had a pale, delicate face and thick clumps of long black hair, streaked with purple. He looked very young, half a dozen thick silver rings in each ear, bangles on his wrists. He was wearing black jeans and a lace shirt not unlike her own.

"Hey, snap!" she said, nodding at his outfit. "Elaine's just making drinks. She'll be up in a minute."

Then Jo saw Niamh, and his eyes lit with delight. He watched her toddle to her mother's lap.

"Hello, little girl. Aren't you gorgeous? You must be Niamh. So you must be Katherine?"

She nodded.

"And you are?"

"Jo."

"Jo the bearer of the voodoo doll?"

"Yes. And now Elaine is hoping I will lead you all to the bag lady again. I've told it isn't as easy as that."

Elaine entered the room as he spoke.

"We'll find her," she said. She was carrying a large, chipped teapot decorated with yellow roses. She dug out three mismatched mugs and poured tea for her guests. Niamh had juice in her beaker. As Jo drank, Katherine observed the red angry weals on the white skin around his wrists, like snakes.

"Eczema," he said, noticing the direction of her gaze.

"Jo's allergic to the entire world," Elaine said coldly. Katherine noted her crisp but faintly proprietal tone. Evidence of an affaire? They seemed an unlikely couple. She recalled Elaine's emphasis on old friend. A past attachment then. An old flame, though he certainly didn't look very old.

Katherine told them about the Morris men, and her talk with Paul the previous evening.

"I saw them too. Just as I was leaving the site. I saw them arrive," Elaine said. "How could they have been faeries?"

"I don't know for sure that they are. Owain thinks so. He was acting very strangely, very aggressive. I've never seen him like it," Katherine said. Elaine considered.

"If he thinks they are, we should believe him," she said. "They were people out of the ordinary, that's for sure."

"You didn't think they were faeries at the time though? Even though they whisper in your dreams?" Katherine asked, a little irritated. "Did you see where they came from?" She wondered why Elaine was getting on her nerves. Were they were collaborating in a fantasy after all? At least Paul aspired to some intellectual rigour. Elaine's credulity always seemed to force her into the sceptical corner, but she knew Elaine could beat her down. So she turned to Jo.

"So how do we find your mystic lady?" she said. Jo looked a little helpless. Elaine sighed with exasperation.

They did not begin the search for several hours. More tea was poured from the teapot with the yellow roses. The sun glittered on the sea of tiled roofs. They talked. The brief alienation was eclipsed. Their endless, rambling conversation, punctuated by fits of laughter, came like a cool draught of water, quenching a deep parching thirst. The day stretched ahead, formless, an empty vessel waiting to be filled with adventures. Jo joined in from time to time, but often he was left at the sideline. Still, Katherine could not help but observe him. His glossy elf-locks hung over his face and shoulders. He was terribly pretty, very fragile and fey. Had this been the attraction for Elaine?

Once the heat of the day had faded, they set out for the city centre. On the broken horizon the sky was smoky rose and mauve. Elaine strode ahead, bolt upright, the white gauze of her skirt floating behind her. The ceaseless traffic poured along the road.

Jo took them to the Chapel, not open as yet though a poster on the door promised live music later in the night. Already a couple of kids in leather and fishnets were swilling cider on the steps outside. He tried to remember the route. They walked back and forth for an hour, but just as Jo had forewarned, the narrow street and the cafe were not to be found. Elaine grew impatient and cursed him. She accosted passers-by with questions about the missing cafe. She pored over paving slabs for bloody footsteps and upbraided a couple of tramps on a bench. Niamh grew tired of the backpack and began to cry and squirm. Jo hovered uneasily beside Katherine, fearful of Elaine's temper. At last she was too weary to continue. They all sat together on a bench near the tramps, tired and deflated. Down the road, they could see the Chapel doors were open, and the kids on the steps were heading inside. Elaine perked up.

"Shall we go?" she said.

"What, with Niamh?"

"I guess not." They remained in silence for a few minutes more and still, Elaine watched the trickle of dark clad, bright-haired people. She shifted on the bench, restless with indecision. Then she dug about in her bag for keys and gave them to Katherine with a flourish.

"You don't mind if we go, do you?" she asked. Katherine felt a pang of disappointment, along with something else. Envy or rejection.

"Of course not." The words half choked her. "Have a great time. I'll see you later." Swiftly she stood up. She nodded a quick goodbye to Jo, and began, once again, the long walk to Ravenscraig.

The long evening was drawing to a close and the twilight settled on the city. The sun declined, spilling lilac shadows in the streets. The spire of grandiose St Mary Redcliffe pierced the sky like a keen, slender blade, amid clouds soaked cherry and gold. Down on the pavement Katherine strode through the gathering darkness, through the purple shade where the walls still breathed a faint warmth from the day. Then the street lights popped on and in an instant the muted tones bleached away. High above the city the first star glistened in a sweep of hyacinth blue. Below her feet the grime and rubbish faded. Niamh slumped on her back, fast asleep, her face resting heavily on Katherine's shoulder. Faintly she could feel her breath, sweet and soft on her neck. She walked on, one step after another. Her feet were bruised, and her shoulders ached. Her thoughts were slow and unreasonable. When she thought of Elaine heading off for fun she felt very sad. But why should her parental obligations stop Elaine enjoying her nightlife? She had practically foisted herself on Elaine after all, Elaine was well within her rights to send her home alone when Niamh fell in the way of her pleasures. But still she felt miserable. Her body was heavy and weary, but the distance had to be covered, so walk she must. One foot after another. She fell into a daze, moving like an automaton. The sky darkened, violet blue, and a huge yellow moon drifted above the horizon. She reached Coronation Road, and the river smelled of rotting garbage and decay. Peering down through the line of trees along the she could see a pale mist rising above the black water. The moon hung like an amber rose, the city crouching in darkness, with Katherine small as a mite in its body. She turned away from the river. The street lights seemed to dim. She fixed her eyes on the moon, bright as a jewel, and strode past the ranks of houses, locks fastened, curtains shut. Every now and then she was aware of other people passing, dark silhouettes, vague and enclosed. She walked on. Surely she must reach Elaine's place soon. Surely. In anticipation her footsteps quickened, her body regained its lightness and vigour. She felt her spirits rise. She turned into the last road.

No. This was not the street. She did not even recognise the name. She stood for a few moments. It had to be nearby. She realised she was surprisingly calm about this new turn of events. Was she lost? How safe was this area at night? She tested her response to the questions, and found that she was not overly alarmed. Some change had occurred. Niamh, still asleep, was not weighing on her shoulders anymore. Her legs itched to be moving. Her feet tapped restlessly on the pavement. She had emerged from exhaustion. She felt hard and bright, like a piece of moonlight. She turned around and headed back the way she had come. She skipped. She laughed. Still she was lost. She turned left and right, but she seemed to fly, her body strong as steel, tireless. She thought she could walk forever. The night air brushed against her face with soft, dark fingers. She moved among unseen spirits, the dreams of the dragon. She was exposed to every thread of scent, each tiny movement, as the path unwound through the great brick forest.

She realised she was not alone. She registered the movement of someone before her, further up the street. She peered through the shadows. Nobody. She had been mistaken. Then the flicker again, the curve of a robe. She had seen no other pedestrian for some time. It occurred to her she might ask for directions. She hurried her pace. She ran. The figure remained at a distance. If figure there was at all. She could not be sure.

"Who is the third who always walks beside us?" she asked the sleeping Niamh. The words, spoken aloud, echoed in the empty street.

"When I count, there are only you and I together...but? Who is the other one?"

Niamh made no response other than to sigh in her sleep. Katherine was afraid she might be cold, but her cheek was warm enough.

"We'll be back soon," she said."Then you'll have somewhere more comfy." Katherine looked along the street again, and there, illuminated beneath a street lamp, the figure was plain to see. Katherine began to run, calling out as she did so:

"Hey! Excuse me! Can you help me?" But as soon as she reached the place the figure had disappeared. Then she saw the shifting form ahead. She felt compelled to follow, mindless of any hazard. How could she find her way back otherwise? She walked on. Whenever she flagged or stopped the figure appeared again, now and then turning towards her, rewarding her patience with a flick of a pale hand, a quick nod. She was closer. The distance between them was falling. Then her guide disappeared altogether. Katherine was standing before a high wall covered with ivy. The nearest streetlight was dead and as she stood in the near-darkness, Katherine felt a sudden lurch of fear. Was she about to be accosted? She stepped forward, cautious, till the wall gave way to an old iron gate, partly ajar. A huge wooden sign hung over the gate, and dimly she could make out 'Suitable for Conversion' in red letters, and 'Sold' emblazoned across the details. She pushed the gate and peered through. A slim hand reached out and held her by the wrist. She pulled away in a panic.

"It's okay!" It was a warm, female voice. A little familiar. Katherine looked up at her assailant. A slender woman with long dark hair. She could not discern her features in the darkness but still she thought she knew her.

"Crow?" she said. As if in answer to a summons, two huge black birds alighted on the gate above their heads.

"This way," the woman said. She lead her across tarmac to a closed-up, semi derelict building. As they moved from the shadow of the wall, the neon glow dusted the ornate stonework at the top of boarded up doorway. It was framed by an arch, and carved in stone at the top Katherine could read 'Highfield Infants School'. An old Victorian building, windows broken and patched with pieces of hardboard. An ancient elder tree, coarse and overgrown, pressed against the side of the building, thrusting coarse limbs through the broken panes into the old school. The tarmac playground was strewn with broken glass, cans and limp plastic bags. Katherine's guide walked to the doorway and tugged at the boarding. One small piece opened smoothly. Katherine stepped inside, and the board shut behind them like a secret door. She felt a momentary doubt. What was she doing? Wandering about in the dark, breaking and entering, taking her precious child into danger? A sharp, sensible voice shrilled warnings in her head, but still she carried the moon's radiance about her like an armour. She could feel its golden glimmer on her face. The scared voice wittered on, but she felt compelled to continue—as though she was asleep, moving through the inevitable turns of a dream, while her half-awake mind interfered with advice and impotent alarm. Inside the school the darkness was complete. She took a hesitant step forwards, when a warm hand reached for her arm and led her forwards. She followed cautiously, kicking through bits of rubbish and rubble with her boots. She sensed space opening around her, as though they had moved into some kind of hall. Her eyes began to adapt to the dark, and dimly she could make out the patched windows. To her left, high up, she could see moonlight trembling through an empty frame. Then the glow was obliterated by a black, feathered body. One of the crows flew in through the frame. Its fellow followed just behind. As Katherine watched the crows, the woman lit a large storm lantern. It spilled huge, animated shadows across the walls and debris as she began to light a host of smaller candles in a semi-circle at the top of the room. The she placed the storm lantern in the centre and sat on a dark red rug on the floor. She patted the space before her.

"Why don't you put Niamh down here? I have a blanket too. She can sleep in a little more comfort."

Katherine nodded. She eased the backpack from her shoulders and gently pulled Niamh free. She laid her on the rug, the colour of wine or blood, and covered her with a torn wool blanket. Niamh turned and sighed, but she didn't wake. Katherine sat down. Her shoulders were stiff. She had been carrying her burden for hours. The hall smelt of crumbling plaster and cold stone. It was empty, beside a couple of decrepit wooden benches, broken and vandalised by earlier intruders. The floor was deep in dust, with clots of plaster fallen from the ceiling, and the ubiquitous sprinkling of litter. The candes emitted a wavering yellow light. The crows stood together on a makeshift table, planks and plastic crates, covered with a torn silk scarf, patterned with purple. It bore candles on chipped saucers, a jam jar filled with sprays from the elder tree and a rose or two, doubtless filched from a front garden. The crows began to groom their thick blue-ish wings, stepping daintily around the candles with their huge, clawed feet. A vigorous skein of ivy had burst through a window and was growing up the walls and across the ceiling, reflecting a verdant light. Katherine smiled.

"I've found the Green Chapel," she said. She looked at her companion. How could this be Crow? Crow had been a young girl. This woman, as far as she could tell in the candlelight, was fully grown, maybe in her early thirties. She had smooth brown-black hair and dark blue eyes. Her skin was smooth and golden brown. Her bearing was calm, distinctly regal, like a queen, or a priestess. She wore a long velvet dress, grass green, and silver hoops in her ears.

"The Green Chapel? Perhaps," she nodded. Katherine was uncertain.

"Are you really Crow?" she said. The woman nodded again.

"You're older than I remember."

"But still you knew me," Crow said. Her demeanour was tranquil and assured. She reached out her hand to stroke the cheek of the sleeping child. Twining blue tattooes decorated her arms and wrists. Niamh stirred and her eyes flicked open for a moment. Then she sank into sleep once again. Crow looked at Katherine.

"So how can I help you on your quest?" she asked.

"You're not a faery," Katherine said. "Who are you?"

"I'm Crow. I am your signpost, your guide."

"You are very familiar to me—even though you are changed."

Crow nodded in reply but made no comment.

"Niamh," Katherine said. "You told me the faeries wouldn't touch Niamh but I'm afraid they have."

"I told you the faeries wouldn't harm Niamh. You are twisting my words."

"So they have taken her?"

"Taken her? She's right here! How could they have taken her?"

"I think," Katherine sighed painfully, "I think this is not my child." It hurt her to say the words. How long had she harboured this unspoken fear? She could scarcely admit the thought. Now she had declared it aloud.

"I am afraid this is not my child," she said again.

"A changeling?" Crow said. "Of course you are right. You're her mother. You would know. Why don't you take one of these stones and smash her to pieces? She isn't real."

Katherine was shocked. She blanched. She looked down at the sleeping baby, this perfect, warm being she had held to her body.

"Are you mad?" she said. "How could I do that?"

"You know it's a changeling. It possesses a glamour that has convinced you this creature, this simulacrum, is your own offspring. But you can't destroy it?"

"Of course not!"

"So you're not convinced it isn't Niamh?"

"No. Not convinced. Uncertain. Even if it isn't Niamh I couldn't do what you are suggesting. It's a living, breathing creature. It's alive."

"It's? Don't you mean she?"

Katherine struggled for words to reply. Seeing her turmoil, Crow smiled gently and broke in again.

"You are right. You could not destroy the child. Your instinct is correct. Your true daughter has been taken from you and here we have a substitute, but the two are connected. Niamh exists in the other place, but it is the shadow of her will that holds the false Niamh together. So nurture her well, she's the link that will reunite you."

"You said no harm would come to her? But how do I get her back?"

"You have to find your way back to the other place, and bring her out."

"How do I do that? I can't even remember what happened!"

When Crow didn't speak, Katherine began to panic.

"Tell me. I thought you were my guide! Guide me."

"You do know the way. You'll find it if you keep looking. I can't tell you anymore."

"What about the other faeries, the succubus, the Morris men? What's happening at the protest site?"

Crow's face remained closed. Katherine's questions ceased. Then an idea occurred to her.

"You were the Bag Lady too? How silly we were to look for you altogether. Of course you would only appear to one of us." She realised she was sounding bitchy. "What about Elaine's doll? Can you tell me anything about that?"

Crow looked up, her clear face lovely in the candlelight.

"That is for Elaine to discover," she said quietly. "Come. I'll show you the way to Ravenscraig." She gathered Niamh into her arms and stood up. She placed her gently in the backpack and helped Katherine lift it onto her back. She took Katherine's hand and led her from the Green Chapel to the street outside. They walked along the pavement.

"Just down there," Crow said. "The first right." She stepped away.

"Will I see you again?" Katherine asked. "Will you be able to help me?"

"Yes. You will see me again." She was backing away, already indistinct. Katherine headed down the road, and when she looked again, Crow had disappeared. She turned as directed, and found herself in a familiar street. Ravenscraig was half way down—so close, after all. She unlocked the front door and headed up through the gloom to Elaine's room. No-one was in. She settled Niamh in a pile of cushions on the floor, and lay down beside her in a sleeping bag. The conversation with Crow had been warm and reassuring, but what in fact had Crow told her? Nothing she didn't already know. Nothing at all. Still, Elaine would be pissed off to have missed the event once again—unworthy moment of spite. She nestled with the child, the sweet simulacrum, and thought of Paul all alone in the house.

CHAPTER THIRTEEN

The girl flipped into a handstand. She stood poised, tiny feet pointed to the sky and a flame of scarlet hair floating to the ground. Then she swung her long, slim legs right over, her body arched for a moment, before lifting herself upright again. She stretched up her arms, took two short running steps, and cartwheeled twice. She laughed to her companion, sitting on the grass, ran again and leapt into a quick somersault, one perfect, fluid movement.

"Did you see that?" James said, his voice full of admiration.

"Amazing. Who is she?"

Paul and James were walking up the Old Lane from the main road. It was Saturday morning. After a night alone, Paul was restless and bored. He had considerable correspondence to work through at home, calls to make, a press release to put together. But it was hot. He listened to the weather forecast, to the dire drought warnings. Global warming? More doom? He couldn't face his computer. The prospect of human companionship won him over. He rang James and suggested they should meet at the protest site, hand out some flyers for the fair—and maybe head for a pub later in the day. James was also at a loose end and he readily agreed. As they walked along the lane, the air shimmered on the track before them. The leaves hung limp on the hedgerow. Huge bracts of hogweed teetered in the verge, the flowers creamy white and coarse on thick stalks.

The nymph was standing on her hands again. When the two men opened the garden gate she glanced at them, and flicked back onto her feet. Her companion, another girl, stood up. Paul and James began to walk towards the cottage, but found their path was blocked. The four people confronted each other in curious silence. James had finally shaved off his moustache. He was wearing a pair of baggy shorts and an old Greenpeace tee-shirt. His hair fell in a big forelock, which he pushed back off his face as he beamed at the two girls. Paul, in the usual jeans and boots, had donned a black vest in view of the weather though already he could feel the delicate white skin on his shoulders beginning to burn. He remembered that he hadn't showered for a couple of days, while James smelled sweet and clean, of soap and, faintly, aftershave. Paul rubbed the stubble on his face.

"Hello," he said, shifting from one foot to another. "You're new arrivals?"

"I'm James," said his friend, offering his hand. "This is Paul."

The girls each shook his hand and smiled, but since they offered no reply, the four people fell into silence again. Both girls were small and slightly built. Their little feet were bare, excepting a couple of silver rings on their toes. They wore leggings and tight, sleeveless tops. The girl with long, scarlet hair was dressed in turquoise. The other wore purple, and her hair, the colour of onyx, was fastened in a pony tail that fell to her waist. Their skin was the soft, pure white of snow.

"Yes, we arrived this morning," said the red-haired girl. "We're here for the fair."

"You're acrobats?" James asked. "We were watching you as we walked up. You're brilliant."

"Thank you." The two girls smiled at each other. They turned from the men and spun away in matching cartwheels to each side of the garden, their slight bodies toned and strong, barely seeming to touch the earth at all. They skipped away, to the rear of the house, out of sight.

"Amazing," James breathed.

"You've said that already," Paul said.

"But they were! Absolutely gorgeous. Surely you agree?"

"Yes, I suppose so." Paul headed on up the path and knocked on the door. Jan Blessing let them in. A pile of blankets and a couple of rucksacks were heaped in a corner, but Jan was alone in the cottage. He noticed how musty it smelled, the air grown stale though the window was open. Sprays of beech leaves lay upon the mantel, and beads of incense smoked on a charcoal block, resting on a chunk of flint. Paul handed Jan a poster to put in her shop window, and a pile of flyers to distribute. He had billed the event as a protest, still uneasy about the unofficial nature of the fair they were planning. He was worried the event might grow out of hand. If they were crowded with ravers they might attract the unwanted attention of the police. They could lose the goodwill of the local people and allow the council an opportunity to be rid of them all the sooner. He didn't want the protest to be sullied. Nobody else seemed to be at all alarmed, but he could not quell his concern. He was hoping he could steer the course of events in such a way as to minimse the chances of trouble.

"Who are the acrobats?" James asked.

"I don't really know. Friends of the Morris men," Jan said. She lit a cigarette.

"The Morris men. Of course. Katherine mentioned them. Are they all camped out at the back of the house?" Paul asked.

"Yep. More Morris men turned up yesterday—another three. And the girls came today, on foot. They've erected a couple of tents in the garden. The men were up all last night playing music and talking."

"Have you spoken to them?" Paul asked.

"A bit. They're not very forthcoming though. They stick together."

"Those girls are fabulous," James said.

"Stop drooling, will you? The men are lovely, too. They look like they belong to one family, all very close. Perhaps they're a bizarre performing troupe."

"Like Circus Archaos? This fair's going to be fun," James said. Paul looked worried. James headed for the door.

"I'm going to talk with them," he said. "Are you coming?"

Without waiting for a reply, James headed out of the cottage and into the back garden. Paul remained inside for a few minutes more, discussing where to hang posters. Jan stubbed out her cigarette.

"Are you okay?" she said.

"Fine."

"Is this all becoming too much for you? You need some help? You know what they're like—unless you specifically delegate some of your load, they'll let you carry on struggling."

"I know. I'm fine. A bit tired."

"Katherine's in Bristol with Elaine?"

"Yes. They're coming back Monday."

Jan could sense some weight bearing down on him, but as he would not elucidate she could offer no more than moral support. She patted his arm gently.

"Have some fun," she said. "Stop worrying. Go and chat to the Family Morris with your friend."

"I'll try," he said. "Easier said than done."

"I know. So many causes, so little time. But you can't dwarf your own life. You've got as much right to happiness as anyone else. You're taking on too much."

"I don't really look at it like that. Right now children are dying because they haven't got clean water to drink. Right now acres of forest are being destroyed. I can't help feeling that unless I give everything I have, my efforts are insufficient. Do you know what I mean?"

"Yes, I do. I do, indeed. But you look tired. Why not take an afternoon off? Just this once? Owain's up at the copse—why don't you ask him to take you across the Pewsey Downs to Honey Street? It's a lovely walk, I'm sure he'll show you the way if you bribe him with a beer."

"Perhaps I will. We were planning to spend the afternoon at the pub anyway. If I can drag James away from the ladies."

Paul emerged from the cool, sombre shade of the cottage into the brilliant heat. He shaded his eyes.

"James?" He headed round the cottage. A black and white pony was tethered near the hedge, drowsing in the shade. As he passed, it snorted and tossed its head, unsettling a swarm of flies hovering above its ears. Behind the cottages, covering the old lawn and vegetable garden, a new encampment had risen from the ground. Chunks of flint encircled a fireplace, a patch of grey and white ash upon the burnt grass. Around it were three ridge tents, simply built compared to the elaborate constructions in the trees, but magical, beautiful, like a knight's pavillion or a storybook circus. The tents were just tall enough to stand in. They were worn and patched, but the fabrics were brightly coloured—diamonds of mauve and burgundy, stripes of orange and peachy gold. The materials possessed a faint sheen, a glimmer in the unrelenting sunlight. Blue and silver streamers hung from the tent poles, dripping with tiny silver bells that tinkled in the faintest breeze. The sound was at once distant and curiously penetrating. The wind rose momentarily, shifting the leaves and the long grass.

"Will you share a drink with us?" A voice broke into his reverie. Paul drew his attention away from the tents to the small man standing beside him. He looked down into green eyes, black and copper hair under a top hat.

"You must be Spring," he said. The man bowed with a flourish.

"And you must be Paul. Will you join us?" He gestured that Paul should follow him. Paul looked down, and saw that he was standing just outside a fragile circle of leaves on the ground. He stepped over and walked towards the fireplace.

"So now I am in your domain?" he said with a wry smile. "I understand you might be faeries, in which case it would be foolish of me to eat or drink while I'm here. Maybe I wouldn't be able to leave?"

"If we were faeries, that might well be the case," Spring replied. "Here. Some wine. You don't believe in faeries so why not take a chance?" His voice was low, equally sardonic. The two men looked each other in the eye, and smiled in a moment of mutual understanding. Paul sat upon the ground near the empty fireplace, and received an earthenware cup, filled with a pale, bitter wine. He sipped it gently. Spring sat opposite and raised his own cup in a salute.

"We shall be comrades," he said. "You are welcome among us."

Paul raised his own cup and drank again.

"Where are your friends?" Paul asked.

"Walking."

"Where is James?"

"Your friend? Playing with the girls." Spring pushed back his hat. His hair shone in the sun like the feathers of a raven. Paul looked across the garden, where James was earnestly attempting a cartwheel, while his svelte companions laughed and skipped about him like butterflies.

"The fool," Paul said softly. "He looks like a bloody carthorse." James thumped clumsily on the ground, and abandoned his acrobatic efforts. He joined Paul, breathing heavily, his face red and sweaty. The girls followed him, perched themselves gracefully upon the pony cart, which was pulled up between two of the tents.

"This is Dawn, with the red hair, and Dusk, the lady in purple," James said.

"Very poetic," Paul said. "I can see you're getting into the scene."

"They're theatrical people!"

"Sure," Paul returned. The wine was already taking an effect, but still his response was sour. He thought Spring was okay—but the girls? He did not think they were here to protest about the road.

Dawn jumped neatly from the cart and landed beside him.

"Don't you like us?" she said. He caught a fine thread of scent from her body. He shivered.

"I've only just met you," he said carefully. He felt a prickling over his skin. She leaned over and whispered in his ear. He felt her fingers brush against his neck. Her breath was cool.

"I can see your dreams," she said. "They drift around you like smoke. I can taste them."

Paul recoiled. He felt her hair, smooth as silk, on his bare arm. Were his thoughts so exposed?

"What dreams do you see?" His voice was curt, but he felt his heart begin to thump in his chest.

"This one," she said. She kissed him, and her mouth tasted of fruit and earth. He trembled, pulled away from her.

"I have other dreams," he said. He looked round. James and Dusk were watching this intimate scene with some curiosity, but they heard voices and looked up. Beyond the tents, the other Morris men were returning. Spring moved towards them, and spoke in a low voice. They eyed the two visitors, greeting them with cool smiles. The three new Morris men closely resembled their brethren, in appearance and clothing. Faded velvet, rich colours, the ubiquitous bells that jingled whenever they moved. They were decorated with feathers and sparkling beads, with flowers and leaves tucked into the brims of hats, pockets and buttonholes. They laughed with each other, exposing teeth too white. Their hands were fine and slim, effeminate, with nails just a little too long. Paul could understand why they made Owain feel uneasy. As they moved around the tents, it was difficult to tell one from another. He could almost believe himself that they belonged to another race. But then, he had drunk two, three glasses of wine by now and the sun was beating on his head like a hammer. With a great effort he rose to his feet.

"Shall we head off?" he said to James. The girls had gone. Paul felt dazed and half asleep. The Morris men watched them turn to leave without a word, but Spring moved towards them.

"We'll be seeing you again, no doubt," he said.

"No doubt," Paul replied. He stepped from the circle. Did he feel a faint resistance? He chided himself for falling in with Katherine's grand delusion. How easy it was to build patterns, if your wish and desire were strong. But what was his wish? They headed for the copse, where Owain was sitting with Violet in the shade. Under the trees, in the cool, the air was clear and the dim light filtered green through the leaves. The earth was dusty beneath his feet, dry leaves trampled into the dirt by passing feet. Paul's mind began to clear. He nodded a greeting to Owain and Violet, and crouched beside them.

"We're heading for the pub," he said. "Jan thought you might show us the way to the Barge, over at Honey Street. Beers on us."

Owain made no immediate response. He looked at Paul, considering.

"Okay," he said. "Violet?"

She shook her head.

"I promised I'd help Mum, cover for her at the shop."

Owain rose to his feet, brushing the dust from his jeans. He looked from Paul to James. Neither of them knew Owain particularly well. Paul wondered if he had made the right decision asking him, though Owain's connection with Katherine and Niamh would, sooner or later, have brought them into closer contact. They headed back to the main road, then across the fields to East Kennett.

Paul walked behind Owain, unaware of his surroundings and lost in thought. He was conscious that they made an ill-assorted threesome. James was a useful promoter of the anti-bypass movement in the local press, and had become a good friend, but he couldn't shed the impression that his companion was essentially an enthusiastic daytripper—out for the experience, curious about the people and events, but ultimately not personally or passionately involved. He kept a good-humoured distance, even when assisting with posters or analysing the protest meetings with Paul. Sometimes this annoyed him, having his passion become an intellectual exercise. At other times it was a much-needed antidote, when he was himself so bogged down and implicated in the salvation of the strip of land around his village. While he pondered on the purpose of his life, while he suffered prickling guilt at his own inability to force a change, James seemed to stride through the days taking in the sights and enjoying the pleasures he found in his way, a warm-hearted and intelligent schoolboy happy to have a good time. Maybe he envied him. Come to that, he understood that much of his dislike for Elaine was based in jealousy. Elaine was free. Elaine had not compromised herself, as he had. He couldn't help but admire her courage even though he rejected what he perceived as selfishness and egotism in her behaviour—as well, of course, as her hold on his partner, who he felt was slipping further and further away from him.

He looked up, to see that James was walking beside Owain, striking up a conversation. Paul smiled. What could Owain, tongue-tied, unworldly old hippie, possibly share with the up and coming career boy? Perhaps James was telling him about his ultimate ambition to work for The Sun? ("It would be a laugh, wouldn't it...") Maybe Owain would gather the words to expound his theory on the old paths running through the Otherworld as well as this one? It occurred to him that the conversation he was witnessing was in some way a collision of the two worlds in just the same way. And sharing the same path too, as they walked through the heat and the dust to East Kennett. But perhaps he was exaggerating. They were two people after all, two human individuals, and although he could not hear what they were saying, he could see that Owain was laughing at something James had said. Then he felt a pang of envy, for James's charm and easy humour.

They passed through East Kennett and turned right along a farm track, and up a steep lane to the Pewsey Downs. The lane ran along the edge of a huge field, the soil thick with flints. Beneath their feet, the lane was deeply rutted, ridges of long, lush grass alternating with narrow troughs of dried, cracked mud. Below them, they saw a huge dry valley, dotted with sheep, while above, a couple of crows were circling in a thermal, on the same level as the walkers. The sun glinted on the birds' backs, so the black feathers shone white as they dipped and drifted in the air. Owain peeled off his shirt and tied it around his waist. Despite his fair hair, his skin was a rich tawny brown. The sun imbued him with colour. His skin glowed golden in the heat. He looked very fit. Paul felt the same sun burning his own skin, and in contrast to Owain, felt himself to be some way disabled. He couldn't even enjoy the summer sun without blistering—suffering damage. He wished he had worn a long sleeved shirt.

At the top of Furze Hill they passed through a patch of woodland. The dead stalks of bluebells stood in endless ranks among the trees. The grass was splashed with the pink and white of campion, the pale, delicate faces of late flowering stitchwort. The old hawthorn trees were laced with tendrils of dogrose and traveller's joy. A little footpath wound through the trees, so the walkers could avoid the deeper, muddy ruts in the lane. They moved in single file, ducking beneath low branches and brambles. At the end, Owain stopped and pointed to a great hump in the trees, stretching off to left and right, covered in trees and bushes.

"We're crossing the Wansdyke," he said. "Have you walked the Wansdyke path before?"

Both Paul and James shook their heads.

"Maybe you could show it to us another time?" James said. "I take it we just cross it today?"

Owain nodded, gesturing out across the fields beyond.

"Honey Street is straight on," he said. Paul slipped through a wire fence, down into the huge ditch on the lee side of the Wansdyke. He was surrounded by a ring of trees, in a green cavern of leaves and branches. Beneath his feet the earth was moist and clinging. He surveyed the great ridge, which spanned miles of countryside, struck by the purpose which drove the ancient people to this laborious task of digging and building. He resolved to learn more about the history and people who had lived and fought and died on the land where he had made his home. He returned to the lane, where his companions had moved out to the top of the smooth, chalky hills overlooking the Vale of Pewsey. Rising to the left, he could see Knap Hill, topped with the remains of a bronze age hill fort. To the right, against the sky atop Walker's Hill, was the long barrow known as Adam's Grave. The blue sky spread all around them like a lake. Before him, the descending field was verdant with glistening grass. Paul's spirits soared, new energy rising in his body. Across the vale, the patchwork fields lay before before him and the sky bending down to meet the land. An unexpected thrill washed through his veins. Maybe Owain had the right idea after all. They walked down the hill, startling half-grown rabbits, and even a huge hare, which hopped in front of them with ears like towers. Then, skirting a field of yellow oilseed, they reached Alton Barnes and tramped down the road to Honey Street.

The Barge was quiet as yet. Inside, traditional country pub decor was mixed with carvings of crop circles on smooth stones, and the mask of an alien Grey. James bought beers, and they sat in the shade, outside, by the canal. The water was blank and murky, and two swans drifted towards them, hoping for food.

The three men drank and chatted for an hour or so. They were pleasantly tired, and often they would lapse into silent thought. The pub filled with families out for lunch, hikers and American tourists. Then Paul caught the gaze of a short, powerfully built man sat alone at a bench on the other side of the garden. A shock of recognition. He looked again. The man was staring at him, and raised his glass. The idle pleasure of the afternoon vanished. He rose to his feet.

"I've just seen someone I know," he told James and Owain. "I'll go over and say hello. I won't be long." He picked up his glass and sat on the bench beside the man.

The man had changed somewhat, in the time since their last encounter. His dark hair was receding, cropped very short, and he had gained a little weight. He was about ten years older than Paul, who deferred to him. He had a bold, handsome face, closely shaved but still swarthy.

"Long time no see," Paul said.

"Three years," the man replied.

"What are you up to? Are you here long?"

"No," the man said, laconic. "Just a few weeks, then out of the country again."

"Where?"

But the man made no reply. He looked straight ahead, and took another sip from his glass.

"So what have you been doing, Paul? Using your time productively? You still with Kate?"

"Katherine? Yes."

"Good grief. You'll be married soon."

"Not married. But we've got a daughter. Niamh—remember?"

The man shook his head in disbelief.

"That's it then. We've lost you."

"Not necessarily. I'm involved with the Locksbury protest."

"That's good. Still small stuff though. We could use you, Paul." He turned to face the younger man, "You've turned us down once—but when this road business is over, you might change your mind." He dug in his pocket for a pen and wrote a name and number on a scrap of card torn from an empty cigarette packet. He handed it to Paul.

"Thank you," Paul said. "Now tell me what you're doing."

Owain and James were curious. They watched Paul and the dark man engage in a heated discussion, keeping their voices low but gesticulating, their faces intense.

"I wonder who he is," James said. "D'you know?"

"No. Never seen him before. I don't much like him."

"How can you tell at this distance? I think he looks rather interesting. He's certainly got old Paul dangling on a line, and I don't know many people who can argue him round."

After a while, Paul rose from the bench, the man still talking and Paul shaking his head. Paul offered his hand, and grudgingly the man shook it. Paul strode back to his waiting friends, with a dark expression, some kind of stress etched on his features.

"Who was that?" James asked. "Aren't you going to introduce us?"

"No. An old acquaintance. Used to be in the party, the SWP, but he left it a year or so before I did."

"And now?" James persisted.

"Just drop it," Paul said shortly, his voice still angry. "Isn't it time we headed back?"

They followed the same route back to East Kennett, and then on to the protest site, where the car was parked. Paul was bound up in his thoughts, blind to the land, indifferent to the conversation of his companions. After a couple of failed attempts to involve him, Owain and James likewise fell silent. Owain left them at the main road, where the car was parked, and returned to the copse. James drove Paul back to his empty home in Locksbury. Paul climbed out.

"Are you okay? Katherine will be back the day after tomorrow," James added hopefully.

"Yeah."

"D'you want to go out tomorrow?"

"No. Thanks. I've got a lot of work to catch up on." Paul relented for a moment. "I'm sorry, I know I've been bad company. I've got a lot on my mind. I'll give you a call in the evening, okay?"

James nodded and the car pulled away.

Paul went inside, straight up to the study, and switched on his computer.

CHAPTER FOURTEEN

Jo pressed his face against the window of the coach, as it drove down Herd Street. Marlborough opened before him like a fairy tale town. Beneath the tall church tower, mismatched stone houses surrounded the Green, gardens crowded with poppies and geraniums at the windows. Beyond the town, Savernake Forest lay dark upon the hills. He felt like a child heading off on a seaside holiday, venturing into a new world. Beside him he had a small bag with his clothes and a couple of books. Sharing the the seat in front, Katherine and Elaine were chattering and laughing. Every now and then, Niamh, who was standing on her mother's lap, peeped over the top of the chair at Jo, who pulled silly faces at her, till she giggled and ducked away.

They disembarked in front of a bank in the High Street. The pavement was full of people. A group of glossy haired girls from Marlborough College passed by. Old ladies carried wicker baskets full of groceries. Poring over maps, tourists sipped coffee around tables outside a cafe. In his torn jeans and jewellery Jo felt uncomfortable and incongruous. He had been nervous about coming at all, and was wearing a considerable layer of make-up as some kind of defence. Now he was completely out of place, though nobody seemed to be taking too much notice of him.

They shared a taxi to Locksbury. Paul was at work, so the house was tidy and quiet when they piled inside. Katherine made cups of tea, and they took turns to bathe and change before sharing sandwiches in the garden for lunch. Niamh seemed very happy to be home, sorting through her toys with squeals of delight, as though she was greeting long lost friends. Jo wandered about in a dream. He thought the garden was beautiful. It was tiny—a shady patch of paving stones at the back of the house, then a small stretch of lawn and an old apple tree. But Katherine had filled terracotta pots with flowers, and an overgrown honeysuckle spread across a trellis on the wall, filling the warm afternoon air with its sweet scent. His room-home, full of clutter, seemed very trashy and tasteless in comparison. He liked Katherine, and found her easy to talk to when she wasn't monopolised by Elaine. When the two women were together he was happy to take a back seat. It was Katherine who had suggested that he join them at the protest site, since he had met Crow, and was thereby implicated in the turn of events. Besides, she thought he might enjoy the solstice celebrations. Jo was at once tantalised and terrified by the prospect. His desire for adventure had eventually overcome his anxiety, but still, he suffered moments of panic, so far away from his home, his familiar territory, adrift amongst these people who seemed so very much bigger than him—even though he towered over them. They acted with such unthinking confidence—bought tickets, made arrangements, chatted to the bus driver and fellow passengers. He felt clumsy and inept in comparison.

At the end of the day, Paul returned from work to a house full of people. He shook hands warmly with Jo, who shuffled and looked at the ground.

They dined in the garden, eating stuffed vine leaves, salad with feta and olives. They drank several bottles of red wine, munched on grapes and strawberries, and ice cold slices of melon. Jo knocked back glass after glass of wine, till at last the alcohol defeated his feelings of inferiority, and he began to witter on to Paul about his life in the city, his adventures at the clubs. Paul listened most politely, but Jo didn't think he was overly impressed. But what else did he have to talk about? He was on a run, and the words didn't want to stop. Paul asked him one or two questions about his interest in the road protest, which Jo found it hard to answer. His mind grew hazy. The light slowly faded, and the clouds above the garden wall were a smoky lavender, fiery on the underside. The moon rose, pale and pink in the sky. The sweet rocket glimmered white, its breath scented like spicy sherbert. Jo shivered. Katherine was clearing away the dishes. Niamh had disappeared, and Jo assumed that Katherine had put her to bed though he couldn't remember when. He began to feel cold. He hugged his bare arms, and the night chill began to clear his mind. What had he been talking about? They went inside for coffee. He was very tired, and profoundly grateful when Paul and Katherine retired to bed. He and Elaine unpacked sleeping bags. She bagged the sofa, and he found a convenient patch on the floor to spread the thin foam mattress Katherine had provided.

He lay in the darkness, looking at the ceiling. Elaine didn't speak to him. Come to think of it, he couldn't recall her sparing him a word since their arrival in Locksbury. Was he such an embarrassment to her? Did she have to create such a huge space between them? He began to worry that he might have said foolish things. He ran over his conversation, as far as he could remember it. But what could he possibly say that would interest or impress someone as clever and accomplished as Paul? He hadn't been anywhere, he hadn't done anything. He was nothing. Why had he let them drag him here?

The street light outside the house stole through the curtains, vaguely illuminating the room. He could discern the mantelpiece, and the profile of a puppet figure perched on the edge. Katherine had told him she made them. He didn't like it, the hooked nose and fierce eyes, like a Punch at a children's show. He had never liked puppets. He had watched the most stomach-churning horror videos without a qualm, but this puppet had him pulling the sleeping bag up to his chin. What if it fell off during the night? What if it landed on him? He began to sweat. Perhaps he should move it out of sight—though the prospect of leaving the safety of his covers and actually touching the thing was not one he relished a bit. Better to look the other way and think of something else.

He turned to face Elaine on the sofa. Through the gloom he saw her eyes were open. She was looking at him.

"Well, Jo, are you happy?" she said softly. "Are you having fun?"

For a fleeting moment, he thought she could read his mind, that she was referring to his fear of the puppet.

"What?"

"Do you like it here, away from the big bad city?"

"Oh. Yes." He remembered that look. He was afraid she could see right into him, that his face was a transparent sheet allowing her to view his private thoughts. He had grown to hate that. She was too clever for him.

He had seen her first at a club. She had picked him up, drawn by his fragile beauty and inebriated abandon. They met again, and again. He was hooked. She had poked and pried into his life, delving into his past, analysing him, all the endless questions, till he felt he was a curious clockwork toy she was taking apart, piece by piece. Though of course at the beginning he had simply been flattered and overjoyed that someone like her should be so very interested in him. He realised he hadn't thought of it quite like that before. He had only remembered the strange, magical times, when they had lain together whispering in the dark, when he understood how much she wanted to know him, to be intimate, till they felt they were cradling each other's souls in their hands. But it had been too much for him. He had pulled and pulled away, choosing all the mindless, silly games with his mates instead. And she had held on to him, raging with incomprehension that he should choose tinsel when she was offering gold. So their final fight had not come out of the blue after all. He could see it now, the pattern that had led to the violence and bitterness of their break-up. For the first time, he felt an unexpected compassion for Elaine. He realised how much he had hurt her, an idea that had never occurred to him before. He began to relax.

"Yes, I do like it. I like your friends, and Niamh. I'm really glad you brought me with you."

"Good. You'll get to see our tree village tomorrow. And we'll be rehearsing the Mummer's Play. Lots of people to meet. Scary, eh?"

He was conscious of her mockery, but failed to rise to the bait.

"I'm looking forward to it."

They were silent for several minutes, but Jo knew she wasn't asleep. He heard her sigh. Then she cleared her throat.

"Can I give you a cuddle?" she said.

"Of course." She wriggled from the sofa, still in her sleeping bag, and nestled up to him, her head on his shoulder. He breathed her familar scent, which carried with it a tide of emotional recollections.

"Oh, Jo," she said. They lay together quietly, but Jo couldn't stop his tears. From the slight dampness on his shirt he knew Elaine was crying too.

He was woken at six thirty when Niamh dropped something on his head. He opened his eyes. He pushed a small plastic dog from his forehead onto the floor. His head ached and his mouth was dry and sour. Elaine was lying back on the sofa, though he hadn't felt her move away. In the kitchen he could hear Paul pouring tea, making breakfast and tidying up the plates from the night before. Just before he left for work Paul brought them steaming mugs of tea.

"Can you look after Niamh for an hour? Katherine's driving me to work so you lot can have the car today, for your rehearsal," he said.

"Yeah. Sure," Jo said, sitting up and rubbing his face. "I hope you're feeling better than I am."

"I don't think I drank as much as you. " Paul picked up a bag and headed for the door. Katherine rushed down the stairs, kissed Niamh, and followed him out. Niamh looked puzzled for a moment, then picked up her dog and sat on Jo's lap. Elaine regarded him.

"Kids take to you." She sounded almost critical.

"That's because I am one," he said. She didn't disagree. In fact, she said very little else to him for the rest of the morning. As Jo dressed and made them breakfast she was positively icy, as though their moment of intimacy had been a weakness, an aberration. Now she had to keep a chilly distance, responding curtly, avoiding eye contact and ignoring his presence, so that he might know how little he signified to her. Jo was not overly surprised, but it hurt nonetheless. He knew her well enough. She might be mistress of the art of self-denial, but she couldn't erase her tears from his memory.

Katherine returned from Swindon an hour later. Elaine was still not dressed, though Jo was tidying up the kitchen. Later in the morning they piled into the car and drove to the protest site. The air was soft and hazy above the fields, the trees were shifting olive forms along the hedges. Jo was mesmerised by the landscape.

"Elaine?" he said, sitting forward on the back seat. "Do you remember laughing at me, because I hadn't noticed how every tree was different?"

"Yes," she said. Jo waited for a moment, but as she said nothing further, he sat back again. He teased Niamh, strapped into her car seat. Katherine pulled into the Old Lane and parked on the verge. A slim coil of smoke rose into the sky from behind the cottage. It was still cool, though the pure sky signalled that the heat would soon be upon them. The only sound he could hear was the reedy, wistful song of a bird in the hedge along the lane.

"A robin," Katherine said, pointing to the small, brown form swaying on a stem of bramble. As they walked past, it flitted onto the lane, then away, with a quick flash of red. Jo was a stranger in a strange land. He found the silence uncanny. The land opened up all around him. The verges were twining with such vigorous growth. Could the plants reach out and choke him? The air was thick with pollen, heavy with the scent of leaf and wood and earth. He was afraid he would begin to sneeze. His arms began to tingle, and itch. He felt exposed. So this was the natural world? He ached for the forest of brick and concrete, for the tarmac pavements, for the endless hum of traffic. He scratched his wrists. The thin silver bangles slid and clinked on his arm.

Katherine knocked on the front door of the cottage. After a minute, they heard the drawing back of bolts, the turning of a lock. A slender, freckled face peered out, a ring through the lip, another in her eyebrow. The girl let them in.

"Violet, this is Jo, a friend from Bristol," Katherine said. Violet looked at Jo, and smiled.

"You're here for the fair?"

"Yes," he said.

"Well, you're not the only one." Violet gestured towards the back of the house. "We've plenty of strange people here for that. Have you seen them?"

Jo shook his head. He was looking at her hair, red and copper, glinting with beads and braids, decorated with tiny shells and feathers. She was wearing a baggy purple shirt, threaded with gold. She looked like a pixie, very small, or perhaps some ancient tribeswoman, elaborately decorated. He realised he was staring.

"I love your hair," he said.

"Thanks," she said, pushing it over her shoulder.

"The Morris men, you mean?" Elaine said, breaking in. "I saw them arrive. Three in a pony cart."

"Well, now we have at least six, and a couple of girls too."

"Where's Owain?"

"He's going to meet us up at Oldbury Castle. He wanted to walk."

Katherine and Elaine looked at each other.

"Shall we?" Elaine said. Katherine nodded. They left the cottage, with Jo close on their heels, and Niamh in her mother's arms. The Morris men were all present, six of them sitting round the fire, not speaking. When Jo saw them, his heart fluttered in his chest. Two girls were sitting together at the front of a tent on a patchwork blanket. Katherine and Elaine exchanged another glance. They were hesitant, unsure how to approach, but one of the men stood up, extending a hand in greeting.

"My favourite ladies," he said. "We meet again. Please join us."

Katherine stepped towards him. The man kissed her on the cheek.

"Hello, Spring," she said.

"Katherine," he said. "And Elaine. And this is?"

"Jo," he said. He took the offered hand. He towered above Spring, but their eyes met with a jolt of recognition. But how did he know him? Jo was at a loss for a moment. He kept a grip of the man's hand. How could he possibly know him? Then the feeling slipped away, like a dream, and he let Spring's hand fall from his own. Beyond the fire, the rest of the assembled company were staring at him, seven pairs of bright coloured eyes, in seven pale faces. Then they all began to talk, and Jo was led to the circle and offered a seat amongst them. Jo looked back, to Katherine and Elaine still waiting on the outside.

"Is this a private party?" Elaine asked. They had been quite forgotten. Spring gestured for them to follow, and they perched on the patchwork blanket with the girls. One of the men handed Jo an earthenware cup. It was cold in his hand, holding a pale gold wine. Jo drank with the men. They began to chat with him, looking into his eyes, nudging him, laughing. He began to laugh too. He turned from one face to another. An amazingly happiness welled. Who were these strange people, who were also so familiar? One of them gave him a top hat, trimmed with black and white feathers, and a waistcoat jingling with little silver bells. He put them on. Then he felt small hands tugging at his bangles, and he surrendered them, still grinning, and watched as they were distributed amongst the men. Their faces were close to his own, too similar, filling his field of vision. It crossed his mind that he was getting drunk, because his surroundings seemed to recede and fade. But he was not alarmed. In fact he was bursting with joy. The Morris men were bright, almost luminescent in the gathering twilight. He was talking with them, grinning, but his words had little meaning and seemed to flow from a source he didn't control. He wasn't making sense, except that on some level it made the most perfect sense and he realised he was home at last. Wasn't he? Home? As the word arose in his mind, he remembered his room in Bristol. But where was Elaine? Why had it grown so dark? How had he found his way in here? He needed to find a way out. What was happening to him? He began to panic. He closed his eyes.

When he opened them again he was standing up, still shaking hands with Spring, Katherine and Elaine standing with him. The other Morris men were sitting in their circle. What had happened?

"Goodbye then," Spring said. Katherine turned away, Elaine close behind her. Jo was confused. He followed them, but the feeling of disorientation didn't fade. Had he drank with them or not? He thought he tasted the wine on his tongue but he could not be sure. He scratched his wrist. The bangles were gone, and he realised he was wearing the hat and waistcoat. The bells jingled as he walked. Had the women noticed nothing untoward?

He caught up with them.

"What was all that about?" he said.

"What?" Katherine looked at him blankly.

"The Morris men. Wasn't it strange?"

"What was strange?" Her eyes were veiled. Already she was focussed elsewhere. She began to talk about the play, and Jo too felt the memory begin to slip away. But he stroked the soft, velvet waistcoat, quartered in red and green. The cool silver bells were tangible enough. He smiled to himself.

They collected Violet, squeezed into the car, and drove towards Oldbury Castle. They passed Silbury Hill, rising from the fields like a smooth green altar, and then the chalk downs rolling away from the road. They parked off the road at the foot of the steep scarp face of Cherhill Down, where a white horse was carved in the turf. Jo shielded his eyes against the sun. The horse looked a little brownish, in need of a cleaning. At the top of the hill stood an obelisk, sharp like a dagger. Or a finger, perhaps, pointing into space, straining upwards. He helped Katherine take up Niamh in her backpack, and together they began to climb the hill. It was a steep ascent, the close-cropped grass littered with sheep droppings. Fragments of chalk covered the narrow soil path, dry and powdery in the June heat. Jo began to sweat. Elaine was some distance ahead, walking with a long, swinging stride despite the incline. At the top of the hill the land levelled out. On the summit, a maze of mounds and banks and hollows were all that remained of the hill fort. Jo was disappointed for a moment, imagining crumbling walls and ivy strewn battlements, but Katherine assured him the site was much older than that. He was walking on ancient history. A swift, cool wind rose, and he ran up and down the banks, the breeze caressing his face and body. He stood on a pinacle, spreading his arms to feel the wind blowing across the downs, passing and heading on again across the land. The view stretched for miles. He was linked by this wind, blowing through him, to the hills on the horizon, and the fields laid out to the skyline. An outsider, yes, but now the prospect before him was paradise. He breathed deeply, then ran again, and skipped down the steep embankment and back up the other side. Suddenly he stopped. At the foot of the obelisk a figure was sitting upon the great steps. Jo walked forwards, cautiously. The man was wearing long leather boots, and clothes of green and brown, much worn. He had long dark blonde hair in a pony tail and a beard, and he was swinging his legs, kicking the stone steps. He was also watching Jo very closely.

Elaine and Violet ran up beside him, Katherine lagging behind with Niamh.

"Owain!" Elaine called. "Have we kept you waiting?" She ran past Jo, and up to the man on the steps. He jumped down, one quick, graceful movement. Elaine embraced him warmly, grinning and chattering. Jo watched her with an unexpected spike of jealousy. She was illuminated, he thought, she simply shone in response to this Owain. Had she ever reacted to him like that? His exhiliration vanished. He felt small and awkward, like a child in comparison. Still, although Owain was warmly returning Elaine's smiles he kept glancing over at Jo. Eventually Elaine picked up on his curiosity and turned round. Jo was introduced as an old friend. Owain stepped forward and shook his hand.

"Where did you get those?" he asked, gesturing towards the hat and waistcoat, a frown on his face as he asked—as though he already knew the answer.

"The Morris men, at the protest site. They gave them to me. Aren't they great?"

Owain looked puzzled but he made no further comment.

The five people gathered in a circle at the top of a mound. Niamh wandered about them, turning to Jo from time to time, for a cuddle. Katherine drew a pile of photocopied papers from her bag and handed them around. They began to read the script.

"We need six for this," Violet said.

"Yes," Elaine said. "But the sixth person will play Belzebub, who only has four lines. I thought we might be able to get Paul to play him?" She looked at Katherine, who didn't seem too sure.

"I'll ask him," she said. "I don't know if he'll want to be involved with this. Can't we just leave that bit out? It's completely extraneous to the plot. He doesn't actually do anything."

Elaine looked shocked.

"How can you say that? This is a ceremony, a ritual—not a television drama. We are not thinking in plot terms. Everything has a symbolic meaning. This is sympathetic magic. By rehearsing the cycle of death and resurrection we are hoping to influence the course of events. We are touching the intangible life beyond the mundane world."

"Okay," she shrugged. "I get the point. I'll ask him."

They allotted the remaining parts. Violet took on the soldier, Slasher, and Jo was given the part of the doctor. He was oddly excited by the idea of performing, particularly when Elaine told them how important it was for all the characters to be heavily disguised.

"If anyone recognises us," she warned, "the magic will be worthless."

They spent the rest of the afternoon rehearsing the play. Elaine was director, as well as Young Woman. Owain and Violet practised their sword battle with bits of stick, acting out their roles with considerable clumsy enthusiasm, upon the ramparts of the old castle.

CHAPTER FIFTEEN

On the morning of Midsummer's Eve the sky was pale, powdery blue, the colour of harebells. Katherine lay in bed. Among a heap of white bedding, Niamh was crawling and hiding, curling under her mother's legs then sitting on her stomach, and diving off again onto the quilt. Katherine was still half asleep, suffering her daughter's early hour acrobatics with a head still heavy with dreams. Upon the old wooden dressing table, festoons of mock-orange blossom in a chipped cream coloured jug filled the room with its musky-sweet scent. Katherine opened her eyes and regarded her daughter. Already Niamh's perfect, petal skin was damp with tiny drops of perspiration. Her dark hair was slick on her forehead. Katherine sighed.

"I suppose I'd better get up," she said. Niamh grinned. As Katherine climbed out of bed, she heard Paul head out the front door.

"See you later," he called out, as he left. Katherine dressed in a yellow cotton dress, the colour of marigolds, embroidered at the front with twining flowers. She plaited her hair. Niamh, dancing about naked on the bed, was captured and covered with a nappy, tee shirt and shorts. Katherine carried her downstairs.

They had the house to themselves. On the table were half finished masks and swords, awaiting a final coat of paint for the play.

Katherine braced herself and walked into the kitchen.

She put on the kettle, willing her mind to be still. Her hand began to shake. She opened a drawer, where the knives glittered. She shut it again. She was gripped by a wave of nausea. What was this? Horror, more horror, now seeping out into the rest of her life like an insidious black tide poisoning her thoughts. Had she never noticed before that her kitchen was a veritable torture chamber? All the knives, the red-hot plates, the electronic machines that chopped and sliced and grated. Why was this happening? What disorder was she suffering? She couldn't enter the room without imagining what all these things could do, how they could be used to hurt and maim. Sick, sick person, she told herself. She willed herself to open the drawer again, withdrew the bread knife and cut three slices from the loaf to make toast. She switched on the grill. The bars quickly glowed orange, and she put the bread on the tray, flinching away from the heat. Was this too part of the faery curse? What had they given her, that in return she must suffer thus, perceiving only pain and mutilation in the most mundane of activities?

She heard a knock at the front door, and ran to answer it. The postman handed her a small parcel addressed to Niamh. She gave it to the little girl, who spent several minutes struggling with the brown paper wrapping before giving it to Katherine. The smoke alarm began to shriek. Katherine remembered the toast and shot into a kitchen full of acrid black smoke. She pulled the grill from the cooker and dumped it outside the back door, opening all the windows till the alarm was quiet at last. Still, a faint pall hung over the kitchen, so she fed Niamh cereal instead. Inside the package was a plastic fish, bright purple, decorated with squiggles, big black eyes with eyelashes and a huge grin. It had a key in its back, which Katherine wound. When she set the fish on the floor it spun and flopped clumsily on the floorboards for a minute or two. Niamh was entranced. She wanted to see it again. After the third exhibition she lost interest. Katherine picked up the letter included, a short note from Niamh's great aunt, apologising for missing Niamh's first birthday. Niamh went into the kitchen, and began to pull the saucepans from the cupboard with a great clatter. Katherine regarded the fish. She detested it. A graceless lump of coloured plastic which Niamh had already forgotten. Then she felt guilty for her ingratitude, thinking how her aunt must have chosen it, bought it, posted it with such good intentions. But how many lumps of plastic did Niamh need? The house was full of all manner of useless lumps, a great burden of possessions. Maybe she was sick. Why else should the arrival of a plastic fish send her into a sea of anxiety and personal doubt? She picked up the fish and carried it up to Niamh's bedroom. She dumped it in a toybox and tried to put it out of her mind. She surveyed the room. The sheets on the cot were decorated with cutesy jungle animals, smiling lions and giraffes. On a chair were piled fluffy teddies, a tiger, a rabbit, a pink wolf. They appalled her. What relation had the smiling lions to the real creature? Was Niamh to grow up thinking lions were such inane, inoffensive beings? It was false. The room was full of lies. It was too comfortable, too bland. When Niamh thought of a wolf she would remember the pink and cuddly monstrosity on the chair. What about the heat and ferocity of the real creature? What about its heart and sinews, its cruel teeth? She wanted Niamh to know the wolf's spirit, to honour the beast, its endurance, its flesh and blood reality. She had a sudden urge to place all the toys, the pictures, in a bonfire, to destroy them. Maybe they should spend days in the forest instead, crawling about in the leaves to watch the rabbits and the foxes—even killing if that's what it took to feed themselves, but still acknowledging the unassailable mystery of the creature. Instead she filled her room with these hideous animal falsehoods, diminishing them, while those of her friends that ate meat bought cleanly packaged lumps of pork or beef from the supermarkets. All lies. What a shallow, insipid life she led. She pictured the bonfire. Then she imagined Niamh in the psychiatrist's chair in twenty years time:

"And your mother burned all your toys, you say?" the psychiatrist said, her voice restrained but appalled. Katherine permitted herself a small smile. Lighten up, she told herself. Yeah, compromise, follow the herd. You can't burn your kid's toys. Perhaps she could just ignore them instead. She wiped her hands on her dress. Her palms were sticky with sweat. She was still shaking. Niamh called out from downstairs. Katherine shut the bedroom door and went to her assistance.

She added the finishing touches to the masks, and sprayed the swords with silver paint. The previous day she, Owain, Jo and Elaine had spent many enjoyable hours assembling their costumes from cardboard, chicken wire, rags and feathers. Katherine plundered her puppet-making stores for shining buttons, hanks of horsehair and sequins. They would perform at sunrise on Midsummer's Day. Owain and Elaine had chattered together with happy, smiling faces. Jo was distracted, still wearing his hat and waistcoat, responding to Katherine's questions but often lost in a dream. He had told no-one about his experience with the Morris men. Katherine and Paul would be taking the costumes over to the protest site in the evening.

The day passed slowly for Katherine. It was too hot to sit in the garden, and after several days of constant companionship, she felt lonely and deflated. Niamh was equally restless, constantly demanding attention, while Katherine simply desired to read, to escape into a novel, to be absorbed. She thought about walking to the protest site but failed to muster the energy. In the afternoon, when Niamh had her nap, Katherine curled up in her own bed and sank into a half-slumber, a hinterland of dreams and thoughts. She counted the hours till Paul's return from work, and as soon as they had eaten, they concealed the costumes in the boot of the car, and drove out of Locksbury.

It was nearly seven oclock, the sun was high and bright, though along the horizon a thin layer of cloud lay like grey lint above the hills. They parked near the foot of Silbury Hill. The little car park was already crowded with an assortment of cars and campervans, a couple of converted buses, with a dozen tents pitched on the grass. A blast of grungey rock music from one of the old buses competed with the gentler acoustic strains of a young man playing his guitar outside his tent. Katherine surveyed the solstice revellers. They were a mixed bunch, some very straight-looking student types, travellers with children and dogs, and some more ethereal pagan people, a couple in white robes. A trio of amazing girls walked past, dressed in bright coloured shirts and skirts, with painted faces, carrying rucksacks and juggling batons. The atmosphere was friendly and welcoming, strangers were shy but eager to talk. Paul handed out his flyers inviting them to the 'Midsummer Protest Rally' at dawn the next day. Despite the admonitions by English Heritage not to ascend the hill, a number of people were already perched on its summit. Katherine and Paul set off for West Kennet long barrow, where another cluster of people were assembling. The lane skirted a pasture, crossing the Kennet over a small brick bridge—then the long ascent up a narrow track to the barrow at the top of the hill. About twenty people were sitting atop the barrow, gazing across the fields, talking and laughing. One or two they recognised from the protest site. Paul walked round with more flyers, and Katherine went inside the barrow. The air was dense with candlesmoke and incense. Through the dark, she could make out a small group of people sitting around the main chamber at the rear of the barrow. Others had taken up residence in the tiny chambers off to left and right. Nightlights had been placed in nooks in the walls, sending shadows flickering across the great stones. She walked to the main chamber, where Owain and Elaine were sitting, with another half a dozen people she didn't know. One of them, a young man in a long grey coat, had a drum in his crossed legs, and he filled the barrow with a rhythm like a heartbeat. When Katherine sat down, Owain smiled at her and squeezed her arm. Elaine was gazing into the flame of a stout church candle burning at the base of a huge stone supporting the roof of the barrow. Beside it a jar had been filled with summer flowers, and on a bed of dried sage rested the white ceramic head of a horse, the size of Katherine's hand. As her eyes grew accustomed to the dark, she could make out a couple of cards stuck in the cracks of the wall— prayers, wishes and poems—as well as offerings of polished stones, fragments of jewellery, the heads of flowers. Niamh quickly grew bored of the confined space, and Katherine was obliged to leave the barrow and return to the open air. So she wandered with Paul on top of the barrow. Across the fields was Silbury Hill, and to the west the glowing, golden sun began to descend. Paul had a flask of whisky in his jacket pocket, and though he was abstaining till they reached the protest site, he passed it to Katherine, who sipped it steadily as the twilight settled over the fields. The girls in the bright shirts arrived at the barrow, and they juggled with flaming brands. A troupe of musicians, in torn silk and pied jackets, sang a folk tale to the accompaniment of a drum, a dulcimer and a mandolin. When they had finished, Katherine told them about the fair and invited them to attend. The cloud on the horizon thickened, burning salmon and pearl and flame-orange as the sun sank upon the hills. The air was perfectly still, freshening as the sun disappeared. For a time the land was cast into a half-light. The fields were dark emerald. The first star appeared, and a delicate half moon. Katherine basked in a sense of peace, Niamh asleep on her lap, the the stray, slightly discordant notes of the folk singers began again.

Paul lifted Niamh from her.

"I'm going up to the site now," he said. They had arranged for Niamh to sleep in the cottage, where Jan was on guard duty. As she was house-sitting, she was happy to babysit too. Katherine decided to stay on at West Kennet and walk over to the site a little later. She kissed Niamh, as Paul enfolded her in his jacket and headed back down the hill to the car. She went back into the barrow. The drummer now had a friend, and they struck up a long, hypnotic tattoo that echoed off the stone walls. The barrow pulsed with sound. The candles still burned, but the shadows were deeper and darker. The faces in the circle, like the stones, were partly illuminated, partly obscured. Katherine joined the circle and sat in a warm daze upon the dirt floor. The barrow closed around them like a womb, like a cave buried deep in the earth. It had been the resting place of the dead, but she felt the spirits of the place were at peace. The atmosphere, thick with breath and smoke, was one of serenity and celebration. Nobody spoke, listening to the beating of the drums, sitting very still in this stone space, within the body of the Earth Mother. Time ceased to have any meaning. When the drums stopped, Katherine felt she had been released from a spell, some mesmeric incantation in which she and all the others in the circle had been participants. She rose unsteadily to her feet and left the barrow. Outside the contrast was absolute. From the confines of the tomb, she stepped into infinite space. The sky opened above her, dark now but glittering with stars. The land stretched away all around. She was hanging in a void, a mote in the celestial stream, but warm and alive, vigorous, her pulse beating fiercely in her body like the drums in the barrow.

"But I'm here," she shouted. "I'm here." Her voice echoed across the fields.

She laughed, standing on the barrow. One or two of the people glanced at her but it was a night for performance and their smiles were warm and tolerant. She thought of Crow. Where was she? Would she see her? Somehow she had to find her way in again. Katherine put her hands against her head. She felt the skull beneath the skin. How was it possible that this casket of bone, this fragile vessel full of soft tissue, could hold the brilliant stars, the black space pouring away for ever above her head? How could it be that in all of time, in all of the vast unfolding universe, she could be conscious, here and now, in this moment? How could it have happened? Her finite consciousness, like a straw adrift on an endless ocean, coalesced from the void but separate and complete. It seemed too unlikely, too impossible to be borne. For a moment, she felt she was losing her mind. Her senses reeled. She staggered. But her nose began to run. She reached into her pocket for a tissue and found salvation in the blowing of her nose. Best not to think about these things too hard. Humankind can not bear very much reality.

She opened the flask and sipped whisky, burning a fiery trail down her throat. The night air was growing cold. Paul had her jacket in the car, so she rubbed her arms, walked up and down. The protest site was some hour's walk away, along the roads—a little less across the fields though walking in the darkness would be difficult. Midsummer—the shortest night. The sun would rise in another five hours, and the solstice would occur at 2.20am. Owain and Elaine emerged from the barrow, and agreed to walk with her to the protest site. With Owain as guide, they avoided the main roads, and used the lanes and footpaths. It was not utterly dark, and though there were times when she walked blindly in shadows, under trees, the fields were gently illuminated. The sky was a very dark, velvet blue. The moon cast shadows upon the ground. The grass crushed beneath their feet smelt sharp and fresh. In the lunar light, the silver grey verges were poised in the still air. Apart from the sound of their boots, the night was perfectly quiet, the leaves motionless. They did not speak, walking through a charmed realm, pearly dust upon their feet, and the trees glimmering argent above them. Two moths flittered in the air by the hedge, with ghostly milk-white wings. They seemed to leave trails behind them, the imprint of soft wings drawn on the air. Katherine touched her face with her fingers. Her skin was cold. She could feel the moonglow, the silver sheen upon her body, as she had donned once before at the Green Chapel. Elaine walked before her, dressed like the moths in white. Indistinct, Owain blended with the shade. They did not look at each other, moving in their own thoughts, and Katherine wondered if her companions were walking in her moon world, or if they perceived a different realm, reflecting their own dreams.

At last they reached the main road. On the other side, the Old Lane led past the cottages to the stone valley. The tarmac shone as they crossed the deserted road. The ribbon of cloud along the horizon was spreading across the sky in heavy skeins, obliterating the stars, though Katherine could not feel any movement in the air. She called in at the cottage to check on Paul and Niamh. Owain and Elaine picked up their costumes, and disappeared up the lane to the copse, though before they left, Elaine admonished Katherine to join them just before sunrise.

Most of the protestors had abandoned the site to pass the night at Silbury Hill, Avebury and West Kennet. Jan was alone in the cottage, apart from Paul, smoking the habitual spliff and engrossed in a discussion. Niamh was asleep in one of the rooms upstairs, wrapped in a blanket on a mattress. Katherine looked in on her. Her eyes were closed, but Katherine saw she was restless. Her eyes twitched and rolled beneath her eyelids. Katherine kissed her gently and went back downstairs.

"Are there many people up at the copse?" she asked Jan. Jan inhaled deeply and nodded.

"A dozen or so, I think. Violet's there, and your friend Jo from Bristol."

"What about the Morris men?"

"Huddled together in their little camp as far as I know. They've been pretty quiet all day." Katherine began to feel very tired. Her eyes felt gritty and leaden. She was torn between the urge to curl up and sleep, and the desire to be wakeful for the whole night, to soak it up. Paul and Jan talked on. She half-listened to their conversation—some consideration of the protest and how they would fend off the bailiffs and the security guards, who might arrive at any time. Katherine began to drift. She knew she would fall asleep if she stayed inside any longer. She was vaguely aware the conversation had moved on and Paul sounded half-choked, Jan listening to him intently. They both seemed unaware of her presence in the room. She didn't want to hear what he was saying, so she willed her heavy body into movement, stood up and left the cottage. It was past midnight. The clouds were massing, obscuring the moon. The darkness thickened.

"Katherine."

She jumped when she heard his voice. One of the Morris men was standing right beside her, though she had not heard him approaching. It was too dark to make out his face, but she knew it was Spring. His eyes shone bright green, like gems, illuminated.

"Come and sit with us," he said. Anxiety seized her, sweat prickling on her skin. Words stuck in her throat. These things didn't happen. She tried to will the event into a new form. She wanted to look the other way.

"Katherine," he said again, insistent. He held out his hand. She placed her own in his. She trembled. His hand was cool. As he turned and led her around the cottage, the sleeve of his shirt brushed against her arm like dead leaves. He didn't enter the circle. He nodded to his companions, and one by one, they stood up and followed him out. They walked in a shifting group around Katherine and Spring, who headed down the garden path and onto the Old Lane. No-one spoke, but Katherine was aware of whispers speaking from the night. As they progressed, the path began to glimmer, as it had that night with Owain and Elaine. This time she had no trouble discerning the light. She walked in the stream, with the Morris men and the faery girls. The shining path stretched out before them, across the land. Beyond her, she knew it would fork and weave, passing through the long barrow at West Kennet, through Silbury Hill, along the grand avenue to Avebury and on again across the face of the earth, one path amongst many in an intricate, ceaseless circulation. She wondered if the other people gathered for the solstice were aware of the realms opening up around them. They passed the copse, and Katherine tried to see Owain and Elaine, Violet and Jo. Surely they could see what was happening. She could make out nothing in the arboreal blackness. The path led her on. They journeyed to the stone valley. The whispering intensified. Spring gestured for her to sit down on one of the flat stones. The others sat around her, their eyes shining, seemingly sharing the same inner illumination. It was very dark, but Katherine could sense that the Morris men were shifting in form. They moved like shadows, blurring and inconstant. They began to talk with each other in low murmurs.

"It is nearly time," Spring said. Katherine discerned movement all around her on the path, walkers passing by, faery forms but also human people, the ghosts and memories of the countless journeys charging the path with dreams. Faces seemed to press against the darkness, peering out at her, pushing against some boundary that held them back. The veil was thin. The voices began to clamour, loud and hectic.

"Now," Spring said, "Place your hand upon the earth."

When she did not move instantly, he grabbed her arm and pushed her to the ground. As she pressed her fingers into the cold grass she felt a movement in the soil, a rippling like a serpent beneath the surface. She tried to pull her hand away, but Spring held her still. The ground began to glow incandescent, and Katherine saw blades of grass, fragments of moss and dead leaf, chips of stone and wood and hide, shifting and assembling before her. Humus, ordure, particles of quartz and chalk and flint. The accretion of matter accelerated. It gained form. It lay before her, discernable as a human figure, stinking foully, as material shifted from the earth and covered the body. Then it lay like a clod upon the ground, till the very moment of the solstice, when the veil was breached and a pale figure stepped through, light as gauze, and sank into the body. The clod girl shimmered. She breathed. A shiver of colour passed across the dark body, which gained a skin, a face, long golden hair. A glamour. The stench of the decayed matter was partially covered by a familiar cloying sweetness. The doll of earth rose to her feet. She drew in a deep breath, like Eve reborn, waking in a new garden, and flicked open her eyes. Katherine realised with a shock she was looking into her own face.

Swiftly Spring was speaking to her again.

"Take off your clothes," he said. "Give them to her. We haven't much time." Katherine nodded numbly. She acted without thought, peeling off her dress and boots, passing them to her reflection, who put them on, laughing, running her hands across her new body.

"Now you must find your own way."

If the faerie spirit had slipped through the broken veil, then so too could Katherine—at this in between time, the moment of transition, of bridges. She focussed on the rent the faery had left behind, a thin effulgence like a thread upon the air, and she stepped through in the opposite direction. She passed from the earth's night into daylight.

CHAPTER SIXTEEN

On the morning of Midsummer's Eve, Jo was sitting high above the ground, crouched precariously on the slippery grey and green bough of a beech tree. Below him, Violet was checking ropes and knots. In another tree house, just yards away, Elaine was huddled out of sight. Jo had spent one night with Elaine but she was so frosty with him, and made him feel such an encumbrance, that he spent the next night on the floor at the cottage. He was beginning to wonder why she had allowed him to come in the first place. But he was not lonely. The other protestors had made him feel very welcome, plied him with food and drink, and offered him various places to sleep. It was Violet's offer he had finally accepted. So here he was, perched like an enormous bird outside her makeshift home, waiting to cross the threshold while she made her final safety checks.

"Okay!" she shouted up. "Go on inside! I'm on my way up."

He slithered carefully from the bough to the edge of the wooden platform. His hands were slippery with sweat, and his black suede boots found little purchase. Violet had eyed them with great reservation when he began the climb—even suggesting he would be better off barefoot—but Jo was loathe to expose his feet to splinters and scatches. As he had climbed step by slow step, guided from the ground by Violet, he realised too late he had made the wrong decision. The ascent would have been much easier if he could have flexed his long feet, and gripped the branches like a monkey.

He pushed back the flap of tarpaulin that served as a door, and crawled inside. Violet had created a makeshift window at the rear of her shelter, with a square of transparent plastic. He pushed the doorflap right back, and the interior was flooded with pale, golden sunlight. Even sitting, his head touched the top though Violet, soon beside him, was not so inconvenienced.

"You shouldn't be so tall," she said.

"It's not something I can help." He looked around in amazement.

"You've made it beautiful," he said. "Like a yurt." The tarpaulin was lined with a white cotton sheet, but this was almost totally obscured by scarves, crimson and gold and peacock blue, embroidered with elephants, stars and fabulous plumed birds. She had the usual storm lantern, and the bits and pieces essential for eating and cleaning, as well as a handful of books, and a huge bouquet of bluebells, now pale and dry, hanging by the little window. A tiny bronze Shiva danced on top of the books.

"Will there be room for me to sleep here?" he asked.

"When I've cleared up, yes. If you don't mind being a bit cosy. I've slept two in here before." Jo's first night with Elaine had been anything but cosy, and avoiding contact in a treehouse had not been an easy matter. And he had felt unbearably precarious, hanging above the ground, worrying that the floor might break beneath him, or that he might tumble through the tarpaulin and off the edge. This time he would not be so anxious. He spotted Violet's patchwork blanket.

"Did you make this?" he asked. The patches were vivid—blue, emerald, scarlet, the yellow of daffodils. Many had been embroidered with shiny metallic threads, depicting crop circles, flowers, suns and moons.

"Yes. Bit by bit. I'm still adding to it. It helps me relax, when this place gets too much."

"It's wonderful."

She smiled in thanks, a faint blush creeping into her face.

They spent the day together, up in the treehouse, in and around the copse. It was Violet's turn for the necessary but unsavoury task of filling in a pit latrine dug some distance from the copse near a hedge. Despite layers of sand and soil the place stank. The earth was as hard as rock to dig, and by the time the job was finished to Violet's satisfaction they were tired and sweating. Jo helped out with good will, and when the work was done they sat in the shade of the copse upon the little barrow. Jo loved the place. The trees had been decorated with clay faces, perched in clefts in their trunks, simply modelled gargoyles and green men. Around the roots some were circled with stones scavenged from fields. Lumps of rock protruding from the soil bore painted spirals and celtic knots. Here and there pieces of stone were threaded with string and hung from the lower branches. It was a veritable sacred grove, a holy space amongst the trees. Jo found it utterly enchanting.

"What are those for?" Jo asked.

"Stones with holes. Protection from faeries."

"Faeries? I thought the faeries were on our side."

But Violet shook her head.

"Then you don't know the faeries."

"But what about the Morris men?"

"They're not faeries. How could they be faeries? They're as solid as you and me. It sounds like you've been talking to Owain."

"Elaine," Jo said. "And Katherine. So you've seen real faeries?"

"Seen? Not exactly. Sensed them. Some nights it has been very eerie here. Some people left. They couldn't take it. Some thought they could see lights in the valley, and Owain told us he saw a faerie procession."

"I've heard some of this before and it sounds amazing. I'd love to see it. I can't imagine why anyone would be scared off. I thought these people would be really into it." Jo was fired with enthusiasm, but Violet smiled thinly.

"Well, maybe you'll see," she said. "It's Midsummer's Eve after all."

"It's like living in a fairy tale already—this beautiful place, all the signs and masks and flowers."

"Don't get over romantic. Just wait till the bailiffs come. Just wait till the weather turns for god's sake. What about the shit we've just been shovelling. Can you imagine what it was like here at the beginning of the year in the bitter cold, perpetually wet and muddy, never having dry clothes, not being able to light a fire, trying to climb the trees when your hands are cold and the bark is slippery with rain, and the ropes are sodden? Can you imagine what it was like having flu, stuck in a tree, the struggle it takes just to go out into the bitter weather for a pee? It's all very well turning up in the dry summer weather, when it's like one long picnic, before the trouble starts, isn't it?"

Jo was suitably chastened.

"I see what you mean," he said. But Violet softened.

"You're right in a sense," she said. "We have tried to make it like a fairy tale. In some ways it makes it more bearable, all the cold and the mud and the struggle. So we have it be magic as well, something precious and extraordinary. We see spirits in the trees, and tell tales upon the barrow, and venerate the earth even as we get bruised when we fall from the ropes, or when we're digging, or disposing of rubbish. Surviving like this, day to day, every activity involves effort, fetching water, lighting a fire, making a cup of tea. Living is such hard work! No turning on the tap, reaching for the kettle."

"But you must get something from it—or you wouldn't be here."

"Yeah. Knowing I'm protecting the land, that I'm speaking out instead of letting it happen. But there is more. A keenness, from living like this. More acute perception. A greater sense of connection."

"Maybe that's why people are sensing faeries?" said Jo. "Perhaps they've always been here, but not noticed for a long time? Books I've got at home talk of people taken into the faerie realm, of meeting all sorts of spirits, trying to please them with gifts and saucers of milk, trying to appease them or ward them off. Bogles and boggarts and pixies and dryads. It seems like long ago, awareness of this whole faerie business was part of everyday experience, part of living. Maybe this isn't something unusual, but something we've lost the sight to see?"

"I know, I know. I think you may well be right. We've been talking about it here often enough the past few weeks. It is threatening though. The atmosphere can be sinister sometimes. If the faeries are true to my perception of them, they most certainly don't fit in the gauzy wings and gossamer image."

"Then what are they like? Evil?" Jo asked.

"No, not that. Uncertain. Unreliable. Illusion and tricks and knowing how to go for your weak point."

Jo laughed.

"Well, that's okay. I think I already have one living in my head. I'm always going for my own weak point. When I have arguments with the voices in my mind, I'm always the loser."

"Don't forget this is all my speculation. My feeling. I haven't actually encountered a faerie face-to-face."

"Unless the Morris men really are faeries. I think they are," Jo asserted. Violet smiled.

"Maybe," she said. "And maybe you are part faerie too. You have the air of a faerie. Not sinister though."

"No. I've inherited the thin and gauzy aspect. Or if I was being particularly unkind to myself, I'd say I'm just weak and ineffective." He looked almost comically downcast for a moment, but Violet took his hand and squeezed it.

"Plunged into a momentary pool of self-doubt, are we?" she said. "Well, you're here, aren't you? We're sharing this time, this Midsummer's Eve. You're part of the adventure."

Jo looked up, into her freckled pixie face, framed by hair and adornments.

"Yes," he said. "I suppose I am."

Later in the afternoon they climbed the tree to Violet's home, to talk and laugh and laze in the pool of sunlight, pouring through the opening. Violet peeled off her jumper, exposing arms golden with freckles. Her hands were small, like a child's, but her nails were chipped and dirty, her palms calloused, from the rigours of her life at the site. Jo observed her with delight. She was very slender, and she looked as fragile as a bird with her delicate bones, though he knew from watching her work and climb that this belied her strength. She was wearing a loose vest the colour of indigo, and when she leaned towards him, he caught a glimpse of tiny breasts, each pierced with a silver ring.

"You've had your nipples pierced too!" he burst out enthusiastically, though he blushed in acute embarassment as the objects of his admiration were swiftly hidden away again. But Violet smiled.

"Yes," she said. "Go on then. Show me yours."

Jo took off the jingling waistcoat and his black shirt.

"What a pair we are," she said. She took off her shirt too, revealing a further, thick embellished ring in her navel. "So that's five, altogether, along with another two in each ear," she grinned. "And you have...eight?"

"Nine."

She counted again.

"Where's the other one?" she said. Jo had the grace to blush, and Violet burst out laughing.

"I see," she said. "Or rather, I don't." She put her shirt on again, and lay on her front in the sun. The light glinted in her hair, spinning stray wisps to molten gold.

"It's funny, isn't it?" Jo mused. "I feel the need to decorate my body like this. Paying homage somehow. A kind of ritual, like a tribesman adorning himself."

Violet reached for her books and rummaged in the pile until she found the volume she was seeking.

"Goblin Market," she said. "Christina Rossetti. Have you read it?"

Jo shook his head. Violet propped herself on her elbows, and began to recite aloud. They fell into fits of helpless laughter when the fallen Laura found redemption, kissing and licking her saintly sister.

When the long evening drew on, they joined their fellows for a meal of curry and rice, cooked over a fire. The atmosphere was jovial, a couple of bottles of wine in circulation, and when they had finished, a half a dozen people headed on foot to Silbury Hill, leaving Jo, Violet, Owain, Elaine, and maybe half a dozen more of the treefolk still in residence at the copse. Owain and Elaine wandered off together down the valley. Violet gazed after them.

"They're becoming an item, I fancy," she commented. Jo nodded.

"I hope Owain knows what he's letting himself in for," she added. She turned to Jo.

"You know her," she said. "You know her from Bristol. Were you and she...?"

"An item? Yes. A long time ago."

Violet narrowed her eyes, and took another swig from a wine bottle. They were sitting in silence. The others moved away, clearing up saucepans and plates, gathering fragments of wood to maintain the fire through the evening. Violet slipped her hand into her pocket, withdrawing a tiny embroidered purse, decorated with mirrors. Tucked into a seam were two white paper squares embellished with a yin-yang circle.

"Shall we?" she said. "It is Midsummer's Eve after all. And you do want to see faeries." Jo felt a fluttering in his stomach, a mixture of excitement and dread. He swallowed to clear his throat.

"Okay," he said. Violet downed one square with a swig of wine, then handed the other, and the bottle, to Jo, who repeated the procedure.

"Here goes," he said, grimacing at the rough taste of the wine.

Some indefinite time later, Violet lay curled on the grass caught in spasms of laughter till tears poured down her cheeks. Jo was sitting cross-legged, a little worried that nothing was happening to him. Or was it? He couldn't be entirely sure. The mental furniture in his head seemed a little out of place, but didn't it always? He couldn't remember. Then surely if he was wondering such a thing he had to be tripping? He pondered. He gnawed his fingernails. Violet watched him and laughed. She writhed on the grass, the blue-green grass, like an animal, her tiny frame possessed by her laughter. Jo was anxious. Was he really so very funny? He pulled his knees up to his chin, hugged his long legs to his body. He felt very small indeed, like a bundle of sticks not held together too firmly. He thought he had better hold onto himself in case he came undone. It was frightening really, just how unravelled he was, how disconnected. What was it that held him together? He had to be careful. If he started to think like this, how far might his mind drift away? How would he get the bits and pieces back again? Which was the bit of his mind that could bring the other bits back? He felt empty inside, like a hollow drum with voices hammering on the outside but a void in the middle where his sense of self should be. Did everyone feel like this? He was missing pieces, big pieces, that should weigh him down and stop him floating apart. How often had he tried to explain this to Elaine?

He felt an aching weight in his stomach. He focussed outwards, to Violet and the trees, where the leaves shifted in their great multitudes on the branches. He realised Violet had stopped laughing, and was lying on her back staring into the sky. Her face looked purplish in the evening light, in the shadows. A flicker of electric blue pulsed across her face, then patterns, restless twists and coils on her skin. Her hair lay about her in a mobile pour of red and gold, spirals of bright copper and cobalt. The weight in his stomach tightened, into an almost-pain. He ignored it. How could he have doubted? He knew where he was. Familiar territory. Home ground. Yet when he wasn't here he forgot what it was like. No, not forgot—he could recall the events, but that was not the same thing at all. He thought back. A long, long time ago he had been wondering if parts of him were missing. Maybe he left those bits here? Perhaps when he returned to that other place, where he was the helpless, incompetent person, bigs chunks of him remained behind. No wonder he was so much smaller than everyone else. How could he rescue the missing bits, take them back from acid land and chase them home again, back to Normal-Jo, however normal that was to start with? It was hard to hang onto his thoughts. They were becoming too swift to catch. He hung onto their tails, as though they were fish jumping in and out of the water, pulling him behind them. He always lost his grip though. The thoughts tunnelled off and he was left adrift in a heaving swell of fragmentary sensations.

Quick panic. He noticed that Violet was saying something. What was she saying? Had he been ignoring her? How long had she been speaking? He looked at her. She was facing him, that beautiful hair streaming in glorious colour down her shoulders. He could lose himself in her hair for hours. He was transfixed. But she was speaking. What was she saying?

"Where are you, Jo? Are you in the same place as me?" It seemed to take him a long time to find the necessary mental connections needed to form words. And what should he say? Best not to think about it too hard. Just go for it.

"I don't know. Where are you?" He gazed into her face.

"You look like a lion," he said. "With a great mane. A magical lion though, a spirit lion." Violet smiled, but she didn't reply. Jo began to worry. What was she thinking?

"Say something," he said. "Tell me what's happening." She grinned again, till Jo was afraid her face would split. They sat and gazed at one another for hours, for an eternity. Jo flipped from freakish paranoia to exuberant ecstasy. How did he get to be in this place, in the middle of a sea of fields, far from his room, lost amongst strangers? But at the same time he was here, where he was most at home. Dull, earthly geography was far less significant than this, the landscape of his mind. The sun was setting. Hours had passed. They grew cold, but the ascent to the treehouse was way beyond him. He watched in terror as Violet skipped up the tree like a monkey, returning with jumpers and jackets. Then they huddled together round the embers of the fire, watching the flames, Jo drifting off into thoughts that opened like chasms and swallowed him up.

He looked up. He felt something brush against him. A presence. A faint scent, a high pitched strain of music. He looked around. The night was black, pressed against him like a huge body. Sheltered by the trees, he could not see beyond the realm of branches. He rose to his feet and moved to the boundary, to the edge of the copse. The darkness fell away. He could see stars, a moon flashing out from behind clouds. The tree shadows seemed to hold onto him, protective, drawing him back, but Jo was a light spirit, intangible, and he slipped through. He stood outside. The land stretched out before him, mauve and tangerine flames flickering above the horizon. The stars spat blood red drops, dissolving into clouds that aped the forms of fruit and faces. Jo stood like a child at the edge of a brilliant, inconstant ocean. He watched waves rise and burn like phosphorus.

Then the presence again. Closer this time, moving towards him. He saw a path, running past the copse and down into the stone valley. It unrolled before him, like a ribbon. It was paved with stones that throbbed with red and gold. Inbetween the bricks the void flashed glittering black, but the cracks were too small to fall through. The path beckoned. It curled and pressed against him like a cat, insinuating, flirting. But he held back. A hiss. A troupe of ghosts stole past, walking the path. He felt them, like silk against his skin. One ghost turned towards him, searching, but she did not see him he was sure. The others looked too, bright-coloured eyes and teeth that glinted, half-alluring, half bestial. Did they hate him so? They were hungry and afraid. They knew him. They wanted him. They passed him by and were gone. Should he follow? Where did the path lead? He trembled. Maybe he could find his missing pieces. Maybe, if he took to the path, he wouldn't have to go back to the mundane world. Was this his golden opportunity? He stepped forwards. His feet were on the path. He was committed. The land fell away and all around him crowds of people passed like shadows. He couldn't see the copse anymore. He began to walk forwards. He was aware that some form of barrier prevented him seeing the land that lay around the path. It had closed behind him. Pale grey skeins, like cobwebs, obscuring his surroundings. Could he pass through? He was torn. Should he head onwards or force a passage through the veil and retreat? Purpose or escape? Put it like that, he thought, it has to be escape. He stopped walking forwards and dived headfirst through the shroud.

CHAPTER SEVENTEEN

Paul was oblivious to Katherine, crouching in the shadows, but when she left through the cottage door he felt her absence like a faint ache. Where was she going? Jan asked him if he wanted a drink, but Paul shook his head.

"I think I'll go outside for a bit," he said. He rose to his feet, pulled on his leather jacket and headed into the garden. He stood on the doorstep, as his eyes adjusted to the night. The silence was absolute. He walked to the back of the cottage, but the Morris men were gone. The tents remained, drab, motionless shapes in the dark. Even the bells were still. He felt cold, and zipped up the jacket, pulling his hands into his sleeves. He returned to the cottage, and sat huddled on the stone doorstep. A hand gripped his shoulder, pressing painfully.

"Hello, Paul. You're slowing up."

Paul looked up. He couldn't make out his assailant's face in the blackness, but the soft, determined voice gave the intruder away. A hot prickle ran along his spine.

"I must be," he said. "What are you doing here? How did you find me?"

"I wasn't looking for you. I was here on my own account, and I spotted you wandering round the garden."

"I never had you down as a pagan. Are you here to watch the sunrise? If you're hoping for a run-in with the police I should head for the Stonehenge exclusion zone."

The man shook his head.

"No. Since our recent chat I've been making some enquiries about this protest of yours. I thought I might be able to help."

"Oh, yes?" Paul said, too quickly. He rubbed his hands together, suddenly feeling sweat on his palms.

"Yeah. Do you know when the eviction will start?"

"No. In the next few weeks I imagine."

"You imagine. Very slack, Paul. All this hippie living I've no doubt, and happy family life. Got your life insurance sorted yet?"

The voice bit into his own troubled conscience.

"It's not like that," he said. "Not the happy family life bit anyway," he added with a short, painful laugh.

"Just the life insurance?"

"Yeah. I haven't just taken all the crap on board though. It still worries me. I've got a kid. I've got to look after her."

"Yeah. It still worries you. How about the guards at Auschwitz? D'you think they went home in the evening and said 'It still worries me'?"

"Shit, Stuart, it's not comparable."

"No? I think so. You've become part of the system you always claimed was corrupt and injust. You had principles, and now you've sold out. You're not happy with what you're doing, but you haven't got the guts to stand against it."

"What about this protest?"

"You've become a hobbyist. You're not even living here. Don't tell me, you've got to get up for work in the morning."

"My kid's got to eat."

"Yeah, hurrah for the family, the tight little unit, holding the whole damn system together."

Paul held himself tight but he knew he would surrender. How could he hold out when Stuart was articulating the argument he continued in his head every day? Stuart put his hand on Paul's shoulder again, gently this time.

"Come on," he said. "I know your heart's in the right place. You've lost your way. Come with me now. See what I've found."

Paul took a deep breath. As he breathed out again, he relaxed. He let go. What was he fighting against, anyway? It always happened like this, with Stuart. He held out, stubbornly, but Stuart was only speaking his own desire. He had avoided him all this time, fighting his true feelings. Now he would face the truth. He stood up, and followed him down the Old Lane. Having given up resistance he felt a surge of exhiliration, a release. He trotted to catch up.

"Where are you taking me?" he asked. Stuart smiled, sensing victory.

"Wait and see. It's a good one. You'll be impressed." Stuart was wearing black. In the darkness Paul could only make out his face, but as the moon emerged from the cloud it shone upon his leather coat, which hung about him like the wings of a bat. At the end of the lane, an old Metro was parked on the verge. They climbed inside. Paul noticed that the window on the driver's side was missing. Stuart was fiddling with wires beneath the steering wheel.

"Stolen?" he said. He rubbed his hands again, wiping the perspiration on his jeans.

"Yeah. Don't panic. Worried about your job?"

Paul shook his head. The engine started, the noise echoing into the night. Stuart was a competent driver, but he pushed the car to its modest limits. Paul sat tense in the passenger seat. They didn't go far. Two miles down the road, they turned off onto a farm track. The hedges were very high. Stuart switched off the car headlights and slowed right down. At an open gateway he turned the car round and parked in the middle of the lane.

"This is where we get out," he said. They walked up the lane, Paul stumbling on the stoney, uneven surface. Stuart had a torch in his pocket, which he handed to Paul. He seemed to have uncanny night vision, walking without misplacing a step. At last, the lane opened up, with a cluster of buildings and an enclosed concrete yard. To one side stood a small mobile home. Yellow light spilled from the windows, though the curtains were drawn.

"What's here?" he said quietly. Stuart didn't answer. He gestured to the yard and buildings, and after scanning the vicinity, walked towards them. Paul followed him. They climbed a pile of mouldering straw bales, and peered over the corrugated iron fencing into the enclosure. Stuart took the torch and shone it inside.

Paul drew a breath. The circle of light glanced off the sleek yellow bodies of earth-movers and diggers. In the limited light, it was hard to be sure how many, but he counted a dozen at least. They were emblazoned with the name and logo of Tarcost, the company awarded the contract for the building of the bypass. He was perfectly familiar with it, having upon his desk at home a generous file of correspondence from them. They had always replied to his letters, polite and bland, full of reassurances.

"Fifteen altogether," Stuart said. From a pocket in his coat he pulled out a brown envelope. Inside it were half a dozen pages, photocopies of faxes and letters.

"Hold this."

Paul held the torch above the pages, trying to read the indistinct text.

"July 26th. That's when the bailiffs are planning to move in. Tarcost have arranged for a security company to fence off the bypass route, beginning the same time. This isn't Newbury, they're not imagining it will be that much of a battle, not for a small village bypass. How many people do you think you can muster?"

"Altogether? On the day? With people from the village as well as those on site, and doubtless a few others keen for some action, maybe two hundred? Most of them will be law-abiding and anxious to avoid arrest. Maybe a few dozen will be prepared to cause a real obstruction."

Stuart nodded.

"About what I thought. Tarcost are imagining it will only take a day or two."

"Where did you get this stuff?"

"We haven't all been enjoying the good life you know. I have my contacts. I have ways and means."

"What are you planning to do?"

Stuart pushed his hand down into the straw bales. He drew out a large metal petrol can.

"I came here last night," he said. "It's all prepared."

Paul gazed at him, appalled.

"You're going to burn it?"

"We've got to do something. You think your hippie friends are going to stop this? You're going to sit in a field and pray?"

Paul was helpless. He didn't know what to say. Could he back out now? He felt sick.

"Why didn't you do it yourself, last night?"

"I needed your help. I couldn't do it all alone. I've done all the hard work. All you need to do is keep out a watch for me. There is only one guard in the mobile. They think this place is secret and they are unforgivably complacent about your competence, though I can quite understand why."

"I don't think I can go through with this."

"Why not? No-one will be hurt. We're only talking about machines. You have feelings for these machines?"

Paul shook his head, and sighed.

"I don't like it."

"Yeah, I guessed. A bit too far out for you? A bit too dangerous? You're prepared to be part of the counter-culture just as long as it doesn't damage your chances in the real world. How long can you sit on the fence?"

"Okay. Okay. I'll do it." Paul was now sweating profusely. He could feel his shirt sticking to his back. He felt a strong desire for a cigarette, though he had given up when Katherine was pregnant.

"Tell me the plan."

Stuart regarded him for a moment. His face became serious. He spoke in a low voice, without expression.

"Stand at the bottom of the bales. From there you can see the mobile, and you'll be able to climb up and warn me if anyone emerges. That is unlikely, as I won't be making any noise and there is no reason for the guard to be suspicious. However, every now and then he does come out and walk around, and if I am inside I will not be aware of his movements. I'll pour quantities of petrol over the vehicles, and when I climb out again, you must scoot down the lane as fast as you can and start the car. You know how to do it."

Paul nodded. Stuart continued in the same intense monotone.

"I'll start the conflagration, and come down after you, so you must be ready to head off the instant I reach the car. Yes?"

Paul nodded again. He slipped down the bales, and peered across the yard to the mobile. Everything was quiet. Stuart clambered over the fence with the petrol can and dropped out of site.

Paul waited. How long would it take? The minutes passed by. The sweat cooled on his body and he shivered, but his pulse continued to hammer through his body. He shifted from one foot to the other. He imagined Stuart weaving through the vehicles, carefully pouring out petrol, leaving trails, completing a thoroughly competent job. The cloud cover thickened, though the air was still. Would it rain? Would the fire be extinguished? The moon appeared momentarily, a bald silver saucer. He thought of Niamh, peacefully asleep in the cottage. He thought of Katherine, and wondered where she was. He heard a hiss. He looked up. Stuart was again atop the fence. He had a glass bottle in his hand, a rag stuffed in its top.

"Go and start the car. I won't be far behind you."

Paul waved quickly, and disappeared into the darkness. Stuart had the torch, and as Paul ran down the lane, his boot caught in a stony rut and he sprawled headlong onto the ground. He put out his hands to save himself, and felt a fiery pain in his hands as he grazed his palms on the road. His knees hit stone, and he suppressed a cry, quickly staggering to his feet again. He headed off again, as fast as he could, ignoring the pain and eager to find the car. He heard a muffled explosion, and turning round, saw a sudden red flare against the darkness. Then Stuart was beside him.

"What are you waiting for? Get going!" he said. They heard some kind of commotion behind them. A door slammed. Someone was shouting. Stuart pushed past Paul and ran to the car. He jumped in the driver's seat and fiddled with the wires. Paul jumped in beside him. The engine started, and they pulled away, the wheels spinning on the stones, bouncing through the potholes as the car tore down the lane and back to the main road. When they approached the Old Lane, Stuart slammed on the brakes.

"Get out," he said shortly. "You've been here all evening, and you haven't seen me, okay?" Paul climbed out. Before he turned away, Stuart spoke again.

"Well done," he said. "You haven't entirely lost it. You've got my number." Then without awaiting a reply he drove off towards Swindon, headlights off, quickly lost in the darkness.

Paul stood by the side of the road. He looked at his watch. It was 2.50am. The solstice had just passed. The silence fell heavy all around him. He had been absent less than an hour. He crossed the road and walked up the Old Lane. Just outside the cottage he saw a dark figure walking towards him.

"Paul!" It was Katherine. She threw her arms round his neck and pressed herself against him. She was very cold.

"Hello," he said. "What's this for?" How long had it been since she hugged him like that?

"Because I love you."

He laughed.

"I was beginning to wonder. Have you been drinking?" he said.

"A little. But I'm not drunk." She undid his jacket and pushed her hands inside, clasping them around his waist. He felt the chill of her body disperse into his own flesh. He kissed her forehead. He caught the scent.

"Is anything the matter?" she said. He shook his head. He put his arms round her and squeezed her tightly. Desire rose up like a flame in his body.

"My god, I want you," he said, his voice thick. She laughed.

"I want you too. Where shall we go? Somewhere outside? It is Midsummer after all."

"The valley?"

"Okay." They walked up the lane. He kept his arm around her, pressing her against him as though he was afraid she would skip away from him. But she gripped him just as tightly, one arm around his middle. When they reached the valley he pulled her to face him and kissed her mouth. She kissed him fiercely, pressing her hips hard against him. He picked her up, and laid her down on her back in the wet grass. He couldn't wait any longer. His whole body shook. He pulled off her underwear, and pressed into her, and in moments she came, thrashing beneath him, and even as he moved in her he watched her face in amazement. It had never been like this before. He could feel her body so distinctly, every muscle, every bone, every thread of flesh, cleaving to him, desiring him. She held him so tightly her fingers bruised his skin, and as he reached his own release she smiled and laughed, kissing his face, and as they lay entangled, together in the dark and damp, his old life seemed to fall away in fragments.

CHAPTER EIGHTEEN

When they returned from West Kennet long barrow, Owain and Elaine dropped Katherine at the cottage and walked up the Old Lane, close together. They were tired from their walk, but bright with moonlight, sharing smiles and glancing at each other in the darkness. Elaine's gauzy white dress fluttered behind her. Her limbs were heavy with weariness, but her mind was light and acute. She felt elated. Owain walked at her side, connected to her by a thousand imperceptible threads. She was keenly conscious of his physical presence, the movement of his body as he walked. He seemed astonishingly beautiful, and she kept looking over to him, grinning foolishly when she caught his eye, and realised he was looking at her in just the same way. When she stumbled in a rut, she caught his arm.

"I can't see where I'm going," she said. She slid her arm through his, and they continued up the hill. The tangible connection gave her a shock of delight. She could feel the warmth of his flesh through the sleeve of his coat. He squeezed her arm, turned and smiled again.

"You look very pale," he said. "And your hair—in the moonlight it looks nearly blue."

Elaine blushed and bit her lip.

"Where shall we go?" he asked.

"My bower? Let's go round the back. I don't feel like encountering the others just now."

They entered the copse from the far side, and made the ascent to Elaine's eyrie. She lit the storm lantern, filling the tiny space with quavering yellow light.

"It's like a cave," he said. "Locked away. Like the barrow, only now we're surrounded by air, not earth. We should be outside."

Elaine nodded, very serious.

"First we must make our preparations," she said.

"What did you have in mind?"

Elaine rummaged in one of her bags and withdrew a tin box, an old biscuit tin with a picture of poppies on the top. She opened it, withdrawing brushes, and she filled a jar with water.

"Face paints," Owain said.

"Seeing as your Fool is going to be more King of the Woods than clown, I thought we should begin our preparations in the hour of the solstice. I want you to feel the part." Elaine shuffled across the floor to face him. She covered a small sponge with pale green paint, and she placed one hand upon his head.

"Keep still," she said. She began to apply the paint. She was intent upon her work, though her face, bare inches from his, and her arms moved so close to him.

She kept tutting and asking him to shift, to keep his face out of shadow. She mixed the green with grey, embellished his cheeks with leaves, painted clusters of acorns growing from his mouth. She was engrossed in her work, though she could feel his breath on her skin. At last she was satisfied. She drew back, but their knees were still touching.

"Not bad," she said. Then, with a laugh, "Why, Owain, you're trembling."

He made no reply, but he held out his hands to her. She took hold of them, and he drew her onto his lap. They sat very close for a few moments, not speaking.

"You're trembling too," he said. She took his face in her hands and kissed him very gently.

"You'll smudge the paint," he said.

"I can always do it again." She kissed him a second time. Then they were still, prolonging the moment, afraid of bruising their fragile, infant intimacy. Owain placed his hands upon her waist, but Elaine held back. They regarded each other and Elaine was curiously afraid to proceed. She felt perfectly exposed. She didn't trust herself. She slid from his lap.

"Take off your shirt," she said. "Let me paint your body."

Owain pulled off his jumper and shirt.

"Lie on your front," she instructed. Owain lay with his head resting on his arms, upon Elaine's sleeping bag. While she worked, Elaine was unaware of the man. She focussed entirely on her painting, swirls of green and ochre, leaves and spirals covering his back. She was slow and methodical, beginning upon his shoulders, noting the honey brown of his skin, soft as velvet, the canvas for her work. His body was lean and strong. A tree sprang up from his slender waist, ascending his backbone, spreading boughs across the back of his ribcage, laden with leaves and fruit. Owain lay as though asleep, though aware of the movement of the sponge and brush across his flesh, because he flinched, ticklish, every now and then. When she told him to lie on his back he covered his face with his arms, unwilling to watch her, absorbed in the sensation of paint upon his body. She marked out a great spiral centred on his navel, uncoiling on the hard muscle of his belly, where a triangle of pale, golden hair stretched down into his jeans.

"Okay," she said, at last. "Finished, I think. Are you cold?"

"No."

They climbed down from the treehouse. Owain was still bare to the waist. In the darkness of the copse they stumbled haphazardly, until they reached the open field where the moon's faint radiance glimmered on the wet grass. They looked down the stone valley. Owain hesitated.

"What is it?" Elaine said.

"Look. The path."

Elaine stepped forward, straining her eyes to see.

"I can't make it out."

"Come with me." Owain took her hand and led her down to the valley.

"Can you see now?" he said. Among the stones a thin light rose from the ground like a mist. Elaine drew back, but Owain stood his ground, unafraid.

"Look at the walkers," he said.

"What walkers? I can't see them," she said, hanging back.

"You're not looking. The veil is thin. They're coming through." Then he laughed, an unexpected, triumphant laugh. He let Elaine's hand drop, and held up his arms like a mage.

"Welcome!" he cried.

"I thought you didn't like them!" Elaine cried, half hysterical.

"This is different. This is their proper time. This is where we share our space, where we can dance on the bridge together. Welcome!" He laughed again, and ran off like a deer into the darkness, darting through the stones until Elaine lost sight of him in the night. She was cold and anxious. She wasn't sure what he could see. The path shone, yes, but who was he speaking to? Were there faeries she couldn't see? She lost her fear in favour of annoyance. She sighed briskly and trotted after Owain. Why had he left her alone like that? She headed down the valley, her bare legs bitten by the icy dew, grazing her ankle on a grey wether obscured by grass and darkness.

"Owain?" she called. "Owain! Where are you?" The moon was blotted out by cloud, and then she could see nothing. She stood still.

"Owain!" When the cloud cleared again, she thought she could see him further up the valley, standing on one of the stones. She walked towards him. He appeared to be holding audience, truly like the King she had painted. He had loosened the habitual pony-tail, and his long, golden hair hung over his shoulders. She noticed with a slight shock that he was now completely naked. He looked like a stranger. The paint upon his face broke up the familiar contours, and when looked over, her heart missed a beat. Who was he after all? Their earlier moment of intimacy flashed into her mind, and she suffered a moment of fear. How truly do you ever know someone? He was entirely other to her now, but he regarded her with fierce familiarity. He held out his hand as though he was making a claim. She heard a whisper in her ears. Her dress shifted in the breeze, which touched her hair. She stepped forward and placed her hand in his. He jumped down from the stone. He took off her dress and her underclothes. Elaine made no resistance. She felt her precious self control evaporate. She stood with the moon beating down on her head, breathing the tart, fresh scent of the bruised grass. She was aware she was cold, but still she was strangely detached from her physical self. He kissed her breasts, and knelt before her, rubbing his face in the soft, white skin of her belly. Gently he touched her sex with his tongue, and seemingly from a far distance, she felt her pulse quicken and knew she was aroused. Then he pushed her onto the grass, looming over her like a black shadow, priapic, like an animal sprung from the woods. She couldn't see his face as he entered her, but his body was hot and coated with sweat. She sank into a trance, dimly aware of the movement of the clouds in the sky, the fleeting appearance of the stars. Ghostly faces seemed to appear all around her, peering into her eyes, teasing her hair with thin fingers, touching her face with their hands. Then she saw a little girl with blue eyes and thick golden hair, grinning and waving, but the woman washing by the river was close behind, a pile of bloody clothes by her side, and her face downcast. She heard a shifting, the sound of a bitter wind lifting dead leaves. Moving towards her was a woman dressed in black and brown and ivory, her robes embroidered with fragments of bone and the torn rags of faded winter foliage. Her hair was grey with cobweb, and dust mottled her skin. She nodded at Elaine, with a blank, beautiful face. Elaine shouted out in terror, and as the sound left her mouth she came to herself, lying inert, Owain's body heavy upon her. He was breathing deeply, his mouth pressed against her neck. Then he calmed, and kissed her face, almost dutifully.

"Are you okay?" he asked.

"Yes. Yes, I think so." They were separate again, a little embarassed. Owain stood up and peered around for her clothes. She quickly slipped them on.

"I seem to have lost my trousers."

"Yes."

"I guess I'll find them on the way back."

"Yes."

They walked apart, Owain shuffling through the grass till he found his jeans, half way down the valley. Awkwardly he pulled them on. They headed back to the copse, almost stumbling on Katherine and Paul, coiled in the grass, on the way.

"Seems to be the night for it," Elaine remarked. But she remembered her vision, and shivered.

"You're cold," Owain said. "Let's sleep for an hour. Set your clock. We've still a little time before sunrise."

They climbed to the treehouse, and curled up close together.

CHAPTER NINETEEN

The solstice revellers did not see the rising of the sun. Crowded upon the summit of Silbury Hill, gathered in amongst the Avebury stones, and standing on the long barrows, they witnessed the birth of the longest day as a gradual paling of the cloud. By dawn the sky was utterly grey, thick unbroken cloud the colour of oatmeal and flour. The pilgrims were cold and tired, some drunk or otherwise intoxicated. The better prepared were huddled in blankets and sleeping bags. A couple of greybeards in druidic white assembled on Silbury and made the midsummer sun a formal greeting. Those on West Kennet long barrow could see their fellows stop the sacred Silbury mound, and across the field they could hear ululating and the deep tones of a horn.

Paul and Katherine walked hand in hand towards the cottage. Paul was tired and stiff, his clothes damp with dew. He thought they must have slept a couple of hours, for although the night had faded, it was still before five o'clock. He smiled at friends at the copse, similarly grey-faced in the early hours of the day. As he walked he warmed up, and he squeezed Katherine's hand. He felt perfectly happy. Then just as they turned into the garden, a police car drove slowly up the Old Lane and the memory of the night's events crashed around his head like rocks. A moment of panic—he had quite forgotten his foray with Stuart. It had fallen from his mind. He stood and waited for the police car to pull up alongside them. Two officers were sat inside, an older man with steel grey hair at the steering wheel. They stopped the car and climbed out.

"Can I help you?" Paul said. He kept his grip of Katherine's hand.

"Perhaps you can," the older man said, his mouth smiling but his eyes cold as stone. "Perhaps you can. My name's Sergeant Gerard. This is PC Lamb. We're from Marlborough. Are you one of the protestors squatting at this site?"

"No," Paul said. "A protestor, yes, but I don't live here."

"And where do you live?"

"Locksbury."

"And your name is?"

"Matravers. Paul Matravers." When he spoke the two policemen exchanged a glance.

"So what's the problem?" he asked. The officer paused for a moment.

"An incident near here, last night. Some property was damaged in a fire. We think it may be arson. We're making some general enquiries, that's all. Could you tell me where you were last night between midnight and three o'clock?"

Paul shrugged.

"Sure. I was chatting with Jan Blessing in the cottage, and the rest of the night I spent with my partner here, up in the stone valley." As he spoke, the younger officer scribbled some notes in his pad.

"The stone valley. Right. Thank you Mr Matravers. Thank you very much. Sorry to trouble you." The older officer spoke very slowly. He nodded to his colleague, and with one last quick, scrutinising glance at Paul, he headed on foot up the lane to the copse. Paul and Katherine watched their steady progress.

"That's one way to spoil the party atmosphere," Paul commented. "I hope our fellows in the trees are straight and sober. And polite. I don't want the police hanging round here too long. People will be turning up for the fair very soon." His voice was level, but he was sweating. Katherine looked at him carefully.

"Don't ask," he said. She shrugged.

"Okay." The breeze tugged her hair, still plaited, though thick strands had worked loose and fluttered into her face. She brushed them aside. The marigold dress clung to her body. Paul looked at her face. She was gazing absentmindedly at her feet, teasing a stone in the dust with the heel of her boot. He observed her eyelashes, dark and curved, and the single delicate line at the top of her nose, which wrinkled when she frowned. He knew her face better than his own—but how long was it since he had noticed these things? She looked up, as though aware she was the object of his attention. She put her arms around him, and hugged him with enthusiastic fervour. She pressed her face into his chest. She was different. Smaller. Softer. When she returned his gaze, he knew she was engaging with him. For months, he had been half aware that he had been little more than an inconvenient presence. Her eyes would skate across him, even as she spoke. She was wrapped up in the baby. She was always tired and she didn't want him. And he had turned away and lost himself, as always, in his work for the protest, in his various lobbying, crusading groups. But now something had changed. His focus had altered. He could see what had happened between them. She had come back to him, renewed.

"We'd better see how Niamh is," he said.

"Still asleep hopefully."

"And we'll have to get ready for this play, or we'll have Elaine on our case."

They walked up the path to the cottage. Jan stood waiting for them in the doorway.

"Niamh okay?" Paul asked.

"Yes. Not a sound from her. What did the police want?"

"Questions about a fire nearby. I don't think they're onto the fair."

Jan nodded and let them in. She stood on the step for a minute or two, shaking her head.

"I don't like them hanging around like this. Maybe they're sussing the situation ready for the eviction?"

"Maybe," Paul shrugged. "But why should they come at this time of day? More likely they're on the prowl for any midsummer evil-doing. Perhaps they're feeling snubbed because they weren't invited to guard Stonehenge from the hordes."

Jan sighed. She shut and bolted the door. Katherine went upstairs, where Niamh was still fast asleep. Paul came up behind her, and slid his hands inside her dress. She leaned back against him. He kissed her shoulders. She tipped her head back, and he kissed her throat.

"Careful. We'll wake her." Katherine started giggling.

"Not if we're quiet. Come over here." They collapsed together on an old mattress by the wall, stifling laughter.

"I fancy you like crazy," he said, wrapping his legs around hers, caressing her neck.

"I fancy you like crazy too." She climbed on top of him and covered his face with kisses.

"What's happened? You never used to," he said. "Not for ages and ages."

"I don't know. Are you complaining?"

"No! Certainly not."

"Then be quiet." She stopped his mouth with a kiss, a taste at once sweet and corrupt, then she reached back to undo his jeans. Outside, the police car cruised lazily down the lane, to the main road.

In the hour after sunrise people drifted from the sacred sites to the stone valley. Some came in cars and vans, which quickly choked the lane. Some walked across the fields, to sit among the stones, to sleep or drink, or talk. Traveller girls, crowned with sprays of ivy, accompanied dreadlocked young men, with beads in their hair. Tidier pagan people had driven from Bristol and Bath, dripping with silver jewellery, robed in red and purple. The Morris men appeared, dancing amongst the assembly, speaking with the visitors. The girl acrobats pranced and pirouetted, streaming hair and rags of brightly coloured silk. The musicians arrived from the long barrow, with the jugglers and drummers, and a fire-eater spraying flames from his mouth like a dragon, orange-gold against the heavy grey sky.

Paul and Katherine lay in the cottage, dozing and kissing. When Niamh awoke, she clambered across to her parents, and lay on her mother, her face pressed into Katherine's chest, one hand resting on Paul's shoulder. Conscious the Mumming was overdue they roused themselves and hastily helped each other with their costumes, much to Niamh's delight. They left the cottage in a hurry, trotting up to the copse with Niamh perched on Paul's hip.

They needn't have worried. Owain and Elaine were still dressing, and there was no sign of Jo at all. They asked Violet, whey-faced, still tripping, but she could only tell them he had disappeared into the night. Elaine fretted and cursed.

"Pretty stupid, wasn't it? You and Jo shooting out your brains like that. You don't know what he's like. Are you up to this performance?" she snapped. Violet appeared to be on the verge of tears. She plucked at her hair anxiously.

"Stop worrying," Owain said. "He'll be here. Get yourself ready. It doesn't matter if we're late."

"We're already late," Elaine said.

"So what? It's of no consequence. Enjoy yourself. The hard work's done." Owain turned to Katherine, already hidden by her costume.

"How are you, Katherine?" he asked.

"Fine," she said. Her voice had a curious tone. It pulled Owain up short. He looked at her closely. He also looked at Paul. Unthinkingly he moved away from them.

"Look!" Elaine beckoned. "Owain. They're celebrating a handfasting. Down amongst the stones."

A flaxen-haired maiden with a coronet of flowers, and a tall young man in a purple velvet jacket were standing together before one of the white-clad greybeards. He was summoning witnesses from the circle of people gathered around them. Owain looked at Elaine.

"Shall we?" he said. Elaine looked at him and grinned.

"Do I understand that to be a proposal?"

"Yes."

She hesitated, but she couldn't stop herself smiling all the while.

"Then I accept. We must be quick!" They arranged their disguises. Then they walked down the hill into the valley holding hands. They attracted much attention, cheers and greetings. They approached the handfasting circle. As they drew near, the crowd opened up to let them through. The pagan priest looked up, taken aback at first, then clearly delighted.

"Welcome," he said, holding out his hands to them. "The King of the Woods and the Queen of May? Have you come to be handfasted too?"

"We have," Owain said. The flaxen-haired maiden, thunder stolen, looked a little disgruntled. They stood, all four, in the centre of the gathering as the priest began his welcome anew.

Owain gazed at Elaine with unbridled admiration. She was dressed in a long, plain gown of her habitual white. Her hair hung unfettered, a pour of black, as sleek as water over her shoulders. She had fashioned a crown of dogroses, honeysuckle and dark, shining ivy which trailed over her brow and hair. Her face was painted white, decorated with flowers, swirls of black for her eyebrows, around her eyes. Her lips as red as holly berries. But she was indeed well matched. Owain stood bare-chested in the morning cool, his hair loose, his skin patterned with foliage just a little smudged. He was wearing a head-dress made of hazel and willow, thin stems woven together with brown twine, like a helmet leaving his eyes and mouth uncovered, but tall around his head, covered in leaves.

The priest asked if anyone present knew of any reason why the couples should not be married. The wind lifted in response. The leaves rustled, but nobody spoke. He bound their intertwined wrists with a cord. Then he drew a long dagger from his belt and cut them free. The crowd cheered, and a horn full of mead was passed round. The priest began to chant:

"Green is gold. Fire is Wet. Fortunes told. Dragons met."

The gathering took up the refrain in a ragged chorus, which swelled into a crescendo.

"What does it mean?" Elaine whispered.

"It's an old Midsummer verse," Owain said. "About Midsummer magic. Wife."

"Don't you dare call me that in public, d'you hear? I'm your mystic, spiritual wife. Don't start getting all possessive on me, will you," she said. Owain looked nonplussed. The priest turned to them.

"Not bickering already are we?" he asked good-humouredly. Elaine scowled her darkest scowl, and the man looked away in alarm.

"Come on," Owain said, tugging her away. "Let's see if Jo's back, shall we?"

The sky was shuttered with unbroken cloud, deepening in colour, now slate grey, here and there a sallow yellow. The sun was masked. The colours of grass and leaf were faded and drab. The fair-goers sensed an oppression, but looking one to another they perceived they had not suffered in the same manner. The land was closing in. The cloud pressed down. But here on the face of the earth, the assembly of travellers and hopeful pagans, the students and protestors, were strangely enlarged and illuminated. The eyes of the Morris men, seemingly lit from within, glowed like the stained windows of a church, jade and amber and crimson. As they skipped and danced through the gathering they leaked an intangible glamour. It seeped like mist into eyes and mouths. The coarse face of a dreadlocked waif began to glimmer, white as a marble. She looked up and smiled, with the blank face of a Bottecelli angel. Here, the leaves of an ivy coronet shone like emerald, and the lips of the flaxen bride were red as coral, as she sat upon a wether and began to sing. The priest, dagger in his belt, rose to his feet and began to proclaim in tongues, his hoary locks fluttering like flames in the lifeless air. They looked from one to another with shining eyes, as though a veil had fallen, as though they had wakened to brightness after long years in the muddy twilight of a tomb. They walked like jewels, iridescent, transformed.

The mummers gathered near the copse, one body composed of ill-matched parts, yet still recognizably a whole. The Doctor appeared, just as the Fool took up his drum and strode through the valley leading the mummers through the crowd. The leaves painted on his face twitched as he walked. The shoots growing from his mouth pressed against his cheeks. The Fool beat a slow rhythm, matching the steps of the players. He was followed by the Maiden, cold and white as a snowdrop. Her eyes were turned to the ground. Behind her the Old Woman, her body bent and thin, arms like winter branches, black with ice. Her cloak was stitched with old feathers, the skulls and bones of birds hung around her neck, glittering oddly with sequins. She nursed a bundle in her arms. Then the Soldier, very tiny, in a red military jacket emblazoned with gold, a helmet with a plume of black horsehair, long leather boots, and a mask like a skull with glass jewels in its eyes. The Doctor next, dressed like an angel in a torn wedding dress, a stream of white netting for wings and a blank mask upon his face, the colour of alabaster. At the rear, Belzebub, in a long red robe with the face of a gargoyle, brandished upon a staff the broken sheep's skull, cleaned and polished but stinking still. The pitted bone was painted with swirls of silver, and two red roses were stuffed in its empty eyes. Glossy ribbons fluttered from its brow.

People gathered together in their wake, quiet and expectant. The glamour focussed on the mummers. Silence spilled about them. The Fool ceased drumming. He put down the drum and stood upon the Speaker's Stone.

"Open your door and let me in," he cried. His voice was fierce and amplified. The Bottecelli angel shivered.

"I beg your favour for to win,
Whether I rise, stand or fall,
I'll do my duty to please you all.
Room, room, it's room I require.
Step forth, sweet maid,
The bride that I desire."

The Fool jumped down from the stone, and drew back. The Maiden stepped
forward, head bent modestly. Then she looked up and spoke with a voice like ice.

"I am Mary, Mary is my name.
Is it my hand in marriage that you claim?"

She turned to the Fool, holding out her hand, but the Old Woman leapt out
and clawed at her sleeve. She clutched the bundle under her arm and called out:

"Hold fast! This Fool is not so free.
This child is his. The Fool belongs to me!"

She lifted the roll of rag and displayed it to the crowd. The crude face of the
Punch puppet grinned out from a pink lacy bonnet. The Maiden fell back,
distraught. The Fool accosted the crone in anger:
"Your daughter's babe is not a child of mine!" he cried, but the Old Woman
persisted:
"You lie! My son will prove your crime." As she spoke, the Soldier put her
hand to the hilt of her silver sword.

"I am a soldier, Slasher is my name,
Sword and buckle by my side I'm bound to win the game."

The Fool responded:

"Draw forth your sword and fight.
Draw forth your purse and pay.
Satisfaction we will have
Before you go away."

He drew a slender wooden stave from his belt, and the two began to battle,
wood against cold metal. They darted around the stones, the dimiuitive soldier
skipping about the Fool, sword flashing in the gloom. Then the Soldier was
knocked to the ground, and the Fool stood over her, stave raised high.

"Stand off, stand off, for your time draws nigh.
Stand off you dog, for now you die!"

He thrust the rod into the soldier's side. It slid through her body, and pierced
the earth beneath. Brilliant blood welled from the wound and dripped upon the

grass. The crowd were fixed, motionless. The Soldier sobbed once, and was still. The Old Woman rushed over and cradled her son's head in her lap, a bird-like *mater dolorosa*, in her dull cloak of feathers. She raised her face to the dim heavens and lamented:

"Oh cruel, cruel Christian, what hast thou done?
Thou hast killed and wounded mine only son.
Doctor, Doctor! Ten pounds for a Doctor!"

Right on cue, the seraphic Doctor minced in, his wedding dress about him like a cloud.

"I am a Doctor good and rare,
I've travelled this country far and near.
Italy, Scotland, France and Spain.
I can cure that man that lays there slain."

The Old Woman regarded him.
"What pains can you cure most noble Doctor?" she asked.

"Hipsie, Pixie, Palsy and the Gout,
If the Old Man's in I'll fetch him out.
I 'ave a little bottle in my left hand
Sleeve waistcoat pocket called okum pokum.
'Ere Jack take a little of my nip nap
Put it up your snip snap.
Rise Jack and fight again!
Ladies and gentlemen standing round
See I've cured this man safe and sound.
I've healed his wound and cleansed his blood
And gave him something that done him good.
Ain't I Jack?"

The Soldier stood up. The blood, like spilt wine, stained the coat only.
"Yes. And I liked it too."
The Soldier bowed with a flourish. The crowd cheered and clapped, like the clattering wings of countless pigeons in the grip of the still air. Then silence fell again, like a stone. The Soldier skipped back. The Doctor lifted his hand to the Old Woman, in a gesture of blessing. Gently he took the baby from her arms. The Old Woman looked up quickly, in alarm. What was he doing?
Belzebug entered, waving the sheep's skull aloft, ribbons trailing.
"In comes I old Belzebub," he said.
"On my shoulder I carry a club."
He gestured to the staff and the skull. The rose eyes twinkled. He took the Maiden by the hand and presented her to the Fool. The couple embraced. Belzebub continued:

"In my hand a dripping pan,
Don't you think I'm a funny old man?"

The mumming was over. The lines were all spoken, a song and a bow still remaining. But nobody moved. The Maiden glanced at the Doctor, holding centre stage. He possessed the audience, although he was standing perfectly still. His net wings rose around him, diaphanous, glistening like dew. Through the mask she saw the shining of green eyes. It wasn't Jo. How could she have failed to notice? The Doctor was at least a head shorter than Jo. His hair was black and copper. Where was Jo? The Doctor turned to her. The grass hissed beneath his bare feet as he moved. He bent his head, with a touch of mockery, and presented her the bundle like a gift. The Maiden fixed her eyes on the angel, but she accepted his burden and pressed it to her chest. The Doctor backed away. The Maiden shivered. She looked at the Punch, and felt a bite like frost in her heart. Peering from the pink bonnet was the Bag Lady's wooden doll, its hank of hair falling on its face. As she stared, the stiff body seemed to twist in her arms, convulsing like a trapped animal. Then for a moment the carved face blurred, assumed soft skin, lips, a pink tongue. It smiled, reaching out a tiny fist from the rags, and its eyes flicked open. Its pupils were yellow, slit vertically like the eyes of a goat, its gaze expressive of a cold malicious humour. Elaine cried out and threw the creature from her in revulsion. It bounced on the ground, and then lay still, a piece of wood once more. The crowd burst into a frenzy of cheering and clapping, and they started to mill about. The stasis was broken. At the same instant the Morris men appeared with a drum, pipes and a fiddle, and they struck up a wild melody, dancing amongst the assembly as they played. How many were there? Four musicians, but half a dozen more frolicked about the stones, with the acrobat girls, leading the men and women into a great circle.

Owain shook his head, clearing the spell from his brain. What had happened? He picked up the doll, now inert and harmless. He showed it to Elaine, but she could not bear to look at it.

"Take it away," she said. "Whose idea of a sick joke was that? Katherine? Did you switch the dolls? Jo?" She spoke his name with special emphasis, knowing full well what face was hidden behind the mask.

"As you guessed," Spring said, revealing himself. "It is only a wooden doll. What did you see?"

"Nothing," Elaine said through gritted teeth. "So what have you done with Jo?"

"Who knows where he is. I thought I would take his part. To help you out."

"Get away from me," she said. Spring smiled sadly and curtsied in the wedding dress.

"As you wish," he said. "We'll speak again." He tripped off to join his brethren. Owain put his arms around Elaine.

"What did you see?" he asked gently. Elaine shook her head and pulled away from him. She walked towards the copse, tearing the crown of flowers from her head. Petals spilled on the grass. Owain hastened after her.

Violet was invited into the circle dance, holding hands with Dawn and Dusk. Katherine and Paul followed them, linking hands. The ring was not complete.

They moved close together in an open semi-circle, stepping forward, stepping back, inching around till Spring, at the head, changed direction and curved off into a second circle, his back now facing the centre, moving counter-clockwise, and leading the dancers after him in the figure of eight. The drumbeat accelerated. The music reached a crescendo as the dancer at the tail end joined the new circle, all backs inwards, progressing widdershins. Then the music stopped. The sky darkened, echoing with thunder. The air was charged with static, and the thin perfume of decayed flowers. The dancers dropped hands and turned around. In the centre of the circle a long white flame hovered above the ground. A thin green girl stepped from its heart. She sat upon the grass, and withdrew a pearl comb from her dress. She began to comb her hair, glancing in a little silver mirror. Then the apparition faded, leaving a pale golden radiance where she had been. Then a second figure emerged, a squat figure with the head and torso of a pig, a great chain about its neck. It gazed about, bent over, as though its head were too heavy to carry, then it too evaporated on the air and the white flame dwindled and disappeared. Another flame sprang up further down the valley, disgorging a rabble of tiny men no bigger than a hand. They ran like ants, lasting a minute or two before they vanished. Then an old hag, gaunt and naked except for a mantle of holly boughs that scratched and tormented her body. The white flames burned and died again. They breathed forth corrupt and fantastic forms which survived for a moment, or a minute, before dispersing like mist in the sun. The stone valley teemed with the dream-forms, moving amongst the fair-goers, who stared about them in a daze, not knowing if their fellows were real or insubstantial.

Then the thunder rumbled again, closer, more ominous. The clouds blackened, and were cleft by a thin blade of lightning.

Warm water splashed on Paul's face. He looked up, and the rain began to pour in a torrent. The dry ground steamed. In seconds he was soaked to the skin, hair dripping, water leaking into his eyes. All around him people were blinking and rubbing their faces, looking about them in amazement. Some dashed up the hill to the copse and the cottage. Some surrendered to the elements, enjoying the rain that fell like a grey and silver sheet to the earth. Paul scanned the valley for the flames. Were they gone? Katherine came up behind him and slipped her arms around his waist. Her skin was wet and sleek. He turned round and kissed her face, slick with rainwater. She laughed.

"Shall we go to the cottage?" she asked. "Get something to eat and pick up Niamh?"

He took her hand and turned away from the valley. What had happened? Already the memory was sliding away, slippery as a fish, impossible to hold. His thoughts latched onto his daughter, the prospect of vegetable curry and the twinge of arousal he felt as he watched rivulets of water trickling along Katherine's arm. They walked up the hill.

Just behind them a stooped goblin clad in leather hopped from a pale flickering on the air. He glanced about, scuffing his boots in the mud, before sinking away again.

CHAPTER TWENTY

Katherine stepped from darkness into daylight. She blinked in the bright light. The sun was low, wreathed in loops of mauve and magenta cloud. The vault of the sky was blue-gold, veils of colour overlayed. Above the dim horizon the atmosphere flickered like fire, pale silver and indigo, a visible discourse between the heavens and the land.

She shielded her eyes. She was standing in a forest of stone. Tall, slender columns rose about her, dark, teetering, as her head swam and her eyes adjusted to the bright light. She stepped backwards. A ruin—or a graveyard? Beneath her bare feet the grass was faded and coarse. Rank weeds clustered at the feet of pedestals, surmounted with crosses, many scarred and broken, granite and marble rimed with green. Amongst the crosses, headstones were lined like teeth, some aslant, others sunk into the earth, consumed by ivy. Katherine walked amongst the stones, where angels rested elegant feet upon fluted pillars, toes stained with lichens, fingers snapped, their smooth, empty faces mottled by the droppings of birds. The silence weighed heavy upon the still air. She trod carefully. She was vaguely conscious of her nakedness, but her body was remote. The stones hissed as she passed. Here and there she was aware of a presence, brushing against her, like a faint mist upon her mind.

She walked as in a dream, hazy and indistinct though now and then a detail, a shape or colour pierced her mind like a vision, the sparkling specks of quartz in a headstone or the curl of a cherub's battered wing. The sky filled with darkness. The night's fingers pressed into the monuments and crosses, where the last light still glowed, dull mauve and crimson. The stones glimmered, casting shadows that fell awry. Katherine shivered. She sat upon a sarcophagus the colour of ash, its cold flanks decorated with skulls and lilies in relief.

She must have fallen asleep. She opened her eyes, and the sky weighed down utterly black. She was lying curled upon her stone bed. The missing time was empty, dreamless. Was the faeryland soaking her up? Absorbing her dreams, her breath, gathering the dead skin cells she shed in her wake, the inevitable decomposition and renewal of her mortal, material body. An intercourse—a sharing, between Katherine's finite earthly self and the shifting spirit of the faeryland. She lay her head upon her arms and slept again.

When she woke a moon was sailing incandescent above the stone garden. She sensed movement, the presence that touched her before, and turning her head she saw the corrupted forms of people huddled amongst the graves. She was not alarmed. She lay upon the stone, the moonlight painting her white, picking out the bones of her thin body, filling the hollows with shadow. Her hair fanned out across her back like a cloak. One of the figures moved towards her, indistinct in the darkness. Shreds of fabric moved about its body as it walked, and when it drew nearer, the moonlight fell upon a face split in two. A woman's face, divided in a ragged line from brow to chin, ivory skull to the left and sleek skin upon the right. Her eyes glittered, two giant sapphires, and a great mane of henna-red hair fell about her shoulders. Her body was held in the ruins of a black lace dress, embroidered still with beads of jet and milky pearls, and through the rents the flesh revealed was also torn, hanging in dry ribbons from the bones. Katherine did not move. When the woman stood over her, she smiled and placed a thin, ringed hand upon Katherine's warm body. Then she turned and beckoned to her companions, who moved from the shadows, and gathered in an uneven circle about her, a mosaic of bone and rags and jewels. Katherine was neither repulsed or afraid. She awaited their ministrations with perfect equinamity. A ring of faces like marquetry, bone inlaid with lapis and agate, flesh like parchment patterned with paint. Amongst the windings of silk and tulle, dead flowers protruded from bare ribs, and silver chains were wrapped about the exposed bones of shoulders and arms.

The red-haired woman pushed Katherine over onto her back, her spine pressing into the stone slab. She stroked Katherine's hair, then she poked her sharp fingers into Katherine's eye sockets and lifted out her eyes. Katherine felt no pain, or indeed any sense of violation. She could still see. Her eyes were resting in the hands of the dead woman, and she observed herself upon the sarcophagus. She watched another of the creatures break off her hand with quick twist, snapping her feet, digging hands into her belly and lifting out viscera, gleaming a dark ruby red in the moonlight. They murmured inaudibly amongst themselves, nodding, gesturing to the patchwork remains of Katherine's body. Then the woman's hands closed about her eyes, and her vision was obsured. She felt a pressure in her eye sockets, a shuffling and reconnection in her brain. Then she could see again. She put her hands to her eyes. They were hard and smooth like stones. She looked at the woman, and realised that her own eyes were now in place in the half-face. The woman drew a mirror from her pocket and held it before Katherine. She looked into the silver surface and saw the sapphires now embedded in her own skull. Then her fellows began to cobble her body together again. They filled the cavity of her belly with roses. They replaced her hand with a bundle of dry twigs, and her feet with heavy marble feet of a felled funereal angel. Then they lifted her from the slab and stood her up.

Katherine blinked. Her vision swam. Amongst the graves she could see the shifting body of a forest. A stone cross sprouted branches and leaves. Vines thrust from the earth. The black iron railings, fencing a tomb, thickened with buds and burst into flower. When she looked at her companions, she sensed the gleam of the spirits lodged amongst the bones and rags. They were bright and malleable. The forest receded a little, though still she was aware of its presence, the barely discernible motion of leaves, the distant scent of earth and foliage. Then she saw the old grey wethers here and there amongst the graves. So she was in some sense still within the stone valley, though here the wethers were patterned with swirls and mazes. Katherine crouched and touched one gently with her human hand, causing the lines to pulse.

A flicker of golden light caught her eye. She turned to see a thin golden man sitting on the grass observing her. He was slight, like a boy, but his eyes were an unbroken black, without iris or pupil, and his skin was a pale, papery gold. He smiled. His lips were tinged with purple, like a plum. He stood up, in one fluid movement. In his face she saw a simplicity, or more, a vacancy. He seemed only partly formed. As she watched him, the golden man began to fade, though he didn't altogether disappear. She detected a golden haze about the grass where he was sitting.

"Who was that?" she asked the red-haired woman. It was the first word she had uttered, and the sound of her voice hung perilous upon the air. The woman turned to her, the fey presence shining through the half-face.

"Another visitor, " she said. Her voice was cold and clear. "Come and see." She led Katherine through the graveyard, where the echoes of the forest were evident in the dappled shadows upon the earth and the dewy brush of imperceptible grass upon her legs. She walked amongst crumbled walls and the remains of ionic columns, a nave still floored with black and white tiles. One gothic arch still stood, a green man carved in the crook between the top of the column and the curve of the archway reaching over to its completing half. The green man was embellished with fruit and birds.

"See, the sun is rising," said the woman, though even as she spoke, Katherine noticed the darkness was shrinking away. The woman stopped before a crude stone font. The water inside was brackish and foul.

"Look," she said, peering into the water. Katherine followed suit. The water cleared in an instant. She gazed into space, falling away beneath her. Down, down at the bottom she saw light, movement, a brightness far below at the bottom of a tunnel. And a figure, tall and thin like a scarecrow, wandering around in a dream, like a lost child.

"Jo," she said. "Is he here?"

"In part. He doesn't know where he is."

"Can I help him?"

"Give me your necklace." Still around her neck hung the carved bone on the thong, Crow's gift. Katherine hesitated.

"You want to help him?" the woman asked. Katherine nodded and pulled off the necklace. The woman held it over the water, where it swung slightly for a moment or two, before she let it go. The necklace sank into the murk, and then it was tumbling through the emptiness and into the light at the bottom. It disappeared.

"Will he find it?"

"He'll find it," the woman said. "Then he can find you."

They left the remains of the church. The forest was gaining ascendancy. The stones were retreating to the shadows, and the tall crosses had been swallowed by boughs and branches. They headed for a brake of aged hawthornes, bent over and tortuous but bearing bright leaves, a summer splendour upon ancient bodies. In their midst rose an elder tree, rising like a queen above her stooped cousins, decked in foliage and their last decaying remains of her spring blossom. As the graveyard faded, Katherine's guide began to alter in accord. The bones and cerements dissolved, and she walked before her like a dryad, greenish, opaque in the early sunlight. Her long hair hung down to her knees and fluttered in the breeze. Her

:yes were the colour of sloes. Her eyes. Katherine pressed her fingers to her own
:yes. The sapphires had gone. The marble feet, the twigs and roses. Her body was
:ntire. She stopped and ran her hands across her bare flesh. Her guide regarded her.

"If I go back to the graveyard?" Katherine asked.

"Your body would be as before. We are passing through. I must leave you here
with the Old Lady. If you wait, she will speak to you." The dryad backed away,
becoming ever more insubstantial, until she disappeared altogether. The last
fragments of the graveyard disappeared and Katherine sat before the elder.

She waited a long while. The sun rose high above the trees, and the forest filled
with birdsong and the movement of animals through the undergrowth. She saw
deer moving like grey shadows through the trees, and a family of fox cubs playing
near the mouth of their den in an earthy bank. Then the sun began to sink, and just
as the first star pricked out in a lake of blue sky, the elder shifted its leaves. A
shudder ran through the tree and it tossed back streams of leaves like wayward
tresses, revealing a pitted, woody hag's face. Spiky fingers poked forwards, twigs
reaching out for Katherine, who winced as they caught in her hair and scratched
her. Grey-green eyes, like knots of wood, flicked open in the trunk and stared
directly at her visitor.

"Katherine," the tree said. Her voice was deep and dry. "Katherine from the
other side. I have felt your presence through my roots. You send out ripples of
disturbance. Wherever you go the grass ripples and the stones start to rattle."

Katherine did not know what to say. The elder hag smiled, sending creases
through bark.

"You want your daughter, yes?"

Katherine nodded.

"But you don't know where to find her?"

"No. Can you help me?"

The elder paused.

"The matter is not as simple as you perceive it to be," the tree said. "We are not
as you are. We have looked through your eyes, we have touched your heart. You
think in straight lines. There is much more for you to learn and understand. Your
daughter is one element only, in a web of difficulty and imbalance. To proceed you
need to return to the beginning. "

"The beginning?"

"The dark space, the curious room."

"My journey with the faeries? You can help me remember?"

The elder bent low over Katherine. Shining on the tip of a twig was a long iron
key. Katherine lifted it free.

"My magic key," she said. "I've been looking for it. I thought it was lost."

"Turn around," the elder said. Katherine obeyed. A scene arose before her. The
mellow red of a brick wall, buried in streamers of ivy and traveller's joy. A tiny
doorway obscured by plumes of dog-rose, stretching up to a pointed arch, and a
wooden door with two long hinges and an ornate, rusty key-hole. Katherine slipped
the key into place and turned the lock. The door swung open. She stepped out to
the open space, to the past, to the copse by the Swallowhead Spring where the faeries
were waiting.

CHAPTER TWENTY ONE

The clouds hung heavy and sodden above the land, and the rain fell in grey sheets, unrelenting. The parched earth, thirsting for moisture, sucked up the rain. Once the soil was replete, the water flowed over the fields, surging into the dry ditches. The grass pushed fiercely through the ground, verdant and revived.

Violet huddled on the barrow in the copse, enfolded in a large sheet of transparent plastic. She was clammy with perspiration, in the hot, oppressive air, and her clothes were moist with rain. Rain fell onto the trees, and dripped off the leaves in a constant irregular patter. The bark was slick and slippery as ice. Within a few hours the earth beneath the trees was churned to a broken mass of mud that clung to boots and clothes. The summer idyll dissolved in the downpour.

In the wake of the rain, the midsummer gathering soon came to an end. A few people lingered on at the cottage, eating Jan's curry, drinking and smoking, some catching up on missed sleep, curled up on any spare patch of floor. Most headed home in cars and vans, tired, keen to be out of the rain. And curiously anxious to . get away...it had been a strange morning hadn't it? Did you see the Mummers? Wasn't it odd? And the circle dance? And the Morris men? And something else too...something the mind didn't like to settle on, a memory that slid away...an unpleasant atmosphere perhaps? Violet watched them trudge away, heads bowed, packs on their backs. Some had transport to retrieve from Silbury Hill and Avebury. Doubtless the Red Lion would be full of tired, gently steaming people before too long.

But what had happened before the rain? Violet pressed on the memory, digging into her mind. Jo was still missing, and she was worried. Where had he gone? She remembered the Mummer's play. With the momentary clarity of a dream, she could see Elaine casting away the wooden doll in horror. Then the circle dance, following the Morris men, and the appearance of so many uncanny creatures...it had happened, hadn't it? They were witnesses, all of them. What group hysteria had infested them? Were they the victims of a practical joker? She didn't think so. Even conjuring up the manifestations in her mind brought on a mental nausea, a helpless vertigo. Was this how Owain suffered in the proximity of the Morris men? Why had this happened? She had spent her childhood hunting for faeries, and now, in their midst, they filled her with unease, even horror. Where were the delicate winged demoiselles sitting in the bluebells? Where the frail, dancing maidens dressed in petals? Perhaps she should be searching for Jo. The rain persisted. She was tired to death, her mind still raw from the drugs and a night without sleep. So she waited, peering out from her sheet across the fields. Soon he would be back. Perhaps he would understand what had happened. She felt a faint tickle on her hand. She looked down. A huge millipede was crawling across her fingers. She snatched her hand up in a moment of revulsion, and jumped to her feet. The enormous beast fell to the grass and continued on its way unpeturbed. Violet rubbed her hand on her jeans. Had she ever seen a millipede so big? As fat as her little finger, and twice as long, surely, black and sleek in its carapace, countless legs moving in waves. She shuddered. After months in the tree house she was used to insects of various kinds, but still, the millipede was a monster. Horrible. A fly buzzed close to her face, and she flipped it away. Despite the rain, she noticed the air was thick with flies. And the grass, alive with insects unsettled by the moisture. Flooded out. She didn't fancy sitting on the ground any longer. She pulled the plastic sheet close around her and set off from the copse to the cottages.

She walked down the lane, avoiding the mud-brown puddles, head downcast, but the rain still pelting into her face. Half way down, she heard the sound of a car splashing through the pot-holes. She looked up. The police car had returned. As it moved along the lane, its smooth white flanks were coated in mud. It pulled up outside the squat, and the same two police officers climbed out and strode up the garden path to the front door. Violet followed them cautiously. They hammered on the door. Doubtless the occupants were debating on the wisdom of letting them in. Violet stood behind them and coughed. She noticed their shiny black boots were also splattered with mud. The older man turned round when he heard her.

"Good morning. I'm Sergeant Gerard, and this is PC Lamb. Could you persuade your friends to let us in?" He spoke smoothly, though the irritation in his voice was barely concealed.

"Perhaps no-one's in," she said.

"I can hear them talking," he said quickly. She saw the rain soaking into his coat. A shower of fat drops fell from the old porch and wetted his hat.

"Look," he said. "This isn't anything to do with an eviction. We need to ask some questions. Of course we can't enter without your premission, but it would not be a problem obtaining a search warrant, and it would make all our lives a little easier if I could have an informal chat about an incident that happened near here last night, okay?"

Violet paused and pondered, shifting her weight from one foot to another. She sucked on her lip-ring.

"I'll see what I can do," she nodded. She stepped forward and banged on the door.

"They just want to ask some questions," she shouted. "I think we should let them in." She heard more movement inside, a hasty discussion. Then the bolts were drawn and the door was unlocked. Jan stood in the doorway. She eyed the policemen with distinct hostility.

"Is this the same incident you were asking about early this morning?" she said. "Didn't you get all you wanted then?"

"Just a few more questions," Gerard asserted. He moved forward, as though expecting Jan to step out of his way, but Jan remained where she was.

With the officer's face just inches from her own, she said in a low voice, "I hope this won't take too long."

She paused a moment longer, then she stepped back into the house. The two policemen followed her, with Violet just behind them. Many of the visitors had made a hasty exit through the back door, because apart from Jan, the only people remaining in the room were Paul and Katherine, with Niamh, and a couple of young lads from Swindon still sleeping off their cider from the night before. Jan bustled about clearing up paper plates, bottles and beer cans in a black bin liner.

"Must have been some party," the younger officer sniffed. No-one made any reply.

"Mr Matravers," his colleague tried, "We meet again. We have already accounted for your whereabouts between midnight and three last night I believe."

Paul returned his stare but declined to add any further comment. Gerard nodded.

"Were there any strangers around the protest site last night? Any newcomers?"

"Lots," Jan said. "It was midsummer's eve, you know? People come from all over the country to celebrate with us." ·

The officer kept his attention fixed on Paul. He ruminated.

"Let me elaborate," he said. "A number of earth movers and diggers, locked in a secure compound, were burned in a fire last night. Damage estimated at hundreds of thousands of pounds. At this stage we are considering it was an act of arson."

"What a pity," Jan commented through clenched teeth. "Do I presume from your presence here that these wonderful machines were destined to plough up the land for the bypass?"

"Well, they were owned by Tarcost," he answered. Jan flashed a look of triumph at Paul and Katherine.

Then the front door rattled. They heard a shout.

"Let me in!"

"It's Jo," Violet cried, jumping to her feet. She ran to the door and pulled it open. Standing on the doorstep, impossibly thin and bedraggled, Jo was soaked to the skin and dripping with water. His face was slick with rain. His shirt clung to his bones.

"Jo! Come in! Where've you been?" she cried, dragging him into the house. Then she stopped. Jo was staring at the policemen.

"Yes," the sergeant added. "Where have you been? Specifically between midnight and three in the morning."

Jo blanched. He opened his mouth, and shut it again without saying a word. His pupils were still a little dilated. He looked very pale and tired. His boots and jeans were covered in filth. His silence seemed to stretch for hours. Then at last he replied, in a rush.

"Running about in the fields," he said. "Getting into the landscape, you know? Had a bit too much to drink I think." He was trying to look confident.

"Why don't you have a cup of tea, Jo? Dry yourself off a bit." Violet tried to usher Jo into the kitchen but the policeman stopped him leaving.

"So no-one was with you?"

Jo shook his head.

"Could you tell me your name?" he asked. Jo hesitated.

"Jo Hoblyn," he said.

"Are you from this area?"

"Bristol."

The younger officer, Lamb, made a note. Violet and Jo retreated to the kitchen.

The visit began to drag on. Paul was convinced Gerard suspected his involvement, though he couldn't understand why. Gerard asked the same questions again and again–wanting to know exact times, precise locations. The stone valley? Where exactly in the stone valley? How could he be so sure of the time? Wasn't it dark? In the end, Jan lost patience and asked the officers to leave. Gerard complied.

"Thank you for your help," he said. "We've kept our distance from the protest. You've got the right to make your feelings known, but this is a different matter. A whole new league. We won't be letting it go."

When they departed, Jan shut and locked the door behind them. She grinned.

"So the event wasn't a total washout," she said. "We failed to make any money, but Tarcost suffered a major loss instead. I wonder who did it?"

Paul shrugged. Jan pondered. She rolled a perfect spliff and lit up. Then she frowned.

"On second thoughts," she said, "I don't suppose it's going to help the profile of the protest. Until now, we've been fairly law-abiding–apart from the car incident. How are the Locksbury people going to react? Won't they suspect it was one of us? We don't want them alienated. Protecting the land is one thing. This kind of destruction is something else entirely. Maybe our mysterious eco-terrorist hasn't done us such a favour after all."

Paul shuffled restlessly.

"What do you think, Paul?" she asked.

"I think you're right," he said. She was still regarding him, wanting more. He was struggling for words.

"I think you're right," he said again. "Tarcost will have more machinery. They'll tighten up security. We can expect them to be a little more belligerent, and we'll have all the press round again looking for a new angle on the road protest."

As he spoke he realised his perspective on the night's adventure had entirely changed. Had he been a fool? How was it that Stuart could always make his argument seem so incontrovertible? Anxiety opened like a pit in his belly. He felt a prickle of perspiration on his face. Why had he done it? What if he was found out? At least he could be certain of Stuart's discretion and careful planning. But how could he be sure they hadn't been seen? Hadn't the police regarded him with suspicion? They certainly seemed to know his name–but then they would, wouldn't they? He was the leading force in the protest. He couldn't give in to paranoia. But now they were suspicious of Jo, feckless Jo, who apparently hadn't a clue where he had been last night. Paul took a deep breath. Katherine placed her hand upon his thigh and turned to him.

"Are you okay?" she said. He nodded.

"Yes," he said. "Tired, that's all."

"Shall we go home?"

"Yes. Better help Jan clear up here though."

Jan shook her head.

"Don't worry. Violet can give me a hand. You go home."

Katherine picked up Niamh and opened the front door. Paul gave Jan a hug.

"See you later," he said. Then he followed Katherine into the garden, and the rain. The car was parked at the bottom of the Old Lane. Katherine was some steps ahead of him. As he walked, Paul was oblivious to the rain, lost in thought. Were the police singling him out? Waiting for him to make some incriminating step? Did they have some file on him, as active protestor, marked out for his contacts with direct action groups? Surely not. He didn't subscribe to conspiracy theories. He remembered some of his student friends fearing their telephones were tapped by security forces because they were members of the SWP. Ye gods! The toytown revolutionaries—as if anyone cared what they were doing. He was not going to succumb to such ridiculous anxiety.

A step beside him. The sound of boots, on the stones and the patina of dust turned to mud. Paul looked up. A dark blue suit? His heart seemed to stop for a moment. He took a quick breath.

"Mr Matravers."

Paul stopped and turned to the speaker.

"What now?" he said. He covered the tremor in his voice with a show of anger. He looked directly at the speaker, into green eyes, brightly coloured.

"Oh," he said. "I'm sorry. I thought you were someone else."

Rain dripped from the brim of Spring's hat, though oddly he didn't appear to be wet.

"It's okay," he said. "I thought I'd walk with you a way, that's all."

Katherine, at the end of the lane, was strapping Niamh into her car seat. Paul saw her glance up, as he talked with Spring. Spring's bells jingled as he walked.

"I suppose you guys will be heading off, now the fair's over," Paul said.

"Maybe," Spring shrugged, "but we like it here. We like you all. I think we may remain for a while longer."

"It's pretty miserable camping in this kind of weather."

"Oh, I don't mind that. Are you trying to get rid of us?"

"No, no. Of course not. We need all the support we can get. The eviction will soon be upon us."

"Ah yes. The eviction. I'm sure we can help you with that—if you wish."

They stopped alongside the car. Paul unlocked his car door. Then he stood still, waiting for Spring to move away. Spring smiled. Paul smiled back.

"Well? Do you wish?" said Spring.

"Wish what?"

"For us to stay and help with the protest."

"Yes, of course," Paul said. "You don't need my permission. As I said, we need all the help we can get."

Spring jumped up and down excitedly, like a child.

"I have something for you," he said. He reached into the pocket of his waistcoat. He drew out a small object clenched tighly in his fist. He put both hands behind his back.

"Which hand?" he asked. Paul sighed. This was infuriating. The rain had soaked through his shirt and was dripping off his nose. Katherine was waiting for him, and this preposterous child-man was playing silly games.

"I don't know. That one," he said crossly, pointing to the left. Spring tossed his head, strands of black and copper hair falling behind his shoulders.

"Good guess," he said. He handed Paul a tiny black box, made of wood, encased in an elaborate lattice of silver vines and flowers.

"It's beautiful. Thank you. Why give it to me?"

Spring shook his head and moved away.

"I can see your dreams," he said, as he walked away. "They cling to you—like smoke." Then he was gone, striding up the lane, apparently immune to the rain and the mud. Paul looked at the box, sitting in the palm of his hand. The lid was decorated with a single, silver eye. He lifted it cautiously. A flame leapt from the box, and hovered flickering above it. Paul nearly dropped the box in surprise. How did it work? Why wasn't the flame extinguished by the rain? He closed the lid and opened it again. The flame rose as before, like a flower, its roots in the blackness held in the body of the box. Paul held his hand near the flame. He couldn't detect heat. He moved his fingers closer and closer, right into the flame. He felt nothing, a faint tingling perhaps...then the flames sprang up all around him. The smell of petrol stung his nostrils, and he saw the blackened shapes of metal machines, but they moved, creeping away from the conflagration like injured animals, struggling out from the heat, bodies charred, paint blistering.

Gone. In a moment. Paul shut the lid. He opened it again. The flame flickered as before. What had he seen? His thoughts raced. Did Spring know? Had he followed them? How could he possibly know? What had he ment about dreams?

No. Did he credit Spring with the powers of a magician, an illusionist? Spring was a strange man, no doubt. Somehow he had conjured up the puppet-ghouls they had witnessed that very morning, though he couldn't quite fathom how he had done it. Marionettes? Some kind of projection? He didn't like to think on it too much. The day's dawning was a long time ago. They had all been out of it, in one way or another, lack of sleep, drink, drugs—open to suggestion. Receptive to the games and tricks of the Morris men—and the Mummers—he himself, of course, had taken on the mantle of Belzebub for a while. A magical morning. A time of deceit and disguise.

He heard a knock on the inside of the car window.

"Are you going to stand in the rain all day?" Katherine looked amused rather than irritated, but Paul jumped into the car and started the engine.

"Look what Spring gave me," he said, dropping the box in Katherine's lap. "I've no idea how it works."

As he drove off, Katherine opened the lid.

"How what works?"

"The flame."

"What flame?"

Paul glanced from the road to the box in Katherine's hand.

"Oh. When I opened it just now a flame rose out, as though there was a candle inside. No heat though."

"Must be special to you, my dear," she said. "It doesn't do anything for me."

Jo and Violet were sitting in the old kitchen, at the back of the cottage. It was the ugliest room in the house. The cupboards had been ripped out, leaving patches of broken plaster. Layers of paint and wallpaper surrounded wounds of raw brickwork. Wiring dangled from the walls for a cooker long gone. The cracked sink, not deemed worthy of saving, was full of dirty mugs and saucepans, huddled in a puddle of cold water from the plastic container on the red-tiled floor.

They were sitting on the grey stone step in the doorway. Jo removed his boots and socks.

"Nowhere to dry these, I suppose?" he said.

"Put them by the fire in the front room. It's still going from Mum's cooking this morning. I'll put more water on and make tea. You look like you could do with some."

When she returned Jo was still on the step. He was shivering, and his gaze was vacant.

"Jo?" she said. "Jo?"

After a moment he came to himself.

"What?"

"Are you okay? What happened to you last night? Why did you just run off like that? I was worried sick."

"I'm sorry," he said. "It's hard to explain. I was there. In faeryland."

"Hmm. Some trip. You missed the Mummer's Play. Spring had to take your part."

Jo didn't seem to hear.

"Look what I found," he said. He held up a thong, dangling a tiny bone, intricately patterned.

"It's Katherine's," Violet said. "Where did you find it?" On the kitchen floor she noticed half a dozen woodlice scuttling through the dust. Jo sighed.

"It's hard to explain," he said. "When I was tripping I had a new idea about why I am like I am."

"What do you mean? What do you think you are like?"

"Lacking."

Violet laughed.

"We all feel we're lacking, sometimes. You've got an inferiority complex you mean."

"No," said Jo impatiently. "It's more than that. Will you listen to me?"

"I'm sorry. Carry on."

"It occurred to me that pieces of me are missing—as though I'd been sliced up, and these fragments lead their own autonomous lives in different places. But all these different slices, although they are complete in a certain respect, are thinner, less substantial, than they should be."

"You seem pretty solid to me. Isn't this some false illumination brought on by the acid? A delusion? You know, Elaine told me off for giving it to you. She said I didn't know what you were like."

"Stuff Elaine," he said bitterly. "She doesn't know what I'm like either."

"So where are the missing slices?" Violet loosened her shirt. The air was stifling. Humid like a jungle, with the rain pattering on on the broken window.

The virginia creeper growing on the back wall of the house pushed questing tendrils through the half pane. Surely it had grown overnight? It must have been thirsty, waiting for the rain. The dark leaves of a fruit tree pressed against another window over the sink. A spider crouched in the heart of its web, spun in the corner of the empty doorway above Violet's head. Most of the doors had been plundered. Violet shivered uneasily. She felt choked and claustrophobic.

"One piece is in acid land, I think. That's why I feel so at home there. For a time Normal-Jo and Acid-Jo are reunited. Twice the size."

"Acid land? It's not a place, Jo. It's a frame of mind."

"You think that makes it any less a place? I don't think of geography only in terms of road maps."

"If I let that one pass, I suppose you're going to tell me that another slice of Jo lives in Faeryland?"

"Yes!" said Jo, triumphant. "Faery Jo. Why else do you think the Morris men recognised me? And I them, for that matter. It all makes sense to me now. They know me for one of them, in some sense. Not a very good faery, not a whole one, anymore than I'm a whole Normal Jo. I live between all these places, and sometimes in extreme situations—"

"Like when you've blasted your brain with drugs?"

"—when I'm in an altered state of awareness, I can reach through to the other pieces. I can join up. Then I can see through the eyes of my fellow me's." Jo sat back, looking pleased with himself. Violet frowned, sceptical.

"It's a nice idea," she said. "But I'm not, as you know, convinced about the Morris men being faeries."

"But Violet, I've been there. I looked into Faeryland."

Violet laughed again.

"Oh Jo," she said. "Lots of people say that when they've taken stuff. It's the same sad old dope dreams, I'm afraid."

Jo looked hurt. Physically he shrank away from her. She nudged him with her arm.

"I'm sorry," she said. "Take no notice. Despite all the regalia I'm not a subscriber to all the dippy-hippy stuff I'm afraid. Defying appearances, I'm a pretty down-to-earth kind of person. Go on. Tell me what Faeryland was like. And tell me where you found Katherine's necklace." Jo sighed. He was downcast. Violet slipped her arm through his.

"Go on," she said. "Please." A huge black beetle scurried from a hole at the bottom of the wall. At the broken window, a strand of the creeper waved up and down in a breeze. A small pool of rain water was accumulating on the floor below the sill.

Jo clasped his hands together.

"Well, I was walking along a bright path, through the stone valley. Somehow this path runs through this world and the faery world at the same time. I jumped off the path into the other place. The trouble was, I wasn't entirely there. Partly I could see this place, and partly the faery world too—vaguely, like a dream."

"What was it like?"

"A graveyard."

"A graveyard? I thought Faeryland was a green-wood—or a shining palace. Or a garden."

Jo shook his head.

"I think, I feel, that Faeryland is more complicated than that. It isn't fixed and stable. It holds many, many places all linked together. I just saw one of them."

"What was it like, this graveyard?"

"Shadowy. Beautiful and decayed. And undead people in rags of black lace walking about with jewels and flowers. I couldn't see much."

"Where Goths go when they die, huh?"

"You still don't believe me, do you?"

"The necklace?"

"I think I met Katherine," he said. "I'm sure I saw her in the graveyard. For a moment I was very much present there, but I faded out. Then I was walking in the stone valley again, not wholly in any place, but I saw her face, and she dropped this to me."

"Dropped it?"

"It fell down to me. I caught it."

"Well that is weird, but as for Katherine—she's here. You saw her yourself, with Paul and offspring. She was here for the Mummer's Play as well," Violet said. Jo was lost in thought for a time.

"Perhaps I'd better talk with her," he said. "She can tell me how she lost her necklace, can't she? Anyway. How did the play go down? What did I miss?"

Having played the sceptical part with Jo, how could she describe the events of the morning? What were the events of the morning? In truth, she wondered how much the drugs had affected her own perception.

"As it happens, I saw faeries too," she said. "I think. It was a very strange morning. A weird atmosphere. Everything looked different. The play went very well, though Spring surprised us emerging from your costume. Then dancing and music, the Morris men led us into a circle dance, and somehow, we started to see bizarre creatures emerging from the air. I don't know how they did it. It's hard to remember clearly. I was still pretty out of it. I saw a maiden, and goblins, and a pig creature. They appeared, and after a few seconds, they vanished again. Puppets maybe. Children dressed up."

"What children?"

"Oh I don't know. I'm speculating."

"Perhaps they really were faeries. Like the Morris men. Something is happening. For some reason the veil separating the worlds has become weakened? Maybe the road building, all the destruction. The faeries are creeping through. Isn't this what Owain and Elaine were saying? I'd better find them. I've got to tell them what happened to me."

Violet stamped her feet.

"Oh Jo, don't!" she cried. "It's all bullshit. Stop it! Listen to yourself. This doesn't happen!" She rubbed her bare arms. Her skin itched and prickled and she was sweating profusely. Hordes of woodlice were climbing the walls, marching on tiny grey legs, and she found them utterly repulsive. She stood up.

"What's happening to this place?" she said, almost in tears. "It's seething. Insects everywhere. I hate it!"

"Hey, Violet, what's up?" Jo looked around. "It's no worse than usual. It hasn't worried you before."

But Violet began to scratch her head. Her face turned very pale. She stifled a sob.

"Jo," she whispered. "Jo. Look in my hair will you?" She sat down again, holding herself. Jo ran his fingers through the braids and curls, the astonishing, beautiful tumble of coppery hair. He parted it carefully, peering at the white scalp beneath. Her hair was alive with headlice. The tiny brown beasts ran for cover whenever he lifted her mane. The size of a match head, quick and purposeful, feeding, vampiric, on the blood of her scalp. Clusters of eggs were visible, stuck at the roots of her hair, and the pearly white cases of eggs already hatched.

"Tell me, Jo," she said, as though she already knew what he was seeing. "How bad is it?"

"Rather bad," he said. "In fact, I should say very bad. How can you not have noticed before? Your head must be itching like crazy."

"It is now," she said. "It wasn't before. Have you seen me scratching?" She felt very small and sad. Her white face lost ten years. She curled up like a child.

"It'll have to go," she said quietly.

"Go?"

"My hair. You can treat headlice with chemical potions, or combing with conditioner and a special comb. But my hair is full of dreadlocks and braids. There is no way I could treat it effectively. It'll have to go." Tears ran down her face.

"Get my Mum will you?" she said. Jo, looking helpless and heartbroken on her behalf, went to the front room and summoned Jan.

Mother and daughter drove off together in the van, back to the flat in Marlborough. Jo stood alone outside the cottage, now the sole guardian of the protest headquarters. The Swindon lads had disappeared. It was up to him to hold the fort, to keep the place secure. He went inside and locked up. He didn't feel comfortable on his own. The building's decay, so picturesquely disguised with paintings and flowers, became more evident now he was on his own. The kitchen was squalid. The front room was now full of mud and Jan's half-filled bin bags. He headed upstairs, and curled up on a mattress that smelt of damp and age. Weariness settled on his body like a shroud, but try as he might, he couldn't fall asleep. His fingers and arms began to tingle painfully, as they often did if he was tired. Poor circulation. He shook them, waggled his hands about, aching for sleep to relieve him. Poor Violet. He thought of her suffering the ministrations of scissors. Her crowning glory. The phrase seemed particularly apt. The tingling spread to his feet, so he was obliged to get up and walk around the room. It was tortuous, to be thus afflicted when tired, if the affliction then stopped you from sleeping. He marched up and down.

Someone knocked on the door. He raced down the stairs and opened it without a thought. A tall man in a green waxed jacket was standing outside. He was accompanied by five colleagues, similarly attired. Before Jo had a chance to shut the door or say a word, the man thrust a piece of type-written paper into his hands. Jo stood open-mouthed with surprise. The man spoke quickly, and he couldn't entirely grasp what he was saying. Without awaiting a reply, the men turned away and walked briskly back down the path. When they reached the garden gate, they turned left and headed up to the copse. Jo glanced down at the sheet of paper. It was a notice of eviction. Without reading further, he chased after the men, overtaking them, and running up the lane as fast as he could, shouting out a warning to the others.

CHAPTER TWENTY TWO

After lunch Niamh fell asleep on the sofa, a biscuit still clutched in her fist, crumbs clinging to her chin and the front of her dress. The rain beat upon the outside of the windows. Plates and mugs were gathered on the table, with slices of apple and cheese, Niamh's scattering of raisins. Paul was sitting on an armchair, with Katherine facing him upon his lap. Her arms were wrapped around his neck with her head resting on his shoulder, breathing the soft scent of his skin. Paul was warm and drowsy, ready for sleep but loathe to move her away. She shifted and looked up into his face. She kissed him gently, once, twice. She drew back slightly, and smiled.

"You kiss like an angel," he said. She tipped her head back and laughed, so her hair brushed against his hands, holding her waist.

"Like a sinner you mean." She kissed him again. "Have you had enough of my kisses yet? Shall I shift?"

"No. Certainly not. I think you are quite precisely where you should be."

"Good. So do I." She pressed herself against him, and he squeezed her tightly. The telephone rang. Paul sighed. He let it ring unanswered for a few seconds. Should he leave it? The noise persisted. Grudgingly he untangled himself and hurried to the phone. It was Violet.

"The bailiffs called this morning. They served the eviction notice," he heard her say, her voice terse and angry. She sounded close to tears.

"Are you okay? Was there trouble?"

"I don't know. I wasn't even there. Mum and I were here at the flat. We missed it."

Paul considered. Was that the reason she was so upset? Because she'd been absent?

"How did you hear about it?" he asked.

"Jo called. He was alone in the cottage. There were only a few people at the copse as well. Everyone was in a state of disarray after the fair. Do you think that's why they called today?"

"I don't know. Don't worry about it. We knew it was coming. We'll just have to step up preparations for the eviction." He heard a muffled discussion in the background.

"Hold on," Violet said. "Mum wants a word." The phone was passed over.

"Hello, Paul? I think we should have a meeting as soon as possible." Jan's suggestion caught him off balance.

"Well, yes," he said, half choked. "How about tomorrow evening?" He waited for an unpleasant reaction. He knew it wasn't what she had in mind.

"Tomorrow? This is a crisis. We've been waiting for this for weeks. Don't you think we should make it tonight?"

"But everyone is exhausted. What kind of attendance could we expect?" he said. Even over the telephone he could tell she was surprised. He certainly didn't want to go out and organise a meeting for tonight.

"But, Paul, I think this is important," she persisted.

"You're right, it is very important. However, meeting tonight or tomorrow night is not going to make any difference, and frankly, I want to stay in tonight."

"This is most unlike you," she said. Paul dug in his heels.

"Well, you organise it for tonight then. I'm just not up to it. You can chair the meeting. It's about time someone else had a turn. Weren't you the one telling me to take things a bit easier?" His suggestion was met by silence. He could imagine her chagrin. He hadn't skipped a meeting since the bypass scheme came before the planners three years ago.

"I suppose you're right," she said, at last. "We'll leave it till tomorrow. I think I'm going to head back to the site though. I understand they're feeling a bit unsupported. Perhaps you could manage to call Locksbury Alliance people and let them know what's happened?"

Paul sighed.

"Yes, of course," he said heavily. When Jan had rung off he spent half an hour making five calls. Each new call required a few minutes explanation and a deal of reassurance. When he had finished, he discovered Katherine was lying asleep on their bed. He carried Niamh gently to her cot, and lay down beside his partner. Katherine was curled on her side, facing him. Her breathing was slow and even. A wisp of golden hair had fallen across her face. Her lips were slightly parted, raspberry pink and very smooth. Her skin possessed a particular dewy sleekness. He wanted to stroke her, but refrained for fear of disturbing her sleep. Despite his weariness he didn't want to stop watching her, as though she might disappear if he let his attention slip. She shifted and frowned, her eyes still closed, and rolled over onto her back. As she moved he caught a thread of scent, her breath, her body. He propped himself onto his elbow. He wanted her even now, seeing her limbs so soft and brown, the delicate skin of her throat and the thick hair falling across the white pillow. She did look different. As he watched her face, relaxed in sleep, he was puzzled. The planes and curves of her face had altered. Was he looking too hard? Was his close scrutiny confusing him? She flicked open her eyes, looking straight into his. Strange eyes. Who was she? No. For a fragment of an instant only. Then familiarity asserted itself again. She peeped at him sleepily. She smiled.

"Hello," she said. "Did you get it all sorted?" She stretched out her arms to him. He wriggled close to her, holding her hot body close to his.

"Yes," he said.

"Do they want you to go out again?"

"Yes. But I told them it'd have to wait till tomorrow."

"Good. I don't want you going anywhere." She slipped her hands into his tee-shirt.

"Don't worry," he said, and he fell asleep at last, with her hands pressed against his chest, and his face in her hair, breathing the scent of soil and petals.

He was woken by Niamh an hour later. He collected her from the cot, and took her downstairs so Katherine could sleep on. She joined them a few minutes later, her face still soft with sleep, and disappeared into the shower. Paul prepared dinner while she washed and dressed, Niamh playing around his feet as he chopped vegetables. When Katherine came downstairs again, her hair still damp, wearing a white dress dug out from the dark recesses of her wardrobe, the table was already laid. He handed her a glass of wine. Her eyes were bright.

"Are we celebrating?" she said.

"It's the longest day. Happy Midsummer."

"Yes. Happy Midsummer." She sipped cautiously.

"Welcome back," Paul added. She looked up at him, a little sly.

"Welcome back?"

"From the distance. Thanks for joining me again."

Katherine regarded him curiously.

"Have I been so far away?" she asked.

"You must have been aware of it too."

"Yes, I suppose I was." She smiled to herself. She turned away and walked to the window, taking another sip from her glass.

When they had eaten, Katherine bathed Niamh, and when the little girl was dressed in her pyjamas, Paul cuddled her on his lap with some picture books while Katherine cleaned up the kitchen. Then Paul carried Niamh up to her bedroom. The window was slightly open. The rain pattered on the glass, but the room was stifling. Niamh lay in the cot kicking her feet in the air, tugging off the thin sheet Paul placed on top of her.

"Go to sleep now," he said. Already Niamh's face was sticky with perspiration, but the girl lay obediently while her father tidied up the room, picking up toys and clothes from the floor. Just as he was leaving the room, someone knocked on the front door. He paused and cursed. Then Katherine walked into the hallway.

"Paul?" she called in a soft voice. He looked down, to where she stood in the shadows by the front door.

"Who is it?" she said. Paul shrugged his shoulders.

"I don't know. I'm not expecting anyone."

"Shall I ignore it? Pretend we're not in?"

Paul hesitated for a moment. Then he shook his head.

"Too late. I think they can see you through the glass."

He felt a mixture of annoyance at the endless interruptions, and shame for his childish desire to hide. He came downstairs. Katherine opened the front door. He stared at the caller in surprise.

"Stuart," he said. Instinctively he glanced outside, up and down the street.

"You'd better come in," he added. Stuart appeared to be perfectly relaxed, even amused. His black hair was wet. Droplets of water clung to his coat, which he pulled off and draped over a chair. He sat down at once, putting his feet on the low table, making himself at home.

"Isn't this a bit risky? I thought you were going to keep away from here. I've had the police asking questions." Paul's voice was low and hurried. Stuart smirked.

"Don't panic. They've absolutely nothing on us," he said. Katherine walked into the room. Paul quickly moved away from Stuart. He stood by his partner.

"Katherine, this is Stuart. We were in the SWP together. A long time ago."

Stuart stood up, and shook her hand with a charming smile.

"Now I understand why Paul has abandoned the Cause," he said, still smiling, still holding her hand.

"Abandoned the cause? He's hardly done that." She slipped her fingers free. "Would you like a drink?" As she spoke, someone else knocked on the front door. Katherine and Paul exchanged a look.

"My, you're popular tonight," Stuart commented, sinking back to his chair. Katherine answered the door. Clad in his leather jacket, helmet in hand, James was standing in the rain.

"Is this a good time?" he said. "Is Paul in?"

"I am indeed," Paul said, peeping over Katherine's shoulder.

"Come in," she said, hesitant, "come out of the rain."

As James stepped over the threshold, he leaned down and kissed her on the cheek. But he drew back. He looked at her carefully.

"Are you okay?" he asked.

"Fine," she smiled brightly. "We have another visitor. An old friend of Paul's. Come and meet him." She put her hand on his arm, but James shifted away. He entered the living room. A sense of alarm flashed through Paul.

"James," he said, a little too loudly. "I'm glad you called round." He turned to Stuart. "James works on the local paper. He's a friend of mine—given us some good coverage."

Stuart, lounging in the chair, held out his hand to James.

"Nice to meet you," he said.

"I've seen you before. At the Barge? You were talking to Paul."

"Yes," Stuart nodded.

"Former political associate, is that right?"

"Absolutely."

"So what brings you to this part of the world?"

"Oh, nothing in particular. I'm between jobs right now. At a loose end. As I'm staying in Swindon I thought I'd check out this road protest, and hey presto, I find it's my old friend Paul Matraver's pet project." Paul bridled. James looked curious.

"And what is your line of work?" he asked. Stuart looked across at Paul with a slight smile.

"How would you describe it, Paul?" he asked. "I work freelance. I travel a lot. I operate as an environmental consultant for big companies. Does that sound about right, Paul?"

"I guess so." He was irritated that Stuart could play on his anxiety so effectively. James sat down and withdrew a notebook from a pocket inside his jacket. Katherine returned with mugs of coffee.

"This is not a social call?" Stuart queried.

"Half and half." He turned to Paul. "I was hoping for two stories? I want to write a report on your Midsummer Fair, and I was hoping for a comment on the arson attack on Tarcost's machinery? Have you heard about that?"

"Uh, yes. The police have been round to the squat a couple of times," he said.

"Bloody good story. I wouldn't be surprised if the nationals pick it up. Hundreds of thousands of pounds worth of damage."

"So I heard. How did you find out about it?" Paul said.

"The police. Told me about it this morning. A bit of adverse publicity for you lot."

"Maybe," Paul shrugged.

"Okay—what's your line? Condemnation?"

Stuart looked at Paul closely. Paul felt an uncomfortable tightness in his chest. He found it hard to swallow. The other two men awaited his reaction, both curious.

"Yes, Paul, what is your line on this?" Stuart echoed. Paul glanced at James. Was he picking up Stuart's sarcasm, his taunting? Paul thought quickly.

"Our protest is based on the principle of peaceful, non-violent direct action," he said. James waited for more but Paul did not elucidate any further.

"Does this non-violence extend to property as well as people?" he asked.

"Yes."

"So you dissociate this action from the bypass protest movement?"

"Yes. Absolutely."

"And condemn the action of the individuals concerned?"

Paul paused.

"Go on," Stuart said softly. "Condemn them." But Paul kept his attention fixed on James.

"I think we must decide who the criminals are in this matter," he said. "Let us consider the damage the road-builders will inflict on the land. The murder of trees and hedgerows. The destruction of unique historical sites. These are irreplaceable. Tarcost's machinery is not. Personally I regard the construction of the bypass as the criminal act."

James scribbled quickly.

"So you're not going to condemn them?" he said.

"That's all I'm going to say on the subject, okay?"

James apparently sensed his unease.

"I guess it's been a difficult day for you. Were the police troublesome?"

Paul shrugged.

"A little," he said. "Of course they suspect it was someone connected with the protest, but they don't seem to have any clear evidence. Doubtless they'll be sniffing about for a while."

Paul fell silent. James swiftly drank his coffee. He stood up.

"I seem to have called at a bad time, so I'll leave you to it. Perhaps you could write a report on the fair and drop it round at the office tomorrow?" he said. "I'm sorry I disturbed you. I'll just use your loo, and head off home, okay?"

Paul began to protest half-heartedly but James shook his head and walked through the kitchen towards the bathroom. Katherine followed him into the kitchen, carrying mugs. A minute later, Paul heard James speaking to her.

"Is Paul okay?" he said.

"Yes. We've had a busy day. He's pretty tired, and this fire business has upset him."

"I'm not surprised."

Paul detected a new tone in Katherine's voice. Was she flirting with James? Jealousy stung him. He made an excuse to Stuart and went to the bathroom himself. When he walked through the kitchen, James was leaning against the worktop. Paul lingered in the tiny lobby by the bathroom door, peering surreptitiously into the kitchen.

"And are you well, Katherine?" James asked. She stopped what she was doing and looked at him.

"Yes, of course," she said. "Why do you ask?"

"You seem different."

Katherine walked towards James and reached out her arms to hug him. In a state of tension, Paul dug his nails into the palm of his hand. But James recoiled from her.

"Don't you like me anymore?" she asked painfully. "I always thought you liked me a lot."

"Of course I like you. And to be honest—you look great. Gorgeous, in fact."

"But?"

"I don't know. Are you and Paul getting on better?"

"Yes, we are."

"Maybe that's it," he said uncertainly.

The three were sitting in silence in the living room when Paul returned from the loo. James picked up his jacket and helmet, and Paul showed him to the front door. James mounted his motorcycle and rode off in the rain, the bike casting a fine spray of water from its wheels.

Katherine and Stuart abruptly halted their conversation when Paul rejoined them. He sat on the sofa next to Katherine, and snuggled up to her. The physical contact relaxed him. He put his arm around her. He let out a deep breath. The tension subsided. They both smiled at Stuart, isolated on the far side of the room. He sniffed dismissively at the display of connubial bliss.

"Difficult time for you, talking to your reporter friend?" he said, digging for another reaction. But suddenly Paul was impervious.

"James is a good bloke," he said.

"Trouble is, however well-intentioned an individual journalist may be, the papers are all controlled by large companies with a major interest in maintaining the status quo."

"True enough."

Stuart turned his attention to the room, to the bookshelves.

"Nice place you have here," he said. Paul was conscious of his comrade's disparagement, but for once it washed off.

"I like it," he said.

"Mortgage, I suppose?"

"Yes."

"So you're harnessed into work for the next twenty five years. Don't tell me, it's better than throwing money down the drain renting. I can hear your father talking."

"I didn't say a word. We could always sell it."

"Isn't it a bit of a pose though, having Marx on the bookshelf? Property is theft—yes?"

"So where are you living at the moment?"

"Staying at a friend's council flat as it happens. And I'm signing on—at three different places," he boasted. "So now you can suggest that I'm sponging off the tax-payer, i.e. your good self, for the housing benefit? For my dole money? Fuck, you're losing the case."

"I didn't say a word," Paul repeated.

"Yeah. But your silence speaks volumes. The whole fucking state is corrupt. Screw it for whatever you can get. Tear it apart, yes? Isn't that what you wanted to do?"

"Yes. I do want something better. But I don't agree that being corrupt is going to end corruption."

"Well, it's all bloody comfortable for you but what about the rest? What about the families without the good fortune to earn a fucking architect's salary? What about the environmental damage created by your middle class lifestyle? Commuting to work? Lead-free petrol, no doubt, and recycled loo paper, and a compost bin in the garden. It's a fucking sham. A con. And d'you know what makes me sick most of all?"

Paul regarded him coolly. Stuart raised his voice. His face was growing distinctly red. He had witnessed these rants before, the outburst of anger. But this time he was unaffected. Stuart sensed his verbal claws were losing their effect. He increased the volume further.

"D'you know what's worst of all?" he said. "What goes on up here." He pointed to his head. "You've caged yourself in with the comfy lifestyle, little wifey, trawl to work and back, the deathly routine, the spiralling path. We're heading down, d'you hear me? It isn't sustainable. You're blind. You're stupid. The Earth's resources are swallowed up. The forests are depleted. Your over-consumption is depriving a quarter of the world's population of sufficient food. You're part of the cancerous growth of humanity on the body of the Earth, feeding and destroying your own precious habitat. You are pollution. Your mind is blinkered. Your horizons will narrow and narrow. Soon you won't be able to see further than your new bloody wallpaper. Do you understand me?" Stuart halted for a moment. Katherine and Paul were staring at him, expressionless. For an instant Stuart looked like a madman. But Paul was free. Stuart had lost his hold. What had happened? Stuart's voice softened.

"You listen but you don't hear," he said quietly. "Have I lost you, Paul?" The question was almost an appeal. When Paul didn't answer, Stuart picked up his coat. His face was dark, downcast, his expression a pent-up mixture of anger and loss. He walked from the room and left through the front door, slamming it behind him.

The atmosphere was still again. Paul and Katherine waited in silence for a few moments, in the wake of Stuart's departure.

"Not a happy man," Katherine ventured at last.

"He feels I've let him down. Deserted him. He's a man who likes his friends to be disciples."

"Is that why you parted company before?"

"I suppose so. Unconsciously perhaps. I still admire him though. That much commitment. He's given up everything."

"Everything? You mean home, family, conventional life? It doesn't seem like that was much of a sacrifice. Isn't that all the stuff he despises?"

"He was the one who dropped me you know. When you became pregnant. He didn't want to have anything to do with me anymore. I kept on writing and calling. I guess it was for that reason—that parenthood would inevitably rope me into a different lifestyle—that he didn't want to know me. I disappointed him. It was intensely painful. It still hurts me now, just thinking about it. Just at a time when I needed his friendship, his support. Just at a time when I needed to keep a contact with what he shared with me—you know, being a free-thinker, being on the outside of Western culture's great human machine. I even sent him a picture of Niamh just after she was born, wanting him to share my new adventure, and he never replied. A double blow. I was heart-broken. I certainly never thought I'd see him again."

"Having Niamh was a blow?" Katherine said. Then, "You've never told me about this matter with Stuart before." Paul put his hands to his face.

"Paul?" she said. "Paul?" His body was rigid—he was holding himself in a tight grip, every muscle tense. When he didn't answer she pulled his hands away. His eyes began to brim with tears, spilling over and trickling down his cheeks. Katherine put her arms around him and held him tightly. His body loosened, convulsing with sobs, long cracks stealing through him, breaking him apart.

Later, in bed, Paul made love to Katherine in a passion of anguish and emotional hunger. As he reached a climax he gripped her wrists in a show of force, wanting to have her utterly, be joined to her—reaching the centre of her being. When she came, her body tensed hard against him, and then as he collapsed upon her, she laughed, holding his face, covering him with kisses. Then they lay quietly together, sweating, arms and legs interlocked. They were silent for a long time, lying in the dark except for the flickering light of a single candle. Finally Paul sighed.

"But, of course, you're not Katherine," he said.

"No," she replied. Paul did not relinquish his hold.

"You're the one who came to me before. When all this started. Hard though I find it to believe. But I can't keep on deluding myself."

She didn't say anything, but Paul persisted.

"So who are you, and where is Katherine?"

The faux Katherine propped herself up on her elbow and looked down at him. Her eyes glinted in the candlelight. Were they green? He found it hard to make out in the slight, quivering illumination.

"The true Katherine is on the other side, hoping to retrieve your daughter."

"Niamh is like you? A changeling?"

"Haven't you always suspected?"

"Yes, I suppose so. Suspected—but found it impossible to actually believe."

"And you do now?"

"I have no choice. I know perfectly well you're not Katherine. Why did you come to me?"

"I felt your desire. Your hunger. You drew me, even from the other land, through the veil and I couldn't resist."

"But what about the first time?" he asked carefully.

"I was needed to distract you."

"While your accomplices kidnapped my daughter?"

"While Katherine kidnapped her daughter."

"Katherine? What do you mean?"

But she shook her head.

"It's too hard to explain right now. You will see the whole picture soon enough."

Paul stroked her shoulder absentmindedly. Then a painful idea occurred to him.

"Does this mean you won't be staying long?" The very prospect engendered an intense feeling of loss, a rising wave of nausea.

"I don't know," she said. "I don't know. I don't ever want to leave you."

"I don't ever want to let you go. When I'm with you, I am perfectly happy. When we're together I feel, for the first time in years, that I'm in exactly the right place in the universe—doing just what I'm ment to be doing. Fulfillment. It is the most amazing feeling."

"Yes," she assented. "I know what you mean."

"When I'm with you I feel that all manner of new places open up in my mind, like rooms that have been locked up for years—or else never opened—revealing magical vistas, strange places, whole new worlds." He looked up at her.

"Shall I call you Kate?" he asked. "Katherine hates it when people call her Kate, but seeing as you're not Katherine, I'd rather you had a different name."

"Yes. Kate would be fine."

"So how do you know what Katherine would know? And what's it like where you come from?"

"Katherine was present at my inception. When I donned her likeness I also took on her memories. Some of them at least—the memories of her recent life. I doubt I'd fool her mother—but then again, you weren't fooled for long."

"No," he admitted. "I knew soon enough."

Kate leaned forward and kissed his cheek. His skin was wet and salty.

"I'm sorry," he said. "I'm crying again. Not like me—to be over-emotional."

"Don't apologise. It's fine. Just cuddle me as well." Kate slid down, resting her head on his shoulder.

"I don't want you to go," he said. "I love you."

"I love you too. Very much."

The candle was close to expiring. The flame sank low, then flared up brightly for a moment, before dying away completely. Paul stared out into the darkness for a few minutes more, until sleep crept over his mind, stilling his thoughts.

CHAPTER TWENTY THREE

As Katherine stepped away from Crow, from the shelter of the copse, the dark, mutable forms closed around her. She felt their breath, the swift brush of their bodies, insubstantial as smoke. Their eyes gleamed like gems in the twilight. A thin hand slipped into hers, a flickering contact sending quick currents thrilling through her veins, through her flesh. The shadows solidified. Beside her, rising like a flower from the earth, a frail, slender form unfurled. Skin the colour of milk, streams of hair like flames, black and green and copper, twining like snakes, like a Medusa. Glittering eyes, bright green, and the pupils black as the void, great pools tumbling away into eternity. Lodestones, the eyes, the only constant, in a face that shimmered, recreated in every moment. The creature released its grip. It looked at its hands, flexed its long, pale fingers, lifted its head, all afire, and smiled. It turned to Katherine, drinking her with its gaze, and it turned to its fellows, which rose from the darkness all around them, clear, white bodies, trailing incandescent clouds, like wings. She stood in a forest of angels.

The night gathered around them. Katherine could not discern the fields or the copse. The stars faded. The faeries looked from one to another, rippling azure, blood red, molten gold, with pure, perfect faces. She heard whispers, though the faeries didn't seem to speak, a rising clamour, like the countless clash of leaves in the wind. She felt a hunger, an emptiness, standing among the faeries. She couldn't hear what they were saying. She couldn't understand them. They towered above her, untainted, and she understood her own corruption, the countless imperfections of her decayed physical form. A clumsy machine, ingesting and excreting, sweating and damaged, plagued by the endless hordes of bacteria and viral invaders. A brief, battling sleeve of bone and flesh dying and decomposing with every breath she took. A heavy, clumsy carcase. It filled her with revulsion and dismay. An affliction—this body—a filthy prison, her bright soul peeping out at the faeries, at purity, with an ancient longing.

The first faery held out its hand to her, and she gripped it again. Its touch was shocking, like plunging her hand into ice-cold water, but she didn't let go.

"Come with us," the faery said. Its lips moved but the voice seemed to come from a distance. "We have a long way to go."

Katherine nodded mutely. She walked beside the faery like a child as the others gathered about them. A path unfolded like a river, a ribbon of electric blue upon the land. They passed through the night like ghosts.

"Are we in Faeryland?" she whispered.

"No. These are the secret paths that run through your world and ours. The border. The point of connection. We're between the two places, not wholly in either."

"Where are you taking me?"

"We have much to learn, you and I. Just as the path is a sharing place, we are connected too. You have taken on aspects of my nature, enabling you to walk with me, to move as we move, but I have drawn from you too. I have a form like yours. I can speak with you."

They moved quickly. Black space pressed against them. Utter darkness. Then illumination.

The path wove through a wood full of bluebells.

The light was gooseberry green, with spears of sunlight piercing the shade and pattering the ground. The trees were widely spaced, sleek beeches, silver-grey bark and delicate new leaves. The bluebells covered the earth, an unbroken, undulating lake of purple-blue. The scent rose like a mist, faintly sweet and heady. The breeze lifted, and clouds passed above the canopy of leaves casting fitful shadows upon the blue pour of flowers. Katherine drew a breath, exultant. They walked along a narrow path through the bluebells. As far as she could see, they stretched in a sea, in deepening tones of blue and lilac through the wood, streaming through the trees, collecting in hollows like pools. She turned to the faery, looked into its green eyes.

Another moment of blackness. The scene collapsed and rearranged itself.

The bluebell wood still. But now she was mounted—riding a horse. The faery had also shifted form. Katherine beheld a medieval maiden, a sorceress from a picture book, sitting upon a horse. The sorceress smiled. Her hair was black and smooth, falling to her waist. She wore a velvet robe, red and purple, with sleeves that widened at her wrists, and a gold serpent circlet on her brow. Katherine, upon a white horse, felt the weight of heavy armour upon her body. The metal plates on her thighs shone dully in the speckled sunlight. The horse's mane was long and thick before her, the beast's crest well muscled. The saddle was decorated red and gold, ornately caparisoned. When the horse tossed its head, the long silver bit jingled like a bell. A sword swung at her belt, sheathed in a long leather scabbard. The horse jogged impatiently, grinding its bit.

"Who are you?" Katherine asked. The sorceress gathered her reins. She was riding a slender bay mare, with a coat the polished brown of conkers and four flinty black hooves beating a delicate rhythm upon the dirt path. The mare pranced, but the sorceress was sitting at ease.

"We are the dreams of the Earth," the sorceress said. Then she relaxed her hold on the reins and the mare leaped forward into a swift canter through the bluebells. With little prompting, Katherine's white horse followed suit, and they passed through the wood at a great speed. The horse swerved to avoid low branches, leaping over ruts and rotten logs in its path. Katherine leaned forward over its neck, wrapping her fingers in its mane, surrendering control to the horse, careering through the trees in pursuit of its companion. The wind whipped tears from her eyes. Up ahead, the horizon lightened. The trees began to thin. They were approaching the edge of the wood. The bay mare disappeared. Katherine's charger hurled itself into the white space at the boundary, and then they were falling, headlong, through darkness, and Katherine felt the breath sucked from her body.

A hilltop. They were walking on foot across moorland. The path wound through bare outcrops of rock. The earth was covered with purple billows of heather. Here and there a gorse bush flowered in a blaze of yellow-gold. The sky was overcast. A faint, light mist drifted over the ground. The path was patched with rough stones. The faery walked beside her, in the form she had first seen, though its original splendour was muted. Its long, thin feet were bare and it carried a staff, like a pilgrim. Katherine looked at her own feet. Her boots were scuffed and worn. The laces were torn. How far had they walked?

"Where are we?" she asked.

"On the path," the faery answered. They continued in silence. The mist brushed against them, and cleared again.

"You are the Earth's dreams?"

"As you are the Earth's waking—its consciousness. And not just the Earth, though this has been our home, our root. You are the substance of the universe awakened, knowing itself. You are the a piece of the Earth, a fragment of its mind."

They walked on to the crest of the hill. Way below, the sea stretched away, glittering like silk, ever restless. Upon the cliffs, belligerent white seabirds had balanced precarious nests on stilts of rock. In crevices, tiny flowers thrust roots into the body of the cliff, tiny pink faces straining for the sun. How fierce the desire for life, she thought. On every bare rock, in every harsh and inhospitable climate, the Earth teems with plants and animals and microbes and insects, all hungering to exist, fighting and suffering and struggling for a place, for a lifetime, however long that lifetime might be. Why bother? When the life might be so cruel and short, so difficult? There was no compassion, in the killing and feeding, in the cutting down of young ones, in the merciless destruction of the old and sick and maimed. What momentum pushed it on, what force filled them all, grass and worm and human alike, that they clung to and fought for their lives so desperately?

And the faeries. Immortals? The being walking beside her was malleable and untainted.

"You're not alive, are you," she said softly. "You don't die. You don't feel pain. You don't suffer."

The faery didn't reply.

"You wouldn't exist without us," she said. "Dreams don't exist in isolation."

"And you can't live without us—though you are trying. You are blocking us out. You are building a world of certainties, measured and predictable. You fill your lives with limits and boundaries, afraid of the precarious, clutching after security." The faery's voice began to slide. Its tone grew more familiar. Where were they now? The moorland melted, the cliffs and the sea.

They were in a room. She recognised it. Yes, the living room in the mouldering flat where she and Paul had lived before they moved to Locksbury. When she was pregnant, and Paul was working twelve hours a day in a packing warehouse trying to find a better job. And she was endlessly ill, wan and nauseous, and Paul was tired and frustrated, trying to be supportive but bitterly unhappy, forcing himself through effort of will to stick to his job, to do the right thing. The ambience of the time washed over her and she shuddered. A bad place, in her personal geography, and for Paul too. The faery was still speaking. The voice had become more accusatory. She recognised her mother's voice, reprimanding her. She picked out teachers, bullying friends. She discerned a strand that could only be Elaine. The faery's words became more personal.

"You cling on to plans. You follow the easiest path, accumulating possessions as though they are going to save you. You are fed with fears and offered methods of appeasing them, only each time you do so you sacrifice a little more freedom, you relinquish your dreams and your brightness. You are beginning to fade. Your mind is cluttered, heavy with wadding."

As the faery spoke, its form began to change, shrinking and shrivelling, head stooped, shoulders hunched and narrowed. It leered up at her. A hideous face—broken teeth and slack, leathery lips, and eyes, still green, full of malice. It hopped up and down like a toad, limbs gaunt and ugly, utterly repulsive. Laughing and jeering, it pointed a misshapen goblin finger at Katherine.

"Nobody's fooled, you know. Everyone can see through your pretence. We all know the truth about you. We all see how weak and useless you really are. How stupid, how afraid. How thin and ugly. Your little facade of confidence, your charade, is no defence against us. You are no good. You are nothing."

Every phrase seemed to penetrate her heart. As she shrank, so the goblin began to swell. Could it see into her secret fears?

No. She had precipated this attack herself. The faery, a dream, was reflecting her own thoughts, like a mirror. She had brought them to this place. She had contorted the faery. Within her make-up, like everyone else, was a huge lake of anxiety. But it wasn't everything. No—to hell with it. She had allowed herself to be engulfed and she had to break free. If she was nothing, what did she have to lose?

"Yes," she said, triumphant. "Yes I am nothing. What of it? What does it matter? Everything springs from nothing. Take me somewhere else."

The room evaporated. She was walking again.

Bright blue sky. The cliff tops, and the shining bodies of the gulls circling in the sunlight. The faery strode beside her, beautiful again, dressed in blue and white. At the bottom of the cliffs the sea crashed against the rocks, the endless rush and retreat of the waves. The sea spread away into the distance, the grey-blue of slate merging with layers of turquoise and below, where the water was clear, the clear blue of sapphire. Her ears were filled with the low thunder of the water on the rock, and the hiss of the sea spray. The sun burned hot on her face, and the air tasted fresh and pure, untainted. The sight of the sea was profoundly moving, like a balm to an unknown ache. She felt an uncurling, and tears prickled her eyes.

The faery reached for her elbow and guided her forwards. Countless shrubs and bushes bordered the cliff path. Clouds of butterflies rose from the flowers and fluttered about as they proceeded. Blue and red and yellow and the clearest white, plain and ornately patterned, like animated petals, the butterflies danced around them in a train.

"Our land is interlaced with yours," the faery said. "In special places, like the paths, the veil between is thin. There has always been limited access between the two places. Vulnerable points. Times of interchange. We are drawn to you. We have taken people with us. We passed through your land, noticed and unnoticed.

But always there has been a balance, a reciprocation. Whenever we take, we have given in return. We have been acknowledged."

"And now you're denied? You want gifts, like in the past? And the shrines to local deities, and the last apples left on the trees, and the last sheaf of wheat to appease the corn god? The old superstitions?"

"Times change. Humankind alters and we follow suit."

Katherine was surprised to see the faery looked confused.

"You don't know what you want, do you?" she said. The faery turned a blank face.

"You are attributing me with too much humanity," it said. "I am reflecting you, remember. In order that we can communicate I have taken on aspects of your nature. Me—I have no such conscious thought or desire. We are not isolated individuals but a web of dreams, riven by storms of passion and fear, our lands built of patchwork pictures, leaking from your minds and feeding them in return. Without you, I have no individual will, but move like water to fill an empty space."

They were walking along a beach. At the end of the bay a long ridge of rock reached out into the sea, where girls in white were throwing garlands of flowers into the waves. At the other end, past the tawny sweep of sand, monks were praying on a holy island, sending streams of incense into the air. Katherine walked to the waves and felt the water on her toes. Holes were worn in the soles of her boots. The faery was fading. For a long time she strode on, as though alone. Distance was hard to judge, with the waves and the sand stretching on without measure. She was very hot. The sun beat down upon her body, till her flesh was inflamed, and her skin burnt. She stepped into the water, pushing through the cold waves till the sea reached her neck, and the icy Atlantic drew the heat from her body, the great ocean pressing against her, swallowing her, so she was cold and elemental, like a fish or a mermaid. Then she waded back out to the sand. She walked on.

Around the skirts of the sea the sand was pocked with countless stones. Smoothed by aeons, as large as her head, as small as a fist, the stones were glossy with water. Black as coal, or striped yellow and white, some brown or red, crusted with crystal, or else the white of ocean surf. Hundreds—thousands—littering the wet sand between the waves and the shore, spread into a vast pattern across the bay, shaped and placed by the infinite ocean. What did it say, this lexicon of stones? What storms, what currents, what earthly shifts had formed each rock, had brought it together with its fellows, and left it, just here and now, in this vast assembly so beautifully spaced? She ached to read it. Then somehow, if she knew the right key, the very heart of the ocean would be hers to understand. How often did she walk blindly? How narrow was her vision after all? Was this what the faery ment? Like reading tea-leaves, or tarot cards, or the fall of raindrops on a window pane. The random fall of cards or bones, reflecting part of the pattern, acknowledging that the conscious, man-made world was a tiny part only, a small bright bubble with the unknown, huge and incomprehensible, all around.

Then, in a sky of ghastly red and orange, the sun shifted in the sky, nauseating Katherine momentarily. A figure tottered towards her, close to the waves. The sea was full of mud or blood, sticky brown. Had the faery found a new face? Another fear, rising from her new understanding? Wrapped in rags, its head bound with strips of cloth, the figure was the same slick brown as the sea, with a face foul and sunken, like an apple left to rot. Lurching like an animated corpse, the creature tried to speak. A witch. It was cursing her. She couldn't make out the words of the curse, but she understood the meaning. She had reached another boundary. She was standing on a new threshold and the witch barred her way. Katherine held her place. This time she was unafraid. The witch kept moving towards her, and her jaw kept flapping, but the body was loosening and coming apart. Then its head dropped off, with a splash into the waves, and the body tumbled like a doll.

The sea was gone.

A sensation of bliss. She was lying on her back. Where? All around space glittered blue and clear. High up, in the sky, or beyond, resting on a crystal column. She held out arms that shone with silver, like the scales of a fish. Her hair floated around her head, irridescent, rippling candy pink and blue and amethyst, and filmy wings spread all about her. Her faery companion knelt by her side, its wings floating above them, silvery, diaphanous, and a face alight with glory. It stooped down to kiss her, radiating joy. Ecstasy filled her body, her being. Was this what she had longed for? The love of immortals, a conjunction of faery souls, the quivering of every nerve, every cell, in a blaze of inexplicable delight?

Katherine came to herself again. The faery held a little mirror in its hand. She took it and looked in. She was a faery, fabulous, multi-coloured. But she looked again. In the depths of the reflection was little Katherine, looking tired, and beneath the shimmering she could see her face was peeling very badly. Her eyes were heavy. Mortal. She put the mirror down and jumped from the crystal column.

A ploughed field. The hedges were dull green, speckled with bright red hawthorne berries, and scarlet rose hips, like beads upon the tendrils of briar. September then, the air cool, scented with blackberries and damp earth. The path ran through the centre of the field. Two fluted marble columns marked each end— cracked and broken, patched with moss. Walking through the field, Katherine and the faery passed the broken remains of statues half buried in the soil. Humans, angels, animals. Kings and crows. Heads and limbs, partly submerged, discarded and shattered by the plough. When the spring came grew, the marble relics would be hidden by the growing wheat, green, and then golden. Who would know what was hidden?

They came to a metal bridge. It was old and neglected, covered in a film of rust. Waiting upon the bridge was a blue horse. Katherine knew immediately it was her horse—the most beautiful creature she had ever seen. The blue of cornflowers, with a shimmer of silver in the sunlight, and a mane and tail of the softest black. How precious it was, like a jewel. She stroked the horse's hard neck, its coat sleek beneath her hand. The faery halted at the edge of the bridge.

"Goodbye, Katherine," the faery said. She understood the horse had been entrusted to her care. She slipped her fingers through its mane to lead it forwards. She stepped across. The metal bridge was hard beneath her feet. The horse's hooves clopped loudly, echoing from the great girders on the bridge. The entire structure floated in a grey cloud. Then she thought she heard someone calling her name. Walking onwards, the grey pressed in on her, till she could hardly see at all.

She clung to the horse's mane, but the animal was hesitant beside her. She urged it on. She stepped blindly, hearing her name called again, and she stumbled. The horse snorted and pulled away.

"No! Come back!" she called, but the horse had already disappeared, its hooves clanging on the metal surface. She felt a gaping sense of loss. The horse was gone. Where should she go? She placed one cautious foot before the other, but her head began to swim. Her mind grew dim. What was she doing? Her journey with the faeries fell into darkness, and was lost. She headed onwards, through the veils.

CHAPTER TWENTY FOUR

The darkness had closed round the cottage and all Elaine could see was the distant light of the farmhouse across the downs, half way up the slope. The leaves of the birch tree in the back garden slapped against the small, dirty window panes and the never-ending rain poured down, down, down and she could hear the tiny, insistent patter of the raindrops on the windows, the walls, the narrow road outside the front door. Inside the air was hot and humid.

Crouched in the hollow of an old armchair, Elaine sweated and shifted her weight from one bare foot to the other, pushing her hair back from her face as perspiration clung to her forehead. It had been raining for two weeks, and the farmers were hauling sodden wheat from the July fields, struggling to wrestle some kind of harvest from the deluge, with grain dryers, while the giant yellow bales sat in the fields, swollen with water. The sky never cleared. The clouds hung in the sky, oppressive, and the heat pressed down on the fields and hedges. When the rain did ease up for an hour or so, the air began to suffocate, catching in the throat like smoke. The summer land stretched gold and a heavy, dull green—the fields full of wheat and the trees torpid and stagnant, as though weighted about the boughs and branches.

Elaine wiped sweat from her neck. The only illumination was provided by a candle on the table, otherwise heaped with dirty plates, books and scraps of paper. The room was very small, with the front door opening into it. On the walls were pictures of flowers, an engraving of of the stone circle at Avebury and a small framed family photo, an Owain of maybe ten years ago, looking scruffy, quite incongruous, with a neat, smiling younger sister and a plump mother. He lived in the cottage during the winter, and he returned there intermittently over the summer months. It was owned by the farmer who periodically employed him.

Behind the house, a long, thin garden stretched in an overgrown green ribbon to the flooded River Kennet at the bottom. It had risen several feet in the last two weeks, and the waters were muddied, pushing a careless course through the old riverbanks, here and there spilling onto low lying fields, to sit in broad, shallow pools on either side of the channel.

Should she go outside? To sit in the rain, surely, would be cooler, to let the raindrops soak into her skin. But for a long time she was gripped by a clinging lethargy and she crouched in the semi darkness watching the sinking and flickering of the candle flame. Then a gust of wind brought a splatter of raindrops across the tiny window pane. Startled, Elaine roused herself. She stood up and moved through the kitchen to the backdoor, stretching. The door had been left open. The cottage was joined to another, larger dwelling but the owners were weekenders from London and she had not yet met them, though she spied antique furniture and oil paintings through the window. She switched the kitchen light on and a halo of light spilled out of the back door onto the small brick sheds on the left. Elaine, barefoot, walked carefully through the uncut grass towards the bottom of the garden. The light from the back door illuminated the first few yards, and then as she headed towards the river the hard electric light faded out and she was feeling her way through darkness. For a moment she was walking blindly, but her eyes adjusted and she began to discern the forms of the old fruit trees, and the coarse green stems of hogweed, over six feet high, with fists of flowers turning to seed at the summit. Owain had told her the soil at the cottage was magic—everything he planted sprang from the soil—but the weeds flourished likewise, and the garden was dense with miraculous quantities of plant material knitted in days from the soil and rain. Fat white cauliflowers and giant cabbages squatted near the ground, unharvested and overblown.

The sound of the rushing water grew louder and at last the river was before her. Nettles grew at either side of the garden, where a thin barbed wire fence separated the garden from the field. The rain seeped through her hair and the water began to drip over her face and down her back. At last by the river she sat in the rich, soaking grass. Ripples shone on the surface of the river. The dark line of the barbed wire sagged on the other side, where the cattle in the field had rubbed themselves, and the posts were loose in the ground. The rain was cold and soothing. She stared at the water, mindless, till the slight, silvery ripples assumed shape and pattern, like a script upon the surface of the water, endlessly radiating, intersecting and repelling. She drifted off into long, convoluted streams of thought, concerning Owain, her future, half-formed fantasies, acting out conversations and scenarios, testing and trying, fishing for clues and ideas. She had come to the cottage to get her head together, had she not? But she couldn't relax. No, she was too restless. Indeed she was fed up. Annoyed. Once again she trailed through the interminable, hopeless thoughts. Her brain ached with the endless repetitions, the dull old ideas revolving round and round without resolution.

She was aware of some disturbance, like an itch. A weight. She was so unutterably tired. Every night she slept for hours, but arose in the morning more weary than ever. So she struggled against it, feeling as though her bones were full of lead, sapping her strength.

The rain ceased, briefly, and the clouds thinned, tearing almost to nothing for a moment so the moon, curved like a hollow shell, blazed out—and was consumed again by the blackness. In those moments the faint light illuminated the garden and the fields beyond, glinting on the turbulent surface of the river. The curve of the sharp sickle moon appeared, quick, like the flash of a dagger. Then cloaked again. A minute passed, in darkness, though Elaine sensed the tremendous rolling weight of the clouds. A sign, yes. Beyond the river, out across the fields, something shifted. Perhaps it was the movement of the cattle, roused by the brief respite in the rain. Beneath the endless passage of the clouds, and out across the field, another, closer activity. Elaine stood up and stared into the darkness. She could see nothing— soaked and vulnerable, standing alone. But a low rumble sounded out across the field, like thunder. Elaine crouched down, and peered across the river. The rumble grew louder, seeming to spread from east to west. The noise increased, and in the darkness Elaine made out the black forms of cattle galloping across the field towards the river, in a mindless stampede. The thunder of their hooves upon the earth grew deafening as they charged towards the river, pushing and harrying each other. Just before they reached the barbed wire, they veered to the left and headed off along the edge of the field down into the hollow at the bottom. The dull thudding hooves grew distant and quiet, fading away into silence again. She waited for five minutes, ten. Nothing else stirred in the field. Why had they stampeded? Slowly she turned from the river and headed back up the garden to the cottage. Yellow light filled the doorway, but before she could reach the comfort and security of the four stone walls she had perhaps thirty paces of dark, tangled garden to traverse. She was filled with a strange reluctance to turn her back to the field but she could not walk backwards through the garden. As she turned she glanced over her shoulder. Was someone was in the field, frightening the cattle? She had an irrational fear they were coming after her. She forced herself to walk towards the backdoor. It was now a dozen steps away and she had to fight with a compelling urge to look over her shoulder with every step she took. She imagined illumination—a glimpse of swaying forests of nettles, and the poppy heads gone to seed. She reached the overgrown brick pathway and the sheds. Then she ran the final steps into the cottage, banged the door shut behind her and locked the door, drawing across the two bolts at the top and bottom.

She peeled off her wet clothes and ran up the stairs to the bedroom. She pulled on a dry pair of leggings and a shirt. But locked in the cottage, her anxiety increased, as though by hiding away and setting up barriers she had named and agreed to her fears. So she sat in the corner of the room, the light off, and waited. After ten minutes or so she began to reason away her anxiety. She filled the kettle with water and turned it on, leaning against the wall as she waited for the water to boil. Suddenly the back door rattled against the bolts, and she heard a thin voice calling her name from the outside. She jumped back into the living room.

"Elaine!" the voice called. "Elaine! Let me in!" A fist hammered on the door.

Elaine realised in a flash of relief who her visitor was.

"Oh, Jo! It's you," she cried. She ran to the door and pulled back the bolts. "Jo, you gave me such a fright. I thought I had a prowler!"

The door swung open, and Jo walked in, grinning foolishly.

"Look, you're dripping everywhere! Take your clothes off. I'll find you a towel," she said. Jo removed his sodden boots, jeans, shirt, and draped them over the furniture. When Elaine came down with the towel she saw how thin he was. Thinner than ever. Down his back the shoulder blades and vertebrae jutted through his skin, so in the half-light of the candle his body was a mass of hollows and shadows. He turned towards her, conscious of her eyes upon his bones.

"Thin, aren't I?" he said, switching from shyness to showing off. He paraded himself. Elaine turned away, passing him the towel.

"Why are you wearing Katherine's faery necklace?" she said. Jo stopped playing the fool.

"She gave it to me," he said.

"Why?"

"When she was in Faeryland she threw it down to me. I asked her about it when I saw her with Paul, a couple of days after, but she couldn't remember doing it. She didn't want it back though. Paul was a bit weird about it."

Elaine pondered. She was reluctant to talk about it further. She moved away.

"I've got another tee-shirt you could borrow," she said. "I suppose you want some tea?"

Sitting together in the lumpy armchairs, she was conscious of his scrutiny. She had changed too. She felt heavier. She thought the lines had deepened under her eyes, and her skin was dull and coarse. She was afraid she looked old.

"So what brings you here?" she said sharply, turning her face from him.

"I've been looking for you. Then I bumped into Owain, and he told me I'd find you here. I haven't seen you for days. Are you hiding away?"

Elaine shrugged.

"He said the Mummer's Play had upset you. Yes?"

"Owain doesn't know everything. I'm fine. Why can't you all leave me alone?"

Jo tried again.

"There's still weird stuff going down at the site," he said.

"Yes. Owain's told me all about it."

"This is Owain's house?"

"Obviously. Well, the horsey people he works for let him live here. Of course he's not here for most of the summer. Look, much as I enjoy our chit-chat, I'm going to bed now, okay? We can have a proper talk in the morning. I'll bring you a blanket down."

"Can't I sleep with you?" he asked.

"I don't think so." Elaine disappeared upstairs. But when she fell asleep she dreamed he hadn't lstened to her, that he climbed into her bed, curling up close with his back towards her as he always had, pulling her arm around himself, and pressing her hand to his heart. When she woke up alone she felt a little raw inside. She remembered their intimate times with a pang. How hard to bear, in the last weeks, those moments of communion, like false jewels that promised endless riches. But he had thrown them back in her face, quite careless. The pain turned to anger.

She sat up in bed. From the chair, half obscured by a pile of clothes, the old lady's wooden doll stared out at her. She detested the thing, but as yet, she had not managed to discard it. Everytime she met its gaze, she remembered the Mummer's Play, and felt a chill in her veins. She covered its face with a jumper.

Her stomach was achey and hollow. She stepped downstairs barefoot, and into the bathroom at the back of the cottage. Outside the rain persisted. The bathroom ceiling sagged down, leaving a hole between the plasterboards. Someone had stuffed a handful of dry grass in the gap. She peered into the mirror, pushing the black hair from her face and observing the dark, puffy shadows under her eyes, and the blocked pores and bumps that had appeared in her skin around her nose. She washed her face vigorously, in cold water. Newly scrubbed, her complexion looked worse than before, but she fastened her hair back, so at least she felt clean, though the face in the mirror still looked tired and ill.

Peering into the front room, she could see that Jo was still asleep, though the stale air in the room and the ashtray heaped with cigarette ends indicated that he had not slept till late. She made tea and toast. She opened the window, over the back garden, with its sprawling beds of mint, thyme and sage, generously mixed with nettles and fingers of lavender. She could smell the rank weeds and the wet soil, and beyond the fat river, she saw the gentle rising curves of the downlands.

When Jo awoke, nervous and edgy, she made him breakfast, and watched him eat. Looking at his wrists and hands, she could see his ezcema swirling in painful, burning swirls, sore and scabby. At one time she had thought his intermittent disfigurement perversely attractive—as though he was so sensitive that the very effort of living in the real world brought out a chronic allergic reaction. Now it revolted her. He rubbed his hands.

"Don't scratch," she said, irritably.

He stopped.

"What's the matter with you? You don't look so good," she added. Jo shrugged.

"I don't know. It's the place. It's affecting everyone. After midsummer—I think we caused some kind of disturbance. That's what I've been wanting to talk to you about."

Elaine looked at the floor.

"Yes. Owain's been saying something similar. But I can't get much out of him. He wanders off everyday and I stay here on my own. So you're all waiting for the eviction."

"Why aren't you with us?"

"I don't know. I just needed to be away for a while, that's all. I'll be back."

"But you're missing all the preparations. We've been working like crazy since order was served. Preparing barricades and stuff. Making plans. You should see it! We could do with your help."

Elaine heard the 'we'. So he thought himself one of them now, another foot soldier in the army of earnest crusaders at the camp. Obviously he didn't need her to do his thinking for him any more.

"I'm not up to it, okay?" she said.

"Come on, Elaine. I think it's time you stopped hiding away, don't you?" Another, deeper, voice. Elaine turned round. Owain stepped in through the back door. He was wearing a dark green oil-skin coat.

"Hello, Jo," he said. Jo was looking at Elaine expectantly. Was he waiting for an outburst of indignation? Well, she could still surprise him. She curled up on the chair, small and meek.

"It's our turn to walk the route," Owain said, more gently. "Come on, Elaine. Do you realise you've haven't stepped out of the house for a whole week? And you've missed your signing on."

Elaine sighed and tutted. She rose to her feet.

"Okay. I suppose it is about time," she said. "Let me put my boots on, if that's all right? Can we catch the bus? I don't feel like walking all the way."

The bus wasn't due for another hour. Owain washed and ate while they waited. The bus dropped them off in Locksbury village. Jo headed back across the fields to the stone valley and the squat, unable to communicate with a taciturn Elaine. She and Owain walked down the road to the intended start of the bypass route, where the new road would fork from the narrow Locksbury road and divert the traffic in the smooth two-mile arc around the village. Three times a day volunteers walked the route—keeping a watch for surveyors, or contractors with chainsaws, vigilant for signs of preparatory road-building activities. As they crossed the first field, Owain pointed out daubs of paint on a string of horse chestnut trees in the hedgerow.

"The marks appeared two days ago," he said. "Which indicates they are soon to be felled." He led her to the doomed trees.

"But look." He stretched out his hand to the bark. The fresh paint was already partially obscured by lichen.

"Is it the weather? Making everything grow fast?"

"I don't know. I don't like it though."

"But nature is protecting the place herself. Isn't that good?"

"I suppose it should be," Owain said. "But it makes me very uncomfortable. Uneasy."

Elaine looked up and down the field.

"Does your magic path run the entire course of the bypass route?" she asked.

"No, not all of it. Most of it. See the little stand of hawthornes down there? There's an old stile in the hedge. A footpath. At that point the energy line curves, and coincides with the bypass route, which follows it across these fields, down the stone valley and the old lane till the bypass ends at the main road into Marlborough."

"And the weirdness you've noticed—your prickly feet and fast growing lichens—just on the energy line?"

"I think so, yes. But seeping outwards." He clutched her sleeve and froze.

"Look down there," he hissed. Elaine turned. At the far end of the field, three men in reflective waterproof coats were setting up apparatus on a tall tripod.

"Surveyors," he said. "Come on." He strode across the grass towards them.

"Owain! Owain—what are you going to do?" Elaine hurried after him, but Owain didn't stop. As he drew near, one of the surveyors noticed him, and spoke to the other two. One continued struggling with the tripod. The other two put their hands in their pockets and waited for Owain to arrive.

"Good morning," Owain said. Elaine stopped beside him. She saw them assess his appearance. Long hair. Scruffy jeans. A protestor. The men stood tall, on the defensive. The third man cursed as the tripod collapsed upon the ground.

"What are you doing?" Owain asked politely.

"That's not your business. Are you aware this is private land?"

"Is it your land?" Owain said.

"Help me with this, will you?" The man with the tripod addressed his nearest companion. He was plainly irritated. "Bloody thing must be broken. I don't know what's up with it," he said. Not perceiving Owain as an immediate threat, one of the others turned to help him.

"Having problems?" Elaine asked. The men ignored her. At last the tripod was erected. It stood like a fragile, metal insect in the wet grass. Then, for no perceptible reason, it began to teeter, swaying drunkenly, before tumbling to the ground again. The first man swore.

"We'll have to get another one," he said. "Come-on." They picked up their equipment, eye-ing Owain and Elaine suspiciously, as though they were responsible. Then they marched across the field towards Locksbury.

"Goodbye. Better luck next time," Owain called. He was resolutely ignored.

"I see what you mean," Elaine said. "That was uncanny. Sabotage?"

Owain started to walk away.

"Or maybe," he said, looking over his shoulder, "maybe they had faulty gear."

They crossed three more fields, before emerging in the stone valley. The grey wethers were largely obscured by long grass. Elaine stopped by the copse. The ground had become a mire. Planks and straw bales had been placed on the ground between the trees to form walkways through the mud. She gazed down the hill to the old cottages.

"Gods, Owain, I see what you mean." Elaine hadn't returned to the site since the Midsummer Fair. She wandered slowly down the Old Lane, staring at the squat. The garden was a jungle. The old rose bushes had grown into precarious towers of briar. Tendrils bowed under the weight of clumps of flyblown flowers, mottled white, and the red of raw beef. The honeysuckle by the door had spiralled up the brickwork, scaling the chimney, and still aspiring upwards, sent stalks clutching at the air above the house. The virginia creeper covered the rear wall and sprawled in a twitching green blanket over the roof tiles. Elaine pushed her way through the long grass and the sword-leaves of burgeoning crocosmia. The garden smelt both sweet and rancid. She halted before the front door, and beheld a monstrous guardian angel, like the cherubim at the gates of Eden, brandishing a flaming sword. Crudely painted, but ferocious, with its violent red eyes, robes burning white floating behind it, and wings like flames. She saw the brickwork had been amply decorated, the brickwork obscured with pentacles, flowers, spirals and mazes, an arcane fortress dripping with leaves. The windows had been barricaded from the inside with a motley collection of planks, and upon these too, were pictures of avenging spirits, angels, faeries and goblins. She walked round the house. How to get in? The Morris men's camp was still present, though she couldn't see the residents, or their pony. They appeared to have beaten back the vegetation, for the circle around the faded tents was clear—not even churned up. But she was disappointed not to see them. She continued her circuit of the house, and, failing to find an access point, tried hammering on the front door.

"Who is it?" she heard. The voice sounded distant, and muffled.

"It's Elaine."

"Just wait there, Elaine. Someone will come out to you."

Elaine stepped back from the door. Jo appeared from the side of the house.

"What d'you think?" he asked, gesturing to the house. "Isn't it amazing? You should have been here!" He was skipping on the spot, quite elated.

"Are you tripping?" she asked, narrowing her eyes.

"Of course I'm not," he said. "You only left me half an hour ago."

"Time enough."

"Elaine! Do I look off my face?"

"Yes, you do. Kind of hectic."

"Don't be silly! Come with me. I'll show you our access point. I bet you didn't find it." His voice was triumphant. Elaine breathed deeply. She followed him to the side of the house. Jo looked around them, furtively. Seeing the coast was clear, he pulled back an old plastic rain barrel from the wall. Behind it was a small hole into the house, just above the ground.

"You crawl through that?"

"Yes! It was some sort of ventilation thing, into the old pantry. We knocked some bricks out to make it large enough to climb through. There's a whole heap of stuff inside ready to block it up completely when the time comes." Jo dropped to his hands and knees, and wriggled through the gap. Elaine followed suit. When she stood up again, her white dress and plastic coat were covered in streaks of mud from the garden path. Jo reached out, and pulled the barrel back in place. They were plunged into utter darkness. The air smelt of mouldering plaster, and stone, and dust. Jo switched on a large torch, and passed Elaine another.

"Come and see," he said. "Come and see."

Elaine flashed her torch about. The squat had lost any last trace of homeliness. In the living room the front door had been barricaded with an old iron bedstead, and layers of planks. A huge railway sleeper had been propped vertically behind the other layers, pinned by another monstrous piece of timber, surrounded by piles of broken breeze blocks and builder's rubble. The staircase had been entirely removed and dismanted, its constituent parts now gracing the blocked windows. A rope ladder provided access to the first floor. A little daylight squeezed through tiny chinks in the windows. She pushed a piece of rock with her foot, disturbing a nest of woodlice which scurried away from the beam of her torch. The walls were crawling with them. Jo led her to the kitchen, where the backdoor was similarly defended. The ceiling moved. Elaine directed her light upwards. The creeper had invaded the room, and the ceiling was covered in reddish-green leaves, which rustled in the still air. How did it grow in the darkness? Elaine shuddered. Jo hopped about with pride and excitement, but she felt incarcerated. The cottage was a dark, miserable cell, crawling with insects and stinking of mould and damp.

"Where is everybody?" she asked quietly. "You're not here on your own, surely?"

Jo shook his head.

"They're upstairs. We've still got a living room." He climbed the rope ladder. Elaine put her torch in a pocket and followed him up. The landing was not so dark. She could make out stacks of wood and a large metal barrel. More breeze blocks had been piled nearby.

"The next line of defence," Jo explained. "In case they get in downstairs, we can barricade ourselves in up here."

"Yeah, like rats in a hole," Elaine agreed glumly. She began to feel a little nauseous. The dust stuck in her throat, and the sense of enclosure made her dizzy.

"Did you say there was a living room?" she asked. Jo took her to the front bedroom. When he opened the door, a deluge of sunlight spilled about them, and Elaine was momentarily blinded. She stepped inside. The window was open and unfettered, though another pile of barricading materials lay close at hand. Six people were sitting on old mattresses round the room. She saw Paul, sitting with Jan Blessing, a couple of young men she had never seen before, probably new arrivals to the camp, a stocky, red-haired girl who had been a long-time resident at the cottage and the copse, and beside her, a frail, freckled girl with a shaven poll, looking little more than a child. It took Elaine a moment to recognise Violet.

"Violet! What've you done to your hair?"

Violet ran her hand ruefully over her scalp.

"Shaved it," she said. "It was infested with lice. I couldn't get them out of the dreads and plaits."

Elaine still looked shocked. She sat next to Paul, but she found herself stealing glances at a Violet so completely transformed. She looked vulnerable, with her delicate head so naked and exposed. She was also very pale.

Jo climbed onto a mattress next to Violet, and stroked her arm. Violet kissed him on the forehead. Elaine noted the connection with a slight pang, but she refused to nurse it. Instead she turned briskly to Paul.

"Where's Katherine?" she asked. "How come you're not at work?"

"Kate's at home, with Niamh. Not really suitable for toddlers here. I've taken a couple of weeks off work. I heard that the bailiffs were planning to strike on July 26. We've been very busy, as you can see. What've you been up to?"

Elaine detected a note of criticism in the inquiry but she ignored it.

"Hiding away," she said bluntly. Paul looked edgy and distracted. She observed them all. Was the stress of the situation affecting them so much?

"It's only the sixth today. You've got another twenty days to go," she said. It took Paul a moment to reply.

"Since that arson business, I've been informed that the plans might be rearranged. The contractors are unhappy and want to get on with it. Could be anytime."

"So where did you hear all this?"

Paul shook his head.

"Around," he said. "On the grapevine." He lapsed into silence again. His focus was vague, as though his mind was elsewhere. He flopped on the mattress, then stood up and paced up and down, before leaning out the window and looking into the rain.

"Who did all the paintings outside the house?" she asked.

"The Morris men," Jo said.

"Where are they now?"

"I don't know. Sometimes they're here, and sometimes they're not."

"Did they help you with all this barricading too?"

Jo shook his head.

"No. They won't come into the house. Mind you, Owain won't either."

"I know. He told me. I can understand why. It's like a hideous prison. And you all look like madmen."

Everyone fell silent. Elaine realised how loudly she had spoken. They all looked at her.

"Well, you bloody do," she said. Jan, who had been sitting curled in a corner, unwound herself and confronted Elaine.

"And what about you locking yourself away at Owain's place? I understand you haven't stepped out of the place for a week."

Elaine shot a malicious glance at Jo. Who had been talking?

"You're not looking so good yourself, Elaine," Violet said. Paul turned from the window and slipped his hand into his pocket. He drew out a tiny wooden box.

"Open it, Elaine," he said. He placed it on the palm of her hand. On the top, a silver eye stared up at her, unblinking. She looked around. Everyone was watching her closely. She quailed for a moment, but mustered her strength for a sharp reply.

"Is this some kind of trick?" she said. She lifted the lid cautiously. She heard the sound of wind through dead leaves, and a chill bit the air. From the dark depths of the box, a woman's form arose, in black and brown and ivory, dusty skin, her hair caught in a skein of cobweb. She nodded at Elaine, turned away and sank back into the box. Elaine heard the rustle of her skirts, and was filled with a heavy sense of foreboding. She choked a cry in her throat. Tears started to her eyes, but she looked up, aware she was being observed, and she struggled to regain her composure. Were they all against her?

"Bastards," she hissed. "I thought you were my friends. Is this more faery trickery?" She looked from one to another, and perceived the hostility was imagined. They were all afraid.

"What's happening to us?" she asked quietly. Then the sound of engines, at the bottom of the lane. Paul rushed to the window. Four vans had pulled up on the verge behind the barricade and trench they had built where the Old Lane met the main road. A herd of men in dark uniforms and hard hats were climbing from the vans, along with half a dozen policemen. Paul turned to the others.

"This is it," he said. "Block the entry points. Phone the others and get them on site immediately. And call the press." For a second or two, everyone stood frozen. Elaine still clutched the box in her hand, where it seemed to burn into her skin. She handed it back to Paul.

"I don't want to be here," she said.

"Too late. We need you. Go and help Jo block the window."

The last window. Then darkness and torches. Elaine thought of Owain outside. What was he doing?

CHAPTER TWENTY FIVE

Through the veil, Katherine could see the stone valley. But it flew away from her, and vanished. She was sitting, once again, beneath the boughs of the Elder hag. The old lady crooned absent-mindedly, trailing soft leaves upon Katherine's head.

"I remember," Katherine said. "I remember it all."

"Yes," said the Elder. "And what can be done?" She teased Katherine's hair with twiggy fingers. Carelessly she scratched the soft, naked skin below Katherine's neck.

"Hey, careful!" Katherine cried. Tiny beads of blood welled, like a string of faery jewels. The Elder wrapped twigs about Katherine's arms, tightened them like ropes. She hoisted her into the air. Larger branches encircled Katherine's waist, her thighs. Thin tendrils coiled around her head, pulling tight, crowning her with fragrant foliage. Katherine let out a small scream of alarm. The bent hawthorns twitched and murmured.

"Stop! Stop—you're hurting me!"

The Elder held Katherine aloft and looked into her face. Now the ancient eyes were brimming with years of malice. Katherine fought to remain calm. Her body struggled ineffectively against its bonds.

"Little flesh puppet," the tree whispered. "I could pull you apart." Green shoots thrust into Katherine's mouth, reaching into her throat, so she gagged and wretched. Another shoot flicked up between her legs, penetrating her sex, expertly provoking a flood of sexual stimulation. Katherine moaned softly. "Puppet," the Elder repeated. "Blind and brief."

Then the Elder withdrew the shoots from her mouth.

"What do you want?" Katherine croaked. "Why do you hate me? Am I going to be ripped up again?"

The Elder tightened the bonds, till here and there, knots and bumps in the bark began to pierce Katherine's flesh. She shrieked.

"Why are you torturing me? Stop! Tell me what to do."

"We've swallowed you," the Elder said. "Here you are in my stomach. In Faeryland."

"Where's Niamh?" Katherine asked. "I came here to find her. Is she here?"

"Oh, yes, she's here. You brought her yourself—don't you remember? No, of course you don't. Your sight doesn't stretch that far, not yet. How painfully slow you are. Maybe you won't be quick enough to catch her." The branches tightened again. Katherine tensed against the pain, running in front of it, in a panic. Blood began to seep from beneath her bonds, but the Elder did not relent.

"How much do you see, Katherine? Do you understand where our difficulties lie?"

She tried to relax, to let the pain wash over her, without fighting it. She remembered childbirth. She drew a deep, slow breath and focussed inwards, to the safe, dark spaces in her mind.

"Disconnection," she breathed. "Humankind internalising—not seeing further than the end of its nose. Turning our backs on the unknown, the irrational—on everything outside our collaborative human consciousness. And shutting you out."

"But you can't, can you? A man deprived of sleep—deprived of dreams—begins to hallucinate. If he won't sleep, the dreams leak out."

"And that is what's happening now? No balance. We won't acknowledge you—but you are irrepressible. Worming out where you shouldn't be—because we have written off our shadows?"

The branches slackened, but the Elder's eyes were full of hatred, black and unforgiving.

"But you seem to me more human than my faery companion on the paths," Katherine tried.

"Don't you listen?" The Elder cracked a branch like a whip. "You've been eaten—and now we are digesting you, here in the guts of Faeryland. You are part of us. We have absorbed you."

"So how do I find Niamh? That is what I came for. What d'you expect of me? Are you recruiting me for your grand crusade? Shall I return, illuminated, and preach to everyone—Hear ye! Believe in faeries, or perish!"

The branches tightened. Katherine tried to wriggle, but the barbs in her flesh began to tear. The Elder made no immediate response, but closed her heavy eyelids, lost in thought. Katherine's wounds began to sting. She hung from the tree, held in its fierce embrace, till the sky began to darken and the moon rose, thin and pale, in the sky. The hours of the night were long and empty. The moon ascended the sky in the north and completed a shallow arc. The cold seeped into Katherine's body, but her mind remained alert and sharp, allowing her no respite. Suspended, bleeding, like a sacrifice amongst the heavy elder leaves, that clothed her body like a robe.

The moon settled below the horizon. The night closed in, silent, except for the sound of her breath. In the vacant hours, her thoughts began to bubble up from the pits of her mind, like long, colourful streamers. The events of the past unravelled before her mind's eye, to be tried and tasted. She thought of her love for Paul, for Niamh. She remembered their setting up a home. How small a life was, how confined. The choices were infinite, every moment branching off with opportunities of which only one could be chosen. How circumscribed, to be human. At any time she could have tried this or that, gone one way or another. Only now she was held without choice, without volition, subject to the will of the Elder hag, who dreamed while Katherine waited and suffered.

She thought of the Morris men, and the girls, Dawn and Dusk. They were an aberration. Owain's instinctive reaction was the correct one. They had stolen through the veil, and they had assumed humanity, after a fashion. They were greedy. Communication between the two worlds should be fragile and elusive—tantalising. Faeries were visitors to dreams, intangible signposts, shadows of fear and desire, beckoning or teasing, pointing away from the world, from the limited human horizon, and beyond their own world too, to the greater realm, to the unknown. Denied access, the faeries had stolen out instead through a rift created by the imbalance. The protest site, on a pathway between the worlds, had become some kind of focus point, a place of weakness, and the faeries had been lured into false flesh by the collective dreams and hungers of the people living at the site. It was beyond her powers to change humanity's course—but could she heal this localised breach? Was this her task?

The sky began to brighten with the dawn. The sun lifted in the sky, grey and insubstantial at first, then fiery red and bronze, bathing her body with heat. Animals began to move among the trees. In the branches of the Elder a robin began to sing. Way below her, Katherine saw a fox trotting in flash of red through the undergrowth.

A ripple seemed to flow through the Elder's limbs. The bindings loosened on Katherine's body, and gently she was lowered to the ground. She half-collapsed upon the grass, free at last, and she rubbed her stiff, afflicted muscles as the Elder opened her eyes and regarded the visitor. The Elder's expression had softened again. Katherine understood that the old lady had eavesdropped on her thoughts— and fed them too—a peculiar faery-human symbiosis. The hag was struggling for answers and understanding, just as she was.

"What must I do?" Katherine asked.

"Go to the heart of the realm. Our land is a spiral path, and you must travel to the eye. You will see what needs to be done."

"Where do I start?"

The Elder laughed. She dropped her branches and scooped Katherine up again. She opened her great mouth, a yawning crevice in the bark, and stuffed Katherine into the dark depths, swallowed her whole.

When the disturbance had passed, the Elder turned to her sisters, with a wry smile.

Katherine was tumbling through space again. After a time, the darkness streamed away, in tatters, and she was sitting beneath an apple tree.

The old tree was shrouded with fine pinkish-white blossom. Its body was thick and squat, lifting a burden of branches. When the breeze lifted, a fine shower of sleek petals drifted from the tree and settled on the grass, and a fragile perfume hovered on the air. The bark upon the trunk was grey-brown and patterned with a rime of green. Beyond the vicinity of the tree, the land dissolved into amorphous mistiness. Katherine was no longer naked, but clothed in a simple green dress, with stout leather boots upon her feet. Where now? She set off from the tree, into the mist.

She walked purposefully for ten minutes or so, unable to chart her progress in the grey cloud, but confident a direction would emerge. She spotted a dark form up ahead. As she drew near, she realised she was back at the apple tree. She tried again, in a different direction, but found without much surprise, that whichever way she walked, she couldn't evade the tree. What was she to do? What key was required? She sensed there was more to be seen. She was too slow, and too heavy. Earthly reality weighed her down like chains, and she had to shed them. She had to clear her vision. She walked again. As her pace quickened, it occurred to her that she had always existed about three steps behind reality. Her mind was closed and fumbling, never and in the now, never in the quick, flashing moment of the present. She lagged behind. But how to catch up? She walked on. She strained her eyes ahead to the place just before her, to the here and now she always limped behind, with her endless churning thoughts, her inhibitions, her self-containment. How to explode into immediacy? How to break down the filter of her restricting, disconnecting ego? She willed herself forwards, reaching for clarity. She began to run. As she moved through the mist, she felt the bindings about her brain begin to loosen. Faster. She glimpsed bright colours, movements. Her limbs lightened. She streamed on, pressing against her own limits, trying to force a new path. She threw herself, grasping for the moment. She burst into light, a leap into a bright pool that embraced her like water. The mist, the apple tree, were folded away and vanished. She landed with an impact that forced the breath from her body. She looked up.

The shifting sea. The sun was swallowed by the ocean. Delicate streamers of cloud glimmered mauve and flaming pink above the broken black forms of the dunes, where the sky faded into aquamarine, and in the heights, the colour of bluebells. Behind her were steep hills, broken with grey rock. The moon hung like a lump of quartz, burning white, and a pale mist rose from the waves, the breath of the sea, clinging to the ground in soft fingers, lying like a thin, intangible shroud above the grass. The stars bloomed like tiny flowers and in the fading light Katherine could see dark shapes moving in the mist, slender, fragile faery people stooping and running and leaping—playing like children. They were indistinct. She crouched close to the land, in the darkness, while the faeries danced, without thought or desire, moving with the same unconscious grace as swallows, or snakes, or fish. The dance was written in the form of their limbs, in the nature of their bodies, and Katherine was apart from them, alone, a fragment locked away but beating outwards. But they were not aware of separation.

The faeries surrounded her, dark and inchoate. One stepped forwards, throwing back long hair to reveal a thin green face, pointed teeth like fangs. A female form, bare breasts covered with thongs and amulets, feathers and bits of stone. Her eyes were a solid shining black, without white or pupil.

"See what I have," the faery whispered. "See what treasure." From the depths of her cloak she drew out a small, soft bundle, that shifted in the moonlight, wrapped in a pale sheet.

"Niamh!" Katherine cried. The little girl was cradled in the faery's arms. She was half-asleep. Her eyelids fluttered, and she peered at her mother. She smiled.

"Niamh! Give her to me!"

But the faery drew back, protectively. She spoke to the little girl, stroking her cheek with a long, green finger.

"I have to look after her," the faery said.

"Give her to me!" Katherine reached out for her daughter, but the faery fended her off.

"You are so lucky," the faery sighed, "Such a treasure. How we love little children. How we ache for them. Like flowers, they are. Mortal. Brief. How sweet she smells, and her skin, like the petals of a white rose. One moment they bloom, so fragile. And then they grow, and rot, and sink back into the earth."

"Give her to me," Katherine repeated. Her voice trembled. The faery shook her head. She turned away, taking Niamh with her. She skipped off with the others, but as she left, she pointed up to the moon.

"You have further to go," she called. Then she was lost in the dancers, and Katherine was stricken with an intense sense of loss. She longed for her daughter.

The faeries moved away. Katherine regarded the moon. What had the faery tried to convey? How could she reach the moon? It was gibbous, bristling with light. Like a huge silver egg, she thought. An egg. What would hatch from such a thing? As the thoughts formulated in her mind, a great black crack ran across the moon. Two thirds of the shell fell away through the sky, down into the sea, and a dragon perched upon the edge of the remaining fragment. It fluttered dark wings and tossed its head. Then it launched into the night sky, and within a few moments had landed lightly on the ground beside Katherine. The dragon was about the size of a large horse. Its body was moist, with a flexible scaley hide. It flicked a long, soft tongue from its mouth, like a snake, tasting the air.

"So where are you going to take me?" Katherine asked. The dragon tipped its head to one side and looked at her with reptilian yellow eyes. It gestured to its back. Katherine climbed on, awkwardly. She wrapped her arms about its neck, and the dragon unfurled its black wings, and lifted up into the sky.

She couldn't tell how long or far they flew. The night opened all around them, the stars as fierce as fires. Then at last, she saw, suspended in space, a circular stone tower. A narrow staircase wound about it, right to the top, where, beneath a turret, an arched window shone with warm yellow light. The dragon landed at the bottom of the starcase, where it clutched the stone with precarious claws. Katherine climbed from its back, and thanked it. The beast nodded, and released its grip on the stairs, tumbling back down again. Katherine peered beneath the tower, and watched it spread its wings, like a giant bat, soaring through the empyrean.

She began her ascent of the tower. She pressed her body against the stone wall as she walked, afraid of the yawning space about the tiny island. She moved slowly, and as she climbed, she began to hear a singing, thin and distant at first, but stronger and clearer as she proceeded. At the top of the tower she peered in through the window. A circular room lay before her, with a fire flickering in an open hearth in the centre. Shelves of books lined the walls. Rails and hooks hung from the ceiling, laden with herbs. A young woman dressed in blue silk was sitting at a desk, writing. She looked up as Katherine appeared at the window.

"You have come this far," the woman said. She put down her pen and stood up.

"Obviously." Katherine climbed through the window, and jumped down upon the stone floor. The woman led her to a wooden seat by the fire. They regarded each other. The woman had long, red hair. Her face was ageless, but possessed a mature gravity.

"So what do I do now?" Katherine said. "Where next? Have I far to go?"

"No. Not far. I can help you." The woman took a silver bowl from the table, and poured in a little water. She placed it before the fire, where the dancing light cast fitful shadows upon the surface.

"What do you want to see?" she said.

"Niamh." Katherine made a quick response, then, more slowly, "and Paul. And Elaine and Jo." And someone else. Who had she forgotten?

Then, just as she had looked into the font in the graveyard, she stared into the churning depths of the silver bowl. The visions swam out to receive her.

A community of people, walking the face of the earth—following the sacred paths. Snow lay heavily upon the ground, crisp and bright with frost, though the sun was high and the sky a brilliant blue. The people were dressed in furs, soft leather boots fastened with laces criss-crossed about their legs. At the head of the tribe, an old woman surveyed her surroundings, a clearing in a forest that spread all about them. She spoke briefly to a tall man, heavily bearded, with long scars stretching across his hand and arm. Beside the old woman was a young girl, maybe twelve or thirteen, keeping close to her side. The girl looked up, to the sky, where a large black bird was circling above the snow. She let out a cry, and the bird cawed hoarsely in response. The girl held out her arms, and the crow flew down, landing lightly upon her shoulder. The old woman smiled and nodded. The crow cawed again, and this time was answered by a chorus from the trees to the north. A host of crows were shifting restlessly amongst the branches of an ash tree, and the sound of their rough voices filled the still, winter air. The old woman pointed to the north, to the birds, and began to walk. The people moved on, following her footsteps.

The snowy landscape receded.

She saw the squat, emblazoned with angels, barricaded like a fortress. Outside the men in uniforms confronted the Morris men. Inside, like a tomb, the air was dark and stale. Paul ached with desire, with love, for his partner. For her? No. She could see her faery duplicate, hovering in his mind's eye.

She turned from him. She saw the woman washing bloody clothes in a river.

"Elaine?" she whispered. Hearing her voice, the woman paused and looked up. She flicked lank black hair over her shoulder. Her face was thin and weary, and beyond her, Katherine heard the sweep of the skirts of Death.

"Katherine?" A familiar voice stretching up to her, from the bowl. Someone was conscious of her presence, her observation.

"Katherine!"

It was Jo. She gazed down.

"Jo! Can you hear me? Yes, it's me!"

He was standing in the cottage under seige. She could hear voices shouting, heavy thuds upon wood and stone. She heard cursing and the thunder of machinery closing in.

"Katherine, I'm coming with you, I'll find you," he shouted. "Give me your hand!"

Without a thought she thrust her hand into the bowl. The liquid burnt like fire, and she howled, but somehow Jo had seized her fingers and she couldn't pull free. She heaved with all her might. She heard a yell. Her hand slipped away and she fell back heavily on the floor. The bowl was upturned, the water split across the floor. Katherine stood up. The woman was watching her.

"What have you done?" she said. Her face flickered. She became the patchwork skeleton from the graveyard. The dryad. Niamh's green-faced custodian, and even, in part, the Elder hag.

"You are all of them, those who have helped me," Katherine said. The faery nodded.

"If Faeryland is a spiral, the faeries are a cobweb upon it. Each of us is a single thread passing through the many mansions, with a multitude of faces."

"And the Elder?"

"Is the mask you made for the fat spider at the hub of the web. But your presence has altered us. You've become part of the web too."

"The breach. How do I seal it?"

The faery, her face mobile and flickering, pointed to a tiny door on the far side of the circular room. There had been no door on the outside. Where would it lead?

The wooden door swung open. The doorway was a narrow, pointed arch, scarcely large enough for Katherine to squeeze through. She stooped. A broken bridge stretched from the tower to a bank of white and silver cloud. She stepped out cautiously. The grey stonework crumbled beneath her feet. Without a handrail, with a path barely wide enough for her feet, Katherine placed one careful foot before another, teetering above a bottonless blue expanse. As she moved from the tower, she saw a rainbow shining beneath the cloud. The bridge reached a peak and then descended steeply. She proceeded nervously, on slipping feet, watching fragments of rock drop away from the bridge, down into the blue. And then at last she was across. She jumped the last step, dropping into the cloud, through a cool veil, to stand at the heart of a forest.

The trees rose up like columns, creating great gothic arches, with boughs and branches interlaced. At the cardinal points, wide avenues stretched as far as she could see, revealing, to the west, a sinking sun, and to the east, a full moon low in the sky. The air was sweet with the scent of flowers and leaves. In the nave, where Katherine stood, the grass was thick with every kind of forest flower—pale anemones, pink campion, stitchwort, and strange spotted orchids. She sensed movement in the trees around the clearing, the shifting of a faery presence. She glimpsed glittering faces, the haze of wings. But none encroached upon this central space.

Katherine took off her boots and walked to the heart of the clearing. She pushed through the flowers, and her legs were coated with pollen. The scent grew stronger. A small mound rose from the earth, covered in bluebells. Upon the mound rested a long white skull. The bluebells caressed it, pushing up through the empty eye sockets. A horse's skull, Katherine thought at first, till she saw the long, crystalline horn, rising from the centre of its forehead. The bone was pale, with a slight shine, caught between the sun and the moon. She looked into its eyes, past the bluebells, into the blackness beyond.

The light fell away. Here at the heart of Faeryland, at its core, was the void. She could go no further. She stared into the skull, into darkness. She dived in.

Katherine was sitting on her bed, alone. Beyond the window, the square view was broken by the parallel lines of the telephone wires, running along the block of terrace houses. The bright, brilliant blue sky unrolled and endless changing vista of faraway clouds. Every few minutes the stillness was cut by the tight, black rush of swifts flying in front of the house. It was nine oclock, the beginning of June. The hours of light were stretching deeper and deeper into the night. The child was asleep, at last, and Katherine's energy ebbed and dissipated in the new calm of the house. Now, however, a small, insistent voice seemed to call from the wide world beyond the window—come out, feel the rush of the sap rising, the slow sink into twilight, this quick June, this summer...I can't go out, she thought. Of course not. Leave Niamh with Paul? He'd manage of course, but would it be fair, after his trials at work today, for me to leave him babysitting while I go out and enjoy myself? She felt a faint satisfactory sense of relief for so neatly concluding the little voice could be disregarded. The hold of lethargy was strong. It was always easy to do nothing... She would go downstairs and make a cup of tea. She would switch on the television. She would sleep. As she always did. For ever and ever Amen. There are no faeries. What was she thinking of? Why pretend, why make up all this stuff? Why cling to phantoms, to the teasing hunger that somewhere there are signs, always elusive, pointing to a greater reality, pointing to a place we have lost—that maybe can be found again? No. Far better be realistic. Far better to fasten her eyes upon the task at hand, to finish that bit of painting, to mow the grass, to make plans for a holiday months and months away. Work hard. Keep busy.

Katherine sank down upon the bed. Yes, she would stay inside. What else was there to do?

An end to our exploring...how did the poem go? An end to our exploring. And here she was indeed. Back where she had started...

The words filtered into her brain. She felt a pain tear through her body, as though her heart was fracturing under an immense strain. Something was wrong. No! This shouldn't happen! Was this the way to heal the breach, for her to un-make the decision of that evening long ago? Some kind of critical point—a gate which now she could choose to close? If she hadn't met Crow, if she hadn't walked with the faeries—would everything be right again? Was that what the Elder wanted her to do? But then I'd keep Niamh, she thought. Right now she is sleeping in the next room, perfectly safe, within my clutches. Erase the faeries. Cut them from my life.

And obliterate all that has happened to us? No. She couldn't do it. If surrender was the Elder's requirement, she couldn't fulfill her task. She had seen so much. They had shared such magic, such adventures—all of them. She had to find another way. She jumped from the bed and ran down the stairs, and out of the front door.

Into another greenwood—shifting and hostile.

And now she had no guide.

CHAPTER TWENTY SIX

Jo pushed handfuls of rubble against the planks, sealing them into the cottage. Clouds of dust swirled in the air, and Elaine coughed repeatedly.

"Help me with this," he urged, swinging the torch beam to the heap of broken breeze blocks. "We'll pile them on top."

Elaine followed his orders, though she was slow, intensely weary. She grumbled at him, that she wished with all her heart she was anywhere but here, building herself into a tomb. But Jo worked on, in a state of feverish excitement.

"Come, quickly," he said, when the task was complete. They climbed back up to the first floor. As soon as they were through the stairwell, Paul helped him push two old doors over the hole, and they heaved the metal barrel on top. Already the last window had been obscured. All was in order. After five minutes of desperate activity, nothing remained to be done—but wait.

The minutes passed.

"I wonder what's going on," Violet said. A storm lantern was burning, illuminating eight faces in the premature darkness. Jo was shaking. He had been waiting for this day, half longing for it. The culmination of their plans and efforts— the confrontation.

The silence weighed heavy. Surely it wouldn't take them long to smash through that first barricade, at the bottom of the Old Lane? It was a slight delaying tactic, to afford them enough time to close up the bolt-hole.

"Shall we sing a song?" Jan suggested. Elaine sniffed.

James pulled up on his motorcycle, wiping the rain from his visor. He parked just behind the police van, within fifteen minutes of Paul's call. He had a camera, as well as his notebook. The photographer was twenty-five miles away, taking snaps of a golden wedding couple. Another reporter arrived as he was taking off his helmet—a girl from the rival local weekly. They nodded to each other.

"Anything happened yet?" she asked.

"I've only just got here myself." He edged round the van and stood at the bottom of the lane. A group of bailiffs—he guessed about twenty—had driven through a wooden barricade and a trench with the help of a small bulldozer. A group of policemen were surveying the proceedings from a distance. He had encountered a few of them before, during the course of his reporting duties at the magistrate's court, and his daily calls to the station, to record the local wrong-doings. He was greeted curtly.

More heavy machinery arrived. A truck carrying a hydraulic platform, a bright yellow digger and a huge metal monster like a crane. More men appeared, in a truck piled high with aluminium fencing panels. The machines crashed through the hedge and parked upon the field, gouging deep muddy wounds in the long grass. The men jumped out, in waterproof coats and hard hats, waiting for orders to proceed. Within minutes, the battalion was fully assembled—ready to attack.

Owain was standing in the copse when he heard a shout. Another girl had taken up residence in Elaine's abandoned tree house, a gawky graphic designer turned eco-warrior, and she shrieked out the alarm.

"The bailiffs, the bailiffs! They're coming!" As soon as she spoke, a dozen people emerged from the shadows of the copse, from the rain-battered benders in the trees. Wrapped in pieces of sheet plastic and elderly waterproof jackets, they looked subdued, inured to the long days of persistent rain, to perpetual mud. Had it ever been different?

But the call to action had its effect. An electric thrill coursed through the assembly. They stood together.

"Should we run down and help them at the squat?" the first girl asked. Owain shook his head.

"No. We stick to our plan. We don't know if they will take the cottage first, or if they're planning to go for the cottage and the copse in one fell swoop. We must stay here and guard the trees, yes?"

The others nodded. Owain was appointed as look-out. The others returned to their aerial abodes, drawing up the access ropes and ladders.

Owain walked a short distance from the copse, down the lane. The cottage lay hidden beneath its blanket of vegetation, though he could still discern the painted decorations on the brickwork. With the windows covered, the house looked blind and mutilated. Had they already lost the battle? The cottage was certainly not a home of any kind. It squatted like some cancerous growth, seething with unnatural vegetation. But people were hiding in its depths—Jo, and Paul, Jan and Violet, amongst others. And Elaine? Where was Elaine? She had gone to the house. He couldn't see her. Surely she must be inside too. He shuddered.

At the bottom of the lane he could see the sharp lines and metallic colours of the heavy machinery, distinct in the grey, rainy haze. A swarm of bailiffs, like ants, were striding to the cottage. Were they nervous? he wondered. Excited? Pissed off to be dragged out in the wet and dirt?

Something happened. Their progress was arrested. The neat ranks broke into a messy rabble. Why? He glanced back at the copse. All appeared to be in order. He hurried down to lane to find out

Four Morris men and the two girls, Dawn and Dusk, stood in the path of the advancing bailiffs. Apart from Spring, Owain could not easily identify the others. He knew they had all been given names, but their numbers varied every time he saw them. Sometimes three, or four, or six. Often they were entirely absent. The girls likewise. But Spring was the leader—the focus of the group. And Spring Owain held in some way personally accountable for the faery corruption eating into the road site, and its inhabitants, after the Midsummer fair. The slippery portal of faeryland had been wedged open and gaping. Faery, elusive and forever just out of reach, was spilling its guts. The Morris men were greedy, too blatant.

An abomination. The longer they remained, the greater the chasm they created. But how could he send them back?

He watched, with a mixture of apprehension and anxiety. What would the bailiffs make of them? He drew closer. He heard Spring speak. His voice pealed like a bell, silvery and precise.

"What do you want?" Spring asked. One of the bailliffs stepped forwards. He wore a large badge on his lapel, from which Owain assumed he must be higher in rank than the others. He was a big man, physically imposing, and he towered over the diminuitive Spring. The bailiff bristled visibly.

"I have the authority to remove you from this site. I am formally requesting you to leave. I am empowered to use the necessary force to ensure you comply with the court order."

The bailiffs resumed their orderly formation in the face of their apparently raggle-taggle opposition. What kind of circus troupe was this? But Spring turned his back on the bailiffs and nodded to his kindred. They joined hands in a long line. They began to encircle the court servants.

How many were there? The original four, with the two girls, became twelve, became twenty-four. Within an instant they had entirely surrounded the bailiffs, who looked around in disbelief. Where had the others sprung from? One or two barged the circle, trying to push a way out, but the circle was resilient. The Morris men began to skip, singing an inane little folk song. The bells jingled.

Owain edged closer.

The bailiffs shuffled uneasily, without trying to escape. One covered his eyes. Owain sensed their growing fear. What were the dancers doing? The bailiff boss began to weep and wave his arms about, fighting invisible ghosts. Two started hitting each other. One man curled up on the ground, in the mud, muttering to himself. The others stared before them, each focussed on some intangible, personal vision. What fears, what monstrosities did they witness? The binding *esprit de corps* dissolved into muddy puddles.

Owain had seen enough. He ran the final distance to the circle, and grabbed Spring roughly by the shoulders. He pulled him from the circle, breaking the ring. The dancers fell apart. The bailiffs came to themselves, confused and uneasy.

Spring was blazing with anger. He shoved Owain from him. He stamped his foot, his face contorted, a thwarted Rumpelstiltskin. He stamped his foot again and raged.

"Why did you do it? Why?" he shrieked. "I'm trying to help you! I'm trying! It's what you want, isn't it? You wanted help—we were asked to stay!"

The Morris men were diminished. Four again. The girls looked bedraggled, rain dripping from black and scarlet hair. They shivered. They clustered round Owain and Spring, like disobedient children. Owain stood impassive before the onslaught. He shook his head.

"It's not right," he said. "It's not what we want. You're causing trouble. We don't need you. Go away, back where you came from." Hands in pockets, he turned away and walked towards the bailliffs. He picked up the man still weeping in a puddle.

"Thanks mate," the man muttered, wiping his face. The others looked disordered, a little vacant, but as Owain turned to walk to the copse, they regained their self control. They looked from one to another, restoring composure, unsure exactly what had happened and not wanting to dwell upon it too much.

Spring was still screeching and jumping up and down.

"I won't go! I won't!" he shouted at Owain's retreating form, "You can't make me! The others still want me. Yes, they do!"

Owain did not respond. He walked on.

James watched the proceedings from a distance. He saw the Morris men make a ring around the bailiffs. How many were there? Six? No. More than that. Many more. He couldn't make out what was happening. Why didn't the bailiffs break out? Then Owain stepped in. Strange that Owain should be helping the other side. What was going on? The Morris men backed away—just six again. Was he seeing things? He must have been mistaken. They walked away and disappeared from sight. The bailiffs resumed their march to the cottage, and the men with the fencing panels drove up the lane behind them. Presumably, they would secure the area around the cottage as soon as they had evicted the squatters.

James followed the bailiffs, camera at the ready. The police remained in a group close by, watching the proceedings with an expression of indifference. The heavy machines started up, and began to close in on the cottage. What hope was there? James thought. Paul had told him there were eight inside, with strict instructions not to let the bailiffs know the exact number. But more were arriving. The news had spread. Protestors from Locksbury and Marlborough appeared. Security guards prevented them walking up the lane, but the keener ones found a way across the fields. The remainder shouted and waved placards by the main road, and the traffic was brought to a halt. Then the police were required to take an active role, ensuring the road remained clear. A fence rose around the cottage, despite the harrying of protestors. Some were bodily removed, but returned. A fight broke out when one of the fencers, provoked beyond his endurance, planted a fist on a young man's nose, spilling first blood. James took a picture. The young man displayed his wound with a mixture of pain and pride. The hostility increased on both sides.

Inside the cottage, the squatters heard a loud bang on the front door. A voice, distorted by a megaphone, coldly and politely asked them to vacate the property. It continued to inform them that the necessary force would be used to ensure they complied. The occupants cheered and shouted out their defiance. Elaine, however, crouched quietly in the corner. Jo hopped about like a bird. Paul made a further phone call. One of his friends outside the cottage had a cell phone and filled him in on the situation, the numbers, and the actions of the bailiffs.

A heavy blow landed on the front door. It fell with a dull thud, and Jo jumped. They heard other bangs, as the bailiffs laid seige, testing the defences. Where would they break in? The cottage roof was already unsafe—on the verge of collapse—so they were confident the bailiffs' obligatory duty of care to the protestors would prevent them breaking an entry from above. They would risk a possibly fatal caving in on the people below. The upstairs windows were the likely target point, if they could get the hydraulic platform up the lane and into the garden.

Jo couldn't keep still. Outside they could hear shouts and bangs, the yells of protestors and the grinding mechanical roar of machinery manoeuvring around the cottage. Yet here, at the heart of the action, at the epicentre, they were locked away in a dark hole, cut adrift from the efforts of their fellows. Although Paul had a phone, Jo felt entirely isolated. Who would he reach out to? His special people were here—his new family. Though Owain was outside, and Katherine was—where? He thought about his life in Bristol, his old friends. Was it only a matter of weeks ago? He lived a different life now, in a new land.

Jan was still singing. Violet pressed against Jo, slipping her hand into his. He saw Elaine hug her knees to her chest.

A cold wind cut through the cottage. Jo's skin tingled. He felt an itch on his scalp. He stood up.

"Did you feel that?" he asked Violet.

"What?"

"That draught. Have they broken in?"

She shook her head.

"We'd have certainly heard," she said. But Jo was uneasy. He walked to the landing, into the other bedrooms. The darkness seemed to press against his face. When he walked, dusty fingers swirled from the floor, and twined into his throat. He felt the wind again. A thickening of the atmosphere. A shift. A ripple of disturbance. A wall flashed white. Then darkness again. He stood motionless, waiting for another clue. What if the walls were doorways, instead of barriers? Where would they lead? Another wall flashed, and he sensed a presence. He was not alone. The bone necklace twitched on his chest. Katherine? Katherine. He shouted at the top of his voice.

"Katherine! I'm coming with you, I'll find you," he shouted. "Give me your hand!"

He heard a crackle of static. The wall shimmered, electric blue, and a small hand reached out to him. He grasped her fingers, though he heard her cry out as he touched her. The hand began to pull back, but Jo held with all his might. He pressed himself against the wall, though it resisted him. He heard a clamour rising in the room, the smell of burning, a tumult of protest as his long, skinny body was torn from one place to the next. Katherine's fingers slipped away. He scrabbled for purchase. His mind blanked.

He plunged into an empty space. His thoughts, his tenuous identity were snatched from him. When the time came, he gathered the pieces together and reassembled them. His actions were slow, without conscious volition. He moved like an automaton.

He wandered in a haze, drifting between clouds of fear and momentary flashes of delight. The landscape quivered and flickered, catching him in a maze of confused images, monsters rising from flowers, fierce admonitory faces, green limbs and twisting bodies suggesting beauty and ecstasy. He was utterly lost.

So he walked, without bearings, through a mist of shifting forms. Instants of panic switched to faint, forgotten echoes of drugged delirium. He floated like a leaf, caught in the fierce winds of his own lost dreams, and in the shadows of a hundred neglected nightmares. Which way to go? He ached for a clue, for a steady landmark —something to hold him steady in the storm. He longed for a respite.

He wandered till his mind reeled, till his fragile sense of self was shattered into pieces.

Then, at last, the fog began to clear. He peered round, sensing something familiar. His environment began to stabilise. Still it was dark, and amorphous, but hadn't he been here before? He halted, struggling to identify the place. He heard music, and sensed the movement of bodies about him. Voices, laughter. The quick, fleeting scent of a cigarette. As he soaked in his surroundings, the fragments began to coalesce. He saw a bar. Beside him, on a little dance floor, a dozen indistinct people were shifting in time to thick, pounding music. In an instant it occurred to him where he was. With a thrill of relief he realised he was standing in the basement of the Chapel. He had escaped. At last, standing in home terrain, amongst friends, amongst his kindred. A fit of laughter bubbled up inside him. Of course. Had he ever left this place? The events of the past weeks dissolved in his mind. Here he was, as ever, perfectly at home. What had he been thinking? What had happened?

He scanned the assembly, searching for his friends. The light was dim, the faces indistinct. He skirted the dancers, and headed for the bar. Here he always had friends. He longed for contact, for an anchor. If he could just find someone he knew—if he could attach himself—he would be safe. He looked among the revellers, pushing through the crowd, glancing into faces. He kept seeing people who looked like his friends—only to find he was deluded. Every time he spotted a familar form, he felt a surge of hope. When he drew closer, he realised he had been mistaken. The familiarity dissolved—he regarded a stranger. He hunted more desperately. He shoved, and ran, and even called out names. White faces, bright eyes heavy with make-up—they watched him with a strange curiosity, from a distance.

Jo slumped on a step by the bar, curled up with his head on his knees. His ears were ringing. He was alone.

Then something brushed against him. He looked up. From the indefinite forms at the bar, his eyes were attracted by the movement of a slender figure walking towards him. As she walked, the others seemed to lose substance, which she drew to herself, gaining in clarity. In the darkness she seemed to shine, distinct from the others, entirely self contained.

As she drew nearer, Jo felt a flush of perspiration. He trembled. His anxiety faded. She was the most delightful creature he had ever seen. He stood up.

She was not tall—her head barely reached his shoulder—and she was very slim, a black-haired waif. And what hair—hanging in thick raven elf-locks as far as her waist, teased a little around her face, forming a dark halo in the flashing lights. She was dressed in a black velvet basque, shaped to a point in the middle of her waist, and a long, narrow purple skirt. Lace gloves reached over her elbows, so her shoulders were bare, a soft expanse of skin as white as snow. She looked up at him, catching his gaze, and smiled quickly, a mix of shyness and hauteur. As she walked past him, she pushed a strand of hair over her shoulder, self-conscious, and Jo saw the basque didn't meet at the back, that a long black lace criss-crossed across her pale skin.

She stopped. Jo's heart stopped, too—for an instant. She hesitated, then turned towards him again. She mooched to his side.

"Are you on your own?" she said. Jo had to put his face close to hers when she spoke, to hear her voice above the music. Her breath smelt faintly of alcohol, and sweet, like violets. He nodded.

"I'm Jo," he said, clumsily offering his hand. She shook it gravely. She looked up at him again, with eyes of bright purple. Her lips were a dark, matte red, like the petals of a rose. Her chin was small and neat, cheek bones high and pronounced. The embodiment of his dreams. The perfect goth girl. Jo's wits deserted him. He struggled for something to say. The girl laughed.

"Come with me," she said. Jo followed like a lamb.

The Chapel lost its clarity, and then dissolved like smoke. Jo hung on to the girl. She led him through a door. As he stepped over the threshold, he began to laugh. He was home. Everything remained in place. The long mirror, the regiments of empty hairspray cans and broken make-up cases. The cheap jewellery, the posters and pictures. His own dear room, his escape—his hiding place. Except it wasn't. The bed was different. Instead of his lumpy double bed, a huge black iron edifice towered in its place. A four poster, hanging with shreds of grey and white tulle, and decorated with goblins and gargoyles, leering from the cold metal. A bracket of candles glimmered on the wall.

The girl watched him.

"Are you glad to be here?" she asked uncertainly. "Do you like it?"

"Like it? I love it. It couldn't be better."

She sat on the edge of the bed. He knelt on the floor before her, feasting his eyes, shaking with desire but unable to bring himself to touch her. She received his homage with good grace, and waited.

"What's the matter Jo? Don't you want me? Would you like me to be different?" Her voice was a little wistful.

"No, no! You're absolutely perfect. It's a bit scary, that's all. You're everything." He reached forwards, and pushed up her skirt. She was wearing short, tight boots and black lace stockings. He half sobbed, and pressed his face against the warm, bare skin at the top of her thighs. He pushed her back upon the bed and kissed her frantically. The girl laughed, pulled herself away, and removed her skirt.

"Take off your clothes, Jo," she said softly, then, "Lie down." She reached down beside the bed, for two long shards of thick satin ribbon. She tied his wrists to the bars at the head of the bed. He was breathing deeply, and his pulse beat hard, but he surrendered himself utterly. When he was fastened, she knelt over him, kissing his neck and chest so her long hair trailed over his body. She tickled his skin with her nails. Then she sat up, straddling him, and lowered herself slowly upon his helpless erection.

He felt he had been swallowed, or consumed. The girl moved upon him, bruising the skin as she clutched his chest with her fingers. She held his legs tight between her thighs, her eyes shut, seemingly oblivious of him, straining to her own climax. As she came, she gritted her teeth, choking a sob, and Jo felt his own release torn from him, a quick convulsion that the girl seemed to soak into her own body. She collapsed upon him, sweating. But Jo was sated for a moment only. He felt an emptiness inside him, a hunger, as though she had stolen something and he was less without it. He wanted her again. He wanted to be satisfied.

The night stretched on. He faded into sleep and woke, still bound, with the girl kissing his belly. He was instantly aroused, and they fucked again. Afterwards the desire continued to grow but his emptiness also increased. He wanted her, more and more, and she took him, time after time.

His mind drifted, alternating between unconsciousness, fierce arousal, and a fleeting moment of satisfaction that led only to a greater need. He was losing himself. He grew faint.

How long did she possess him? Time faded, a confusing stream of ache and distraction, and endless, deepening hunger. When his mind cleared, the girl reared above him, naked, and around her eyelids, upon her cheeks, silver scales glittered like sequins. From her shoulders towered huge, fragile wings, streamers of gauze, black and white and grey. Her hair was threaded with strands of silver. Jo was defenseless before her, caught in the honey of his lust.

"Do you love me, Jo?" she crooned. "Stay with me. Stay with me forever."

She held out a black glass, filled with a viscous fluid, scented like wine and glinting darkly red in the candlelight, like the ripe flesh of a pomegranate.

"Drink, Jo. Stay with me." She lowered the glass to his lips.

Jo fought for breath. An unexpected sense of panic spread through his body. He began to struggle. Where was he? Didn't he have something to do? She drew back the glass and kissed him.

"Who would you like me to be, Jo?" she whispered. "I can be everything you want."

"Do you want me?" said Elaine, sitting upon him, in a white dress.

"Or me?" Little Violet, cascades of hair intact.

"What about me?" It was his mate Steve, smudged with beer and lipstick.

"Who do you want, Jo?" The faces flicked from one to another, in rapid succession. Jo shouted out. He strained against his bonds. To much. It was too much. He had to pull free before she drank his soul. He had to wake up.

He fought like a trapped animal, thrashing and kicking on the bed.

"Jo! Jo! Stop! I love you, Jo!" The girl attempted to sooth him, then tried to contain him, but Jo bucked his body, casting her away. He yanked at the ribbon, yanked again, and at last his hand came free. He knelt up, pulled his other hand from its binding, and stumbled towards the door. The faery lay upon the floor screaming and kicking in a fury. She had lost her allure. The glass had spilled its gluey contents on the floor. He kicked the door open, without looking back. He escaped into the maelstrom.

Into the green wood. The twisted forests. Oh yes, he knew this place. The chasms of space, the winding green, where every moment yawned like a pit, ready to swallow him up. He didn't need to be afraid. He walked through a subway, where the walls were covered in scarlet graffitti, and nodded to the shadows in the dark. He travelled through a park in a city, where children were playing. He saw a tramp on a park bench, a derelict body that shuffled like a sleepwalker, as though its mind had already vacated the premises, but the body moved on, out of habit. He saw the smart city folk, so neatly dressed, so co-ordinated and complete. Did they see him? Did the tramp cast a glance, did the children alter their game? Did the city folk step out of his path, or were their eyes fixed in the opposite direction?

He remembered his mother, and his sister. How long since he had seen them? In accordance with the thought, he moved into a strange flat, where his mother was sitting with a balding, middle-aged man he had never met. His mother wore a new engagement ring. Was she marrying again? Had she not bothered to tell him? He reached out his hand, to touch her. She shivered and rubbed her arms.

"We must invite Jo to stay," she said. "I'd like you to meet him. He's a little strange." Jo detected a faint pride in her voice. He was surprised.

"Yes, I'd like that," said the man. His voice was gentle. Jo saw a photo of his sister on a shelf, with a partner and young baby. She was only eighteen. How long had he been away?

He moved on.

He stood in his little room. His aunt, official landlady, was dumping all his possessions into black bin bags. She swept the junk from the dressing table in one swoop. She stuffed in the clothes from his drawers, picked through the jewellery, tore down the posters. When she had finished, his clutter filled three and a half bags. His room. A storage place for so much garbage. The lowest hole in the great rubbish heap. So much rot and decay. So much corrupted, corroding waste. He shuddered. He moved away.

Had these events occurred? Or were they still possibilities, forks on the branch yet to be chosen? He trod lightly. He looked and marvelled. Each scene opened like a box of shiny treasure—or, instead, a can of worms.

He had to find Katherine. He knew she was near. He tried to call out, but the wind seemed to snatch the words from his mouth. He wasn't otherwise hindered in his search, though the faery girl had tried to detain him. The land heaved about him like a restless beast. He moved through its mind. He sensed confusion, and conflict.

"Jo. Let me help you." The shadows gathered, and the faery girl stood beside him. Had she heard his thoughts? The scales shone at her eyes. Her wings trembled. He drew back.

"Don't be afraid," she said. She put her hand out to him, and he pulled away.

"I'm not trying to trap you," she said. She looked around, as though she was nervous.

"I do love you, Jo. I'll help you if I can."

He was suspicious.

"In exchange for what?" he said. She shook her head.

"You need to find her."

"Why don't you help her?"

"Elements are working in conflict with one another. The left hand doesn't see the actions of the right."

Jo shrugged.

"What have I to lose? I can't find her on my own."

The faery held out her hand again, and Jo clasped it tight. She led him through the glittering green wood. And she took him to the edge of a deep pit, like a well. They leaned over the top, peering into the blackness beneath.

"She's in there?" Jo asked. The faery nodded. She was loathe to let him go but she was trembling. She backed away, and flitted off amongst the heaving trees.

CHAPTER TWENTY SEVEN

Jan was pulled unceremoniously through the window, struggling and screeching. More reporters had arrived, from Swindon and Bristol, and Jan's eviction, a flare of red hair and blue-clad flailing legs, was recorded on video for the regional news. A crowd of about a hundred protestors had gathered, and they stood around the new fence enclosing the cottages, while the bailiffs removed Elaine, cold and aloof, and finally Paul, from the squat.

They had broken through one of the back windows, two men on the hydraulic platform battering the planks with huge sledgehammers. They entered the cottage, broke down the door into the front bedroom, and picked off the squatters one by one. Paul gave them the most difficulty, hanging onto the doorway, clinging with the tenacity of a limpet. In the quiet gloom of the cottage, away from the cameras, one of the bailiffs kicked him hard in the stomach. Paul doubled up, his hands slipped from the frame and he cradled his body, in a red fog of pain as they bundled him through the house, and pushed him, curled and bruised, onto the platform.

He lay on the floor, fighting for breath. Violet crouched beside him.

"Paul? Paul? Are you okay? What happened? What did they do?"

"Kicked me," he choked.

"Bastards. Report them."

"I was the last one—nobody saw. No point."

Two men arrived to remove them from the compound. Another shouted out:

"The coast's clear. They're all out. We'll pull it down."

Violet paled.

"No!" she shouted. "No! There's still someone in there. Jo's still inside. You can't pull it down!"

The men looked from one to another uneasily. She sounded convincing.

"Is she telling the truth?" The tall man, the one in charge, turned to Paul with a cold stare, waiting for confirmation. Paul nodded.

"Yes. One more. Jo Hoblyn. He left the room. He must be hiding somewhere in the house, but I don't know where."

"Great," the man sighed. "Go in again. Apparently there's someone else in there. Look again."

"We've already trashed it. There's no-one left."

"Try again. Just in case."

The bailiffs shook their heads, but returned to the hydraulic platform. The first man addressed Paul.

"You'd better not be making this up," he said.

Paul and Violet looked at each other. Where was Jo? They had no idea where he was hiding. He had effectively disappeared. What if the bailiffs couldn't find him? Paul and Violet were led away, to be ejected from the new enclosure, but the tall man gestured that they should be detained till Jo was found. They waited.

After ten minutes the bailiff reappeared at the window.

"We can't find anyone. The place is empty."

"Okay. You can begin the demolition," he shouted to the contractors, casting Paul a look of contempt. Paul was filled with panic. What about Jo? Had he slipped outside? Two men took hold of his arms to lead him out. The crane swung into position, dangling a wrecking ball like an absurd iron conker.

"No!" Paul shouted. He pulled away from from his captors, shoving and fighting, "He might be still inside! You'll kill him!"

The ball swung, and hit the side of the house. The stonework split and crumbled.

"Wait!" Paul struggled with his captors. He lashed out, kicking and fighting, and a flailing fist landed on the mouth of one of the men. He felt his knuckles crunch against teeth. His hand exploded with pain, and blood sprang to the man's mouth. Paul stood motionless for an instant, in a state of shock, but half a dozen bailiffs charged in, jumping on top of him, pressing him to the mud. A boot grazed the back of his head. Another landed in his ribs. Then he was lifted up, dazed and filthy, and dragged from the site.

"Hello, Paul."

He looked up into the face of Sergeant Gerard. Paul's mind was dim. The policeman's face loomed towards him. He looked faintly amused.

"You've got yourself into trouble this time," he said. "Take him back to the station."

Paul was pushed into the back of a van, and fifteen minutes later, found himself locked in a police cell.

He was released in the early evening, without charge. The bailiff had a split lip, but Paul had an impressive array of cuts and bruises. Retribution had been swift and perfunctory.

Kate picked him up from Marlborough, and drove them back to Locksbury. Niamh was fastened in her seat in the back.

"How are you feeling?" she asked.

"Were the cottages demolished? Did they find Jo?"

Kate shook her head.

"James rang, just before I left. He said the cottages were flattened. And no sign of Jo. They're assuming he must have got frightened and slipped out before the eviction."

Paul saw a faint smile playing at the corners of her mouth.

"What's funny?" he asked. "You know where he is? You do, don't you."

She shook her head. Her hair caught the sunshine, filaments of gold in the tumble of brown. He studied the side of her face, the graceful curve of her cheek, the pale, golden glow upon her skin. Despite the familiarity, there were subtle changes too. As the days passed, she looked a little different. He thought he influenced the changes—a response to his dreams, to his love. She bent like a reed, in the wind of his hopes and thoughts. Did no-one notice these alterations? Very slight, the deepening colour in her hair, the shift in the shape of her face, her lips. She was becoming his own Kate—no longer a carbon copy of the weary partner, Katherine. Friends had commented—had Katherine been to the hairdressers? Katherine was looking well these days—was Niamh sleeping better? Had she gained a little weight? Changed her make-up? They smiled, Paul and Kate, hugging Niamh, nodding and agreeing. How happy they were together. How radiant. And did Paul feel guilty? Was he worried about Katherine? She had, after all, been missing for a fortnight. He prodded himself mentally. He chewed over his irrational behaviour. No, he didn't feel in the slightest bit guilty. Katherine had made it abundantly clear she didn't want him anymore. How often had he seen her wiping his undesired kisses from her mouth? How many times had she been repulsed by his desire for her? He doubted she would even be jealous—a thought which gave him a slight pain. And as for her safety? Kate assured him Katherine was in safe hands. Why should he distrust her? Yes, Katherine's in Faeryland, and here I am, in a car with a faery who looks rather like her, with a changeling daughter in the back. After all, can faeries drive cars? Kate obviously could. She had soaked a certain quantity of knowledge from her model, so she said. Why should he dispute it?

It always went the same way. As soon as he was close to Kate, the questions began to fade away. In fact, a great deal fell from his mind. By the time they reached Locksbury, the day's events at the cottage seemed very far off. His involvement with the bypass protest receded. The interminable ache of wrongness went too, and he basked, instead, in a blaze of peace that flamed in his heart like a torch.

They parked in front of the house. Kate lifted Niamh from her seat, and they went inside. Paul soaked in the bath, soothing his wounds, and washing the mud from his face and hair. They ate baked potatoes and fish and peas, many of which Niamh pushed onto the floor, where they rolled like soft green marbles. Then chocolate ice cream, which Niamh consumed with considerable relish, till it covered her face, and her arms, up to her elbows.

When they had cleared up, they relaxed in the front room, and Paul read stories to Niamh, before putting her to bed. When he came down again, Kate was tidying, picking up toys and clothes from the floor. He stepped towards her, and wrapped his arms around her waist. She squeezed him in return.

"Ouch," he said, flinching.

"I'm sorry," she said, loosening her grip. But he restrained her.

"It's okay. I'm a little delicate, that's all. But don't let go."

She held him more tentatively, and he kissed her gently.

"So are you going to show me your special project?" she said.

"Yes. Yes! Good idea." Paul led the way to the study upstairs. He drew down the blind. A pile of unopened correspondence waited in a plastic tray. Another heap, of opened letters, required him to write replies. He pushed both piles out of his way, disturbing a slight cloud of dust. The particles danced in the sunlight.

"Amazing how much work I accumulate in two weeks," he commented. He began to rummage in the desk drawers.

"Here it is." He withdrew a large green file and spilled its contents onto the desk. Detailed plans and projections. And a coloured picture of his scheme—a school, built largely of timber. A huge tree grew in a central courtyard. The lines of the buildings curled and curved.

"It's beautiful," Kate said. "You have lots of others?"

"Mostly at work. I have them pinned over my desk—to remind myself what I should be doing when instead I'm putting together a plan for an extension, or an executive home."

Kate sifted through the plans. She sighed.

"It's great," she said. "What do your colleagues think?"

"I reckon they like it—but in an academic way. It's not going to earn our bread and butter. I keep entering competitions though. It might be a way to circulate my creations—maybe to put one into action one day. Who knows? No luck yet though."

Kate pondered over the plans. She chewed her lip. Paul slid his arm around her waist.

"Have you thought about this?" she said. She took a pencil, and on the back of an envelope sketched an alteration to the plan, creating platforms and levels, adding space.

Paul frowned. He felt a moment's irritation. What did she know about these things? But then he looked again. He took the pencil from her.

"I don't know. Access is important. We'd have to add ramps too." He thought for a minute or two, added details of his own.

"Hey, I see what you're getting at. Yes, it could work. I love the new proportion. What about this?" He handed over the amendment. She made another suggestion. Paul pulled a clean sheet of paper from the drawer, and they outlined the new scheme for the school. Paul sat down and pulled up another chair for Kate. They worked for hours, discussing and arguing and altering. Paul sketched, erased and sketched again. The time passed quickly. The plan rose, collapsed, and rose again in more vigorous form. Paul was elated.

A glance at his watch revealed it was midnight.

"I think we ought to go to bed," he said. "Look at the time." But first he pinned up the new design. They stood back to admire it.

"We make great partners," he said. Kate assented.

"But tomorrow you've got to go back. To protect the copse."

It was not a pleasant reminder. He sighed. His bruises began to ache. For a couple of hours, the subject hadn't entered his mind.

They lay close together in bed. Paul was very tired, but his mind was alert, inspired by the new plan, looking for fresh ideas. Kate stroked him gently, cautious of his wounds.

"How long?" he said at last.

"How long what?"

"How long will you stay with me?"

Kate didn't answer.

"Why can't you stay forever?" he pressed.

"Katherine will come back. I will go."

"I want to keep you," he said, piteously.

"I know. But it doesn't work like that. Can't you be happy with the time we've had together? Isn't that better than nothing?"

"Is it? I don't know. How can I go back to how things were? Now that I've been happy—now that I love you."

Kate sighed.

"I'll always love you," she said. "Wherever you are, I'll be with you, in some sense."

"But it's not the same, holding onto your memory, like something to shore me up against the hard days ahead. I want to wake up with you, and work with you—like tonight. I want our lives to be shared. I know it sounds twee, but it's true. I feel it."

"But Paul—I don't belong here. If I tried to stay, the memory of my own home would become a torment."

"Then let me come with you."

"You can't."

"But what about Katherine? And Jo? Is he there too? So why not me?"

But Kate put her hands to his face, lightly touching him, as though she was trying to memorize the form of his skull, the texture of his skin. She brushed his hair with her fingers. She traced the line of his eyebrows. Her touch was intense, but impersonal. What was she trying to learn?

"This is it, isn't it?" said Paul, in a quick, intuitive flash. "Our last night. You're going. When the copse falls."

"I don't know. Perhaps. Do I sense our imminent parting? Yes. Though maybe that is only in response to your fears. Do you know how much I am your creation?"

"Is it narcissism, then? My love for you?"

Kate held him tight, and gazed into his eyes.

"Remember me," she hissed. "Don't forget." Paul was taken aback. Was she cursing him?

She climbed on top of him, peeling off her white nightdress. As she bent over to kiss his face, he remembered her first visit, a strange, stinking night creature, slating and then inspiring his thirst. He recalled the goat's eyes, the horrible odour. Were her eyes inhuman now? He couldn't make them out, in the dark, but he fancied they were. The thought inspired a fierce passion. They rutted like animals, without tenderness. He caught her narrow waist, and held her, strong though she was. He felt her vigour and hunger. The faery tore at his flesh and sank her teeth in his soft skin, fighting for her own pleasure. She pressed against him in a frenzy, biting his lip, pulling his hair. He rolled her onto her back, and when she came, she twisted and screeched like a wild creature, then clutched him to herself till their breath and sweat were intermingled.

At last she fell asleep, curled up, her hair spread across the pillow. But Paul refrained. He kept himself awake, till the dawn grew pale in the sky. He lay propped on his elbow, watching Kate as she slept. Was this truly their last night together? He didn't want to miss a moment. He stroked her long, soft hair. He held his face close to hers, to catch the scent of her breath.

He switched off the alarm, minutes before it was due to ring, at six thirty in the morning. Heavy with weariness and a premonition of loss, he crept downstairs to make tea.

CHAPTER TWENTY EIGHT

Katherine stared into the depths of the black pool. Thin staves of sedge rose around the water. Broken reeds pushed through the mud. The sky was dark and heavy. The scene possessed great weight—an inevitability. She would wait, and watch. Nothing changed. She slept and dreamed. Sometimes she saw the bright faces of children, peering up through the water. She tried to catch them, but her limbs were slow. The children laughed and skipped away, slippery as fish.

Once, when she slept, she heard a thin, musical voice singing to her, but she woke and the singer was gone. It irked her. The song echoed in her mind, playing on her nerves like an itch. How long had she been here? A new consideration. What was she doing? When she slept again, the song began anew. It was clearer, and closer. It streamed through her mind like a wind.

The pond was a timeless bubble—a pocket of infinity.

She was caught in a bowl of nowhere, another catacomb, in the endless spiral of faeryland.

She sat up and gazed into the water, straining her eyes to see into its still, glaucous heart. A flicker in the deep, dark space—a pearly glimmering. The song drifted from the water like a mist. Was someone calling her?

The glimmering became a white robe, floating in the water like a cloud. A pale, beautiful face, and streamers of black hair like water weed, trailing in the cold currents. An undine—lifting its face to the very surface of the pool. The water rippled over clear, calm eyes, dimpling over cheeks and forehead. It beckoned with a hand as cool and white as the petals of a lotus. Signalling. Luring.

Katherine stood up. Crusts of mud fell from her bare skin. She lifted her arms above her head, poised on the edge of the pool. How could she leave? She bent her knees, and dived. The water embraced her, hands and arms, face and shoulders, body and legs and feet. She slipped through, like an eel. As the pool closed over her, Katherine strained to reach the undine, retreating before her, still beckoning. Its lips moved, but she couldn't hear what it said. The face shifted, acquiring a certain familiarity. Memories fell into place. The last shreds of the trance fell away.

"Jo?" she called out. "Jo. Is that you?"

Jo called out again and again. Then movement, the rush of water, and Katherine burst from the well with her hands high above her head. Drops of water glistened on her body, coursing from her hair. They exchanged a quick, painful glance but a shadow crept over Katherine's body, clutching it in a shapeless maw. She was thrust up into the air, high above Jo's head, as a monstrous yew tree erupted from the well.

Katherine was flung free, tumbling from the summit of the tree to land unceremoniously at Jo's feet. She curled up, bruised and winded. Jo bent down beside her, offering comfort.

"How strange," she breathed, "to see you here. Another person! Are you real? I think you are."

He nodded.

"Yes. And as real as I ever am."

They both smiled, in a moment of shared understanding. A thick, coarse voice interrupted them.

"Much as I hate to disrupt your little reunion," she said. Katherine looked up. The yew tree enclosed them like a cave, with her long ebony branches. Despite her change of form, Katherine recognised the Elder Hag.

"You are not so pretty," Katherine said. The hag laughed. Her branches were hanging with black rags and decorated with the bones and skulls of animals. The crania of little birds, parchment yellow, twisted on narrow ribbons. Thigh bones clanked together like chimes. Her bark was embellished with teeth. A funereal reflection of the May Day willows by the Swallowhead spring.

"Your cerements, yes?" Katherine asked. The hag sighed and grinned at once.

"You refused your chance to undo events, Katherine," the hag said. "What shall we do now?"

"Where's Niamh?" Katherine said.

"You didn't complete your quest. Perhaps I shall keep her."

"There must be another way."

"I am suffering, Katherine. I am caught. My children have been sucked into your world. My offspring, my branches, held fast in your hard, unyielding home. Should I cut them off? Shall I sever my own limbs?"

"You want them back? Spring, and the others? But it won't stop the greater imbalance."

"No. Times change. We are at a loss. But a new pattern will unfold. The land will shift. Your world is a hectic puddle, and if it dies you will take us too. Your collective strife is echoed in the corridors of faeryland. We have made an exchange, but each of us has made a sacrifice in return. I have learned from you, but I pay a price in pain. You have enriched the land, and in return your world will be enriched. You have a sacrifice to make."

"What?" Katherine said, though a chill in her heart suggested that she already knew the answer.

"You have walked, a stranger, in our land. Now one of our kind must make the same pilgimmage in yours."

"What about the Morris men? Isn't that what they're doing?"

"It doesn't work. They are confused and transient. They have failed. They have too much faery and too little humanity."

"So what d'you want?" Her lips were dry, and as she spoke they began to tremble. Tears sprang to her eyes.

"I want Niamh," the yew tree hissed.

Hot tears leaked from Katherine's eyes. She was choked by sobs. Jo, standing silently, stepped forwards and put his arm about her shoulders. Niamh—most precious.

"She doesn't belong to you, Katherine," said the hag. "A mother doesn't own her child. Children are a loan only, entrusted to your care while they grow. They have their own destiny. And she will return to you. No harm will come to Niamh. She will be like a seed, nurtured close to my heart. She will live in many times and places. She will stand with her feet in both worlds."

"But she won't be the same," Katherine said. She had stopped crying. Her voice was flat and dull, burdened with resignation. "She won't be my daughter anymore. She'll be something else." But she had known, hadn't she? With Crow, sitting by the fire, she had suggested, instantly, the price to be paid. Only part of her mind had been fooled by the maiden's cryptic reply. Oh, yes, she had understood, and still she had taken the chance. She had run with the faeries.

"You have something to do," the yew tree said, interrupting her thoughts.

"Yes," Katherine nodded. She wiped her eyes.

"Wait here," she said to Jo. "I'll be back soon." Jo looked at her.

"Are you sure?" he said quietly. "Do you know what you're doing?"

"I'm sure. This is unfinished business. There is a gap in the pattern still—a missing thread."

Gravestones emerged from the shadows. Tombs and broken angels. A huge sarcophagus laden with ivy. They flamed into being, and died away again. The decorated undead flitted amongst the stained marble, the granite patterned with lichen. The scene loomed, and faded again. Katherine held up a hand of twigs. Jo, through sapphire eyes, was a thin, golden man with purple lips.

"I will wait," he said. He crouched upon a fallen stone.

"Which way do I go?" Katherine said. The door of a tomb yawned open. Steps wound down, into the earth. Katherine placed grey, heavy feet upon the steps. A slim figure walked before her in the darkness. She looked back at Katherine, over her shoulder. She urged her to follow.

At the bottom of the steps she emerged in Locksbury. It was night time. The air was faintly scented with lilac. The moon shone yellow, like a yolk. She was standing on the pavement in front of her house. A woman was hammering on the front door.

Katherine drew closer. The woman, the slender figure who had led her here, turned again and nodded. Katherine was looking at herself—a mirror image—though the doppelganger's eyes were shadowed and belonged to a stranger. The woman handed Katherine a piece of wood, crudely carved. It was not unlike the doll entrusted to Elaine.

The door opened. Katherine saw Paul take her duplicate's hand. The woman-creature walked past him and led him upstairs. She saw Paul's face, sallow in the moonlight, entranced by the new arrival. While he was distracted, she slipped in the front door, and walked up the stairs behind them. Why did he not see her? She climbed noisily, tempting him to notice, but Paul was caught up in the allure of the faux Katherine. They disappeared into the bedroom. Katherine opened the door into her daughter's room, and walked across to the cot.

The little girl was fast asleep. Her covers were thrown off. Her perfect, chubby arms were flung in abandon across the pillow. Katherine bent over Niamh, and stroked her smooth, warm cheek. Her lips were slightly parted, her breathing slow and even. Katherine stood and watched. How many hours had she spent, like this, watching her daughter sleep? What did she dream, this child? What phantoms played in her mind, what prompted the sighs, the wriggles and smiles? She lent over her, to breathe again her daughter's fragrant breath. The hag said Niamh would return—but when and how? And she would be different. She would not be the same child at all.

Indistinctly, through the wall, she heard Paul shout once. Then silence was restored. How much time did she have? The darkness faded a little. She heard the sound of typing. Paul was working in the study. What was happening? They were heading back in time again, to the evening. Paul hadn't gone to bed yet.

Katherine felt sick, and her mind reeled. How much longer would it go on? She was so tired. She longed for rest and sleep. She ached for an end to the adventure. How much more of this inconstancy could she stand? She yearned for solid earth beneath her feet—to be immersed in the forward current of time, to be home again. Such irony, she thought, as I stand here, in Niamh's bedroom, but home still feels so far away...

She stooped to pick up Niamh. The little girl woke briefly, and smiled sleepily at her mother. Katherine undressed her, sat her on the floor, and put the clothes on the piece of wood instead. Was it wood? It stank, like the earth doll Spring had made at midsummer. She placed the doll in the cot, its head on the pillow. The doll twitched and opened its eyes. It waved its limbs. It donned the likeness of the flesh and blood child. It began to cry.

Katherine lifted her own child again, and kissed her tenderly.

"I love you, Niamh," she said. "More than anything."

Niamh looked into her mother's eyes, her little face very serious. Then she twisted. She slipped from Katherine's grasp and fell to the floor. Her body was gripped in a spasm. She curled up. Black sprouts pushed through her skin like quills. She began to dwindle, shrinking and compressing, and the feathers erupted thickly as her form changed. In an instant—the child had become a crow.

The changeling cried again. Katherine heard Paul curse, and stamp across the landing. She hid behind the door as it opened. When Paul let the crow through the window, Katherine crept from the room. She left through the front door. It clicked shut quietly behind her.

The steps appeared before her, vanishing in mid-air. Katherine began her final ascent.

Jo was still crouched on the gravestone.

"All done?" he said. Katherine nodded.

"And you?"

"I had my chance," he said. "I could have stayed." His voice betrayed sadness.

"You're not sure? You want to stay?"

But Jo shrugged.

"I thought I would," he said. "I have a feeling I will never feel quite at home, wherever I am. And I want to see Violet too. And my Mum and sister."

"I didn't think you were very close to your family," she said gently.

"Nor did I," he said.

"I want to go back. I am so unspeakably weary of this place," Katherine said. "And just look at the state of me." She held up her twig hand, indicated her belly leaking roses. They fell into an extraordinary fit of helpless, painful laughter, like children.

"Come on," Jo said at last, wiping tears from his eyes. "Let's go."

They travelled on, heading outwards. Jo's feet found a true path. He led the way, surefooted through each immeasurable moment. The veil thinned and parted. The earth rose, solid and incontrovertible, beneath their feet. For Katherine—what profound relief, what peace, to be home again. For Jo—did some part of his soul howl when he committed himself to the unyielding world again? His heart was heavy as lead.

They walked up the stone valley. The copse was surrounded by men and machines.

CHAPTER TWENTY NINE

After a quick breakfast Paul and Kate set off on foot for the protest site. They walked through Locksbury High Street, where the early lorries rumbled. The shops were still shut—except for the newsagents, where Paul stopped to buy the Marlborough Guardian. Emblazoned on the front cover was a photograph of the cottages crumbling to the ground. Another, smaller picture showed Jan being manhandled from the window of the squat. The man with the bloody nose featured on a third. The story filled the entire front page, and promised comment and further news on pages five and seven. It was a big story for a small paper. James had the by-line, and the headline proclaimed, "Violent clashes as bailiffs struggle with protestors."

Kate and Paul walked on. Niamh rode in the backpack, on Paul's shoulders, wrapped in a pink and orange raincoat. The roads were wet and shiny, but the rain had eased off at last. The cloud thinned. Momentarily the sun broke through, glinting on the puddles. Paul scanned the paper as he walked.

"Thanks, James," he grimaced.

"What?"

"Listen to this: 'Prominent protest leader Paul Matravers was arrested after a confrontation with a bailiff. Three other arrests were made, but all four people were later released without charge.' Nice of him to mention me by name. I wonder who else was arrested."

"You didn't see anyone else at the police station?"

"No. Did you?"

"No. They kept you well apart. Is the rest of the story okay?"

"As far as I can see. He's sitting on the fence, of course, but the comment section might be more sympathetic."

Kate held her hand out to Paul, and they walked close together. They left the village, and headed across the fields. The grass was thick and wet. The earth was churned into mud in the gateways, and by the hedges where the cattle had been sheltering from the rain. Paul kept glancing at Kate. She had tied back her hair. Her perfect skin still possessed its faint, golden sheen. She turned to him, squeezing his hand.

"But you're going," he said. "If you loved me you'd stay."

She shook her head.

"It doesn't work like that."

"Why not?"

"Because I'm not real."

"What about last night?" he demanded. "You were real enough then. What about now?" He gripped her hand still she winced. She stopped walking.

"If you go, I'll die," he said.

"No, you won't. Don't be stupid."

"I might as well." His voice was petulant and sulky. He could hear himself, like a besotted schoolboy, and he was ashamed. But still he persisted. He couldn't let her go. He wittered on. He pleaded.

"After all this time, my life, I should find you only to lose you? It's not fair." The eternal childish cry. It's not fair. Far away, his reserved, calculating self curled up with embarassment. Kate seemed to diminish before his emotional assault. She began to weep.

"Would you rather I had never come back?" she asked. "Would it have been easier for you?"

Paul paused. His face was clouded.

"No," he said. His voice was subdued. "No. I'm glad we had this time. That I knew you. But I sense—I'm afraid of the loss. I can feel the cold blast of it, opening in front of me. Not exactly courageous of me is it? But what about you?"

Kate shook her head.

"It is different for me."

"What do you mean? You don't love me?"

"No, I don't mean that at all. But I'm not like you. When I return—"

"You'll forget me?"

"Not entirely. But a lot will go. I mirror you, remember? I respond to you."

"So the more I love you, the more you become the kind of person I will love?"

"In a way, yes." She lifted her eyes to him, her lashes veiled with tears. "I am a conduit for your feelings. Faeries are passionate, but they don't hold on to their feelings. Emotions—they blow through, like the wind."

"So you are a kind of curse," he said. "Loving you was inevitable. You trapped me, and then you fly off untouched." His voice was bitter and choked. He pulled his hand away from her and walked up the field in long, angry strides. Kate ran after him.

"Wait! Paul! Wait!" She grabbed his arm. He pulled it away, but swung round to face her.

"Paul—don't be angry with me. You called me and called me, and I came. If it was possible for me to stay, I would. You could marry me."

"And give you a soul? You've already taken my heart." He took her into his arms and pressed her to his body. Niamh reached over his shoulder and patted Kate's head. Paul refused to let her go. He squeezed until his arms ached, as though he could imprint her on his bones. At last she drew away.

"Come-on," she said. "We have to help at the copse. We don't know what's happening."

Paul nodded dutifully. He sniffed. He looked away. Kate took his hand again and led him up the field. When they crested the hill, the stone valley came into view. A little further, and the vista of destruction opened before them.

Metal fencing had encased the Old Lane, from the road to the copse, creating a wide, muddy channel. The stoney track, the hedges, and a swathe of the field had been obliterated. The cottages had disappeared, except for a sad mound of stone and rubble. A shred of muddy velvet flapped in the wind, sole sign of the Morris men's magical encampment. Even faery glamour had collapsed before the onslaught of men and machinery. A compound had been constructed off the main road, to protect the equipment and building materials. A portable building perched on the field, and a block of toilets. Even at this early hour, a team of surveyors were taking measurements, and a truck was manouevring into the compound. Half a dozen security men were wandering about, drinking tea, grimacing at the clouded sky.

Paul's heart sank. So much change in less than a day. Their protest was pitiful—trying to hold back an ocean with their bare hands, through an effort of will. Failure was inevitable. What use were their fragile tree houses, the painted pebbles, the banners, the flimsy letters and petitions? In the face of the corporations, the big money. No. He refused to baulk in the face of the corporate Big Brother. What were they, but seas of individual people? And the security men—earning a pittance, mostly, recruited on temporary contracts, to be used as and when required, then returned to the dole queue. No clear lines. Did the security men really give a shit if the road was built or not? Did the surveyors, for that matter, or the road builders? They cared about the job, yes, the money it offered—but did they have a personal interest in Locksbury having a bypass, in paving over this particular stretch of land, the copse, and the stone valley? For the most part—no. But the protestors, the passionate few, cared very deeply. Didn't that count for something? Their will to protect and cherish the place? Paul mustered his courage. He refused to be dispirited by the mass of the opposition, the uniforms, the heaving machinery. He scrambled over the stile and strode towards the copse. Kate half ran beside him.

Owain felt sunlight splash onto his face. He looked up to the sky, where a quick splinter of blue appeared in the sky, a fleeting shaft of golden light, before the cloud swirled over again, turbulent, boiling billows of grey and brown. His boots and jeans were covered with mud, splatters reaching his knees. His hair was wet and greasy. He thrust his hands into his pocket, watching the purposeful activity of the surveyors, and the meandering trails of the security men, and the ground workers waiting for their shift to start. In his green coat, head down, he mingled without causing comment. He was adept at maintaining a low profile. He loitered near the guards, picking up fragments of conversation. The atmosphere was tense. He sensed a rallying of strength. The police, he heard, were due to arrive at eight thirty. The assault on the copse would begin soon after. He wasn't surprised. The fences were up. The copse was a stronghold immersed in enemy territory. The protestors would be picked off one by one, and the trees would be felled. He had no doubt about the outcome—but how long could they resist? He slipped away from the mobile, and walked up the field to the copse. It was flanked by the bleak fence. The tree houses were cut off from the ground—ladders pulled up, ropes cut. But walkways still joined them, one to another. When the time came, a few brave souls might cling to the walkways, hanging precariously above the ground, hampering the efforts of the bailiffs to evict them.

A few dozen protestors, people from Locksbury, and supporters from Marlborough and Swindon, were turning up with placards. James appeared with a photographer. He nodded at Owain, but kept a distance, chatting and smiling with a few other smartly dressed press people.

At the copse Owain bumped into Paul and Kate.

"Hello, Paul," he said. He looked at Kate without greeting her. She smiled at him, but he wouldn't meet her eyes. A faery, yes, Owain thought, and Paul caught up in her glamour. Did he know what she was? And where was Katherine? The thought troubled him briefly. The faery double clung to Paul, tenacious as ivy, sucking his strength. She was poisonous.

"Are you okay, Paul?" Owain asked quietly.

"Of course. Why shouldn't I be?" He sounded irritated, as though he sensed Owain's discomfort around Kate.

"I heard you were arrested. They roughed you up a bit?"

"Oh. That—yes. I've got a few bruises. Nothing much. They didn't press any charges."

"Good," Owain said.

"Is Elaine coming?"

Owain shook his head and looked away.

"No," he said, distantly.

"Why not?"

"She's not well."

"She was okay yesterday. No," he conceded, "on second thoughts, she wasn't her usual self. What's up?"

Owain shrugged.

"I don't know." He refused to elaborate and sidled away.

"Did Violet manage to get into her tree house?" Paul persisted.

"Yes. There were security guards hanging about all night, to make sure no-one else got in. But she was determined. She slipped through. She's up there now."

"Good. Have the Morris men gone?"

Owain halted.

"I don't know," he said. "I haven't seen them since they were fooling around with the bailiffs. Their pretty little camp was flattened."

Kate shivered.

More people arrived, locals mostly, distinct from the resident protestors, clad in coats and boots, brandishing umbrellas. Some had flasks of tea and sandwiches, and cameras. A few were reading the Marlborough Guardian. Passions were running high, but the atmosphere was, as yet, good-spirited. People were chatting and laughing. A few security guards moved amongst them, making their presence felt but unable to move them for the time being.

Then someone shouted. The chat immediately ceased.

"They're coming! The bailiffs!"

Bailiffs, more guards, men armed with chainsaws, and behind them, a truck struggling through a river of mud, bearing a hydraulic platform.

The security men tried to move the crowd away. More fence was erected, and Owain, with several others, climbed on it, the better to view the proceedings. The platform trundled through the mud, into position. One at a time, the squatters were plucked from their arboreal homes, screaming and kicking, watching in tears as their dwellings were trashed, and the chainsaws bit into the flesh of the trees.

The air was filled with noise, taunts and shouts, the whine of chainsaws and the thunder of machines. Violet was the last. She climbed from her house onto a walkway. She balanced upon the thick rope, lying on her front, her hands clasped behind her back. She challenged the bailiffs to remove her.

"If you touch me I'll fall!" she screeched. "I'll be killed!"

The men manoeuvred around her. She clung to the line, shaking. They cursed and deliberated. They brought up a second platform, and it sat in the deep mud, so they could cradle her on either side, and pick her free without her tumbling to the ground. When they grasped her, she fought them, tooth and nail, and in the throng of bodies when she stepped from the platform, she received an anonymous blow on the back which knocked the breath from her body. She was dumped, unceremoniously, outside the new fence.

Paul picked her up. Her face was flushed, stained with tears, and fierce with a rage for revenge. She heard the groan of a felled tree. She saw her home crumple and collapse with the tree, a quick flash of silk and colour, as the bender tore open, and crashed to the ground amongst the branches.

The copse was lost. Six large trees remained standing and a yellow earth mover grumbled up to the little barrow.

But the engine cut out. A sudden silence descended, upon both sides of the divide.

"What the...I thought we'd got them all clear."

From behind the trees, four Morris men and the two acrobats stepped out. They smiled. They bowed.

Spring drew a long, green silk streamer from the pocket of his waistcoat. He was the absolute focus of attention, and reflected in nearly two hundred pairs of eyes, he seemed to grow in stature. He glowed—the colours of his clothes, his black and copper hair, his bright green eyes. He bowed again, with a flourish of the streamer, which floated on the air like smoke. The assembly of road builders were held motionless, utterly in his thrall. Spring split the streamer, and handed its various parts to his fellows. He approached the earth mover, and jumped lightly to the driver's seat. The man watched in helpless amazement. Spring tore another strip from the streamer, and bound the man's eyes. He skipped back to the ground. The driver lifted his hands to his face, but he groaned, and doubled up. He fell heavily into the mud. His body twisted. Spring gestured to the others, so the three remaining Morris men, Dawn and Dusk, flitted amongst the various ranks of road builders, binding each with Spring's green silk. The protestors watched in silence. The first man was pulled to his feet, like a puppet in invisible strings. A thick root, like a rope, sprang from his foot and slithered into the soil. A second, and a third, a web of tendrils snaking from his body into the earth. His form stretched and writhed. His hands reached up, and up, impossibly high, and a skein of grey erupted from his fingers, reaching across his hands and his arms. His face was engulfed in bark. His clothes were swallowed in a tide of sap. Hundreds, thousands of bitter green leaves exploded from the burgeoning limbs, from twigs and branches. The man was obliterated. Swallowed up.

It had taken a few seconds only. The others looked at each other in shock, and fear. Their time had come. One after another, the new occupants of the copse, the victorious army of road builders, sent swift roots into the ground. Branches tore from their bodies. The enchanted forest advanced. The fence was flattened. The protestors woke from their trance and screamed, backing away from the assault of the new trees.

Owain stood his ground. He watched a ripple in the earth by the barrow, as though a huge hand was moving beneath the turf. He heard a groan. The barrow split open. A fierce golden light spilled from the wound. It engulfed the new man-trees. It spilled like a wave upon the fleeing protestors, upon Kate and Paul and Niamh, upon Violet and Jan, and James and his colleagues, and the folk from Locksbury. And Jo and Katherine running up the stone valley to join the confrontation. They were swallowed up. A moment of blindness, and fighting for breath. Then—peace.

Owain opened his eyes. Where were they? A forest. Fruit hung like gems upon the trees. The emerald grass shone. The sky above was a perfect blue. Paul appeared beside him.

"Where are we?" he said. They wandered, in a haze, to a clearing, where a unicorn lifted its white and silver head from a pool, still as a mirror, where lilies grew and a water nymph was sitting upon a stone, her hair drifting in a non-existent wind.

"Faeryland, of course," Owain said.

"How did we get here?"

"I think it's more a case of how it got here. We're still in the same place. Look." He pointed to a grove of stunted trees. Paul recognised the mutated forms of the tree-people trapped in the compound.

The protestors, on the other hand, were drifting about in a mixture of euphoria and stunned disbelief. One of the hippie girls stripped off her clothes and dived into the pool. Another was trying to approach the unicorn. An elderly lady was drinking tea from her flask, engaged in a conversation with a green man, sitting beneath a tree. Others were talking and smiling and marvelling.

"It's all a bit...cute, isn't it?" Paul suggested. "Like a theme park."

Owain nodded.

"I think we've got to find Spring," he said.

Katherine shook her head. How long had it taken her to escape? And now, back at the copse, she was back again, held tight in the palm of faeryland. Beside her, Jo twitched with excitement.

"We're back," he said. "We're back. Have the faeries followed us here? What's happened?"

A couple of huge centaurs trotted past. Katherine recognised one of them. A thin, angular young man with trails of dreadlocks, one of the tree dwellers. Now those same dreadlocks had become a mane. From the waist down he was a horse—a strapping stallion with a glossy black coat, and four fierce hooves.

"I think Faeryland has been spewing its contents into our world—don't you?"

"But it's not like...where we've just been."

"No," Katherine said. "What shall we do? How to put the genie back in the bottle?"

"We've got to send the faeries back—that's what the hag said. D'you think we're too late? Are we trapped?" Jo jumped up and down.

"Calm down. I don't know. Come on."

They walked through the wood. They saw the reporters sitting outside a witch's cottage, dark windows, and a low roof dangling with herbs to dry, and various portions of mummified animal remains. They found Violet lying on the grass, staring into a mirror.

"Jo," she cried, jumping to her feet. "Jo, look what I've found." She passed him the mirror. In its depths he saw a mermaid, sitting in the waves, with a tail of sleek, irridescent green. Her skin was white, opaque, revealing a circulation of turquoise veins. Her hair was long and red. The mermaid turned and smiled. Her nipples were pierced, and her navel. She wore Violet's face.

Violet took the mirror back from him.

"Are you okay?" he asked.

"Yes," she smiled brilliantly. "All my dreams, all around me." Her gaze was bright and blank. Jo felt a chill in his heart.

"Come with us," he said gently. He took her hand and followed Katherine through the trees. Violet trailed behind him obediently, but her eyes were drawn to the mirror.

They came upon a clearing. In its centre, a hawthorn tree, covered in creamy blossom, towered above a delicate maiden in white. She was sitting on a cushion of moss. Her hair was crowned with spring flowers. Her needle shone in the sunlight, as she embroidered a piece of linen. She glanced up as the walkers drew near.

"Katherine?" Jo said, uneasily. He looked from the maiden, to his friend.

"Hello again," Katherine said sharply. "Been having fun, have we?"

The maiden placed her needlework gently on the ground. She stood up. Her feet were smooth and bare.

"I am Kate," she said. She held out her hand. Katherine ignored it.

"I bet you are," she said. "Where's Paul?"

"Katherine," Jo broke in. "You know her? Who is she? She looks a lot like you. Not exactly the same though."

"No. I fancy she's rather prettier, don't you?"

Kate smiled and wrung her hands, dancing a couple of dainty steps on the spot.

"Where's Paul?" Katherine repeated.

"Somewhere. I don't know."

Katherine sighed with exasperation, and turned away.

"He's mine now," the faery called after her. "He's mine."

"Well, hurrah for you. I hope you're very happy together," Katherine muttered. She stomped from the clearing, Jo and Violet following in her wake. They set a course for the heart of the wood.

They walked for an indefinite time. Although they never changed direction, they seemed to be walking in circles. Trees and pools were repeated. A rock, left behind, appeared in front of them again. Kate followed, at a discreet distance. They met other protestors, some transformed, like the centaurs, into storybook characters. One girl had red and gold butterfly wings, and she perched on a branches amongst screeching peacocks. Jan, glaring from the mouth of a cave, had the beautiful androgynous face of a gorgon. Her skin was hard and green, like malachite. Her hair hissed with snakes, but nobody turned to stone.

Jan left her cave to follow them. The butterfly girl fluttered from her tree to join the procession so that Katherine began to feel like a dowdy pied piper. Where would she take them? Why did they follow? With the exception of Jo, her human companions seemed only partially conscious—like sleep walkers. They latched onto Katherine as some kind of centre of gravity. The Kate faery twirled and danced.

A strange grove loomed up ahead. The six beech trees at its heart looked familiar. Around them, a host of smaller specimens were growing, each decorated with a band of green silk. Sitting on the broken barrow in the centre, Katherine saw a bearded man in a green coat. His eyes were clear and focussed. He came out to meet her, surveying her trail of pixie folk.

"Hello, Katherine," Owain said.

"Where's Paul?"

"Over there. I lost him," he said. "Hello, Jo. You're still awake too? In the land of the living?" Jo nodded. Katherine looked across at Paul. He lay beneath an apple tree, drowsy, clad in armour and holding a sword across his chest. A white pennent fluttered beside him. His white horse cropped the grass. In the distance, the black knight was waiting on a bridge.

"A grail knight?" she said. "I should have guessed." She walked to him, and looked into his face. His eyes were dull and sleepy. He didn't seem to recognise her. Katherine returned to Owain.

"What do we do?" she asked. Amid the trees, Dawn and Dusk practised their perfect cartwheels. They leapt out, flipping onto their hands, and over, onto their feet again. Two flames of hair, scarlet and black. Two lean, flexible bodies.

They were followed by the Morris men. Spring, flanked by his fellow seasons, replaced Owain as master of the barrow. He stood on its torn summit. He surveyed his kingdom, his empty-eyed citizens. His face beamed with happiness. He held out his arms, in a greeting, or a benediction.

"We are victorious!" he cried. "We have vanquished the destroyers of the land, the money men, the ravishers and rapists of our woodland. We have turned them into trees. You are safe. The land is free. I have played my part. I have given you dreams to play with. Isn't this perfect? Isn't this what you want? Your wishes?"

The citizens smiled at one another. Owain was less impressed.

"Oh, dear," said Spring. "We have dissenters. But wait, the magic will work. Tell me your wishes. Whisper them in my ear. Share your secrets." He reached out to Jo, brushed his hand over Jo's eyes.

"But you refused your chance," the faery hissed. "You came back."

"What about me?" Katherine stepped towards. She grasped Spring's arm. She stared into his eyes, green as apples.

"I know you," she said. "We've met before."

"Of course," he said. "At the cottages, in my little camp."

She shook her head.

"More than that. Before."

"Yes," he said. His voice changed, stirring chords in her memory. He leaned forwards and kissed her, and in an instant, the answer fell into place. She remembered the high crystal tower in the sky. The ride through the bluebell wood, the pilgrim walking with her across the moor.

"You're the first one, aren't you? The faery that led me along the old tracks, who talked with me. Is that why you're here? Because of me?"

"We shared so much, Katherine," he said. "You gave me a glimpse of the world. I understood, in part what it was to be human, to be complete, to have separation— individuality. I was tempted. I was so, so very hungry. I wanted to try it. I yearned."

"And you brought the others," she said.

"And we helped! We were asked to stay—to join the struggle."

"By whom?"

"By Paul—he said you needed all the help you could get. So much you wanted to save this place. So we saved it!"

"And now we all live happily ever after in the faeryland theme park?" Owain broke in. "You've got to go back."

"No," Spring said. "The others want us here."

"What about the men in the trees?" Owain said.

"But they're the enemy. You wished for their destruction."

"No," Owain shook his head. "It isn't right. These are matters for us to sort out. We don't want your help—not like this anyway."

"Your presence here is causing as much turmoil on the other side too," Katherine said.

Spring backed away. The other Morris men looked from one to another, then to Spring again, looking for a cue.

"Wake the others up," Owain said.

Spring trembled. He shrank and his colours faded.

"You don't want me here?" He turned to Katherine, pleading.

"The hag wants you back. You're hurting her."

"We are part of her. Her pain is ours."

"Then why tarry? Go back."

"You'll lose the copse."

"I know." Katherine's voice was sad. "I know we will. But we have to find our own balance." The enchanted citizens began to stir and look around them. Paul woke from his half-sleep and staggered to his feet. The armour evaporated. Kate ran to his side and pressed against him. He wrapped his arms around her.

"Where's Niamh?" Katherine asked. Paul looked puzzled.

"I don't know."

The real child was...in the hands of the Elder Hag, and safe, so she had been assured. But what had happened to the changeling? Paul held his True Love close to him. She was trembling.

"Go back," Owain repeated.

Long white roots streamed from the broken barrow. Seven tendrils, shining, flexible like silver cord. They separated. They reached out. Two latched on to the beautiful acrobat girls, and plucked the pale, shimmering faery essence from the earth bodies. Four attached themselves to the Morris men, sucking out the ethereal forms. Devoid of life, six heaps of soil and stone and decayed vegetable matter tumbled to the ground. Ashes to ashes. Dust to dust. The tendrils withdrew into the barrow, with the harvest of faery folk. Except one.

Paul held onto Kate with all his strength. The cord fastened itself upon her, but Kate was torn between them.

"Let me go, Paul," she said. "I have to go. Please."

"I love you, Kate," he said. But the spirit was ebbing away. It slipped from the body. For an instant, Paul was cleaving to a carcase of dirt, till the body fell apart. Then his hands were full of crumbled earth and dead leaves. The decomposing matter tumbled around his feet.

He stood in a state of shock. The impact of the bereavement took a moment to take hold. He looked at the contents of his hands in disbelief. He was aware of a distant pain, closing in. What hollow spaces were these, opening in his body? He had never been aware of them, these empty parts, till Kate had filled them. And now she had withdrawn. She was gone.

The golden light faded and dispersed. A cold wind blew through the trees. Katherine looked at her feet. The emerald grass had disappeared, and she waded through mud. Rain had seeped through her clothes. She shivered. She turned to face a cold metal fence. Beyond, a man in a yellow digger was tearing a piece of green silk from his face. No-one spoke. The protestors looked at each other, uncertain what had happened.

"We've lost," someone said, a small voice breaking the silence. "We've lost."

The foreman heard and nodded. The chainsaws started up, with a tearing whine. The remaining beech trees were hacked to the ground.

Owain wandered away from the scene of destruction. The sky was clearing. The rain eased off. He saw a small white form clambering across the field, just beyond the copse. What was it? He walked closer, curiously. Quickly he realised it was a child, a small, naked child with wavey brown hair. Why was she bare? He ran towards her, speaking gently, anxious not to frighten her.

"Niamh?" he said. The little girl looked up at him. Her hair was full of earth.

"Niamh. Let's take you to your Mum," he said. "She's worried about you."

Niamh fixed him with a penetrating gaze. She smiled.

CHAPTER THIRTY

In the evening the heat began to fade, but the sky blazed with gold and crimson above the hills in the trail of the falling sun. In the still, dry air, the fields rolled over the downs, a heavy green, or pale yellow stubble, and the verges were high with coarse, bleached weeds. Upon the trees, dull, weary leaves waited for the cool, crisp bite of autumn, then to burn with colour.

A woman was toiling up the field, in sandals, walking through the stubble. The sharp, broken wheat stalks pricked her legs. The rain was long gone, and the baked earth was hard beneath her feet. She wore a white cotton dress, flowing to her knees, and her hair hung silky black down her back. At the top of the hill she paused, and wiped her face with the back of her hand. Her skin was moist with perspiration. She looked across the vale, the field dotted with barrows, topped with trees, like islands in the golden plain. On the main road at the bottom, a couple of cars passed by, shedding a sharp, metallic glint in the sunlight. She thought of summer holidays, trips to the seaside, shoes full of sand, and sunburn, and buckets full of pebbles. She thought of the ocean, the sound of waves, and the cool, salty water brushing against her body. She ached for the sea. She longed for the past, for an irresponsible childhood, for the long lost carefree days.

Under her arm she carried a crude doll—a clumsy lump of wood carved with a face, crowned with a wisp of hair. Now she knew what it meant—what it signified. Oh, yes, she knew. They had trapped and tricked her. She smouldered. She raged. But now, at last, she would be rid of it.

A movement caught her attention. She was being pursued. Quickly, she turned away and walked on across the field.

"Elaine! Elaine! Wait for me!"

Her heart sank. Was she never to have a moment's peace? And least of all did she want his company. Why did he pester her all the time? She ignored the voice. She hurried.

"Elaine! Stop!" He was running. She heard the labouring of his breath. He caught her up.

"What do you want?" she said. "I was hoping for a little solitude."

"We need to talk. We can't go on like this. You've got to tell me what's going on." Owain was wearing a blue tee-shirt. His arms were bare and brown. He had trimmed his hair and shaved off his beard.

Elaine turned to him. She regarded him coldly. He had shorn himself to please her, but she found him ridiculous. He looked younger without the beard—softer too, more vulnerable, with the soft skin of his face exposed.

"I've got to tell you, have I?" she said bitterly. "Why? What obligation do I owe you?"

"I thought you loved me. We were married, remember?"

"That little charade. Forget it."

"Aren't we friends, at least? I don't understand. What have I done to upset you?" He sounded hurt, and desperate. She walked away, contemptuous. Owain trailed behind her.

"Elaine, please. Talk to me."

She detested him. He trotted after her like a dog. She could see the hunger and desire in his eyes, the greed to possess. Yes, she thought, like a male. She remembered the little bitch she had seen, not long ago, in season and pursued by half a dozen relentless fevered dogs, eager to copulate. Or the drakes, in the spring, when four or five might be clambering upon one unfortunate female, half-drowning her, blind to everything but their own selfish lust. They were all the same, males, dragged around by their genitals, hateful and childish, slaves to the insatiable penis.

"Fuck off," she said. "I've had enough. Go away." But Owain persisted.

"Not this time. Explain."

"Explain? Why I'm fed up with you? For fuck's sake, isn't it obvious? Just look at yourself. You're an ignorant hypocrite. You're a waste of space. I don't understand what I saw in you. I was deluded. You want more?"

"Yes. You're not explaining. You're just insulting me. It isn't the same thing."

"Right. Here we go. Your job. You spend all winter looking after hunters and racehorses, and the spring helping with the lambing. What kind of job is that? Exploiting animals. Being part of the fox-hunting scene even if you don't agree with it. Joining in the machinery of the meat market, breeding sheep to be slaughtered and eaten. That's how you make your living?"

Owain was silenced. She had flung the words in his face, like a blow, and he was taken aback. He flushed and struggled for words.

"Not so long ago you were telling me working with animals was good work—real work," he said.

"Well, I'm starting to see a little clearer now. I'm starting to think."

Owain was thunderstruck. He walked beside her, looking at the ground.

"Elaine," he tried. "Elaine. Why do you say these things? Do you know how much I admire you? You are amazing. You're beautiful—the embodiment of the goddess. You are all women to me."

But Elaine was distant. She observed him cruelly. Every time she veered away, he followed her. Had he no self-respect? No dignity? He was stupid and inarticulate. An embarrassment. Wandering aimlessly, sleeping rough—why, he was little better than a tramp, in reality. She could see him, in thirty years time, one of the derelicts carrying plastic bags full of rubbish. He revolted her.

Owain took hold of her arm.

"Stop," he said. "Stop insulting me. Why, Elaine? Why?"

She stopped and stood before him, face to face.

"Why? I'll tell you why. You've destroyed me, Owain. You've ruined my life—spoiled everything. And I hate you for it."

"How?"

Elaine paused. Could she utter the words? By speaking them out loud, she was making the situation a colder reality. She forced herself.

"Because I'm pregnant. Okay? Because I'm pregnant."

A tumult of emotions flowed across Owain's face. Surprise, anxiety—a quick flicker of delight. But Elaine regarded him with hostility. He suppressed the delight. He reined in.

"Elaine," he said gently. "Is it such a disaster? I would...I would love to have a child."

Elaine turned away. Her eyes filled with tears. She broke down. She crouched in the stubble, and cried. The wooden doll rolled away from her.

"Well, you be bloody pregnant then," she sobbed. "It's not fair. I hate it. I've lost control. I feel ill and tired. I'm sick all the time. My face is exploding with acne. My boobs have swollen like barrage balloons. And this is just the start. I don't want to be pregnant. I don't want a baby."

Owain sat beside her, stroking her back. He couldn't help smiling.

"Oh, Elaine. You're beautiful. You'll stop feeling ill. You'll look amazing. Pregnant women are gorgeous. I would be so happy. You, me and our child..."

"I don't want it," she said. She regained her self control. "I don't want it. Lose my freedom? Give up? That's what it is, isn't it? When you have a child, you're giving up on your own life—henceforward you are living for the benefit of the next generation."

"You think your life stops when you have a child? I don't think so."

"Yes, it does. Running round after someone else. A free agent no more."

Owain sighed. He straightened up. He steeled himself.

"If you're sure that's how you feel, you'd better get it sorted out quickly," he said. "I'll do everything I can to help, of course."

"Yeah. Quick trip to the abortion clinic? Submit myself to the medical procession—lying on the slab while they dig into my intimate places—and tear the brat apart."

"Then have the child, and give it to me to care for. I'll be its parent, and you can be free." Elaine looked at him quickly.

"You'd do that?"

"Yes."

But after a moment or two, Elaine shook her head.

"No. I don't know. I don't want to be pregnant, to give birth, or to have a termination. It's not fair. Just the one time—"

"Midsummer's Eve?"

"We've taken precautions ever since, haven't we? Just once—fate kicks me in the teeth."

"We had unprotected sex. I don't think you can blame fate. It was our own act—our own irresponsibility."

"It's all very well for you to be philosophical about it. I'm the afflicted one."

Owain sighed.

"I'm sorry. If I could be pregnant instead of you, I would willingly take the burden. What can I do? What more can I say? Take it on board, Elaine. Make a decision. Take the bull by the horns. Whatever you decide I will be with you all the way."

"Yeah," she said. "You'll be with me. But it'll still be me that goes through it. Fuck off, Owain. Leave me alone." She picked up the doll and stood up. She walked away, and this time Owain remained where he was, sitting on the ground, watching her diminish in the distance.

Elaine walked for an hour or more. The sky darkened as the evening drew on. She approached the bypass site, work well underway, though now the land was quiet. A couple of security men remained on duty, but the protest had fizzled out. A few dedicated souls continued to harass the contractors, but the loss of the squat and the copse, and the surrender of the stone valley had knocked out the heart of the opposition. Elaine clambered over the hedge, and crossed the field flanking the new road. She was unbearably tired, choked by perpetual nausea. Her mouth tasted foully metallic. She felt she was being poisoned. The child was a parasite, feeding from her, remorseless.

What was she to do? Bear the child? She did not reckon herself to be mother material. What would she do with a child? She was afraid. So many aspects to fear...the terrors of childbirth—and that was just the beginning. Her life would be circumscribed from then on. A cosy home with Owain? But life would become predictable. She saw the iron tracks stretching out before her, the direct route—marriage, home, work, death. The express line, unfaltering. She didn't want it. She had to escape.

Always, chewing at her heels, the urge to fly. But where to go? Why was she never happy, never satisfied? She wanted to live forever in the moment—for the day—not hungering for yesterday or tomorrow, not planning and confining, or imprisoning herself with things. Leave that for the others.

She wandered on, slowly, lost in thought. The night closed in. She kept the doll pressed against her body. The faeries had trapped her.

She stopped, and looked up, at a full moon brimming with liquid silver. The sky was clear, burning with stars. She heard a rustle, the sweeping of skirts.

"Who's there?" She swung round, peering through the darkness.

"Who's there?" she repeated. A cold wind rose from nowhere, cutting her to the bone. She shivered, wrapped her arms about her body. Again, the swish, and a thin moan on the wind. She turned around again, filled with unease. A white face appeared like a flame. A tall woman. She stepped towards Elaine without a word. She was dressed in long, torn robes, brown and black and ivory, covered in a fine dust, tangled with cobweb. On her fingers were rings, decorated with fragments of bone. She pushed back a hood. Her nails were long and sharp.

"Elaine," she said. Her voice echoed with the sounds of winter—the crack of ice, the whine of a north wind. "Do you know who I am?"

"The first faery—the first one I've seen for sure. After all this—after all that's happened."

"Do you know my name?"

Elaine nodded.

"Do you want to leave here," the lady said. "Do you want to come with me—to be free—in Faeryland?"

"Yes," Elaine said, though her throat was dry. "It's what I want. More than anything."

"There will be a price."

Elaine's hand moved to her belly, instinctively. She gave a brief laugh.

"I know," she said. "I'll be glad to pay it."

"And then—complete simplicity," said the lady.

"Costing everything? I think you've been talking to Katherine."

The lady inclined her head in agreement. She moved to Elaine, carrying a cloud of cold like a cloak.

"You know what to do," she whispered. Elaine trembled. The chill crept into her body.

"Yes," she said. She turned from the faery and focussed on the wooden doll. Its eyes shone in the moonlight. Did it blink? Elaine took up a stone. It lay heavy in her hand, dull black and smooth. She tenderly laid the doll in the grass, raised the stone above her head, and brought it smashing down in the face of the lump of wood. It crunched and splintered. She bashed it again and again.

When the head was obliterated, her rage began to dissipate. The stone fell from her hand. An emptiness seemed to open in her chest. Perfectly calm, as though from a distance, she picked up the broken wooden stock gently and cradled it to her chest. In the unrelenting ground she began to scrape a shallow grave. She worked for a long time, scratching into the soil with her fingernails, with a piece of stick. When a hollow was carved to her satisfaction, she placed the doll inside it. She scattered a handful of leaves and a few fading pink campion flowers upon the body. Then she covered it, weeping quietly, her grief a thin veil upon an icy sense of peace.

The ceremony complete, she turned to her companion. The lady was watching her. She took Elaine's hand, and together they walked for a time, along the hidden paths, poised between one land and another. The dawn came, grey and rose above the hills. The air was still, the trees huge and black, motionless in the pale morning. The last star glittered silver above thin skeins of cloud. A red butterfly flitted among the crisp stalks and seedheads of the dead summer flowers.

A sharp pain flared in Elaine's belly, to the side. She bent over, for a moment, gripping Death by the hand. The pain receded. They walked on again, talking awhile. The pain returned, and Elaine curled up upon the ground, moaning softly. A moment's respite—then it hit again, worse than before, fingers of agony tearing into her body. She shrieked. The cold lady stroked her forehead and Elaine's mind began to dim. She lay a long time, in the grass. The blood seeped out, covering her legs in a dark red river, soaking her white dress. Her thoughts drifted. She couldn't move. The sun ascended the sky, like a chariot. Death leaned over and kissed her.

CHAPTER THIRTY ONE

Paul stood outside the house, in Avebury, smoothing his hair. It was Saturday, and although the sky was overcast, the stone circle was hectic with tourists. Among the hedges, the first leaves were shading red and brown, and the briars were thick with blackberries. Paul was scruffier than usual, in torn jeans, muddy leather boots, and a patched green coat. He climbed the three stone steps to the porch, cleared his throat, and knocked on the door. After a moment it opened.

"Paul. Come in."

Paul's boss, John Halvard was short and a little portly, looking dapper in a white shirt and a red waistcoat, grey-haired, sporting a neat beard. Paul stepped in, and followed him into a cosy study.

"James not in?" Paul said, making conversation.

"No. He's gone up to Oxford for the weekend. Looking for accommodation. He's got a new job, did you know?"

Paul nodded.

"Yes. On the Oxford Mail," he said. " A step up the career ladder I suppose."

"While you, in comparison, are planning to step off it entirely. Isn't that correct?"

"As you well know. That's why you invited me here, isn't it? To try and persuade me to change my mind?" Paul exchanged his nervousness for a slight belligerence. He took up the offensive.

"I have made up my mind," he added. "You're wasting your time."

Halvard regarded Paul coolly for a moment or two.

"Calm down. You mistake me. I just wanted a chance to talk with you—to hear your plans. You've lost weight, haven't you? And you look tired. Perhaps I could buy you lunch? At the Red Lion?"

Paul shrugged.

"Okay," he said. Halvard picked up a jacket, and they walked through the stone circle to the pub. It was already busy, with foreign visitors and weekend pilgrims. They moved through the main bar, into the restaurant at the back. Halvard ordered roast pork. Paul opted for the vegetarian pie. They made polite conversation over their meal, and Halvard downed three pints of beer in quick succession.

While they were waiting for coffee, Halvard reached into his pocket, and drew out the three page letter of resignation, that Paul had handed in two days previously. It had taken him hours to compose.

"Well then," Halvard said. "What's all this about?"

Paul blushed helplessly. For a moment, the entire enterprise seemed irredeemably foolish. What was he doing? He fiddled with a napkin, feeling like a recalcitrant son, caught on the verge of running away to the circus. He assembled his thoughts.

"What it looks like," he said. "I want to leave."

"But, from the looks of this, you haven't another post to go to."

"I made my reasons perfectly clear in the letter," Paul said, his voice rising. "Why are you making me go through this? Didn't I make my position explicit? I don't owe you any further explanations."

Halvard sighed. He crumpled up the letter in his well-manicured fist, and threw it upon the table.

"It's nonsense. You can't do it. Losing you to a bigger firm would have been bad enough, but I would have expected it to happen sooner or later. But this? An adolescent crisis of confidence? You've got a wife and daughter, for god's sake. What are you going to do with them?"

"Partner."

"What?"

"She's not my wife. We're not married."

"Amounts to the same thing. What about them?"

"We're splitting up." Paul flushed again, wringing the napkin in his hands. Halvard was stopped in his tracks.

"I see," he said quietly. "Is this why...?"

"Why I'm leaving? No."

"Is there somebody else involved?"

"What?"

"With your splitting up?"

"What the fuck's that got to do with you?" he replied angrily. Halvard was taken aback.

"I'm sorry," he said. "Look, Paul—I care about you. And about your career. You could go a long way—if your heart was in it. I'd hate you to throw it all away, because of an emotional upset. You'll get over it. Take a couple of weeks' holiday. Take a month."

"It's not because of the break-up, okay?"

"So this stuff," Halvard gestured to the ball of paper on the table, "this wanting to live outside western consumer culture yarn, this is the real reason?"

"Yes," Paul nodded.

"A revolutionary, yes?"

Paul shrugged.

"I don't know about that. An activist maybe."

Halvard thought for a time. The coffee arrived. He drank it black, sipping carefully.

"You're doing good work for us, Paul. I know you're fed up with the donkey work—but more interesting projects will come. What about the little innovations you're introducing? What about your scheme for the sustainable village? If you drop out now, won't you lessen your chances of ever putting it into practice?"

"Change from within, you mean? Working in the great machine, trying to alter its course? No. It's not enough for me. A bit of tinkering here and there, on the edges of my life? It has to be everything."

"You being so much better and worthier than the rest of us?"

"That's not what I'm saying at all. I have to follow my heart—my conscience."

Halvard finished his coffee and paid the bill.

"I think you're making a foolish decision," he said. "If you change your mind, come back and see me. We'll always have a place for you."

Paul looked at his feet.

"Thanks," he said. "But don't hold your breath."

They walked back to the villa. Halvard invited Paul inside, but Paul shook his head. He climbed into the car, and drove back to Locksbury.

His house was empty. Katherine and Niamh were staying with Jan Blessing, in Marlborough. They had only taken a few things. The house was much as always, though a little dustier and a little less chaotic. Paul wandered slowly from room to room. He looked into the bathroom, at the mermaid mosaic Katherine had spent so many hours creating. He stood in Niamh's room, staring out the window at the garden, the old apple tree and the terracotta pots, still drowned in geraniums. He picked up toys, lingering over the pictures pinned on the wall. He walked round the bedroom he had shared with Katherine—and with Kate too. He sat in the living room, and regarded the floorboards they had never got round to sanding. Had he thought it would be easy? To leave? How this house had weighed upon him— imprisoned him. And now, considering the months, the years he had spent here, with his family he was afflicted with a terrible sense of sadness—of loss. What was he doing? Chasing dreams? Would he never be happy?

They had been polite, he and Katherine—affectionate even. But the chasm was too great. She didn't want him. No effort of will could engender an emotional connection. He ached for Kate. He thought of her constantly. He found himself looking for her in the street, in crowds of people. He conversed with her in his mind, and when he lay in bed at night, he imagined her slender arms about his neck, her kisses and whispers. When he slept, she haunted his dreams, so he woke with a pain in his heart. A physical sensation—a weight.

He grew distant. He retreated into his study, writing letters on the computer. Niamh considered him coolly, with dark eyes. She climbed onto his lap, and placed her little hands on his face.

"You understand what I've got to do, don't you?" he asked her. "You know what I'm feeling." Niamh made no reply, but she held his gaze. Paul had the uncanny feeling the little girl understood him exactly. Her face expressed compassion—or pity. She hugged him, pressing her lips against his cheek. The warmth of her response brought tears to his eyes.

Now Katherine and Niamh were gone. He had slept in the house alone for the last few nights. Katherine had the keys, and would make the arrangements with the letting agency.

He walked around one last time. Then he dug in his pocket and withdrew a scrap of paper. He picked up the telephone, and called Stuart.

Katherine walked along the narrow lane, beneath the hazel trees. Here and there, the first leaves were paling to yellow. The ground was littered with greenish nuts, and the blackthorn bushes were decked with purple sloes, shining a muted purple-black on the spiny branches. Among the trees, sprays of wild rose were gemmed with scarlet hips, glowing in splashes of sunshine. Niamh, in the backpack, beamed with smiles. Owain, walking just in front of her, stooped beneath a bramble, picking up pretty stones and stray feathers for Niamh to look at. Katherine marvelled as she walked, caught in the delight of a perfect spider's web, glistening with moisture, or a patch of moss glimmering green in the shade, or the copper brown edging of leaves on the horse chestnut tree, growing in the middle of a field. Had she never seen these before? Of course she had—but now, at this time, the season seemed miraculous—a festival of fruitfulness, of colour, shading imperceptibly, day by day, towards winter. She observed the subtle changes. She felt the rhythm of the autumn beating in her blood. The land seemed to reach directly to her heart, to her flesh. Every night she lay in bed with the curtains open, with the moonlight pouring into her room. She slept with its beams upon her face.

Never had the world seemed so beautiful, so astonishing. The vigorous ivy growing on a wall, the pattern of red bricks, the rising of the sun above the storybook town, the jumble of roofs. She was fiercely happy. There was so much to amaze.

On the outside—she had little to be cheerful about. Paul was leaving. Elaine, her friend of sorts, had died alone, a wasteful, shocking death. The bypass was well underway. Even Jo and Violet were planning to move on. Owain, ahead of her, was tired and gaunt, burdened with a double loss. What right did she have to be so happy? But the feeling was almost impersonal—like a river welling up from an unknown source, using her as a channel. She was mad with joy. Joy at being alive. And as when she was miserable or depressed, she could only conceive of misery and depression, now joyful, it was hard to comprehend any other state. She had tapped into a vein, a stream of happiness.

When they returned to Marlborough, Katherine took Owain to a cafe and they sat outside, in the sunshine drinking coffee and eating pastries. Niamh stood upon a chair, her face sticky with icing. Owain began to talk at last, and Katherine pulled her attention away from the complex patterns of cups, plates and decorations on the table, with its spell-binding conjunction of shapes and shadows.

Owain had found Elaine, lying stiff and white in a field, covered in dark blood. He had searched for her all night, trawling through the dark fields. He chanced upon her late the next day, far from anywhere, though he knew she lay upon a faery pathway. He blamed them. He picked up her body and carried her all the way to his house. Then he phoned the hospital, though she had obviously been dead for many hours.

Then a week of horror—dealing with his own bereavement, and the visit from her parents, who travelled down from Manchester to see their dead daughter, to talk to the doctors, and to meet with the man who had fathered their unborn grandchild. They were polite and sympathetic, but Owain sensed that they blamed him in some way. He was mortified. They held the funeral in Manchester, and made no effort to include Owain in the ceremony.

He talked to nobody, walking alone for miles and days. He couldn't sleep or eat. Then he was ill for a week, and lay in bed, in a kind of fever, till Katherine, concerned by his absence, called by and pushed her way into the house.

They struck up an alliance of sorts. They shared their mutual bereavement. They talked of Elaine for hours. Owain told her what the doctors had said. It was an ectopic pregnancy. The embryo had attached itself to the fallopian tube, rather than the womb. It was an occasional occurrence, they told him, but not usually a fatal one. When it grew, the embryo burst its ill-chosen bed, causing copious internal bleeding. Elaine had suffered a massive haemorrhage. She had bled to death.

Owain sipped his drink.

"What about Paul?" he said. Katherine drew herself to the present. Niamh spilt squash upon the table. Katherine mopped it up with paper tissues, and Niamh crawled onto Owain's lap. They seemed to have an affinity, the man and the child —an understanding. Niamh listened to him attentively.

"He'll be off soon. A new career as eco-terrorist, I imagine. Or that's what he'd like to think." She was tight-lipped and dismissive.

"You don't want him to go?" Owain asked. Katherine shrugged.

"I don't know. We couldn't stay together. He hasn't been happy for a long time, and we haven't exactly been lovers since Niamh was born. And I know he's still bewitched by that Kate woman, hopeless as it may be."

"Human men are often supposed to pine away and die if they fall in love with faery maidens—and the maiden vanishes, as she invariably does," Owain said.

"Well he's pining for something. It seems a bit self-indulgent to me, his running off like this. What about his daughter? Doesn't she need him? He thinks he owes a greater loyalty to his unknown cause. He even suggested to me that she might one day be proud of him—the hero—saving the planet."

"Maybe she will," Owain said simply. Katherine tutted and shifted in her chair.

"Here they are," Owain said. Katherine looked up. Jo and Violet appeared, and joined them at the table. Katherine ordered more coffee and cakes.

Jo's hair, uncombed, was falling into dreadlocks. He had traded in his black clothes for motley patchwork. He still wore the Morris men's waistcoat, and Katherine's bone necklace hung at his neck. She hadn't wanted it back. Violet's hair was growing again, and she wore bright orange leggings and long green boots. They attracted looks from the other cafe patrons.

"So you're off to the next protest?" Katherine said. Jo nodded.

"Yeah. A motorway extension, down in Dorset. D'you fancy joining us?"

Katherine gestured to Niamh.

"A bit difficult—with a kid," she said.

Jo had spent a couple of weeks renewing his relationship with his mother. Then he had hitched back to Bristol, to see his mates again. They were just as he had left them—doing the same things. He was bored by them, but sad as well, to have left a part of his life behind.

Now he was back—and he and Violet were planning to spend the foreseeble future wandering hand in hand from one protest site to the next. Then maybe a trip to Europe, or South America. Maybe they could travel indefinitely, working a passage, or trading—two colourful gypsies moving across the face of the earth, not putting down roots or hoarding possessions. He smiled at Violet. She smiled back.

Later, Katherine took Niamh up to the common, and pushed her on the swings. Owain had wandered off again. Jo and Violet were toasting their imminent departure with friends in the pub. It was late, and growing dark. Niamh should soon be in bed. The sky was darkening over the town. Savernake Forest was black beyond the rooftops. The church bells began to ring.

Katherine thought of the faeries, and faeryland. She could remember it, but the experience was very far away. She could point to the trip mentally—she could say this happened, that happened. But she could not actually recall what it was like. It was as though the memories belonged to such a different part of her life, that now she was back here, in the mundane but endlessly beautiful world, she had lost the means of accessing that other realm—even in her own head. Jo had told her he felt the same thing. But he was restless and eager to move. She suspected that perhaps, deeply buried, he harboured the desire to find Faeryland again—perhaps, if he travelled far enough, and long enough. But Katherine had no inclination to move, for the time being. She was held in her own happy valley. She revelled in the riches it had to offer. She knew it wouldn't last forever—but what did? She would take each day as it came.

Niamh squawked indignantly. Lost in thought, her mother had stopped pushing the swing. It had come to rest.

"Time for us to go home," Katherine said. She lifted her daughter from the swing and carried her down the hill into the town. Niamh's eyes were shining. Katherine found her hard to fathom. The little girl cuddled close to her mother, sweet-smelling and adorable. She was quite delightful, and utterly charming, but still... sometimes she seemed to look from very far away. And sometimes she looked uncannily grown-up. Would it be fanciful to think she was ancient? Katherine pressed Niamh against her. Soon the little girl would learn to talk, and they would get to know each other better. Till then, she was entrusted with her care. Niamh, like any other child, had her own path to follow.

The bypass was opened by the local MP six months after the eviction. The two-mile stretch of even, gently curving road was soon busy with cars and lorries. Locksbury traders lost trade and grumbled. The flower shop closed down. Other residents, who worked outside the village, rejoiced that the endless noise of traffic had abated. They pointed out the benefits for road safety.

It was a curious stretch of road. It required frequent mending. Cracks appeared. The tarmac suffered unexpected frost damage. For an open road, it attracted more than its fair share of accidents. The roots of trees grew up and pierced the surface, as though they were breaking it up, and dragging it back into the body of the earth.

CROW

In the early morning the old woman felt a prickling in her limbs. She stood up, stretching her arms, and she left the fireside to walk out into the forest. The spring was slow this year. The winter was tenacious, refusing to yield its grip on the cold land. The wind was bitter. Patches of snow, tired and icy grey, clung to hollows in the ground. But the sky was a clear blue, and the first flowers were creeping from the earth, a splash of golden yellow or mauve in the sallow grass.

The old woman pulled her furs tightly around herself. She carried a pointed wooden stave, as some defence against wolves, lean and desperate after a hard season. She walked briskly, till her blood began to stir, and she warmed enough to throw back her hood and expose her long, grey hair to the sun. The sun stretched brilliant fingers through the branches, touching her face. The wind seemed to lift and drop as she passed, the branches shifting, the flowers nodding their fragile heads. She dreamed of the summer, of heat and plenty. She willed the sun to travel high, to be true.

She was not alone, she knew. The others walked beside her, though she couldn't see them. She began to hear their voices. She continued on her way, patiently, opening her mind to the shallow ripple of words, and songs, and laughter. She waited for them to draw near.

All at once she saw them, milling about her in a crowd. Intangible shadows, now and then thrown into sharp focus—the flash of a face, the sliding of sunlight on trails of hair. She became aware that one of the others was keeping pace with her. She looked across, cautiously, not looking her new companion in the face. She saw a green woman, wearing a cloak, and carrying a young child on her hip. The little girl was soft and pale, quite unafraid. The green woman set her on the ground, with a sign to the old woman. Then the faeries were gone.

The girl smiled at her new protector. A sleek crow flew down beside her. Another perched on a tree, folding its wings fastidiously upon its glossy back. The woman picked up the little girl, and carried her back to the camp. The crows followed.

When she was seventeen the girl was called again by the others. She left the old woman, and her tribe, and passed through the distant realm. She was guided by the faeries, who revealed the hidden and multifarious vistas of their own land. Then they took her to the Swallowhead springs, which she visited in a dream, seeing the long-lost familiar face, offering wisdom, demanding sacrifice. She saw her mother move amongst the faeries. The circle was set into motion.

The faeries guided her again, taking her to a community living on the Wessex chalklands, growing wheat and raising animals. They built barrows for the dead, interring skulls and long bones in their own stone caverns beneath the earth. She was revered as an intermediary with the spirits. She presided over offerings at harvest time, in the fields of wheat, and the weaving of a green god in the spring, decorated with fresh leaves and flowers, to be feasted and paraded, and finally drowned in the springs rising into the river.

But she became restless, and she waited to be summoned. In the depths of the winter the faeries came again. They took her to a new world, to a forest of brick. The air was tainted, and noisy. She made a shrine. She was clothed in green velvet, and silver. She waited for her mother.

She led her to the green chapel, and watched her cradle the child that both was, and wasn't, herself. Her mother slipped away again. How many years till she would see her again? Her heart ached. She carried a perpetual shadow in her mind.

Then for many years she lived without a home. She stepped between the two worlds, belonging in neither. She acted as guide and intermediary. She was a witch and holy woman. She trapped Merlin in the cleft of a tree.

But the faeries were a family without compassion. Her life was an artifice. When her body was old and tired she travelled once again to the city. Bent and weary, she appeared in a mismatch of clothes, carrying bags of tinsel garbage. She predicted a future. She left a wooden doll from the faeries.

In the last days, the faeries returned her to the barrow builders on the chalk downs. What manner of life had it been, she wondered, so fierce and quick—but equally so very, very long. She was tired. Had they stolen her life, the faeries? She had seen such things...but hadn't she been a slave? A puppet? Death drew near, with her sear breath, and cold, brittle clothes. Would Death be a new beginning? She dreamed of the long-lost face, nearly forgotten.

Her bones were laid in the barrow. Beneath the earth, in the stone womb, she curled in the dark, like a seed.